THE
HESPERUS
PROPHECY

THE HESPERUS PROPHECY

Anthony M. Caterina

Close To The Bone
Publishing

Close To The Bone
an imprint of Gritfiction Ltd
Northampton
Northamptonshire
NN4
www.close2thebone.co.uk

First published in Great Britain in 2025 by Close To The Bone

ISBN 979-8-99215-780-2

First Printing, 2025

*In memory of my father Corrado,
my earliest and staunchest supporter*

Prologue

March 24, 1939

He bolted upright, suddenly awake and unsure why. Despite tinted goggles, he squinted at the visual assault, the world an endless blanket of whirling snow and opalescent ice. The sun dominated a cloudless sky and set the world ablaze, drawing attention to a solitary monolith, a crystal pyramid, jutting out from the wintry plains and fracturing daylight into prismatic rainbows. He trudged through the snow towards the towering crystal, inexplicably drawn towards it, when a soft vibration underfoot escalated into thunderous heaving. He sped into a full sprint, the icy expanse splintering, webbed cracks expanding in all directions and large chunks of ground collapsing into an inky abyss. A deep fissure opened beneath him, gravity dragging him down when an impossible shape formed inside the otherwise featureless crystal. With all his might, he lunged forward, and just as his fingertips danced across the smooth pyramid, he began gasping for air. Drowning in blistering cold water, a distant voice called to him…

"Get up, maggot! This ain't sleepy time, Fritz, it's talky time." Snapping back into reality, Declan choked and sputtered, a guard standing over him, holding an empty bucket and laughing.

"Foul man, you should be ashamed," the handcuffed professor scolded the guard, the bucket's contents flowing down his face and soaking through his shirt. "I want answers," he insisted, standing to leave when he realized his feet were chained to the floor. After noting the blood splatter on the cinder block walls, he sat back down, unwilling to risk physical confrontation. Instead, he demanded, "Where am I?"

"Welcome to Dante's Inferno," the young guard drawled, straightening his military jacket, "you're in purgatory, here for your last chance at redemption."

"You uncultured philistines," scoffed Declan, "purgatory and the inferno aren't the same place. If you understood anything about Christian theology or read Dante's *Divine Comedy,* you'd realize how ignorant you sound. Obviously you're not too keen on details. You'd fit right in with my Intro to Bio students."

The guard laughed even harder. "Keep it up Fritz, that sarcastic tongue of yours ain't doing you any favors. You're our guest because the United States government wants information ground out of you, and nobody cares how. You've been a naughty boy, Fritz, and we can be very persuasive in helping wayward souls such as yourself remember the truth."

"Stop calling me Fritz," Declan shot back, "I've already told you people multiple times. My name is Declan Riordan. I'm a college professor from UCLA. This shouldn't be difficult to comprehend."

A second, heavy-set guard with a smug grin approached the self-proclaimed Declan. "There you go again, Herr Fritz, with shameless lies and deceit." He held up a tiny metal swastika. "The Navy scoured one thousand square miles of open Atlantic and found you, the *Valencia's* only survivor, along with several crates full of Wehrmacht rifles and these Nazi trinkets."

"Who's not too keen on details now, Fritz?" ribbed the young guard. "Declan Riordan died in a lab accident last year. On the other hand, you're a piece of German scheiße that nobody will miss. Next time machen Sie better with your research."

Fueled by vitriol, Declan promptly declared, "I'm not wasting any more time arguing with you knuckle-scraping troglodytes. I demand to speak to whoever's in charge."

"You wanna speak to Hoss?" repeated the stocky guard, chuckling. "For somebody pretending to be a college professor, you sure are stupid."

Hoss emerged from the shadows. "I'm Officer Burke," he said, his leathery face curled into a sneer, "although you can call me the Finger of the Lord. As for you, we're gonna keep calling you Fritz. I suggest you worry less about semantic nitpicking and more about your fate, which has been placed squarely in my hands and so far doesn't look promising. If you can't be honest about your identity, let's try something else." Hoss reached into his pocket and pulled out a small vial. "What's this?"

Using his cuffed hands, Declan swept the drenched hair off his face and looked at the label. "Penicillin," he read, shrugging his shoulders. "Is this supposed to mean something to me?"

"It should," Hoss replied, "they found this vial taped to your chest. An overwhelming infection should've killed you. You were in rough shape with pus oozing from multiple wounds, except this vial of penicillin saved your life."

"I don't know anything about this vial," Declan replied, "and I've never heard of penicillin."

"Neither has anybody else, Fritz, but also taped to your body were instructions on how to administer the solution. Convinced you'd die anyway, the medics shot you up with this liquid, and to their surprise, your fever vanished and wounds healed. You're luckier than Lazarus."

"Saved by a magic potion? That's preposterous. I'm a biology professor, and I'd know if something like this penicillin existed."

"First, I'll remind you, Professor Riordan is dead. The only biology he's dealing with now is decomposition.

Second, we found a research lab at Oxford University extracting compounds from fungi. Their most promising candidate, an antibacterial agent isolated from Penicillium mold, matches what was inside this vial. One wrinkle, they haven't isolated enough to begin clinical tests, and their entire supply wouldn't be enough for a single dose. So where'd you get this?"

"Like I already told you," Declan said, "I don't know anything about that vial or its contents. Why is this such a hard concept for you to grasp?"

"Look Fritz, you leave me no choice. You've given us nothing, and down here, we don't stop at the third degree. We pull out all the stops. It's time for you to experience some divine intervention." Hoss nodded, and the stocky officer with a smug grin approached.

The officer raised his left fist. "Here's divine," he said, without warning, punching Declan in the gut.

The professor doubled over and fell off the chair, already squealing in pain when the younger guard walked over. "I warned you against wagging your tongue," he said, kicking the professor squarely in the jaw. "And that's intervention."

Hoss knelt next to Declan, splayed out on the ground, writhing and moaning. "Now that you've experienced some divine intervention, I hope we can start making progress. My superiors want answers, and believe me, I will extract them. I just hope for your sake you wise up and start talking before we need to introduce you to the Power of Christ. Let's try something really simple. What were you doing in Antarctica?"

"Please, stop this," Declan pleaded, sobbing. "I'm an American citizen, not a German spy. The only *Valencia* I know is an orange fruit and I've never been to Antarctica."

"What a shame," Hoss sneered, shaking his head, "I thought we reached an understanding." He walked over to the wall and pulled down a long leather strip. "This here's a cat o' nine tails. As a traditional Navy instrument of correction, usually a few lashes were ample punishment. However, down here in Dante's Inferno, we report to a higher authority and follow rabbinical law, forty lashes minus one. That's why I call this beauty the Power of Christ," Hoss said, stroking the nine knotted tails, "because if He can't compel you to speak the truth, nobody can."

Chapter 1

December 14, 1799
Mount Vernon Plantation
Fairfax County, Virginia

Tobias gripped the banister and vaulted up the stairs, two per stride. His friend's illness had significantly worsened since Caroline fetched him, and the best opinion of two well-regarded physicians merely resulted in summoning a third. While Tobias was not privy to modern medical treatments, he recognized the general had undergone enough bloodletting to make a butcher swoon.

Tobias approached the bed, weaving between doctors and servants. "General, I am here."

"Oh good, Tobias, you have come," the ailing man replied, his voice coarse and rattling. "I find I am going. My breath cannot last long. I believed from the start this disorder would prove fatal."

"Please do not speak of such things," Tobias pleaded, "it merely emboldens the enemies of life. You are strong. You can fight this."

"Oh, my dear friend," the general paused, struggling to refill his lungs, "long have you been my loyal liege, but in this late hour, the time has passed for beguiling chinwag."

"My apologies, General, you are correct," Tobias contritely replied. "I quibble no more. Your desires are my pleasure to execute."

The old general focused his gaze on Tobias, the sharpness and clarity of his steely blue eyes unaffected by the failings of his body. "Organize and record all my military letters and papers. Arrange my accounts and settle my books, as you know more about my affairs than anyone, save me." The general coughed and gurgled, retching forth a brown stream down his robe, the regurgitated potion of butter, vinegar and molasses quickly blotted up by the servant girls.

"Please, Master Washington, have a sip of tea," Caroline pleaded.

"Do not be afraid. I am just going," the general said. He waved Tobias closer, grabbed his shoulder, and drew him near. The wretched stench of acid and death burned against Tobias' cheek as his dying friend whispered into his ear.

"I understand, sir," Tobias repeated several times, noting the strength of Washington's grip even in this waning hour of life. Ultimately his pale, clammy fingers loosened their hold, and the general fell back into the pile of bedding. "It has been my pleasure to serve you," Tobias added, tears rolling down his face.

"'Tis well," the general whispered, one long, guttural exhalation, and there was no more.

"He is gone," one of the professional exsanguinators flatly noted, rendering the first accurate medical diagnosis of the entire debacle.

Tobias offered his condolences to Martha, and she accepted with grace. He hastily retreated downstairs and poured himself a snifter of the general's favorite liquor, cherry bounce, the fruit-infused brandy a reminder of happier times. He lifted his glass. "A toast to my dearest friend and most exalted general, your bidding will be done." Tobias sipped the sweet liquid while walking into the study, setting down the glass on Washington's desk before searching his inner pockets. He pulled out a large, ornate golden key, using it to open the desk's singular locked drawer. After rifling through the jumbled papers and journals, he declared, "Aha, this is the one," tucking a thin, red leather-bound tome inside his vest. "You will not leave my side." The remaining drawer contents, letters bound and free, he jumbled en-masse, walked them into the kitchen, and threw the pile upon the last remaining embers of the suppertime logs, using the poker to aid the flames in the digestion of their inky carcasses.

Chapter 2

October 11, 1816
The Sanctuary of the Epistolith
City of Washington, District of Columbia

Tobias Lear requested this emergency meeting just a few hours earlier, and despite the risks, dozens of cloaked figures answered the call. A quorum of the secret society's members gathered inside the Sanctuary, milling about, eagerly awaiting an explanation for Tobias' visible perturbation.

Tobias did not join the crowd. He needed a few minutes to steel himself and organize his thoughts. He made a concerted effort to admire the rotunda's beauty one last time, his gaze tracking along the massive granite pillars as they rose to meet the vaulted ceiling, so distant the flickering candles below failed to illuminate. He took a deep breath. No more delay. It was time.

The collected group circled around the base of the Epistolith, the massive diamond-shaped monolith occupying the majority of the vast space. Repeating a time-honored tradition, those gathered stood hand in hand, completing a circuit around the singular diamond, which stood taller than an oak and wide as a house. Encircling the crystal's base served as a reminder that each member was equally important in the chain. In this space, neither societal class, profession, sex, nor color ranked one soul above another.

Their hooded reflections danced off the glossy surface of the perfect octahedron, like two pyramids joined at the base, forming a diamond of remarkable geometric precision. Perfect was not hyperbole. The surface smoother than glass and sparkling like the finest crystal, surpassing natural creation and mocking humanity's humble abilities. Whether it was a masterwork of God or perhaps the motley menagerie of lowercase pagan gods, the origins were unclear, lost to history.

The rotunda housing the massive diamond was an architectural wonder unto itself, rivaling the Pantheon in scale but much older, skillfully crafted in times long before Siberian land bridges or Viking ships ever brought men to this continent. Known as the Sanctuary, the rotunda existed with the sole purpose of keeping the Epistolith concealed. The object required no protection as tests proved the crystal impervious to all known degradants. Resistant to fire, chemicals, and brute force, neither stone nor metal damaged the unblemished surface. All attempts just ground them into dust and filings. Even more improbable, the building-sized behemoth hovered a few feet above the floor, quietly defying all physical rules of the Universe, suspended by nothing more than unseen forces.

Tobias approached the roughly hewn podium, built from the reclaimed wood of a tea chest thrown overboard during the Boston Tea Party of 1773, a reminder of how a small group with virtuous intent can change the world. "Good evening," he started, loudly clearing his throat to settle the chatter. "I have gathered together the Clypeate, our clandestine organization, on short notice because the reason for our existence, safeguarding the Epistolith, will be tested tonight. Sadly, General Washington is not here to guide us. Even as we approach the seventeenth anniversary of his departure, I still miss his steady hand and thoughtful guidance. Instead, responsibility for tonight's tribulation falls squarely upon us. While I express remorse and sadness at the loss of our great leader, I rejoice in the strength and wisdom he imparted. My stewardship soon faces the ultimate challenge, and I have made every attempt to faithfully emulate our founder's fortitude. For what we protect, what this Sanctuary holds, is far more valuable than any shiny bauble or sorcerer's stone. The Epistolith is an object of power beyond our creation and a store of unknowable knowledge."

The chamber erupted with shouts of assent. Tobias waited for them to fade before continuing. "As recounted by his hand, in General Washington's seminal journal, are the words of prophecy handed down to him from Hesperus, the original guardian of the Epistolith."

Tobias held up the small red tome, the same book he spared from the kitchen embers on the night of Washington's death. "Here is the Book of Prophecy. Inscribed in these pages are the General's sole accounts of his interactions with Hesperus the Guardian, the last of the ancient Clypeate, from whom our protectorate's name originates. Hesperus put forth these prophecies, which the great General recorded in these pages," Tobias reminded the group, gently cradling the leather-bound journal. "I will now read a few select passages, for they are most pertinent. I wish we had time for more, but tonight, there are far more pressing matters at hand."

Tobias solemnly flipped to the bookmarked page, one he'd read many times before, though never with such gravitas. "On page forty, entry number fifteen, General Washington wrote:

And as Hesperus and I walked along the Tiber Creek, sunset's fading rays dancing across the water, his mood darkened and he walked no further. Hesperus turned and said, 'As days pass, the future becomes more defined, like mist thinning on a cool morning, I can see what comes next more clearly. Your time upon the land will end before the year eighteen hundred arrives, and it saddens me deeply.' I responded to him politely, sharing my appreciation for his concerns regarding my welfare, whilst gently adding only our Lord knows the true path ahead and number of our days. He smiled, the gentle, knowing kind reserved by the wisest elderly for the most foolish youth.

'Indeed,' Hesperus replied, 'and though my existence is not measured in your time, I have seen how remarkably textured your tragically fleeting existences can be. Now pay heed, for the reason I share news of your impending departure is to enlighten, not sadden you, for the time has come to prepare. I must leave you and travel far afield, there is a great disturbance which I failed to see and may already be too late to correct, yet I must try. I will be gone, for how long I cannot say for certain, but your death will precede my return, so we must choose your successor as Commanding General, the Chief Guardian of the Epistolith. I see a path forward with Master Tobias Lear, despite his spotty past he harbors a goodness within that will serve him well.'''

Tobias paused after the last sentence. He always struggled at the reference to his past dubious dealings, although with time, he'd learned to own the truth of the statement. "Fair enough," he conceded, "my only hope is through faithful service, I have repaid my debt in full. Now I shall resume the General's discourse:

'When I return to this place, many years will have passed,' Hesperus revealed, 'even Master Tobias will be gone before that day arrives. But in that time, he will protect your legacy through a great tumult, for the Britons, from whom you have gained independence, will once again attack these shores, even unto this very spot, they will prevail, and the newly created city bearing your

name will blacken with conflagration. Fear not, however, for your new nation will prevail, and the secrets Master Tobias protects will remain safe."'

The Clypeate once again applauded, this time because the last prophecy referenced their heroic efforts during the War of 1812. "Yes, go ahead and cheer, you have earned it," Tobias said, "when called you performed admirably, protecting both this city and our Epistolith, muskets loaded and ready even as British Redcoats marched above our Sanctuary towards the President's House. But I must continue, for the hour grows late. We have all borne witness to how several predictions have already been fulfilled, and now I arrive at tonight's most pertinent and personally distressing prophecy." Tears momentarily welled in Tobias' eyes. "However, there is no time for self-pity," he added, quickly regaining his composure. "As the General's journal details, Hesperus further elaborated upon my fate:

'Unfortunately, Master Lear will meet his unsavory demise at the hands of the Obturavi, the sworn enemies of knowledge and progress, whose twisted truths and lies have brought down my kind. Their selfish desires for power cloud their judgment, and they blanket the truth under blood and domination. I have not felt their influence grow this strong for many centuries, though now I am certain these destroyers are coming, and they are powerful adversaries. I foresee Master Lear suffering horribly at their hands, but the Epistolith must not be discovered. He will know the time approaches when the natural world enters a great upheaval, and the day arrives when his lintel is marked. The sun will not rise again before Master Lear's blood rains down like forest

leaves in autumn. Throughout his tribulations, he must stay strong and true, for the Obturavi will try to twist the truth from him, and while there are no endings that spare his life, any clues he gives will lead them to the Epistolith. He must know his sacrifice is necessary and noble, otherwise, all I can see is failure.'"

Tobias closed the book. "My brethren, by all accounts this year, the natural world has been out of sorts, dry fog all down the Atlantic seaboard, ice and frost late into the summer months, crops withering in the fields. For months, I have felt the tendrils of prophecy creeping into my soul, and this very morning, upon leaving my house, after seventeen years of checking, I found the fateful mark carved into my lintel. I know Providence awaits me when I return home. That is my reason for summoning you all here one last time. Tonight, I shall meet my Maker, with full knowledge I have served my General and our Clypeate with honor and dignity." He unfastened a silver, diamond-shaped pin from his lapel and held it up. "I leave you the task of choosing your next leader, the Commanding General and Chief Guardian, a distinction both noble and fraught with peril."

He then placed Washington's red journal on the podium. "The Book of Prophecy is no longer safe with me. Protect it with your lives. Some entries have yet to be fulfilled, and while I fail to grasp their intent, I trust future leaders will discover their import." Finally, Tobias held up an oversized, wildly ornate golden key with spiked millings resembling a startled porcupine. "Lastly, I hand over the Master Key of Hesperus, necessary to gain access to this Sanctuary of the Epistolith," he explained, laying it on the podium. "When I leave, I trust you will all stay here through the night, guarding the Epistolith from our enemies. Even as I speak, they are surely on the prowl. I will lead them far afield, and when you emerge tomorrow morning, you shall learn of my sacrifice."

Many Clypeate came up to Tobias, some to shake his hand, several to share a hug, though he allowed none to slow his exit from the Sanctuary. "Time is wasting," he warned, reminding them, "as the night draws darker, the wolves are closing in," before slipping alone into the narrow, brick-lined tunnel sloping up towards the surface. The guards monitoring the entrance rolled back the door, a thick stone slab cleverly obscured by the marsh grass and thick weeds growing along the nearby riverbank. Tobias dared not use artificial light, instead relying upon the waning moon to illuminate his path towards the empty home of the nearest Clypeate.

Once inside the darkened home he lit his lantern, taking pains to shout farewells at imaginary hosts upon exiting, feigning his departure had come after a lengthy visit, hopeful any watchful eyes fell for the deception. He walked over to the stable, saddled up his horse, and rode off into the night with great haste. While Tobias had no proof of being followed home, he knew many eyes tracked his progress. Upon entering his home, dark and silent, he proceeded to the study and sat down at his desk.

"Tonight, I decide my own fate," he muttered, "Lord forgive me." Tobias stirred a small bottle of solvent before carefully yet generously pouring it over select pages of his personal diary. "I should have never committed these wild ideas to paper," he chastised himself, then watched the ink disappear everywhere it was applied and smiled thinly. "Though now I've made amends and 'swounds to the fool who tries interpreting these musings," he proudly announced. Tobias looked out the study window and, in response to the handful of dark figures lurking amongst the bushes, retrieved a pistol from his desk drawer. He then poured out a snifter of cherry bounce, the last of General Washington's supply gifted to him by Martha, held up his glass and proposed a toast. "This one's for you, my dearest friend. Even beyond your time, I have faithfully served you." Tobias took a generous swig, but it never reached his gullet; instead, the sweet scarlet brandy joined most of his pulpy cerebellum on the floral wallpaper several feet away.

Chapter 3

June 4, 1898
The Powell Home
Foggy Bottom, City of Washington, District of Columbia

Well past midnight, Mary Elizabeth woke to a loud pounding on the front door. She listened intently while Father lumbered down the stairs, grumbling as he interrogated the visitor, demanding to know what could be so important. While the little girl didn't hear any conversation details, the rationale for the late-night disruption must have been compelling. When the door closed, Father hastily scrambled up to his bedroom, only to race back downstairs a few moments later.

As the eldest of six children, Mary Elizabeth learned self-reliance early, developing maturity far beyond her eight years of life. She'd also been instilled with a keen sense of stewardship over the little ones, and it was those matronly instincts, combined with a curious mind, compelling her to creep out of her room to investigate stealthily. The girl artfully tiptoed down the steps and peeked around the corner. Father was already dressed, wearing a cloak she'd never seen before, as he hurriedly searched through his gun cabinet. Father finished packing his hunting satchel, slung it over his shoulder, and then adroitly holstered a pair of pistols before pulling up his hood. When Father turned back towards the stairway, he jumped, startled by the dark shadow crouched on the landing. Father drew his pistol, causing Mary Elizabeth to squeal in response. He quickly lowered his weapon, realizing the intruder was his daughter. He placed a single finger against his lips, signaling for silence. He walked up the steps and whispered in her ear. "I'm so sorry, my sweet girl, but dangerous men are afoot tonight. Please help Mother get your brothers and sisters dressed and downstairs as quickly and silently as possible."

She dutifully followed instructions, assisting Mother in bundling up the little ones while quelling their tizzies over being abruptly woken from a deep slumber. "Father has a wonderful surprise in store for you," she lied to her four-year-old brother. Although Mary Elizabeth was herself terrified, there was no benefit in alarming the others.

"What is it, Mary Beth?" her six-year-old sister demanded.

Mary Elizabeth lied a second time. "Wouldn't be a surprise if I went around blabbing about it." Of course, she knew lying was wrong. The Good Book spelled it out bluntly, but in her defense, whoever wrote that bit hadn't provided any guidance on handling five grumpy siblings at once. "You'll see soon enough. Father would be quite angry if I spoiled it," she added, ending the inquisition.

The family was ready within minutes, and when Mother led them downstairs into the parlor, Father no longer stood alone. Several men filled the room, all dressed like Father in dark cloaks, all equally armed. Thankfully, the children old enough to ask questions sensed the tension and kept silent. Mother was already busy enough keeping the baby from fussing, while Mary Elizabeth was occupied cajoling the next two youngest of the brood. It was an ominous sign when the assembled group did not leave through the front entryway, instead slipping out the kitchen door into the side alley.

It was late spring, and on this warm Foggy Bottom night, a complete moon shone brightly onto their party. The air hung heavy and calm, accentuating the gravity of the moment. Although Mary Elizabeth usually loved adventure, she didn't tonight, for she saw fear on the faces of the armed, hooded men surrounding them.

Mary Elizabeth's family lived just a few blocks west of Lafayette Square, so she wasn't surprised when their stealthy alleyway trek ended at the park facing the President's House. That was not tonight's destination. Instead, the men led them toward the adjacent State, War and Navy Building. Many people, including Father, had other names for the massive government building, such as the "ugly monstrosity" and the "overdone wedding cake." To Mary Elizabeth, it looked like a fairytale palace, inside and out, an opinion formed through numerous visits. Father worked there and frequently asked his oldest child to accompany him, a special treat she really enjoyed. Not only did she get Father's undivided attention, but she also benefited, getting a reprieve from helping Mother tend to her younger siblings.

Best of all, Father's work friends treated her very well and were extremely kind. They kept her busy and entertained throughout the day, playing and talking with her. Plus, Father's office was always loaded with limitless art supplies, so she spent a lot of time drawing pictures. Sometimes his friends would quiz her, which she enjoyed because they always praised her for being so smart and clever.

Of Father's friends, Mr. Tesla ranked as her favorite. He always surprised her with fashionable outfits from New York City, stuffed animals from Germany, and dolls from France. She also enjoyed Mr. Edison's visits from New Jersey, but not because he was any fun. He was a tad cranky and nearly deaf. Rather, he'd bring along his daughter Madeleine, just a year older than Mary Elizabeth, who made a fabulous playmate.

Despite all these excursions, she'd never seen the building at night before and, with menacing dark windows and moonlight casting wicked shadows off the ornate exterior, hoped there wouldn't be a second time. A handful of the cloaked men darted across Pennsylvania Avenue first, summiting the building's front steps and positioning themselves around the entrance, making certain it was safe for Mary Elizabeth's family to proceed. Once given the signal to cross, they swiftly reunited under the Wedding Cake's portico, only to learn they weren't alone. The silence was shattered by howling whoops erupting all around them. From behind the building's many pillars, hidden in the shadows, ominous figures emerged and bolted towards them.

"Quick, inside the building!" shouted Father, the cloaked men picking up Mary Elizabeth's siblings and carrying them into the dark interior. Father locked the door and addressed the group. "They are already here. Our plans have changed. Take my family down to Lincoln's Tunnel and secure them in the Library of the Ages. Alert the Jefferson Pier guards as well. A few men need to stay here with me and defend this building against the Obturavi as long as we can."

"No," Mother protested, "you aren't leaving us. You're not a sacrificial lamb. The Clypeate, these men, promised to protect our family. All of us." Mary Elizabeth had never heard the name Clypeate openly used before, only when her parents talked in whispers late at night when they thought no tiny ears were eavesdropping. She'd never heard them speak of the Obturavi, but Father spoke their name as if uttering a blasphemous curse.

"Please, Clarissa, we have no time to argue. I am putting Gregory in charge of your safe passage," announced Father. A large, imposing man stepped forward, the only one with a silver diamond pinned to his cloak. "Gregory is the Clypeate's Commanding General," Father explained, "he can deliver you safely to the Library of the Ages. He knows how to best defend against attacks, not I, and he will keep you and our children safe. I am far more useful up here defending against the Obturavi's attack and buying time. If these men are brave enough to stand and protect our family, I must be willing to do the same."

"We won't let anything happen to your husband, ma'am," offered one of the cloaked men.

"And I won't let harm come to your family, Mr. Powell," asserted Gregory.

Clarissa shook her head. "I don't like this idea, not one bit, but the children and I must go. If anything happens to you, know I will be very displeased." She frowned, then gave Father a kiss, which normally grossed out Mary Elizabeth, yet tonight felt comforting. "I love you," Mother added, "so make sure you don't disappoint me."

The Clypeate remained with Father save five men, three carrying Mary Elizabeth's youngest siblings and another pair holding lanterns, pistols drawn. These men led the family down several flights of stairs to an area of the building Mary Elizabeth had never been. They entered a tall room lined with larger-than-life portraits, presumably very important people, all of whom appeared to be scowling down at the group as they raced towards a door along the far wall.

Gregory pulled out a large, ornate golden key and unlocked the door, swinging it open to reveal a restroom. He motioned for them to enter, and while Mary Elizabeth's family and the other cloaked men dutifully filed in, as there was plenty of space inside, the little girl did not budge.

"How is this appropriate?" Mary Elizabeth asked, "I'm not sure Father would approve of such an icky hiding spot."

Her protest was interrupted by sounds from above, multiple pistols unloading and glass shattering, effectively modifying her attitude. Without further resistance, she hurried inside, the door locking shut behind her. Despite the solid wooden door muffling the noise from outside the bathroom, the shouts and gunfire grew ever closer. From amongst the handful of stalls, Gregory picked one and walked inside. Mary Elizabeth, confused and indignant, wondered why this man picked such a terrible time and immodest way to conduct his personal business. More bizarrely, Gregory waved for the group to join him, and once everyone, including Mother, disappeared into the stall, Mary Elizabeth had no other choice than to investigate. She saw the stall floor was bare, with no toilet, and the back wall hid a secure doorway, metal several inches thick, leading into a narrow passage.

A passage so tight it necessitated a single file exit, all the while the commotion growing closer until the sounds originated just outside the bathroom door. Only half the group entered the passage when the building fell eerily silent. Mary Elizabeth hoped this meant the Obturavi were defeated, although ill-timed squawking from the baby proved otherwise. Suddenly the bathroom resounded with a loud thump, the wooden door shuddered, and all her siblings screamed in response. Mary Elizabeth turned to see an axe blade poking through the door. Mother tried to quiet the children, but it was too late. "They're inside here!" a burly voice shouted, and soon, several axe blades were hacking into the bathroom door.

"Faster! Hurry up," barked Gregory. Unfortunately, the narrow door and equally tight passage hindered progress, and Mary Elizabeth's panic-stricken, flailing siblings further slowed the group. Gregory waved Mary Elizabeth forward, exiting the bathroom stall last, swinging the thick steel door closed behind him. Sadly, the attackers, the ones Father referred to as the Obturavi, crashed their way into the bathroom and rushed towards the steel door, wedging their fingers into the frame before it fully shut, preventing the bolting mechanism from engaging.

"Run! Everybody run!" Gregory shouted as he gripped the door handle and leaned back, using all his strength and weight to keep the door closed. Mary Elizabeth tried to help, grabbing onto the door, the tips of numerous bloodied, mashed-up Obturavi fingers poking around the edges. "Grab the key!" Gregory yelled. "The key! It's in my pocket. Take it and run!" he commanded, his strength waning as more Obturavi fingers wormed their way into the gap.

This time she didn't hesitate, grabbing the golden key and running through the passage to catch up with the others. After several yards, the tight passage opened into a wide space occupied by a pair of horseless carriages. Mary Elizabeth had seen a few of these vehicles in the streets, peppered amongst the horse-drawn wagons, usually stuck in the mud or broken down. Father distrusted them and called them the whimsical toys of men possessing more money than sense. Mary Elizabeth had never ridden on a motorized carriage before. Father felt they were too unpredictable and dangerous. While the family loaded onto the bench seats, motor cranking into action, she wondered if Father would approve, though more importantly, she hoped the Clypeate were honoring their promise and keeping him safe.

"Where's Gregory?" one of the Clypeate asked Mary Elizabeth.

She shook her head. "He was closing the door, and the bad men wouldn't let him. I don't think he's coming," she replied, saved from elaboration when the cloaked man nodded his understanding.

The remaining Clypeate loaded onto the second carriage, using their pistols to engage the Obturavi emerging from the narrow bathroom passage. When the carriages rolled forward into darkness, both drivers turned on electric lamps that illuminated Lincoln's Tunnel, which was wide enough to accommodate the carriages side by side. Behind them, more Obturavi flooded the tunnel. At first, the Clypeate were able to deter their advances, but quickly, there were more Obturavi than Clypeate bullets. Although the Obturavi didn't stand a chance against the speed of their horseless carriages, the attackers relentlessly pursued them, running and shooting even as they fell behind until the tunnel's inky shadows enveloped them.

The bumpy ride didn't last very long, only a few minutes, and while slowing down, they were greeted by several Clypeate guarding this end of the tunnel, rifles aimed and ready. "They ambushed us at the War Building," their driver explained, "most of our men stayed behind to give us a head start, but we're still being pursued," he added, underscored by the shouts and taunts of the approaching Obturavi. He turned to Mary Elizabeth's family. "Now, children, we need to pass through the Research Hall to get to the library," he said. "It's a bit cluttered and treacherous, so don't touch anything."

The Clypeate escorted Mary Elizabeth and her family into the expansive Research Hall, an inventor's paradise, a warehouse-sized science lab. Sturdy shelves loaded with jarred chemicals lined the vast wall space while dozens of workbenches filled the room, every surface occupied by scientific instruments, glassware, and exotic gadgets. The group carefully navigated across the crowded space, weaving between stacked equipment even as they gazed up to avoid random wires dangling from the ceiling.

Passing the work benches, Mary Elizabeth's eyes widened with wonder. It looked like the future exploded all over this room. Oddly, the little girl didn't feel surprised by the array of amazing technology on display, instead wondering why it all looked uncannily familiar. These impossibly complex creations reminded her of something, a dream perhaps. Still, she didn't have time to figure out the connection because the Obturavi reached the Research Hall and were hurling flaming bottles inside. Where the bottles landed, small fires grew into larger ones, and the room filled with thick, dark smoke. Mary Elizabeth's family hurried towards a second door at the far end of the room, this one leading to an even grander, more cavernous space as wide as Pennsylvania Avenue and the length of a city block.

Clypeate guards locked the Research Hall door behind them, giving their group a chance to pause and recuperate briefly. They all coughed violently. Mary Elizabeth wasn't the only one whose eyes watered, nose burned, and lungs felt like the air had been replaced with hot volcanic ash. While recovering, Mary Elizabeth scanned the long, rectangular room, the near end organized like a military camp with precise rows of tents stretching to the walls. Massive wooden towers dominated the far side, each topping out halfway to a ceiling higher than her house.

They didn't linger. Wisps of black smoke flowed under the Research Hall door, and whooping shouts reminded them that the Obturavi weren't far behind. All of Mary Elizabeth's siblings devolved into blubbering, hysterical blobs requiring them to be carried. This allowed the group to run swiftly across the room, although their squeaky cries only emboldened the Obturavi now banging against the locked door.

Mary Elizabeth and Mother kept pace with the Clypeate racing across the room, darting between tents and gear towards the massive towers. Mary Elizabeth noted the wooden structures were alive with movement, at first glance looking like a forest's worth of timber randomly swaying. On closer inspection, she realized the motions followed intricate patterns. The towers consisted of spindly beams organized into complex machines, all with ribbons of hole-punched plates circulating through them. Jacquard looms, she concluded, each plate encoded with information. She'd only seen analytical machines like these in pictures, though her wildest imagination never contemplated devices of such grand scale. As they hurried between the looms, Mary Elizabeth turned her attention to the tangled web of wires and cables dangling above their heads, connecting all the looms before descending into a wardrobe-shaped box, a dozen feet tall and peppered with blinking lights, dials and levers. When the group approached the box, they paused, the Clypeate nervous to carry a group of flailing children further into the wire jungle. Their indecision gave Mary Elizabeth time for closer inspection. While the men plotted the least dangerous path through the chaotic maze of electrocution risk, she decided the box must function like a control panel. The young girl marveled at the complexity, how these ostensibly isolated towers were arranged to operate as a single coordinated machine.

She didn't have long to indulge her curiosity, however, because the Research Hall door burst off the hinges, spewing forth billowing smoke and many Obturavi, their pistols ablaze, immediately turning tents into flaming torches. Mary Elizabeth's hope wavered. These attackers were relentless, and just as tears welled, a door beyond the machine stacks opened, and waves of Clypeate streamed out. With guns drawn, they flew past her family and towards a confrontation with the Obturavi. Only one man stayed behind, holding the door open and waving at them, welcoming them. It was Father, he was alive! Mary Elizabeth raced forward to hug him, and soon, her entire family was secure inside the Library of the Ages. The circular room was grand in scale, big as a circus tent, though instead of flimsy canvas, these walls were lined with dark, richly carved bookcases. An equally ornate spiral staircase led up to a series of tiered balconies lining the room, providing access to all the shelves as they extended towards the ceiling several stories above.

They were finally safe, with Father's friends battling the awful Obturavi in the other room and a dozen more men guarding them inside the library. Throughout this ordeal, Mary Elizabeth kept her feelings bottled inside. Her family needed it, but now she felt comfortable enough to flop down onto one of many richly upholstered chairs and sob along with the rest of the children. Mother was occupied calming down her siblings, so Father came over and put his arms around her. "Thank you for being such a strong, brave girl," he said, stroking her hair.

Mercifully, it didn't take long for Mary Elizabeth's brothers and sisters to settle. The men who'd carried them took special care to shield their innocent eyes from the worst of the violence, and with thick walls now blocking them from the melee, the other children gleefully played as if the entire night had never happened, engaged in a game of tag. With Father once again occupied guarding the door and Mother busy tending to the baby, Mary Elizabeth decided to explore the room. She scanned the shelves loaded with books of varying shapes and sizes, some old and fragile, others glossy and new, but all locked behind glass doors.

She noticed the shelves along the upper terraces did not possess these glassy barriers, so she walked up the spiral stairs to the next level. Mary Elizabeth strolled along the balcony, getting a bird's eye view of her siblings at play and the men of the Clypeate assembling a blockade of furniture against the door.

While these shelves also contained books, some held piles of rolled-up paper, stones with funny markings, or stacks of clay tablets. Being a curious child, she grabbed one of the paper rolls to examine it, but pulling the ancient papyrus scroll off the shelf caused it to crumble between her fingers. She looked around. Thankfully, nobody noticed. All the adults were otherwise engaged, so she kept moving, vowing to keep her hands to herself. She didn't wait long to break her promise, though now, with good reason, standing in front of a binder labeled "Mary Elizabeth Powell". An entire shelf loaded with binders, in fact, all titled with her name. She picked one at random and opened it. Every sheet of paper inside was a drawing of her creation, without a doubt, each clearly signed and dated. What they were doing in this place, she didn't know, giggling with pride to find her artwork so lovingly cataloged.

Mary Elizabeth didn't have a chance to share her discovery with anyone before getting distracted by loud clanking noises from above. She looked up, shocked to see a ladder dropping down from a hatch in the library's ornate ceiling and a procession of cloaked figures descending along it. Judging from Father's excited reaction, these were fellow Clypeate. As the men rushed down multiple flights of stairs to reach ground level, one stopped and walked over to the little girl. "Hello, Miss Mary Beth," the cloaked figure said, pulling back his hood.

"Mister Edison!" she exclaimed, glad to see a familiar face. "Bad men are trying to hurt us."

"Yes, I know," he replied. "That's why I'm here, to rescue your family." Mr. Edison continued downstairs to speak with Father, visibly relieved to see the reinforcements.

Mary Elizabeth followed Mr. Edison and listened as he spoke with Father. "The Jefferson Pier is secure; there are no signs of Obturavi outside, and the marsh grasses are tall enough to hide our escape. We have an armored gunboat waiting in the Tidal Reservoir, and we can be several miles downriver before daybreak."

Father shook his head. "I prefer to save that strategy as a last resort. Given how well this attack against us has been orchestrated, I fear there may be more surprises lying in wait." The men spoke a little longer, interrupted by a loud ringing coming from inside the grandfather clock dominating the room's center. Mary Elizabeth hadn't paid much attention to the massive clock tower, only now admiring the beautiful, intricate spire reaching the second terrace with an elaborate pedestal fanned out wider than a door is long.

Mr. Edison opened the clock belly and, to Mary Elizabeth's surprise, reached in and pulled out a telephone receiver. She'd seen telephones before, mainly in the Wedding Cake Building, though she rarely witnessed them in use. The single time she got close enough to touch a phone's shiny brass candlestick, her attempt ended with a stern reprimand for how it wasn't a plaything for children, simply making the forbidden fruit more tempting. Mary Elizabeth didn't enjoy being treated like a child. While admittedly, yes, she chronologically met the criteria, she knew what Mr. Edison and Mr. Tesla always told her: she wasn't like other children.

Under normal circumstances, with such a tempting target within grasp, Mary Elizabeth would have seized the opportunity to examine the electronic marvel, except the longer Mr. Edison listened to the caller, the paler and sullener his face became. Suddenly, the little girl knew things weren't going to be okay. She ran over to Father and hugged his leg.

"Don't worry, sweetie, we're safe," he said, except mere seconds later, Mr. Edison turned Father's reassurance into a lie.

Returning the phone to the cabinet, Mr. Edison ran his fingers through his hair and folded his arms. "The waiting is over. The Research Hall is engulfed in flames, the analytical machines are shot to pieces, and our men defending the library entrance are cornered. They will fight to hold the room as long as possible, but they will be overwhelmed shortly by the Obturavi. We must evacuate immediately."

"This library cannot fall into their hands," Father replied. "The knowledge of the ages resides here, and if they breach the Sanctuary, all will be lost."

"Then it is time to activate the Axyn Kirox and summon Hesperus," Mr. Edison decided. "His prophecies described the arrival of a great upheaval, a time when his presence was once again required, and tonight surpasses my worst expectations."

Father reached into his hunting satchel, the one Mary Elizabeth watched him load with supplies from his gun cabinet, and he pulled out a small, shiny object. A pyramid several inches tall, the surface of silver-white metal so smooth and highly polished it reflected light better than any mirror. Whatever this Axyn Kirox was, Mary Elizabeth needed to touch it. Father must have read her mind because she hadn't fully crafted a plan when he said, "Children, you must stop playing and sit down next to your mother. I'm not entirely sure what's going to happen." Then, he looked directly at Mary Elizabeth. "This includes you too, Mary Beth," he said, "I don't want you getting hurt, and I need you to make sure none of the little ones get too curious, okay?" he added, shooting her a quick wink.

Although Mary Elizabeth felt indignant at being grouped with the other children, she also enjoyed the opportunity to boss around her younger siblings. She eagerly shepherded them towards Mother, who gently rocked the baby while occupying the only chair not piled onto the library door barricade. Mary Elizabeth corralled them all, driving them back against the bookcases while standing in front of the wrangled herd, spreading her arms out to create a boundary line they dare not cross.

Father gripped the short, dull gray handle extending from the base of the shimmering pyramid and lifted the Axyn Kirox. The room grew silent, from the men guarding the door to the normally rambunctious children, all watching Father hold the object like a mighty king wielding his royal scepter. Meanwhile, Mr. Edison reopened the enormous grandfather clock, pulling out a coiled bundle of cable thicker than the python she'd seen at the National Zoo. Father flipped the Axyn Kirox, now holding the silver-white pyramid instead of the gray handle, and inched closer to the grandfather clock. Mr. Edison dragged the thick cable towards the Axyn Kirox, the cable's end splitting into wiry tendrils. Once the delicate fibers wrapped around the stubby handle, the clock's towering spire began to rotate, spinning ever faster until it emitted a high-pitched humming sound.

"Is this normal?" Father asked the genius inventor. Mr. Edison shrugged his shoulders. The vibratory hum evolved into a rhythmic thumping until the phone rang, the noise stopping as soon as Mr. Edison picked up the receiver. This conversation was short, animated, and desperate. Mr. Edison hung up, the clock spire slowed down, and the cable unraveled from the Axyn Kirox, dropping the small pyramid into Father's hands.

"Well, the clock functioned perfectly. It's the response which fails us," reported Mr. Edison, who was obviously displeased with the outcome. "Tonight, we're on our own."

Father placed the Axyn Kirox back in his satchel and joined the other men surrounding Mr. Edison. Mary

Elizabeth seized the opportunity. Instead of listening to the conversation or tinkering with the telephone, she headed straight towards Father's satchel, still ten feet away from the leather bag when the silver pyramid floated out. The Axyn Kirox levitated at eye level, lit up bright as the sun, and whirled like a spinning top while slowly drifting towards Mary Elizabeth. Her eyes glazed over, trance-like, blankly staring at the glowing pyramid. Father noticed too late. He tried pulling Mary Elizabeth away from the Axyn Kirox but couldn't, her feet budging less than if they were nailed in place.

Suddenly, the pyramid stopped spinning, Mary Elizabeth snapped back into reality and hugged Father. "The Axyn Kirox spoke to me," she cried out, "don't stay here, don't stay! They're all going to die!" With her face buried deep in Father's chest, the Axyn Kirox tilted over until the pyramid's tip aimed at Mary Elizabeth, speeding like a bullet into the back of her head. She went limp in his arms.

***

Mary Elizabeth woke to many faces staring down at her. "What's going on? Why is everyone looking at me?" she asked.

Mother pulled the little girl tightly to her chest. "My daughter! My sweet girl! You're alive!" her mother rejoiced, sobbing and gripping her even tighter.

"Mary Elizabeth, do you remember anything?" Father asked.

"Why? Am I in trouble?" she replied, her Christian name typically evoked only when she'd done something wrong.

"Oh, no, sweetie, not one bit," Father replied, turning to Mr. Edison. "What just happened?" he demanded.

"The Axyn Kirox disappeared inside my daughter's head, and now she's babbling about explosions in the sky. What's it doing in there?"

"I have no possible way of knowing," Mr. Edison admitted, "Hesperus didn't mention anything like this during our short conversation. Mary Beth seems fine now. I don't believe the Axyn Kirox is causing her any problems, although Hesperus will know better than I, and we certainly don't have time to discuss the finer points any longer. Hesperus is too far from here to be of any service tonight. In the morning, we can meet him at the rendezvous point."

"You're right, of course," Father conceded, turning to Mother. "It's time for you to leave, Clarissa, though I must stay. Tonight, the Clypeate cannot spare a single man, and it would be unfair to leave when I am needed most." This time, Mother did not protest; instead, she quietly hugged Father. "Now, Mr. Edison, take my wife and children with you and make haste. Keep them safe and get them as far away from here as possible."

Mr. Edison shook Father's hand. "You are correct, Mr. Powell, we need to depart this moment. And even though you will wonder about your family's safety, rest assured, Hesperus already rushes to meet us. You are a good man, Mr. Powell, the Clypeate has never been served by better."

Mary Elizabeth hugged Father as well. "Don't make me leave you," she sobbed.

"The Clypeate is strong," he replied, "but I must stay and help them defend this place to keep you all safe. As soon as I can join you, I will, my dear one."

Already, explosions from outside the library rocked the walls and shook the room. Mr. Edison and Mother carried the youngest children and urged the older ones to hasten their ascent, climbing the staircase and spiraling up towards the library ceiling. Mary Elizabeth proceeded last, giving Father one final hug. "Be strong, my daughter, and help Mother as best you can," he said before joining the men taking up positions to defend against the Obturavi.

When Mr. Edison reached the upper terrace of the library, he helped the family carefully climb the ladder into the ceiling hatch, Mary Elizabeth demanding to bring up the rear. As she navigated the ladder, the Clypeate below began unloading their pistols. She looked down several stories to the ground and trembled at the height. Mr. Edison called to her from the top of the ladder, extending his arm to help.

"Dear Miss Mary Beth, please hurry. We can't let the wicked men know our escape route." Once she was through, Mr. Edison pulled up the ladder and shut the hatch, leaving them in total darkness. "Please keep calm, children," he said, "I'll soon fix our predicament," and the tunnel suddenly shone brightly as day, light coming from the end of a foot-long cylinder in Mr. Edison's hand.

The children "oohed" and "aahed" at the magic stick.

"Torchlight," he explained, "something I've been working on for years, though I just can't seem to keep it lit very long. More like a flash of light, if you ask me. I may keep tinkering with it but it's not yet worth my time filing a patent." The group followed Mr. Edison through the winding passage until the tunnel abruptly ended against a gray stone wall. He stopped in his tracks, looking confused and upset. "They closed the Pier Stone," he growled, pounding on the rock, "I told them to leave it open! We don't have the key, and Commander Gregory has the only copy. We won't be able to get out of here without it."

Mary Elizabeth felt her pocket, and there it was, the large golden key she'd taken from Gregory while he struggled to keep the Obturavi from getting into Lincoln's Tunnel.

Under all the duress, she'd completely forgotten about it. She held it up to Mr. Edison. "Is this the key you need?" she asked, noting the diamond shape carved into the handle.

"How did you get that?" he wondered. "Never mind, child, you never fail to amaze me," he said, patting her shoulder and taking the key. He fed the ornate golden key into an imperceptible slit between roughly hewn stone blocks, and suddenly the wall shuddered, slowly tilting back to reveal an opening above their heads. Unfettered moonlight poured down on them. Mr. Edison turned off his flashlight, and they all climbed the angled stone like a ramp, emerging into marshy fields. Mr. Edison made a birdcall. Mary Elizabeth guessed an oriole, and instantly, half a dozen cloaked men rose out of the surrounding swamp grass.

Mr. Edison looked pleased. It was safe, they were Clypeate. "The monument grounds are clear and secure," one of them whispered. Mary Elizabeth looked up the hill towards the Washington Monument, only a few hundred feet distant, scanning for signs of unwanted movement and finding none, the calm in stark contrast with the battle raging beneath them.

"Why was the Jefferson Pier locked?" Mr. Edison demanded. "We would've been trapped down there if it weren't for a bit of luck."

"Mr. Tesla made the decision," the guard explained while continuing to scan the horizon. "After you traveled down the tunnel, he decided to lead a few men to the rescue boat to make sure the path was clear. He didn't want to leave the Jefferson Pier open, so he manually overrode the closing mechanism. He deemed it strategically wiser to lock everyone inside rather than leave it vulnerable to Obturavi exploitation."

"Calculations of a coward," Mr. Edison hissed. "We are fortunate Miss Mary Beth came to possess the only key, although at what cost I hate to ponder. The Research Hall is already lost," he explained, "and the attackers are breaching the Library of the Ages. Behind us lies a scene of horror and chaos. Your men would serve better down there, defending the Sanctuary rather than escorting us to the Tidal Reservoir. If the Obturavi planned to attack us here, at the Jefferson Pier, they would have done it by now."

The Clypeate guards agreed and raced down the stone ramp into the tunnel, rifles and pistols in hand. Once all the children were counted, Mr. Edison looked at Mother. "I don't know if I can do this. Once I lock the Jefferson Pier from the outside, their only exit will be back through Lincoln's Tunnel, and that path is now a fiery hell."

"Then I will do what must be done," Mother replied, putting out her hand and taking the key. "You have always been a great support to my family, and it is only fair I relieve you of this burden."

Mother approached the stone block and searched between the carved markings. Finding the proper slot, she inserted the key. The stone block rotated back to an upright position, resealing the tunnel and leaving just a few feet of the gray stone peeking above ground, serving as a reminder of the spot where she sealed the fate of her husband and dozens more brave men. On this night, when good fortune was found in short supply, the Washington Monument cast its long shadow in their favor, the obelisk providing cover as they trudged through the swamp grass toward the rescue boat.

Chapter 4

December 22, 1938
Bureau of Engineering
City of Washington, District of Columbia

TOP SECRET - EYES ONLY

Filed 22 December 1938

FROM : GENERAL MALIN CRAIG, US ARMY
CHIEF OF STAFF
TO : REAR ADMIRAL HAROLD BOWEN, CHIEF
OF THE BUREAU OF ENGINEERING

<u>URGENT</u>

On the morning of 12/18/38, British Royal Air Force (RAF) routine aerial surveillance noted unusual German maritime activity. Reconnaissance photos identified the MS *Schwabenland,* a German civilian commercial freighter, traveling through the North Sea following a route deviating well beyond normal shipping channels. The *Schwabenland* was flagged by British Military command, and additional RAF flight time was dedicated to tracking the vessel and gathering further data.

Two days later, the MS *Schwabenland* entered the Celtic Sea, still heading southwesterly. Analysis of aerial photos revealed a deck overloaded with supplies, including airplane catapults and two planes secured to the deck. Both planes were identified as Dornier Do 18s, maritime patrol planes of the German Luftwaffe.

Britain's military command sought input from their Secret Intelligence Service, and their analysts confirmed a prior awareness of the freighter. Their embedded intel network inside Germany noted atypical behavior while the MS *Schwabenland* was still docked in the port city of Hamburg. Their sources reported the civilian freighter under tight security, with constant military supervision during the loading of high-grade Wehrmacht equipment and vehicles. The ship was also packed with enough food rations for several months of travel, as well as vessel modifications for ice-breaking and prolonged sub-zero conditions.

Unfortunately, due to building German aggression in Europe, the British government could not spare the resources to pursue the freighter more vigorously. Thus, they shared their concerns with the United States through the State Department attaché on 12/22/38. The United Kingdom intelligence community, with their limited information, thought it possible the vessel was heading into Atlantic waters to interfere with United States interests and wanted our government aware in case further actions were merited.

President Roosevelt tasked the US Department of the Army with obtaining actionable data. The limited information described above was distributed to US Army intelligence this morning, and I requested we also share this information with you. I've heard rumors swirling that you've quietly amassed an intel team with remarkable analytic capabilities. Therefore I'm eagerly looking forward to your suggestions. And speaking of circulating gossip, congratulations are in order. It seems you'll soon be promoted to Director of the Naval Research Labs, although if your team is as good as they say, you already know that.

DISTRIBUTION: REAR ADMIRAL HAROLD BOWEN

COPY NO : 1 of 1

Bureau Chief Bowen, soon to be Director Bowen, folded the letter and leaned back in his plush chair, a thready grin erupting across his wizened face. While Harold Bowen knew for weeks about his yet-to-be-offered promotion to Directorship of the US Naval Research Lab, he'd been waiting for the other opportunity included in this memorandum much longer. Cold weather gear and ice-breaking modifications hinted at Germany's destination, and despite not having his players fully prepared, the game had begun. He picked up the phone and dialed an old friend, one he'd met years earlier while they were both many pay grades younger.

After hanging up, Rear Admiral Bowen crafted his response, returning it within hours. He recommended a limited response. No reason to muddle the plan. Without consulting a single soul, he typed out a short reply.

General Craig:

While I can neither confirm nor deny these rumors, thank you for including my team in your intelligence analysis. Based on the information provided, we conclude the German voyage most likely represents a non-aggressive exploratory mission. This scenario poses little risk for US interests, but tracking using available resources already deployed in the Atlantic theater would be a prudent compromise.

Harold Bowen, Chief of the Bureau of Engineering

He read it over once, sealed it in a TOP SECRET envelope, and handed it to his secretary. "Please have a courier pick this up now and deliver it immediately," he requested while donning his jacket, "and cancel the rest of my schedule for today. I have some affairs that need attending to. In fact, cancel tomorrow as well." After driving downtown to pick up a traveling companion, he filled the gas tank and set course for New York City. While soon-to-be Director Bowen couldn't be certain of this journey's outcome, the potential reward was worth the effort, just as long as they remembered to bring plenty of birdseed.

Chapter 5

December 24, 1938
University of California - Los Angeles Campus
Los Angeles, California

Professor Riordan sighed while grading another egregious display of mediocrity, slashing red marks down the completed final exam. If these were the future's brightest thinkers, he mused, I might as well give up teaching. Maybe learn to ride the rails like a hobo. He wanted to scribble, "You should apologize to me for wasting my time", across the top of this lackluster effort, having little patience for anything less than perfection in his classroom. Clearer judgment held back his pen. After all, he was only an assistant professor, on the track though not yet tenured, and while such admonitions might be immediately gratifying, they could be frowned upon during his professional review. Tenure, the holy grail of academia, was still several years away, and in this pursuit, he'd been a very patient man.

Declan was reminded of his place in the academic universe every time he sat at the tiny desk of his equally petite office, the smallest in the biology department. Perfunctory quarters for the most junior professor, having only started his professorial trek the prior summer. Upon taking reign of his tiny domain, the other professors, all with notably larger offices, gleefully shared campus apocryphal with him regarding his office's origin. The prevailing theory involved construction crews beginning at both ends of the building, creating equally sized offices, until they reached the middle and realized only a few extra feet remained, inadequate for a proper office. They would have turned the space into a broom closet had it been roomier, so instead, they hung a door and labeled it the junior faculty suite. He didn't believe these stories until the first time he peeked inside the broom closet and realized the janitors had better bargaining power.

Declan used the tiny space as best he could, shelves stacked to the ceiling with scientific equipment and notebooks tracking his research projects. If offices were allocated by intelligence and ingenuity, Declan would dwarf the other faculty, but as a rambunctious upstart, he was being fed a healthy serving of humble pie. Nothing more eloquently demonstrated his place in the professorial hierarchy than his ability to simultaneously flat-palm both walls of his office.

Declan leaned back, ran his fingers through his dirty blond hair, and yawned. He took one last look at the newspaper, the first one he'd purchased in months. He didn't normally make time for inconsequential drivel, but there was an article about this year's Nobel Prize winners. He shook his head in disgust. Heymans won for slicing off dog heads, a decidedly barbaric choice, and Fermi won for his work on radioactivity. "Nothing will ever come of it," Declan commented, "just some glow-in-the-dark paint for alarm clocks. Maybe next year a radioactive decapitated puppy will win the prize," he scoffed. While crumpling the newspaper into a ball, the front-page headline caught his gaze. "Declaration of Lima Secures Peace for the Americas," he read. "Well, at least that's some good news, glad to see we'll be staying out of Europe's messes for a change."

The professor yawned again. Time to call it quits for the evening. Despite the sun having dipped below the horizon hours ago, by Declan's standards, this was an early night. He spent most of the holiday break brainstorming a new research project, and after several all-nighters, even the strongest coffee no longer supported his eyelids. It was December, and night began much earlier, although even in summer's prime the young professor rarely left before streetlamps flickered on. After all, there weren't any particular reasons to rush back to his tiny studio apartment. He lived alone, rarely socialized, and thoughts of a reheated casserole didn't set a fire under him, either. For Declan, work was his passion; his family, friends, hobby, and mistress all rolled into one.

He donned his lab coat before heading upstairs for one final check on his personal research, the extracurricular projects he hoped would build and cultivate his scientific reputation. Walking up to his laboratory, Declan debated curving the final exam for his graduate-level class and, despite giving them the screws-to-the-wall version of the test, decided against the reprieve. "Cocky bastards will benefit from getting knocked down a few pegs," he muttered, fumbling for his lab key.

Although the students were gone, home on break, the quad below wasn't entirely empty. Unbeknownst to Declan, on the grassy expanse stood a pair of men in dark suits meticulously tracking his movements. When Declan flipped on the lights in the biology lab, the taller man looked at his watch. "It's Saturday night, after eight pm, on Christmas Eve, and there's only one creature stirring on this entire campus," he remarked. "That'll be our guy."

Meanwhile, Declan darted between bacterial incubators, jotting down temperatures and documenting the expanding circles on Petri dishes. Bacterial growth velocity with variable substrates and nutrient density wasn't sexy biology, but his approach was unique and should merit publication in a reputable journal. He looked up and shrieked in surprise as the two figures from the quad now filled his door frame. Although the sky had already darkened into the inkiest shades of night, both men wore fedoras and sunglasses as black as their suits. Neither smiled. "Good evening, professor. Doctor Riordan, is it?"

"Yes, that's me. Now, what are you doing in my lab?" he demanded. "There are sensitive experiments in here. Can't you frat boys find more creative ways to amuse yourselves and cause mischief besides mucking around the biology building?"

The men scanned the dimly lit hallway before shutting the door behind them. Declan's annoyance turned to unease. He was trapped, the two men positioned between him and the only escape route not requiring a window jump. "Look, if this is about your grades, I'd be happy to address this during my regular office hours."

"We're not here about grades, professor," the taller, spindly man replied, stepping forward. Declan stood an inch north of six feet, yet this stranger still towered over him. Declan backed up, calculating the odds of surviving a four-story dive. The second man, stockier and slightly shorter than Declan, reached into his jacket pocket.

Declan shielded himself with an errant textbook. "Don't shoot!" he pleaded, eyes clenched shut. Instead of gunfire, Declan heard chuckling.

"*Angels with Dirty Faces*, am I right?" the shorter man asked. Declan opened one eye and peeked over the book binding. "I just saw the flick last week. Jimmy Cagney is the best. Don't worry, professor, we aren't gangsters. Although my name, coincidentally, is James," the shorter man said, holding out a badge as he slowly approached Declan, who now held the book like a batter ready to swing for the fences. Declan deftly plucked the badge from James' hand before returning to his defensive posture.

Declan glanced at the identification card, "United States Navy", in bold lettering, along with the name and picture of a young, dark-haired man. "James Fischer," read the professor. He'd never seen an official military badge, but this looked legitimate, at least more professional than anything fraternity hooligans would produce. "Do you mind taking off your sunglasses so I can compare your face with the ID picture?"

"I'm afraid this location isn't secure," James replied, "and I'd rather not take the chance of being identified."

Declan was puzzled. "By whom? We're four stories up. Why would anyone go through such trouble?"

"We work for a very specialized branch of the Navy. Even the most mundane activities are of paramount interest to our adversaries. Since this is a time-sensitive matter, we've already taken risks to locate you quickly, which means I can't guarantee the privacy of our meeting for much longer. Doctor Riordan, we have a very attractive professional opportunity for you, but it requires you to leave with us immediately."

"Wow," Declan replied, "I didn't realize Navy recruiters used such high-pressure tactics. You must really be desperate," he chided. "No, I'm quite happy in my present employment, although thank you for stopping by unexpectedly and freaking me out." When Declan picked up a notebook to return to his research, the visitors did not leave, budge, or even twitch. "I'm sorry," Declan said, "I thought I made myself clear. I'm not interested in joining the Navy."

James stepped forward into Declan's personal space. "You misunderstand our intentions. We're not asking you to join the Navy. We're offering you something unique. A winning lottery ticket, the opportunity of a lifetime, served up on a silver platter. You're Snow White, and we're the seven dwarfs and prince all rolled into one." James checked his watch. "But we need to get moving, so you need to decide quickly." James fished around in his pockets again, this time pulling out a plain white envelope. "Look, if a moral obligation to serve your country doesn't light your fire, you'd also be serving your own best interests." He handed Declan the envelope. "This is just a small token of our appreciation. We hope you'll come along with us and see what else we can offer." James turned to leave. "Mull it over. We'll be in the hallway waiting, though make it snappy. We've already spent too much time here."

Declan's logical mind wanted to immediately return the envelope; however, curiosity won. He opened the envelope and unfolded the contents. The first page Declan recognized immediately, a picture of gleaming white polar bears roaming the ice pack as a seaplane flew overhead. It was the September 1929 cover of *Nature*. He'd read every issue of the magazine since middle school. The second was a handwritten letter. Declan read it carefully, twice, before running out into the hallway.

James didn't look surprised to see the professor. "So, what's your decision?" he asked.

Declan held up the letter. "Is this for real?" he asked, waving it for emphasis. "This is a handwritten letter from Sir Richard Gregory, editor of *Nature*, the most respected biology journal of our time, guaranteeing me two published articles in his magazine. Do you know what that would do for my career?"

"Yes, you'd instantly be the darling of your department," James replied, "and no more broom closet offices for you."

Declan scrunched his forehead. "How'd you know my office was a broom…"

"We know more than you'd care to hear," interrupted James. "And, of course, the letter is real. Wouldn't be a very good negotiating tool if it weren't. And it's yours, no strings, whatever you decide. No cow flop, no flea circus. We're the real deal. And that letter is only the tip of the iceberg, so to speak." James looked again at his watch.

"Professor, we really need to get moving. Don't worry. Your students won't even have time to miss you. We'll have you back here playing with your slimy petri dishes before you know it." James checked his watch again. "We're really cutting this close." James and the lanky man walked over to the stairwell. "Times up. My apologies, Doctor Riordan, we really must go." As James started down the stairs, he added "I know you're conflicted. Sometimes you have to roll the dice," he turned, before quickening his pace.

Declan's mind swirled. He was a man of science, not whimsy. Curiosity may have killed the cat, but doesn't chance favor the prepared mind? By the time Declan made his decision and chased after the men, they were nearly at ground level. "One last question," he shouted down to them. "Why me? This letter from Sir Gregory wasn't a generic letter. He addressed it to me by name. You picked me for a reason. What is it?"

James stopped and smiled back up. "You're very perceptive. Maybe that's part of why you were chosen. Truth is, I don't really know. My higher-ups tasked me with finding and procuring you, and I don't question orders. You know yourself better than anyone. Maybe you know what makes you so special."

"But there's nothing," Declan answered.

"Sorry to hear that," James replied before resuming his descent. "Perhaps they were mistaken about you."

Declan looked back at his lab, thought about the pile of ungraded finals still awaiting his rebuke, and muttered, "What the hell" before dashing down the stairs.

Outside, the professor found James standing next to a dark sedan, holding the rear door open. "I didn't doubt you for a second. Not special? Ha! Only a rare few could appreciate and embrace this kind of adventure, that makes you very special. Now climb in, and let's get rolling."

Declan slid into the back seat, followed by James. The tall, lanky man sat behind the wheel, his fedora rubbing against the ceiling fabric. Declan barely settled his bottom onto the upholstered bench when a cushioned bar rose from the floor and settled across his lap.

"What's this?" Declan asked, squirming to get free. "I'm trapped!"

"Not trapped," James said, "you're secured. So am I." Declan looked over and saw a similar bar across James. "I should have warned you. Bruce has a lead foot, so the ride can get a little bumpy. Think of this like a roller coaster. Extra precautions don't hurt." James tapped the lanky man's shoulder. "Hey Bruce, we're all set back here."

"Sounds good," Bruce replied, picking up a clunky, brick-shaped black box. He held it against his ear and said, "Admiral, last package secured. We're delivering him now."

"Who is he talking to?" Declan asked. "There's no way you have a telephone line in here."

"Of course not, that's absurd," James replied, "he's on a portable handset."

"A what?" asked Declan. "I've never heard of such a device."

James groaned. "Oh, I forgot, that's classified tech. I'm not sure what clearance you'll get, so I could get in big trouble for that. Do me a favor. Just pretend you didn't see anything."

Not so easily dissuaded, Declan would have pursued the matter further, except his focus shifted to the rising pressure against his chest. At first, like a small child sitting on his ribcage, the automobile's acceleration felt like nothing he'd experienced short of a carnival ride. Before he could ask where they were headed, his body pushed ever deeper into the seatback until the force increased to somewhere between a portly man and a petite elephant. His vision grayed, and within seconds, he drifted out of consciousness.

***

Declan woke to bright daylight streaming through the car window. Rubbing his aching temples, he decided a hot cup of coffee would help. Alone in the car and with lap restraint lifted, he ventured outside to find James and Bruce leaning against the trunk. The breeze felt nice, warm and briny, although he didn't understand why they were parked at a naval base.

"I must have fallen asleep," Declan remarked, surveying the row of towering US Navy warships docked alongside the pier. "Where are we?" he asked. "This port doesn't look familiar, certainly not Long Beach. Did we drive to San Diego?"

"No, Doctor Riordan, welcome to Norfolk," James said, "home of the Navy's oldest and proudest shipyard."

"Is that north of Santa Barbara?" Declan asked before his brain caught up with his mouth. "Scratch that. You don't mean Norfolk, as in Norfolk, Virginia?"

"Indeed, that would be the one," Bruce replied. "Impressive, isn't it?

"Impressive?" Declan replied. "That's not the problem. The place you picked me up, where I work and live, happens to be Los Angeles. It would have taken days to drive here. You must have drugged me. How long was I out?"

"No, we didn't drug you. Look, I could lie to you and feed you some BS that would make more sense, but the truth is that we made it here overnight. I thought I'd have more time to fill you in on the details, but as it turns out, you can't handle more than a couple g's before passing out."

"So, you're telling me we drove thousands of miles in one night?"

"Of course not. That would be absurd. Just the tire friction alone would make it impossible. You're a scientist. You should know these kinds of things." James looked at his watch. "We really don't have the time to discuss this right now." He pointed to a nearby freighter. "See that big ship, the USS *Milwaukee*? You'll be traveling onboard as part of their research team. But the gangplank goes up in twenty minutes, so we better get you moving."

"What do you mean? You still haven't explained anything to me! Am I getting on a boat? Where are we going, and what am I doing?"

"Look, Doctor Riordan, you're in good hands. It's the United States Navy. You're going to love it, an all-expense paid research trip sponsored by the federal government. When you get back, not only will you have two published articles, we'll make sure you're immediately eligible for tenure at the university of your choice. The sky's the limit. Not to mention, we've got the best technology money can buy, and other things so top-secret no amount of money can buy. It's going to be a research nerd's paradise, I promise. And they'll explain all of it when you get on board, but ya gotta get moving. I told you we were in a tight time crunch."

"I've never been on a boat," Declan replied, "what if I get motion sickness?"

"First, there's pills for that, and second, please stop calling it a boat. Sailors don't have a sense of humor about this. The big gray floating thing is called a ship. Big difference."

"But this is just so sudden," Declan hemmed. "Can you promise me this isn't a scam?"

James threw his hands up in exasperation. "What could we possibly be scamming you for that would be worth this amount of effort? You're just gonna have to trust me."

"I prefer evidence over trust," Declan replied.

"Professor, take a look at the big, shiny metal ship behind you," blurted Bruce. "Does that look like a scam? What further evidence can we provide?"

"Valid point," conceded Declan, "although this still feels like a Faustian bargain."

"Well, color me red while 1 strap on some horns," James responded, exasperated. "This is your government, for Pete's sake! How 'bout we skip ahead through some of this drama, and I'll promise you one more thing. All your grant proposals, rest of your career fast-tracked. Do we have a deal?"

They did. Every man has a price, and James led the professor along the dock and up to the quarterdeck. A young naval officer guarded the gangway. "This gentleman is the officer of the deck," James explained. "Officer, my friend here is a civilian, and he's requesting permission to come aboard."

The naval officer looked Declan over. "Is he drunk?" the officer demanded, watching Declan struggle to regain his full faculties.

"No, just adjusting to a new time zone," James reassured him. "Now, Doctor, show him your boarding papers."

"What are you talking about? What papers?" Declan asked.

"The boarding documents, the ones in your pocket, my good man," answered James.

"There's nothing in my..." Declan started but stopped when he dipped his hand into his jacket pocket and felt something. He pulled out an envelope, stamped across the face in bold red letters, "UNITED STATES NAVAL DOCUMENTS".

The naval officer took it from his hand, looked it over, and compared it with his paperwork. "This man is Professor Riordan? My apologies, sir, we've been waiting for you. All of your personal belongings have already been loaded, and the rest of your team has already boarded. I'll have someone show you to your quarters."

He turned to James. "What does he mean, my belongings?"

"He means exactly what he said," James replied, waving him forward. "Now get going." As Declan crossed the gangway, it pulled up behind him. James waved from the dock and shouted, "This is the trip of a lifetime; try to enjoy it!" James watched as Declan was escorted inside the ship by crew members, giving a final wave before returning to the car.

"Nice work," remarked Bruce. "He was a tough one. Too many smart questions for his own good."

"That was exhausting," replied James, "took a lot to get him on board. I made some big promises, not sure how much he believed. But curiosity and greed won him over. Always does."

Bruce nodded. "The Admiral will be pleased. We presented our offer to every last one of them." They waited by the car, watching as the mighty ship pulled out of its slip and headed towards the open bay. "Man, I'm starving," Bruce said, squeezing behind the wheel. "Let's go grab something."

"Agreed," James said, taking a final look at the now-distant vessel. "Sorry, Doc, just doing my job," he muttered, climbing into the passenger seat before they peeled out of the base.

Chapter 6

March 29, 1939
US Naval Research Laboratory Campus
The City of Washington, District of Columbia

"I'm too old to play these high-stakes games," sighed Harold Bowen, the recently appointed Director of the US Naval Research Labs. He placed the report, explicitly marked "Eyes Only" for the Army Chief of Staff, on his desk as gingerly as if it were made from glass rather than paper. Simply possessing this document, military intelligence's summary of what transpired once the USS *Milwaukee* left Norfolk Naval Station already constituted a treasonous act.

Director Bowen stared out his office window at the Potomac River, mulling over his options. The research lab campus occupied prime riverfront land immediately downstream from the nation's capital, and his third-story office afforded him a commanding view of the riverbanks swollen by springtime thaw. He sipped his morning coffee while watching a particularly large branch bob along in the brisk current flowing out towards the Chesapeake. He wondered if Benedict Arnold felt this conflicted over his decisions. When he grew weary of delaying the inevitable, he picked up the report and began reading, consummating his criminal act.

TOP SECRET - EYES ONLY
CODENAME CRACKED SNOW GLOBE
Filed 28 March 1939
FROM : US ARMY CORPS OF INTELLIGENCE POLICE
TO : GENERAL MALIN CRAIG, US ARMY CHIEF of STAFF, FOR HIS EYES ONLY

URGENT

WARNING: ANY COPIES, PHOTOGRAPHS, FACSIMILES, REPRODUCTIONS, OR VERBAL COMMUNICATION OF CONTENT HEREIN WILL BE CONSIDERED A TREASONOUS WAR CRIME AND SUBJECT TO MILITARY LEGAL JURISDICTION PER 1917 ESPIONAGE ACT and 1918 SEDITION ACT.

CONSENSUS SUMMARY OF THE UNSANCTIONED 1938-39 SS *VALENCIA* MISSION TO INTERCEPT THE MS *SCHWABENLAND* EXPEDITION IN ANTARCTICA

This compilation spans December 1938 through February 1939, serving as the sole record of the incident heretofore known as **CRACKED SNOW GLOBE.**

In late December 1938, the US Army became aware of irregularities in the route traveled by the German commercial vessel **MS** *Schwabenland.* With solid evidence that Wehrmacht equipment and personnel were on board, the vessel potentially threatened US interests at home and abroad. In response, the US Army Chief of Staff, General Malin Craig, sought the opinion of multiple intelligence agencies on how to manage the matter with a tempered, strategically appropriate response.

On the morning of December 23rd, General Craig met with President Roosevelt to discuss the consensus strategy of active observation. The president readily agreed to the plan, which consisted of aerial surveillance launched from US aircraft carriers already on drills in the Atlantic Ocean.

Military intelligence, however, soon learned of a rogue operation illegally using US Navy vessels and equipment to intercept the MS *Schwabenland*. These unauthorized actions were traced back to the morning of 12/25/38, two days after President Roosevelt agreed to a minimalist approach for tracking the German freighter.

Irregularities began on 12/25/38 when the USS *Milwaukee* left Norfolk Naval Station, though at the time, no concerns for aberrant activity were raised. The *Milwaukee* was scheduled to participate in US Naval Fleet Landing Exercise Number 5 (FLEX 5), and the *Milwaukee's* captain incorrectly assumed their two dozen civilian passengers were the Navy's neutral evaluation team for the FLEX 5 exercise.

These passengers boarded the *Milwaukee* carrying written orders from the Commandant of the Marine Corps, Thomas Holcomb, with explicit instructions they were not to be questioned, asked for further identification, or interacted with, except for safety purposes. The *Milwaukee's* crew did not recall any useful identifiers; these individuals dressed in nondescript attire, occupied separate quarters and did not fraternize. Even the ship's security officers were given strict warnings that any interaction could jeopardize the validity of the entire FLEX 5 exercise.

The USS *Milwaukee's* passage remained otherwise unremarkable, and the vessel reached port in San Juan, Puerto Rico, six days later on 12/31/38. The USS *Milwaukee* spent four days in port resupplying and refueling. When the USS *Milwaukee* left port the next week to participate in fleet maneuvers, neither the extra supplies nor the mysterious occupants remained on board.

Rumors of the USS *Milwaukee's* unusual passengers circulated through the San Juan bars, and this gossip reached Naval Intelligence's attention. When Commandant Holcomb vehemently denied authorizing a special team aboard the USS *Milwaukee*, their mission orders were examined and determined to be perfect forgeries.

Our intelligence services immediately launched a full investigation and hunt for these unauthorized passengers. We learned that on 12/31/38, approximately eight hours after the USS *Milwaukee's* arrival, a commercial vessel of Panamanian registry, the SS *Valencia*, left port. The harbormaster documented the transfer of supplies from the USS *Milwaukee* to the SS *Valencia*, and several of the unidentified travelers were seen boarding the vessel in question.

Analysis of the SS *Valencia's* port documents revealed the country registry and ship name failed to match any existing vessels. These documents described the SS *Valencia's* voyage as a research mission, carrying scientists and equipment to survey the coral reefs and aquatic life surrounding the nearby islands. The purpose of their subterfuge was unclear, but with obvious implications for national security, finding these rogue players became a top priority.

Upon questioning, San Juan dock workers reported design elements on the SS *Valencia* unique to the US Navy's latest cargo vessel, the EC2-S-C1. This revolutionary model, manufactured at the Bethlehem-Fairfield Shipyard in Baltimore, is wholly sailed by the US Merchant Marine. All vessels are accounted for during this time-period except one, a prototype freighter that went missing in 1936. That incident, codename RED BUCKET, occurred when the ship disappeared off the coast of South Carolina during seaworthiness trials.

Although wreckage was never recovered, two days later, the entire crew was found wandering around the Kaibab Plateau on the north rim of the Grand Canyon. All sailors were unharmed and in perfect health, yet with zero recollection of what transpired. Navy officials told the sailors they'd been rescued and taken to Arizona for debriefing and reassignment, and the cover story held. At the time, the EC2-S-C1 vessel was still a top-secret research project, so this information never became public knowledge. The final Navy report concluded that catastrophic failure resulted in the ship sinking off the coast in deep waters.

Given the possibility the SS *Valencia* was this missing vessel, the threat level increased and merited allocation of additional resources. Not only had this unidentified group forged military documents authentic enough to procure unfettered passage aboard a US Naval vessel, but they also possessed a stolen US military cargo ship with gear capable of receiving and descrambling top secret USN communications.

We tracked down the rogue vessel's next port of call, several days later resupplying at Base Naval de Aratu, a Brazilian military port in the coastal Bahia Provence. The SS *Valencia* docked within a highly restricted area. While the Brazilian government denies awareness of special treatment for the Panamanian vessel, several port supervisors received large deposits into their private bank accounts from an untraceable source. Unfortunately, we received this information too late to request Brazil's detention of the SS *Valencia.*

However, we used this updated location to calculate the SS *Valencia's* route, discovering a potential intersection with the MS *Schwabenland.* Without knowing the SS *Valencia's* intentions towards the German freighter, our intelligence services recommended aerial surveillance of the German freighter as long as feasible while allocating resources to hunt for the SS *Valencia.*

The destroyer USS *Benham* was reassigned to the South Atlantic to assist with the search. While efforts to locate the SS *Valencia* proved futile, we tracked the MS *Schwabenland* as the vessel headed south. Plausible routes ranged from the tip of South America to the Cape of Good Hope in Africa, fanning out over several thousand miles, and on 1/15/19, US Navy air reconnaissance reached the limits of flying range. Upon the MS *Schwabenland's* final sighting, 1400 miles due east of South America's southernmost tip and 500 nautical miles southeast of South Georgia Island in the southernmost reaches of the Atlantic Ocean, we calculated the German freighter's most likely destination as Antarctica. Lacking vessels properly equipped for subzero temperatures and iceberg-laden seas, the US Navy halted further pursuit of both vessels and ordered the USS *Benham* to patrol the waters off the southeastern coast of Argentina.

One month later, the MS *Schwabenland* was once again sighted by US Navy air reconnaissance, heading north past the South Sandwich Islands presumably back to Hamburg, Germany. Just a few days later, on 2/21/39, the SS *Valencia* was detected by the USS *Benham,* also sailing north from similar coordinates.

Despite attempts to gain further details on both vessels' whereabouts during the one-month time gap, we found no information regarding the *MS Schwabenland's* location or activity during this time-period.

As for the SS *Valencia,* we learned the ship docked at South Georgia Island on 1/20/39 in the whaling harbor of Grytviken. Supplies were transferred from the SS *Valencia* onto the FV *Melville,* a local whaling vessel, including equipment described as sophisticated exploration supplies, advanced communications devices, as well as camping and climbing gear.

After the FV *Melville* left port, the SS *Valencia* retained a skeleton crew for dockside maintenance and security. The SS *Valencia* spent three uneventful weeks in port until 2/17/39, when the FV *Melville* sailed into harbor. Local dock workers noted the FV *Melville* returned with more boxes and crates than upon departure, including several large pieces of equipment wrapped in tarp. One dock worker claimed to see what looked like human remains but was told they were sea lion specimens.

On 2/21/39, when the USS *Benham* located the SS *Valencia,* the ship immediately launched an intercept course. On 2/24/39, while still 150 nautical miles apart, the USS *Benham* picked up a distress signal from the SS *Valencia* and navigated toward the last radioed coordinates. During their approach, the USS *Benham's* sonar detected 3 large objects, presumably German U-boats heading toward the SS

Valencia (echo signatures consistent with submarine Type 7A).

Soon afterward, the USS *Benham* lost contact with the rogue vessel and two hours later entered a large debris field including floating crates and one lifeboat with a single survivor. Amongst the crate contents were German weapons and Nazi propaganda, indicating a likely rendezvous between the SS *Valencia* and MS *Schwabenland.* The sole survivor proved uncooperative with our investigation, claiming to not remember any meaningful details, necessitating his transfer to our advanced interrogation center.

END OF REPORT. DURING TRANSPORT KEEP CHAIN OF CUSTODY LOG WITH REPORT AT ALL TIMES.

"Sole survivor," Director Bowen quietly repeated, closing the folder before taking the secret intelligence report into his private restroom. The Director felt along the vanity mirror edge, releasing the securing clasp, which allowed the mirror to swing wide, revealing the door to a hidden safe. Not his official one, but rather the clandestine repository he'd personally installed for precisely such documents.

He deposited the folder, closed the mirror, and flushed the toilet, largely for effect, before returning to his office. Harold Bowen leaned back in his plush chair and sipped coffee while gazing out at the Potomac. The intelligence community hadn't pieced together anything, and for the first time in months, since before his Manhattan excursion, the Director unclenched his jaw enough to sigh with relief. Director Bowen's role required a spotless reputation, Washington's power brokers needed to trust him a little longer, and the report's giant goose egg felt like a personal victory. Too bad the US Army failed to grasp the serious threat posed by the rising turmoil in Europe, though if Mr. Tesla was correct, Germany wouldn't be able to conceal their global ambitions much longer.

As for the fate of the SS *Valencia* and her crew, the news sounded less encouraging, reportedly destroyed by German U-boats. However, Director Bowen did not immediately despair. He did not have time for distractions, even ones that were potentially catastrophic. His indifference was not entirely callous. The Antarctic expedition's chief architect was his mentor, Nikolas Tesla, a master at manipulating perception to suit his needs. Harold Bowen knew whatever the truth, he would never find it inside the pages of a government document.

Instead, he retrieved a second, potentially more illuminating document from his briefcase, a plain manilla envelope, soiled and severely creased. It arrived earlier that morning through his home mail slot, slipped inside the daily newspaper, scrawled with just "H.B.". Harold felt the envelope flap and found the Clypeate's signature insurance policy, an incendiary strip designed to set the contents ablaze if opened incorrectly, guaranteeing no sneaky peeks.

"Gently," the Director reminded himself, carefully slicing the envelope open from the other end, retrieving a document hinting at a more textured story than a sunken ship and drowned crew. He only gave the document a cursory perusal, knowing any truly important details would never be shared so flippantly.

Since the Obturavi attack thirty years earlier, the Clypeate retained a post-traumatic distrust of the outside world, the paranoia worsening in the last few years after a car struck Mr. Tesla while crossing a busy Manhattan thoroughfare. Ruled an accident, the genius scientist instead believed the incident represented a failed assassination attempt, and the Clypeate now conducted affairs like Obturavi lurked around every corner. Despite the document's utter lack of insight into the true fate of the SS *Valencia's* crew, Director Bowen still smiled, the broadest since Harold Junior was born, as the only question that truly mattered was answered on the first page.

Director Bowen needed to act swiftly. He knew the current location of the SS *Valencia's* only known survivor, and recovering the government's detainee justified the countless untold sacrifices. Energized by bullish urgency, the Director made one quick phone call before grabbing his blue officer's peacoat, still wriggling into the sleeves as he flew from his office. There was no time to waste. Craig's top-secret report called the detainee an enemy combatant, a term the military used to condone morally flexible interrogation.

The Director's abrupt exit startled his secretary. "Sir, is everything okay?" she asked, looking up from the typewriter.

"Yes, Darlene, everything's fine," he reflexively answered before pausing. "On second thought, no, I'll be gone for a while. Hold all my calls and appointments. Tell them I went home sick for the day. I need to find that analyst, the Fischer boy. He dropped a report off on my desk earlier today."

"Oh, you mean James," Darlene recalled, "what a polite young man. Would you like me to place a call over to the labs? He works in Building G."

Director Bowen thanked her but declined. "No, I'll find him myself. After that delicious cake you brought in yesterday, I could use the exercise," he jested, finally settling into his overcoat before trudging outdoors into the muddy yard between buildings. The labs didn't have enough funds to build proper sidewalks, so by the time he entered the communications building, his boots and pant cuffs were a splattered mess.

The Director walked the length of the stout building, past shelves stacked with electrical equipment, some semi-functional, others outdated, with even the newest pieces arriving as hand-me-downs from other government entities with meatier budget appropriations. Every piece of old military hardware with a knob, dial, meter, or cord ended life in this junk heap. He walked past some of his engineers sifting through the collection, looking for treasures amongst the trash, feeding off the table scraps.

There was one division under his command, however, that wasn't cash-strapped. The Director reached a locked door and knocked. An armed guard checked his credentials, and a quick elevator ride brought him to the USNRL's officially nonexistent intelligence unit. While at the Bureau of Engineering, Harold Bowen gathered the intelligence community's brightest minds and, upon moving to the USNRL, cherry-picked the best to accompany him. Not only was his team logarithmically better at obtaining and interpreting data than any other government agency, but his analytics team accidentally stumbled upon a very lucrative side hustle. They did not suffer from funding issues like the rest of the USNRL because they didn't rely upon meager Congressional stipends. Instead, this intel unit ran using generous donations from the many political and government figures they'd caught in compromising career and marriage-ending situations. If the Director weren't ethically averse to true extortion, he could've funded the entire facility many times over with the information they'd uncovered. Instead, he was happy with this compromise, having one unit function like a champion thoroughbred, and it was this bullpen which procured him the exceedingly illegal copy of General Craig's report.

Director Bowen beamed with pride. The intel unit was furnished with the best equipment other people's money could buy, and cutting-edge communications gear ran the length of the room. The analysts functioned like a hive of busy bees frantically buzzing about, racing between monitors, radios, and rows of beeping and ringing machines. Instead of honey, this hive churned out the highest quality intelligence data in the executive branch.

"Hello," the Director bellowed above the din. "I'm looking for Lieutenant James Fischer."

Director Bowen's booming voice froze everyone in place, and one raven-haired young man poked his head out from behind a switchboard. "That would be me, Director Bowen, I mean Admiral Bowen, sir."

"Well then, son," the Director commanded, "grab your uniform jacket and come with me." Without offering further details, the Director headed back to the elevator, with James trotting to catch up. In silence, the pair headed outside, chilly breezes balancing against the sun's radiating warmth, trumpeting forth the promise of impending spring. James fell a few paces behind Director Bowen. The older man walked more swiftly and purposefully than expected, and it wasn't until the Director slowed down near the river's edge that James caught up. James shuffled his feet, partially because he was nervous but also because he was slowly sinking into the wet, spongy soil, and his shoes were taking on water. "This is close enough to the Potomac," Director Bowen decided. He did not turn to face James, instead focusing his gaze south down the river. "Lieutenant Fischer, do you know what lies that way, past the river bend?"

"The Chesapeake Bay, Director Admiral sir?" James answered, trying to sound less intimidated than he felt.

"True, and fair enough," Director Bowen said, "although just pick Director or Admiral, not both, you're driving me nuts. No, I'm thinking a bit closer. Did you know it's only ten miles to Mount Vernon, George Washington's home? Sometimes, I wonder what he would think about what our nation has become. Would he be proud? Would he even recognize us? During my many years of public service, these thoughts have grown to haunt me, how Washington's words have been misinterpreted, twisted, and manipulated. They say history doesn't repeat itself, but it certainly rhymes, and the older I get, the more I can hear the echoes of its melancholic song."

James had a tough time deciphering the Director's cryptic musings, the young analyst's face contorting into a decent impression of a puzzled deer caught in the headlights of a big rig. The Director took note and dialed back his rhetoric. "You look nervous, James. May I call you James?" The young man nodded. Of course, the Director could call him Little Orphan Annie. "Well, James, you needn't be alarmed. I'm not planning on tossing you into the river; I just needed a spot where no errant ears could hear. You should know I've been following your progress for a while. I didn't mention this when I hired you, but I knew your father quite well. Same class at Annapolis. We also served together during the Great War. He saved my hide more times than I care to admit. James, you remind me a lot of him, the way you carry yourself, and your dedication to the mission. Tragic what happened to him and your mom."

"I miss them both," James responded, turning to hide the embarrassing and unprofessional tears welling in his crystal blue eyes.

The Director spoke softly. "Don't be ashamed, son, I miss them too. They were good people and dear friends. But that's not what landed you this job. No, you did that all on your own. As one of the highest-ranking cadets in your class, this post is well below your value. For me, it's like getting filet mignon at ground chuck prices."

"Director Bowen, sir, I can explain…" James started before being interrupted.

"No need to explain, James. I've seen your records. I know what happened. And, of course, you were right, although that's not what our military wants from their future leaders, they want mindless obedience." The Director looked down at his muddied boots. "Disgusting piece of land, there isn't a swampier spot north of Lake Okeechobee. But I digress, my purpose is not to dredge up painful memories or remind us of your missteps. James, during my time I've witnessed some strange things, and the older I get the less I believe in coincidences. The time has come to learn the real reason I hired you. Did you happen to read the report you intercepted this morning? The pursuit of the German freighter heading towards Antarctica?"

"Yes sir, I did," James admitted, "and that's why I chose to pass it along directly to you without involving anyone else."

"A wise decision. Now what made this particular memo seem important?" the Director queried.

"Well, sir," James replied, "it referenced the USS *Milwaukee*. I thought it would be of utmost interest to you."

"And it was," the Director agreed. "Continue wearing your analyst hat, what did you gather from that report?"

"Speaking frankly, sir, somebody pulled a fast one and got away with it," James concluded.

"Interesting interpretation," the Director mused. "But what about the men you finessed onto the *Milwaukee*? They're all drowned except one, and the US Army is holding that one as an enemy combatant. Doesn't that strike you as a sloppy job, letting someone get caught?"

"Well, sir, I think there's more to the story. If I were going to treat a US Navy cruiser like my personal chauffeur, then flaunt a stolen Navy cargo ship in plain view of military intelligence, I'd also be clever enough to make sure nobody came looking for me. I'd want intel to believe the stolen ship sank, the entire crew drowned, and there's only one sad sack left behind to take the blame. A clueless rube, left to wash up with a box full of Nazi trinkets, swearing up and down he knows nothing. US intelligence thinks they have their man, the more he protests the further convinced they become, and nobody looks any further for the mastermind. Pretty brilliant."

"Good analysis," the Director lauded. "High marks for crisp insight, intelligent data synthesis and solid inferences. You possess an uncommon skill, the ability to gather information like bits of string and weave them into a cohesive tapestry." Before proceeding the Director reflexively scanned the area once again. Mr. Tesla preached habitual vigilance. Satisfied, he continued. "Now James, that intelligence report did a fine job of recounting the deception on the *Milwaukee* and the tragic journey of the *Valencia*, but it utterly failed to recognize the overarching issue. Do you know what I'm talking about?"

"I believe so," James grinned, "because I wondered the same thing. Our government is totally distracted by this sideshow, when they should be much more curious to know why the Germans are poking around Antarctica."

"Exactly," the Director affirmed. "Even though I'm no marine biologist, I'm fairly certain you don't need a company's worth of Nazi infantry, weapons and armored vehicles to search for whales. Unsettling events are transpiring, and if my suspicions are correct, the world is about to have extra helpings of unprecedented despair shoved down its throat. The reason I brought you out here, James, is because you've impressed me thus far and if you're up to the challenge, I have another document for your consideration. I am instilling a lot of trust in you, and if you continue to earn it, I have bigger plans in store for you."

"Thank you, Director Bowen," James replied, smiling appreciatively, this was not a man who dispensed undeserved praise or minced words. "I believe I'm up to the challenge, and I'll do my best to meet your expectations."

Moments later they were heading towards the USNRL's puddle-dappled parking lot. "Some days I wonder why I don't just build a dock and sail to work," the Director mused, "I'd undoubtedly arrive less mud-caked." James smiled as he slid into the passenger seat of the Director's Buick Roadmaster, carefully maneuvering his soiled shoes onto the floor mat, the plush upholstery a pleasant upgrade from the rigid bus seat of his usual commute. The Director pulled out the manilla envelope, the one he received this morning, from his jacket pocket. "This report is your next assignment. The US military doesn't appreciate looking foolish, and they think their detainee is the key to finding out what happened in Antarctica. It will get ugly when he can't provide them with meaningful details, and to his detriment the more sincerely he professes ignorance the worse his interrogators will react."

The Director handed the manilla envelope over to James. "I only glanced at it, so save your questions for someone who'll have answers. Knowing less serves me better, and I already know too many details, ones the intelligence agencies will never discern from their nosebleed seats." Director Bowen drove out of the facility lot and turned north onto Overlook Avenue, towards downtown. "I apologize for not engaging in mindless small talk," he said. "Navigating out of this bayou requires more concentration than it should, and you're better served reading that entire letter before we get to the Navy and Munitions Building. I wish I had more time to ease you in, to mentor you, unfortunately the forces working against us are stronger than I feared. I need you to get up to speed quickly, to have enough background so you can formulate intelligent opinions when we arrive."

James nodded, opened the tattered envelope, straightened out the wrinkled, stained pages, of which there were several, and dove in headfirst. The report began with a cover letter:

2/17/39
SUMMARY OF "ALLEGORE'S SHIELD"
SURVEILLANCE OF THE MS *SCHWABENLAND*.
Greetings Harold:

I am sending this report out with a whaling vessel headed to Rio de Janeiro and have paid the captain a ridiculous sum to guarantee it arrives at your doorstep. If you are reading this, the expense was worthwhile.

We have returned to South Georgia Island and will push out to sea within a few hours. I am sending this record of what transpired in case we sustain further setbacks. Bluntly, our surveillance mission didn't unfold as expected. Not only did our forces make unwanted contact with the Germans, but our mission attracted US Navy attention sooner and with more vigor than anticipated. I fear our journey will end poorly.

First Officer Riggs typed out the attached summary, representing the most credible consensus of events. There are many unverifiable elements, so take this report with a sizable grain of salt.

F Noonan, Captain SS *Valencia*

PS: It wasn't all for naught, one candidate demonstrated great potential.

James shuddered. The late Captain Noonan's introduction was just as ominous as it was prescient. The young analyst already knew the mission's fate, according to General Craig's report only a few days later Nazi U-boats would sink the SS *Valencia*. Now he'd learn what other disastrous events befell the men he cajoled into joining the voyage before sentencing them to a watery grave. He continued:

MISSION SUMMARY OF "ALLEGORE'S SHIELD" - SURVEILLANCE OF THE MS *SCHWABENLAND'S* ACTIVITY IN ANTARCTICA.

Recorded by First Officer David Riggs

On 1/20/39 we arrived at South Georgia Island where Captain Noonan docked the SS *Valencia* in Grytviken Harbor. Our crew took immediate possession of the whaling vessel FV *Melville*, as negotiated prior to our arrival. We transferred supplies and 36 hours later sailed the FV *Melville* out of Grytviken Harbor without incident, leaving the SS *Valencia* and a small maintenance crew behind.

Once at sea, team leaders shared our real mission objectives with the entire crew, including the non-Clypeate civilians. The stated mission goals included finding the MS *Schwabenland* in order to secretly observe and document all German activity. The civilians were told their participation was vital for the protection of the entire team, providing legitimate cover should we be discovered by the German expedition. The civilians were reassured their safety was of utmost importance, and if any were perturbed by the deception these concerns went unvoiced.

Sailing from South Georgia Island to Antarctica proved treacherous. Rough seas and numerous close misses with potentially hull-splitting icebergs were common, so the crew's overall mood improved greatly when the Queen Maud Land ice shelf came into view on 1/28/39. We spotted inland mountain ranges between coordinates 70°16'44"S, 4°08'27"E and 74°08'58"S, 22°01'50"W, but due to thick iceberg fields did not attempt a closer approach than several miles out. We traced the coastline for nearly sixty miles before visualizing the MS *Schwabenland* on the evening of 1/29/39 at coordinates 69°14'14"S, 4°30'16"W. We backed the FV *Melville* out into open Atlantic waters, beyond the horizon, awaiting a potential reaction from the German freighter. By the next morning, when no signs of German pursuit or investigation transpired, team leaders determined ground surveillance could proceed.

On 1/30/39 in the early morning hours we launched three prototype Higgins Eureka LCP watercraft into freezing, choppy waters. We enveloped each craft with white tarp and lightly sprayed them with water, creating an icy effect mimicking the naturally occurring icebergs around us, attempting to camouflage the vessels against aerial sweeps by the MS *Schwabenland's* seaplanes.

Three mission teams - Alpha, Beta and Gamma, were each assigned a watercraft. Each team brought along two civilians to support the cover story, Alpha Team included the mission's geologist and the academic biologist.

By early afternoon, the three small craft headed en masse towards the frozen continent, making the journey of a few miles through a shifting field of floating ice. Once again, we backed the *Melville* out towards open ocean, putting the vessel beyond German aerial interest and aligning our sailing pattern with the cover story, tracking whale migration patterns and other marine animal activities.

Along the coast, the three landing craft encountered steep ice cliffs. They proceeded with great caution due to many icebergs and the jagged ice shelf, scouting for several hours before identifying a potentially scalable region on the morning of 1/31/39. They decided upon an area of recent iceberg calving, which left a more advantageous climbing angle albeit with a 90-foot summit.

Before disembarking each team received a two-way field radio packset, the type currently under joint development by Donald Hings and the US Department of the Army. These prototypes, unofficially referred to as "handie-talkies", function like two-way radios. While this communications gear is still a few years away from official rollout, I can report the equipment performed well and allowed wireless communication between teams.

Alpha and Beta Teams began their icy climb in the early afternoon. Gamma Team took command of all three watercraft before continuing east, planning to skirt along the coast in order to establish and maintain visual contact with the MS *Schwabenland*.

The teams used mountaineering gear to scale the icy cliff without incident, and within hours all members of the Alpha and Beta teams summited the glacial plateau. They established basecamp half a mile inland, shortly after midnight, although with continuous Antarctic summer sunlight the midnight sky was equally bright as noon. After a short rest the

Alpha Team headed south into the continent's interior, and that was the last visual contact with Alpha Team.

On 2/6/39, several days after Alpha Team's departure and nearly 48 hours since the team's last check-in via handie-talkie, Beta Team was already planning an inland search and rescue mission when Gamma Team witnessed the Germans rapidly loading the MS *Schwabenland*.

Within hours the German freighter sailed away into open waters, and once it disappeared beyond the horizon Gamma Team landed at the MS *Schwabenland's* docking site. They assembled their long-distance radio equipment and signaled the FV *Melville* to return ASAP, then traced the ice road south to Germany's inland camp. Gamma Team followed the ice road under the German fortifications, into a tunnel leading down from the surface into an icy cavern. The cavern functioned as a motor pool, occupied by several abandoned German military vehicles including transports and Panzer tanks. All the vehicles were checked for booby-traps and explosives, none were found. Their fuel tanks also held plenty of gasoline and were loaded with supplies, making it readily apparent the Germans were in a rush to vacate the continent.

Gamma Team radioed the German camp's coordinates to Beta Team and they rendezvoused at the site. The joint Beta and Gamma Teams searched the area, finding scattered garbage but also piles of useful supplies, unopened food rations and gear ranging from tents to Howitzers. They also discovered a series of tunnels starting at the motor pool before branching out in multiple directions. Heading deeper into the ice sheet, these tunnels were carved with precise rectangular cuts, rising several feet high and double in width. Most angled down or were level, a few drifted up, but they all ran for hundreds of feet and were lined with smaller side chambers.

Some areas had been clearly occupied by the Germans with cots, blankets and toiletries strewn about. Some rooms contained boxes of random equipment, one looked like a makeshift kitchen and several were obviously used as latrines. One room contained empty crates and packing material, likely used to prepare retrieved artifacts for the return trip, but most rooms were entirely bare.

One hallway distinguished itself as the main avenue, vastly wider than the others and running level and true for one fifth of a mile. Traveling down this particular tunnel the floor gradually transitioned from ice to pebble, then further along the ice walls and ceiling were replaced by red stone. The walls consisted of car-sized blocks of this ruddy stone, precisely shaped and aligned, indicating this was not a natural structure.

At the corridor's end the tunnel opened up and the ceiling rose to meet a towering wall, a wide swath of dark green stone. Carved into the facade were several massive, beautifully sculpted columns running from floor to ceiling. A ten foot hole had been punched through the wall's center, more than two feet of solid rock, blasting caps found nearby pointing to German handiwork. Our men noted hinges along the wall, suggesting it may have once functioned like a door, but the extensive damage impeded further analysis.

Venturing through the jagged, dynamited hole they discovered the most spacious cavern in the complex, six stories high and similarly wide. Towering above them and dominating the room was a flawless diamond-shaped object. Height estimates range between 50 to 60 feet, and while it is impossible to identify this artifact with certainty, it likely represents a novel Epistolith.

The large diamond's upper apex extended through a defect in the cavern roof, allowing sunlight to stream into the space. They found the floor covered in a heaping pile of stone and ice, consistent with a recent ceiling collapse, and were horrified to discover the remains of Alpha Team members amongst the debris.

They immediately hunted for survivors, amongst the bodies finding two men clinging to life, Alpha Team leader Captain Joshua Vanmore and the team's geologist. Captain Vanmore was alert but in significant pain, suffering from severe blunt trauma to the head. The geologist was unconscious and in more dire condition, his legs crushed, the left side of his face macerated, jawbone nearly separated from his skull. A nearby mallet was identified as the likely weapon.

They carefully extracted both men as quickly as possible, using one of the German trucks to race north to meet the incoming FV *Melville* at the edge of the ice shelf. The geologist never regained consciousness and rapidly succumbed to his injuries.

Captain Vanmore remained lucid for only a short while, and despite his significant injuries refused medical attention until he gave a report on Alpha Team's misfortune.

According to witnesses, this is Captain Vanmore's statement:

> Once my (Alpha) team located the German expedition and gathered intelligence on their camp, we decided

to survey the surrounding area before heading back to the extraction point. In the process we encountered a crystal pyramid towering above the icy plain. Being a safe distance beyond German patrols, we paused to rest and give the geologist time to further investigate the unusual stone.

It wasn't long before I heard the ice cracking, and next thing I remember I was staring up at clear blue skies. It took a few minutes to realize the sky was visible through a gaping hole in the ice sheet above me, and I concluded Alpha Team fell through the ice. I judged the fall to be 50 feet or more, and I credit my survival to landing atop a pile of our team's gear.

My left arm shrieked in pain, dangling at an unnatural angle. Except for a few other sore spots, I was lucky to be alive, and I began climbing through the piles of rubble looking for other survivors. I found random limbs jutting out beneath thick plates of rock and ice but no movement, and I was losing hope when I heard groans from a nearby mound of gear. I dug down and found the team's geologist, his legs trapped under an ice slab, too heavy to move.

I searched our packs for something to pry the ice block off the geologist until I was interrupted by renewed rumbling. Initially I feared a second collapse and braced myself, but this time the vibrations came through the ground. I heard the sounds of heavy machinery and hoped it was a rescue team coming to help us, except when the machines quieted the jumbled voices were shouting in German.

Since my team was unarmed and dressed in civilian gear, I hoped to explain that we were a lost research team who accidentally stumbled upon fellow explorers. I hesitated when I saw the Germans dressed in Wehrmacht uniforms and carrying rifles, so I instead crouched down next to the trapped geologist and quietly watched the soldiers approach a motionless body on the other side of the debris pile.

One soldier nudged the still form with his rifle and waited for a response. When the fallen man groaned the soldier fired a single round into his head, sending further pieces of ceiling raining down. The Germans started shouting at each other, giving me just enough time to scurry deeper into the fallen pile. I covered myself with rock and ice chunks, scooping them over my torso and face. I lay as still as possible, listening to footsteps crunching all around, accompanied by agitated and alarmed German chatter.

At one point a German soldier paused near me for several long moments, a rifle poking into the ice and snow pile covering my motionless body. I braced for the worst but the geologist's pained moans caught the soldier's attention and he moved on. From under my ice pile I watched the soldier strike the geologist several times with a large mallet until he stopped whimpering, blood rivulets dripping down his forehead.

The sound of wet thuds and shrill screams continued to echo through the cavern for many long minutes, replaced by a sickening silence ending when engine noise resumed. The machines were much louder now, echoing inside the icy cavern, and I used the opportunity to slide out and check on the geologist, who was still alive but unconscious.

I thought I moved unnoticed, except it wasn't long until I heard grinding ice behind me. I turned to see the butt of a German rifle coming towards me. I woke to find total silence, no machines, no shouting Germans or cries from Alpha Team.

My skull raged with pain, I touched my head and my glove returned with clumps of bloody hair and scalp. With continuous sunshine there was no marking of time, I could not tell if I'd been down for minutes or days. I spotted the handie-talkie, within arm's reach, but it was crushed to pieces. Without hope and in excruciating pain I expected to perish alongside my team, dispassionately wondering how long it'd take to die before drifting out of awareness.

I don't remember anything else until the other teams found me. I'm surely leaving out huge details, I'm having trouble focusing, my thoughts wander as the pain overtakes me. I'm fighting best I can, I need to tell my story before I get doped up with meds.

I don't expect to survive the voyage home, I've spent enough time around death to feel it hovering, standing over me with a cold, patient, knowing grin. Please believe I led the Alpha Team best I knew, I wish I could have done more to save them and I hope their spirits have gone to a better place where they can forgive my shortcomings as their leader. If I remember any more details I'll pass them along.

Shortly afterwards Captain Vanmore lapsed into a coma and never regained consciousness. He died three days later.

Captain Vanmore's statement remains the only record of Alpha Team's mission. After several hours of recovery efforts we accounted for the remains of all but one member of the Alpha Team. Post-mortem exams showed multiple team members survived the initial fall, their deaths caused by German cruelty, evidence of stab wounds and weapon-inflicted blunt force trauma. Because we could not positively ID many of the Alpha Team members, their features badly distorted, it was impossible to determine which team member was still missing.

While waiting for the FV *Melville* to reach land Beta and Gamma teams sent search parties sweeping through the underground ice complex, hopeful the last Alpha Team member was still alive and hiding somewhere in the underground complex. Although these searches failed to locate the last Alpha Team member, they did uncover a surprising number of unusual artifacts. Many of these objects were in the process of being packed into shipping crates, left behind by the Germans in their hasty exit, so our teams finished packing the crates before shuttling them to the makeshift dock. Our men also mapped the tunnel system and photographed some exotic carvings in the red stone walls, every discovery increasing their conviction the Germans were not the original builders of the underground complex.

As for the presumed Epistolith, while further investigating the area beneath the giant diamond our men discovered thick, shredded ropes secured to a Panzer tank. From the tank's numerous tread marks it was apparent the Germans attempted to drag the crystal and failed, the ropes apparently snapping under the strain. Amazingly the German efforts did not damage the crystal, the diamond's surface remained without flaws, superficially shiny with a gray milkiness clouding the interior. Ultimately we reached the same conclusion as the Germans, the presumed Epistolith was immovable and would need to remain in Antarctica.

When the FV *Melville* arrived at the ice shelf the Beta and Gamma Teams performed one final sweep of the tunnels, making sure they'd found every valuable clue to help explain the Alpha Team's tragedy or the German mission's intent. While checking the grand cavern one last time, searching the icy rubble pile beneath the massive diamond, they heard a loud thud and suddenly the Alpha Team's biologist was on top of the debris, curled in a fetal ball.

While nobody witnessed his sudden arrival, everyone present agrees the biologist hadn't been there just a few seconds prior. We think when the cavern's ice ceiling collapsed and Alpha Team fell through, the biologist got trapped in the fractured ceiling and hung suspended above the cavern until gravity and melting ice loosened him. Miraculously the biologist was alive and relatively unharmed, his vital signs stable and no life-threatening injuries identified, just mild frostbite and several minor lacerations. He was limp and unconscious, however, necessitating immediate transport to the waiting FV *Melville* for a complete medical exam.

Before leaving the camp our men erased all signs of human activity and rendered it inhospitable should the Germans return. Using the German vehicles they pushed all the remaining gear and equipment off the surrounding Antarctic surface into the tunnel, burying the entrance under piles of snow and ice in anticipation the harsh elements would blend it back into the surrounding icescape.

When the FV *Melville* was ready to embark, our men drove all the remaining German vehicles over the edge of the ice pack, sinking them in the Antarctic waters, first removing any electronic equipment or supplies that looked potentially useful.

On 2/10/39 the FV *Melville* left Queen Maud Land, after an uneventful passage the vessel reached Grytviken Harbor on 2/17/39 and the waiting *Valencia*.

END OF REPORT

Chapter 7

March 29, 1939
Navy and Munitions Building
City of Washington, District of Columbia

Director Bowen kept his word and rarely spoke the remainder of the drive, only breaking his silence to curse the country lanes leading from the USN Research Labs into the city. Spring thaw caused the roadways to behave less like gravel and more like chocolate pudding, the car tires sinking into the mud like saber-tooth cats trapped in a LaBrea tar pit. James was convinced he'd be pushing the vehicle at some point but Director Bowen drove with gritty determination, his foot doggedly assaulting the gas pedal, and by the time the Washington Monument's spire rose above the tenements they were smoothly sailing on asphalt. James raced through the Antarctic report, a tough feat to manage because hidden amongst the pages of bland operational tactics and logistics were some of the most unbelievably perplexing and fantastic yarns he'd seen spun outside a Jules Verne novel.

"I'm finished," James said, looking up as they passed the Capitol Building and turned onto Constitution Avenue, "and that was one heck of a read," he added, resealing the document. He'd skimmed through the report twice with enough cushion to circle back to recheck the facts, hoping he'd retain enough details to impress the Director.

"Good timing," Director Bowen noted, once again addressing James, nodding his approval as they drove past the massive federal buildings, each the length of a city block. "What did you think?"

"The Germans went to Antarctica for a specific purpose, and they didn't expend all those resources to plant a flag in the ice," James concluded. "A small group of unarmed, civilian-attired men crashed their party and the Nazis turned tail and bolted, even though they could've hunkered down inside those fortified ice tunnels and defended themselves against an attack from a much larger force. And judging from what they left behind they had enough supplies to withstand a months-long siege. So why bring along that much gear and military muscle if you're going to run at the first hint of trouble? Doesn't add up, unless they didn't travel to Antarctica to defend a property stake or track whales. They fled because they found whatever they were looking for, and didn't want to risk losing their prize."

"That's my biggest fear," Director Bowen divulged before changing subjects. "Now James, here's a little history lesson. Were you aware this road, Constitution Avenue, sits atop a creek?"

James shook his head. "No, I was not, sir," he admitted.

"Don't worry, it's not common knowledge anymore," the Director responded, "but yes, it's true, beneath us once flowed a natural creek. Originally called Goose Creek for obvious reasons, given the ubiquity of the honking grass-munchers, waddling and defecating wherever they please. The name was changed to Tiber Creek back in the sixteen-hundreds, when the Pope family settled along the creek banks. Keeping with their Papal surname they whimsically called their farmlands Rome and renamed the nearby stream Tiber Creek."

James grinned. "Clever, naming the creek after the Tiber River flowing through Rome."

"I'm glad you appreciate the reference," Director Bowen replied. "Of course, back then the pastoral creek was quite picturesque, meandering down from the northeastern hills of the city, curving west near Capitol Hill, and babbling past the White House before joining the Potomac. In time progress beckoned, as it always does, and eventually the city enclosed its banks, sealed the creek over and turned it into a sewage drain. A fitting metaphor for this city. A lot of history has been covered up here, and not all of it smells like springtime flowers. Might not be as ancient as some other places, but the District's still layered with plenty of mucky secrets."

James didn't have time to muster a response before the Director parked the Roadmaster in the lot surrounding the squat Navy and Munitions Building. Prior to World War One this drab asphalt tundra was part of the National Mall, a grassy expanse of verdant lawn carpeting the space between the Washington Monument's hill and the Lincoln Memorial's steps. Now it served as testament to government bloat, built twenty years prior, when military bureaucracy ballooned like an overfed tick and outgrew the Executive Office Building adjacent to the White House. This series of ugly, boxy buildings repeated their way down the length of Constitution Avenue, transforming national parklands into an overgrown trailer park. The structures were a grotesque eyesore, contrasting sharply with the classic Greco-Roman buildings surrounding them. Instead of striving for timeless beauty the architectural theme here was undoubtedly inspired by filing cabinets.

Once successfully parked under the shadow of the towering Washington obelisk James handed the report back to the Director. "Quite a story," James noted, "by the end I expected Paul Bunyan or King Poseidon would make an appearance."

"I entirely understand the sentiment," Director Bowen chuckled, "because once upon a time I felt the same way. Tell me James, do you feel like you have a good handle on the information contained in this report? If asked, could you summarize the contents?"

"I don't claim to understand it all, but yes, sir," James proudly replied, "would you prefer oral or written?"

"Neither will be necessary," the Director said, pulling out a matchbox, lighting a single match. The flame barely licked the pages when the entirety erupted into a fireball.

By the time James yelped with surprise the flames were gone, as was any evidence suggesting the document ever existed. "What was that?" James squealed, searching the car interior for damage or charred debris and finding none.

"Flash paper," the Director responded, "the kind magicians use. Nitrocellulose-soaked paper disappears without leaving residue, no need to worry about bad actors piecing together that document." Harold pulled out a towel and wiped the mud from his shoes before offering James the same courtesy. As James buffed his dress blacks and restored their high sheen the Director gazed up at the Washington Monument, the obelisk perched upon the hill just beyond the parking lot. "I've just made you exceedingly valuable, James, you're the only person who knows the full details of that report. Think of it as a gesture of benevolent intent."

Unsure how to respond, James politely said, "I appreciate your confidence," then carefully positioned the muddy towel on the floor mat, hoping it would absorb some of the lagoon left by his soaked shoes. James didn't wait long for the next surprise, when instead of walking towards the Navy Building the Director trotted off towards the towering monument. For an older gentleman Director Bowen was spry, James jogged to catch up.

Director Bowen paused and turned to James. "Impressive, right?"

James straightened his military jacket and nodded. "Indeed, sir. It's majestic."

"As you know, millions of tourists travel to this spot each year to gawk, snap a few pictures, patriotically ooh and aah before quickly shuffling along to the next national treasure. But there's something even more significant right over there," Director Bowen said, pointing towards a squat, waist-high stone rising from the Washington Monument's gently sloping hill. Before James could ask questions the Director was already walking towards it, crossing the road and following a path towards the singular block.

James cut across the lawn to shave time off the Director's head start, not realizing the unmowed expanse was sopping wet. New puddles flooded his recently cleaned shoes, causing him to wonder how long it would take to develop trench foot. Harold stopped just short of the gray stone. "A nubby hunk of granite, unassumingly anchored into this grassy slope just a few hundred feet from one of our nation's most visited treasures. Ever notice it before?"

"No, can't say I have," admitted James, "and I've been down here to see the Washington Monument a bunch of times since moving into town. I would remember it, too, reminds me of a tombstone," James flippantly added.

Director Bowen recoiled at the comment, causing James to immediately regret wagging his unbridled tongue, relieved when his boss quickly regained his composure. "Well, Lieutenant Fischer, it's not a grave marker, at least it was never intended as such," the Director answered solemnly, "though given this site's history your observation is disturbingly preternatural." The Director reverently placed his hand on the stone, continuing without elaboration. "In 1889 this stone replaced the original 1793 wooden marker, and you're not alone in failing to notice it, nobody does. It's called the Jefferson Pier, and it hides in plain sight, casually ignored. Thomas Jefferson first marked this spot when it was part of the Potomac riverbank. Boats could tie up to this very spot, that was, of course, until the marshy swamps were backfilled to create the land now occupied by the Navy and Munitions Building."

"If Jefferson placed a marker here, he must have intended for this location to be important," James deduced.

"Yes, he did," the Director confirmed. "This stone marks the original prime meridian of the United States, the spot where imaginary lines drawn from the center of the White House and Capitol Building intersect at a ninety-degree angle. It's the singular point from where our entire country radiates outward, and here it resides, barely a historical footnote and just narrowly avoiding a new life as part of that parking lot. You'll be amazed at what people don't see when they aren't expecting it, hidden in the blind spots of our minds."

"That's a fascinating story," James replied, careful to avoid putting his other foot in his mouth.

"Oh, I haven't even started," Director Bowen continued, "I'm still setting the table, we haven't even reached the appetizers. Everything I've shared so far you could find in a history book, I'm merely prepping the scene, readying your mind," he said, turning to James. "Now, think about this, if Thomas Jefferson, a sentinel founder of this country, wanted the nation's center to lie here, then why build the Washington Monument all the way over there?" he asked, motioning at the distant obelisk.

"Maybe the hillcrest made more sense, because this area would have been too marshy to support the weight?" James ventured.

"Nice effort, makes sense," the Director replied, "but incorrect. Don't worry, soon enough you'll understand. I'm just planting seeds, hoping to make the truth a little easier for you to digest, less jarring than it was for me." Director Bowen ran his fingers along the stone block, reading as his hand danced along the engraved statement. "'Position of Jefferson Pier, erected December 18, 1804. Recovered and re-erected December 2, 1889.' Now, how about the next line, can you read what follows?"

"No, Director, it's chipped away, looks like someone exerted a lot of energy chiseling off that line," James noted, a jagged groove extending along the otherwise smooth surface.

"Yes, a long time ago, someone defaced the next phrase, 'Being the center point of the District of Columbia'. Now why would anyone go through such an effort to remove this line?"

"To erase the importance of this marker?" guessed James.

"You're very perceptive," the Director replied, "however you only get partial credit. The complete truth is far more complicated," he intimated, opening his briefcase and pulling out a shiny golden key, long as a ruler with jagged teeth and an ornate loop handle. While James debated whether the oversized key looked better suited for a treasure chest or medieval castle, Director Bowen searched along the obliterated line of text and gently inserted the key, burying it to the hilt. "The marker was vandalized in an effort to prevent this," he explained, turning the key several times before returning it to his briefcase.

Nothing happened. James wondered if he'd missed some critical detail, but the granite block looked no different than prior to the key's interaction. Although terribly perplexed James kept silent, having already used up his verbal mulligan on the tombstone comment. Without further explanation on the matter, the Director headed back towards the parking lot, quietly pensive until after they'd passed through the Navy Building's security check. When Harold Bowen finally spoke it wasn't to discuss their awkward interaction at the Jefferson Pier, rather breaking the silence to gently remind James to keep pace instead of ogling the young ladies in the typing pool.

Worming their way deeper into the complex James found his first visit to the central nexus of the nation's military underwhelming, quickly realizing his expectations were naive. James imagined these hallways would be pumping with energy, critical decisions getting hashed out and crises managed, yet he'd seen more exciting drama play out between library stacks. Each bend in the hallway simply revealed more disappointing generic corporate doldrums, the only differences were the military garb and hyper-patriotic display of American flags.

While James' daily exercise regimen kept the young officer physically prepared for the lengthy march through a maze of corridors, the water sloshing inside his shoes left him hoping for a rapid conclusion. His frigid, shriveled toes appreciated a momentary break when they stopped in front of an elevator, a pair of armed guards blocking their entry. James fiddled with his pocket, he'd slipped his badge inside for safe keeping, wondering what could be important enough to merit this additional layer of security. Cleared to proceed they entered the elevator, Director Bowen selecting the elevator's only button, basement level, before asking, "James, do you know why you were offered this job?"

James was taken off guard by the blunt question, and with his tongue already loosened by nervous adrenaline, answered more honestly than he would otherwise. "Now that I'm aware of your connection to my parents, I'm assuming some nepotism was involved."

"That's a fair concern," the Director conceded, processing the response. "You're not entirely wrong, though for different reasons than you might think. I will explain. You weren't the first person selected for this position, years ago there was another but he lost faith in our mission, couldn't believe what he was shown. When it came time to replace him, I devised a method for choosing more wisely. As I reviewed the stack of resumes, on paper you weren't the most qualified candidate, not even close. Although your educational background is impressive you lacked practical experience, competing against people with equally excellent credentials plus decades spent in the field. Then I saw your name, and thought I'd at least give you a chance to hone your interviewing skills. And I admit, a bit selfishly, I couldn't pass up the chance to see you, to meet the man my good friend's son had become."

The elevator doors opened into another generic, whitewashed cinder block corridor, except this hallway differed in one striking regard. It was entirely empty, notably devoid of people, equipment, or any hint of activity. Once the elevator doors closed behind them Director Bowen resumed. "But I digress," he continued, "none of those reasons are relevant to why I chose you." James obediently followed the Director down the long, sterile hallway, noting a disconcerting lack of doors and every step a reminder of his wet, raw feet.

"Do you remember the details of your interview?" Director Bowen asked. "When we met, I answered a phone call about halfway through, and I told you to remain seated, correct?"

"Of course," James answered, he remembered it well. "It was several months ago, but yes, I recall. I didn't mean to eavesdrop, yet you spoke passionately and frankly about a secret government plot you had uncovered. Afterward, you apologized for burdening me with this knowledge, warning me that no one could be trusted with this information, and it was now my responsibility to guard it."

"Yes, although there were more details to the story," the Director prodded, "do you recall?"

"Poisoned crops," responded James. "Corn crops in Kansas, from Abilene to Weskan, to be precise."

"Exactly," the Director grinned, "I knew you'd remember." He stopped and turned to James. "Your interview wasn't the impressive part, it's the next piece, when later that week several large men flashing government credentials stormed into your home in the middle of the night. They tied you up, demanded you tell them about that very conversation, told you national security was at stake. They threatened your friends, your family, even your dog. Hell, they even roughed you up a bit. But you refused to tell them anything, correct?"

"Well, I did tell them where they could stick their threats, which they didn't like very much."

The Director chuckled. "No, I doubt they appreciated your sass. But you held your own."

"Indeed, sir, a promise is a promise. I assumed you had your reasons."

"And that's why you're here," Director Bowen revealed. "Those were my men. It was a test that only you passed. Every other person we interviewed folded like a deck of cards. Hell, two of them didn't even last until the home invasion, they tattled to the FBI as soon as they left my office. So being your father's son got you the interview, but you earned the job on your own merit. You demonstrated loyalty and courage, and if you continue to prove yourself worthy, the man of integrity I believe you are, your job at the research labs is just the beginning. My aspirations for you run deeper, and there are much bigger opportunities in store."

"I appreciate the confidence, sir," replied James, blushing at the unexpected praise.

"Don't thank me yet son, the day is just getting interesting. And don't forget, I had high hopes for your predecessor, too, but he couldn't handle the paradigm shift. It broke him. Now he's chief of the Navy shipyard's hull descaling and barnacle removal division in Ketchikan Alaska. And he's happy enough to be doing it, trying to forget what can't be forgotten."

"If you don't mind me asking," James probed, "aren't you worried he'll spill secrets?"

"Oh, not in the least," the Director replied, "he's a good enough fellow. Plus, he knows we have dirt on him, and he was into some weird stuff. He likes 'em young. Real young."

"Gross," James groaned.

"Indeed. Really had a thing for runty little bitches" the Director continued.

"Wow, a pedophile. But runty bitches, sir?" James asked, incredulous. "Isn't that a tad bit insensitive, after all you're talking about innocent children."

"Oh no, my apologies, you misunderstand," clarified the Director, "he wasn't a pedophile. He really did like runty bitches. Small female dogs. More like a pet-ophile. After working in our intelligence division, witnessing our nation's most powerful politicians diving headfirst into twisted shenanigans, you must realize everyone has some combination of disturbing fetishes, unique vulnerabilities, or a price tag."

"Yes, I've arrived at that conclusion, although I still cling to the hope that I'm mistaken," James responded to Director Bowen's glum summation of humanity.

"Cynicism is healthy, and a dose of reality won't hurt you during the journey ahead. I've been inside the government long enough to know most people are merely an amalgam of their most rudimentary desires, the four F's.

Food, fame, finances, and you can guess the last. As Director of the Naval Research Labs I deal with political turds every day, treating us like a frivolous side note, an appeasement to Thomas Edison so he'd stop harping upon the importance of technology in future wars. You know what works even better than blind optimism? Gratitude that I don't suffer under the same cloud of ignorance they do, unaware of the truths I've learned and plan on sharing with you. Only a select few ever journey to where our world meets its destiny. Your finger won't just be on the pulse of the future, you'll have both hands wrapped tightly around its aorta."

While James wasn't sure where this path led, it sounded a hell of a lot more interesting than blackmailing smarmy politicians. "Thank you for the edification," he humbly replied, "and I'm eager to learn more."

"I'm glad to hear that," Director Bowen said, turning to James, "because we're just beginning our descent and we've got another twenty thousand leagues to go." The pair slowed down as the hallway ended abruptly and without obvious reason, having remained empty and featureless the entire length. The Director walked over to a seemingly random section of the solid cinder block wall and said, quite clearly, "I'd like to order a ham sandwich, but hold the anchovies." Nearby one solitary cinder block slid back into the wall, leaving a small gap.

From the other side a voice replied, "Anchovies are a salty kind of fish, but they do make the sandwich."

Director Bowen bent down and spoke into the opening. "You're mistaken. People make the sandwich, anchovies do the swimming." The Director leaned over to James and whispered, "I've heard some goofy passphrases, this one deserves a prize." Nevertheless it worked, and soon the sounds of clinking gears vibrated through the wall, followed by grinding as a door-sized section of the wall slid back and out the way. The opening led them into a newly exposed chamber occupied by four armed guards, all positioned between them and a row of several barred cells. James immediately understood where they were. He'd only heard rumors of their existence, but this was an interrogation pit for high-value detainees. Peering through the metal bars he noted only one occupied cage.

"Welcome to Dante's Inferno," the lead security officer drawled, the cinder block wall closing behind them, bolts grinding into place. "Down here they call me Hoss," he smirked, "but y'all can call me Officer Burke. This is where we keep the big trophies, the ones the guys upstairs want disappeared, but not before they spill their beans. Most start off as tough nuts to crack, but we have our softening methods. And we're quite effective."

"Did you say Dante's Playground?" asked James. "Sounds raunchy, there's a burlesque club on 9th Street with the same name," he commented, though as his eyes acclimated to the dim lighting he noticed the foot-high letters painted in crimson along the wall opposite the cells. "'Abandon all hope, ye who enter here'," he read. "Now I get it, the writer Dante, not the nudie girls. Really leaning into the *Inferno* underworld theme, how medievally dungeon-esque of you."

"That's right," another guard smugly responded, "we ain't pussy footin' around down here."

"Indeed, you aren't," James stated, focusing his attention on the scraggly, solitary figure huddled in the corner of a cell, visibly trembling. "Though I wonder which of Dante's nine levels of hell involves bullying unarmed civilians."

"Hey, kiddo," Office Burke growled, "before you come down here passing judgment remember we're just the instrument, the big brass upstairs is the hand that wields us.

And believe me, they don't care how we get information, they just want results."

"My associate meant no disrespect, Officer Burke," the Director intervened, diffusing the situation. "He is young and naive, we realize your job is very critical. Now if you could kindly allow us time with your detainee, we'd greatly appreciate it." After another round of ID checks the two men were allowed inside the cell.

Director Bowen motioned for the detainee to join them at a table and chairs, all bolted to the concrete floor. "Please sit. We mean you no harm." The cell's poor lighting blanketed the cowering prisoner in deep shadow, but as the crouched figure stood James gasped, instantly recognizing the man he'd cajoled onto the USS *Milwaukee* three months earlier. Unmistakably Declan Riordan, the biologist, though he looked vastly different, with a thick beard and unkempt hair. James recalled the professor was a slender man, but now he looked emaciated with visible bruising on his face and arms.

The Director shook his head. "Wow, they put you through the ringer, didn't they?"

Declan didn't look up. "Yes they have, and I believe they're not finished with me yet. Will you please tell me what I've done wrong? I have no idea why I'm here, and nobody will answer my questions."

The Director once again motioned for him to join them. "Please, come sit with us, and we can talk about it."

James took a seat and noticed blood splatter on the table surface, clear evidence as to why the professor did not blindly comply with the Director's request. Instead the doctor hunkered down more firmly against the far wall. "I've heard all these bullshit promises before," Declan snapped back, "you're not selling me anything new."

The Director also sat down. "Please, sir, we know who you are. Doctor Declan Riordan, Professor at UCLA. And I can assure you we speak with our mouths, not with our fists."

Declan's interest was piqued, nobody'd addressed him by name in days. "Everyone else down here's told me I'm lying, Doctor Riordan is dead," he started, "some sort of accident in my biology lab. I'm guessing you know something they don't."

"How about we all sit down and find out," the Director pressed, opening his briefcase and pulling out a Snickers bar and a bottle of Coca-Cola, waving them in the air for Doctor Riordan's inspection. "You see these, right? They're for you, no strings attached, just come over here and join us."

Curiosity and hunger trumped fear. Since waking from the coma Declan had been tempted with false promises of leniency and freedom, almost as often as he'd been threatened with physical retribution, but this was the first candy bar. "Damn you if this is another trick," Declan announced, muttering "we'll see how you like getting punched in the face."

"No tricks," the Director reassured him, "and if you could kindly keep the face punching to a minimum, Doctor, I'd be thankful. My pugilistic days are far behind me."

As Declan cautiously moved closer they saw how gaunt and drawn his face had become, his prison uniform disheveled and sullied with blood and grime. James averted his gaze, horrified to see the full extent of the swollen bruises on Declan's face and the burn marks peppering his neck and hands.

"Shouldn't he be recovering in a hospital?" James asked.

"Oh, he already did," the Director replied, "and reportedly healed up nicely. No, these injuries happened since getting transferred here. All these wounds are from, how do they phrase it? Detainee motivational techniques."

When James spoke Declan immediately recognized the voice, the same one that tricked him out of the safety of his laboratory. "You," Declan growled at James, glowering at him, "you're the one who got me on that boat."

"Ship," James instinctually corrected.

"Boat, ship, friggin' Noah's Ark, it doesn't matter what you call it, you son of a bitch, you sent me on that death cruise. Great for my career? You liar! And now they're blaming me for, well I'm not entirely sure what, but obviously something bad. I bet you're the reason they think I'm dead, too, right? You've got a lot of nerve showing up here." Declan walked over to the cell bars and banged on them. "Guards! Hey, guards, the guy you really want is in here with me! This guy is the one you want," he shouted, pointing at James.

"Doctor Riordan, that isn't productive. Please relax and join us," Director Bowen pleaded.

"Hey, bucko," Officer Burke threatened, "if you don't calm down, you're gonna have another accidental tumble."

Director Bowen placed the Snickers bar and Coca-Cola on the table. "Please join us, Doctor," he reiterated. This time Declan begrudgingly accepted the offer, although the idea of sitting near James was only marginally better than another round of face versus fist. "Well, they certainly take their job seriously," the Director said, surveying Declan's face, "and this is not James' fault, he was simply following my orders, so direct your anger at me. My name is Harold Bowen, I'm a Rear Admiral and the current Director of the US Naval Research Labs, and I was acting upon recommendations from men with even more impressive credentials. I can assure you we had zero inkling the mission could veer so terribly wrong, or the military would allow such harsh interrogation. As a small peace offering, please enjoy these refreshments."

"If it helps, I'm sorry as well," James chimed in.

"It doesn't," Declan replied, wanting to reach across the table and tear out James' smarmy, smug larynx, but knew in his weakened state he'd barely break skin. Instead he compromised and shot James a nasty look. "And you are not forgiven," he added before tearing off the Snickers wrapper with great vigor.

"Fair enough," conceded James, disturbed but enthralled watching Declan throttle that candy bar with such vigor it would make an Amsterdam red-light girl blush.

As Declan guzzled down the cola, the Director continued. "I'm sorry you've been treated so shamefully. I had no control over the matter. The United States military does not appreciate looking foolish, so they took it personally when a phantom crew illegally tricked their way aboard one of their battleships and used it like their private taxicab. In the course of their investigation they also determined the SS *Valencia* was actually a stolen Merchant Marine vessel, and they're taking that even more personally. All that anger and frustration has been wrongly routed in your direction, being the sole survivor recovered from the *Valencia's* wreckage. I'm sure they've asked you many questions about the expedition, and your lack of answers would not have sat well with your interrogators. Now, just between the three of us, do you remember anything unusual about Antarctica?"

"I wish I did," replied Declan, "I don't even remember going there. I'd really like answers as well but my mind is so foggy, the harder I try to recall details the more they slip away."

Director Bowen pressed further. "While in the hospital you mentioned crystals in the ice, and a girl trapped inside, do you remember saying this?"

"No, I don't," Declan said, shaking his head. "There's not much I can say for certain, though I don't recall any women traveling with us."

"I didn't say a woman, I said a girl, a young girl," the Director corrected, looking around Declan's cell. "You know what? I've heard enough, we're done here," he announced, standing to leave.

Declan panicked, spilling half his soda when James rose. "No, you can't leave me here! Please don't go! Just give me some time to gather my thoughts, I'll tell you whatever you want to know!"

"That's entirely unnecessary," Director Bowen reassured him, "in fact, I'd prefer if you didn't tell me anything. I don't need, or want, to know what you know, although I have some colleagues who'd love a good chin wag. You misunderstand my intent, Doctor, we're not leaving you here, you're coming with us," he said, motioning for the prisoner to follow them.

When all three men exited the cell, the startled guards drew their pistols. "Get back in the cell!" Officer Burke barked at Declan.

"Officer Burke, have your men stand down," the Director commanded. "This man is no longer your concern. He's in my custody now."

"Over my dead body," snapped Officer Burke.

"I appreciate the offer," Director Bowen calmly replied, "but that won't be necessary at this time. A simple release of this detainee will be sufficient."

"Released? On who's authority? Because with all due respect, sir" Officer Burke sneered, "you are not our commanding officer. You're a Naval Research officer, which frankly, is kind of a joke, sir." All the guards chuckled.

"Hmmm," the Director mused, "that doesn't sound very respectful, and, frankly, not very nice. I hope you weren't trying to hurt my feelings, although I can handle your sticks and stones. What upsets me most is the condition of your detainee, you did not treat him hospitably, and I'm a bit perturbed. Now, what's going to happen…" the telephone rang, interrupting Director Bowen, "is that. So go ahead, pick it up," he calmly suggested.

Surly Officer Burke huffed as he picked up the receiver. "Yes?" he demanded, though immediately fell silent as his face turned ghostly pale. "But, but, but," he sputtered. "I'm sorry, sir, yes, I'll shut up and listen, sir." This continued for another minute before he hung up the phone, his head hung low like a scared puppy. "Doctor Riordan, you are free to leave. On behalf of the United States Army, I apologize for any mistreatment you may have received while under our security detail."

One of the other guards looked bewildered. "Are you out of your mind, Hoss? We're under strict orders to make sure nobody…"

"Just shut it," Officer Burke hissed back, "we're letting him leave, with our sincerest regrets over our misconduct. So unless you feel like spending the rest of your military career cleaning latrines with a toothbrush, zip your yapper."

"Thank you, Officer Burke, for your change of heart," the Director resumed, "now where were we? Oh, yes, Doctor Riordan certainly can't be seen wearing these dirty tattered rags, can he?" the Director posited, surveying the guards. "Too short, too fat, this one's just right," he said, pointing to the one closest to Declan's build. "Please give the Doctor your uniform," he commanded.

"But, but," the young man stammered.

"Just do it!" shouted Officer Burke.

The young man began undressing, unbuttoning his shirt very slowly, after each button looking back up at Hoss to make certain this was for real. "If you could hurry this up a bit," the Director snapped, "that would be great. And you don't have to keep checking in with your superior officer, he won't be changing his mind." The young man pulled down his pants, put his fingers on his underwear band and paused, eyes pleading for mercy. "That's enough," Director Bowen declared, "keep your tighty-whities and pistol, but everything else goes." The young guard was so relieved he hurried through the rest of his disrobing, handing each article of clothing to Declan who unsteadily yet cheerfully dressed. When he took off his prisoner's jumper the Director gasped. Declan's skin hugged each rib and scabbed over whip marks criss-crossed his back. "You're lucky I'm letting you off this lightly," he said, scowling as he berated the guards.

James seized the opportunity. "Excuse me, Director Bowen, but if you'd like to teach them another lesson, my shoes are really soaked," he explained, "and my feet would appreciate a dry pair. I'm a size ten."

"Certainly," the Director assented. "Any of you a size ten?" he queried. No answers. "Come on, anybody close?"

"I'm a size eleven," Officer Burke begrudgingly admitted, unlacing his shoes without further prompting.

Once Declan donned his military attire and James finished tying his loose but arid shoes, the Director addressed the guards. "Men, you have been very cooperative, and I will pass that along to your superiors. Officer Burke, you are relieved of your command. As for the rest of you, your duty here is complete and you are all summarily dismissed." With bewildered expressions the guards opened the secret door leading back into the hallway. The undressed guard grabbed Declan's raggedy jumper and tied it around his waist like a towel before trailing after the others.

As Officer Burke exited, he apologized to Declan one more time. "You shouldn't be apologizing to me," Declan sharply replied, "you should be apologizing to your high school biology teacher. Anchovies aren't a type of fish, they're a whole group of fish species, and they aren't necessarily salty, some live in freshwater. So there you go." Officer Burke's face contorted with perplexment, and unsure how to respond and unwilling to expend the mental energy, he simply turned and followed his men down the hall.

Director Bowen smiled. "Now Doctor, this uniform does wonders for you, though a hot shower, hearty meal and a break from being used like a punching bag are also on the docket." He looked at his watch. "We need to hurry, time is not our friend, and at the risk of sounding like the White Rabbit, if we keep up this pace we too shall be late."

The three men navigated a serpiginous journey through the Navy and Munitions Building, lengthy enough James wondered if they'd crossed into Virginia. Declan kept stride remarkably well, courtesy of the adrenaline surge resulting from his snack and change in fortune, and despite his conscripted uniform hanging baggily off his emaciated frame, thankfully neither his outfit nor battered face garnered unsolicited attention. They transited a series of lengthy hallways, actively avoiding interaction with other people milling about the corridors, until they reached a far less trafficked one. "The Judge Advocate General's office is down here," the Director explained, "this is where the provisions of the Articles of War, the real heavy-duty disciplinary actions, get handled."

"Why are we going there?" Declan asked, "I thought you were coming to help me, not deliver me to the executioners."

"Relax, Doc," James replied, "the JAG is run by Army lawyers. They only prosecute military personnel like me. Hey," James paused mid-thought, "wait a minute. Director Bowen, why are we heading here?"

The Director slowed down. "James, consider taking your own advice," he suggested, "there's no reason to be so skittish, my intent will soon become apparent," he hinted before resuming his brisk pace.

The JAG reception area was populated with only two occupants, a secretary, and an armed MP, guarding the rows of closed office doors behind them. "Good morning miss. Hello officer." Director Bowen nodded to the pair as he casually walked past. "The JAGs are almost never in their offices," he explained while leading them down the hall, "and since they handle sensitive, top secret documents this area is always monitored. Great place to have our office, and here we are," he said, arriving at the last door, the only one with a glass pane, labeled in gold lettering "Office of Promotion Crippling Infractions and Wickedly Harsh Disciplinary Reprimands."

The Director entered the ominously monikered room without hesitation, the door shutting behind him as neither James nor Declan were eager to follow. Director Bowen swung the door ajar and poked his head out. "Come on," he insisted. "Don't mind the sign, I forget how foreboding it sounds." He held the door open and waved the two men inside the small waiting area. "The intimidation is intentional, keeps away the Looky-Loos. And if that doesn't stop unwelcome guests, the decor certainly will." Declan surveyed the small waiting room, it was a disturbing mess. Heavily stained carpet matched the motley array of equally ragged chairs, cushion stuffing extruding from various tears in the fabric. Against the wall stood a pair of leaning, rickety cabinets, sagging shelves piled with canisters labeled "Hazardous chemicals - do not inhale toxic fumes" accompanied by ominous skulls and crossbones.

Centered along the far wall was a single black door, on one side a framed newspaper clipping of a ship disaster, on the other a photograph of a devastated landscape of twiggy, flattened trees. "Tunguska, Siberia, 1908," James read off the bottom of the frame, "what uplifting choices in wall art," he muttered.

"Fits nicely with the room's welcoming vibe," Declan added, pointing to the large sign nailed to the inner door. 'OFFICE. DO NOT ENTER - KEEP OUT!' in tall, bold letters. "Are you sure this is the right place?" he queried.

"Nothing to worry about," the Director reassured both men, approaching the black door while carefully navigating past the dilapidated furniture and potentially deleterious bric-a-brac. He knocked.

A deep voice bellowed from behind the black office door, beckoning them to enter. The Director charged ahead, leading them into the back room where Declan anticipated further unsanitary surprises. Instead the office was spotless with glossy white walls, matching linoleum tiles and spartan yet clean furnishings, a simple card table and folding chairs. Behind the table stood a slender, towering figure dressed in an all-black civilian suit, smiling broadly. "Welcome, men," he said, grinning, "I hoped to see both of you again."

It was a race between James and Declan to see who could be unshocked enough to speak first. "You? I remember you," Declan spoke first. "Bruce, I recall. You helped this one," pointing to James, "sucker me onto that ship. Thanks for the career opportunity, you ruined my life," he snidely jabbed.

"Indeed, I helped James," Bruce calmly responded, "and your feelings of anger towards me are justified. Please believe our intentions were benign, we never imagined the mission would turn out so poorly. The entire expedition was meant to be a reconnaissance mission, a sightseeing tour. At worst we thought you'd get some mild frostbite or slip on penguin guano. And might I say, Professor, I'm thoroughly impressed you remember my name."

"Oh, that's simple," Declan replied, "You're very tall. Bruce rhymes with spruce, like the tree."

"Makes sense," Bruce mused, "glad my name isn't Buck Chase."

Meanwhile, James recovered enough to join the conversation. "Bruce, it's nice to see you again. Although just because you're new at the Research Labs doesn't mean you should be stuck with these crummy accommodations." James turned to the Director. "Is Bruce also here to discuss the Antarctic…"

"Hold your thoughts a moment," Bruce interrupted. "Excuse me while I guarantee us some privacy." The lanky man walked through the grungy waiting area, locked and deadbolted the hallway door before pulling a CLOSED sign down over the glass panel. Bruce rejoined them, sitting and motioning for them to do the same, even as he struggled to settle his sizable frame into the petite chair. "Not particularly accommodating," he conceded, his knees thrust awkwardly into his chest, "but sturdy," he remarked, noting James and Declan hesitantly eyeing the chairs. "Don't worry," he reassured them, "these aren't like the waiting room chairs, those are intentionally distressed, purely for shock value, guarantees any accidental interlopers don't linger. These chairs aren't fancy, or particularly comfortable, which is fine because we won't be staying here very long."

"Both of you must be terrifically confused by now," Director Bowen started, "Bruce and I will try our best to answer your questions as we move along, however keep in mind we've got a lot to unpack and we're incredibly short on time. Miles to go before we sleep. First, James, I must apologize for misrepresenting Bruce's role at the Research Labs, he isn't a recent hire."

"I'm not following," James admitted, "I was given specific instructions to guide Bruce, show him the ropes," he recalled, assessing the tall man. Bruce appeared to be in his early 40s, face tan and leathery, hints of gray peppered into his chocolate hair, dark eyes gazing upon them with disarming kindness and piercing intensity. Even folded into the chair like an origami giraffe he posed an intimidating figure. "I'm sorry if I misunderstood my role."

"I'm the one who needs to apologize for this deception," Bruce reassured him, "it was my idea to misrepresent my credentials. I convinced Harold to play along, place you in charge of our assignment so I could watch you in action. You don't learn about a person's character from how they treat people they fear and respect, only when a man feels superior to another does he reveal his true nature. I wanted to meet the real James Fischer, and since you're sitting here now, assume I liked what I saw."

"I've known Bruce for many years," the Director explained, "when we were both newbies at the Bureau of Engineering, and I convinced him to follow me to the Research Labs. I've been mentoring him for a very specific role," Director Bowen added, "one that defies simple explanation. I hoped to continue his apprenticeship longer, however recent developments have accelerated our timetable. I'm an old man playing a young man's game, so I've handed off the torch."

Bruce focused his intense gaze on James. "I'm putting together a team, and I need trustworthy men. I'd like for you to come work with me."

James' mind raced. "I'm a bit confused," he responded, "it sounds like you're offering me a job, but I already have one. And that gentleman," he said, nodding at Director Bowen, "is my boss."

"Bruce isn't offering you a job," the Director clarified, "he's offering you an opportunity. And don't worry about my feelings, I'm the one who recommended you. Ostensibly you'd still be working for the Research Labs, just in a different capacity. My directorship duties stretch me too thin to meaningfully assist Bruce, and I think you'd be perfect. Bruce works on special projects deviating beyond normal channels, outside the purview of government interference. Our organization operates behind the Wizard's curtain, and I think you'd fit in well back there."

"I agree," Bruce nodded in assent, the awkwardly seated man now turning his attention to Declan. "As for you, Doctor Riordan, I know we'll need to earn your trust, so let me start by saying goodbye."

"You're not making any sense," a wary Declan replied, "what kind of clever ploy is this?"

"None. I'm not trying to deceive you," Bruce affirmed. "I understand your skepticism, I just want you to understand that you aren't our prisoner. You can leave whenever you'd like. The Army's official intelligence report concluded you were an innocent bystander vacationing in Miami, had one too many pina coladas and accidentally wandered onto a military base. Your record is wiped clean, purer than Ivory Soap. So if you truly desire your old life, you can walk out of here right now. We'll fly you back to California, let UCLA know you're very much alive, and provide you with everything we promised. Published papers, tenure, grant funding, the works. You can settle back into your studio apartment, return to your position as the lowest man on the academic totem pole and rekindle your sorely uninspired social life."

"Hold on," Declan protested, "you're offering deceitful James a chance to be a part of something amazing, your secret organization, and I'm getting the consolation prize?" The professor had never viewed his life as ordinary or boring before, though now he couldn't articulate a reason for rushing back to it. He didn't know why, but now the prospect of spending a lifetime growing bacteria in petri dishes sounded like punishment. Declan struggled to understand his feelings, all evidence suggested he shouldn't trust these men, yet an inexplicable nagging in his mind overpowered these rational hesitations. "Maybe I'd be interested, too. I still can't figure out how you drove us from California to Norfolk in one night, why you sailed to Antarctica, or did any of the other wildly incredible things our government has accused me of doing. And the masterful way the Director handled Hoss and the other guards, your organization must carry serious clout. However, what interests me the most is whether you're just a one trick pony or are there other rabbits up your sleeve?"

Bruce smiled. "Illusionists rely upon sleight of hand. We're like you, Professor Riordan, men of science and technology. And by the way, the government can only guess at our true capabilities, and that's the way we like it."

"Now I'm even more intrigued, perhaps I would consider an offer," Declan hinted. "No commitments, of course."

"Naturally," Bruce responded, "and I'm pleased your gears are spinning, because we're equally excited to learn more about you. I appreciate your willingness to give us another chance. While I can only apologize for the way you've been treated thus far, going forward I can promise you marvels beyond comprehension. Nothing can erase how you've been wronged, but if you work with us, maybe we can square things up a bit." Bruce offered his hand. "Become part of a grander vision of the future."

"You got one thing right, none of what happened to me was fair," Declan passionately replied, "first you and that snake oil salesman James lied to me, then left me to rot while my own government kicked my ass. Your apology is a pathetic consolation, nonetheless I appreciate the gesture. So thank you," he said, shaking Bruce's hand, "and I'll stick around for now, see what you've got to offer. If it's anything short of spectacular, I'm gone."

"Of course, you may leave at any time, Professor," Director Bowen reassured him, "although it shouldn't take long to realize you made the right decision. Your presence will be of tremendous help, even if you don't remember much about your time on the *Valencia* or in Antarctica. Before the *Valencia* sank her crew scripted one final report, a summary reaching the obvious conclusion that the mission could have gone better. The report also indicates you were embedded with Alpha Team, our elite squad of highly skilled professionals. Alpha Team was tasked with the most crucial assignment, surveil the Germans and discover why they were in Antarctica. Your team was the only one in direct contact with Nazi forces, resulting in all our men being killed, while you survived this hostile encounter virtually unscathed. We are left with a lot of unanswered questions."

"Like I already said, I don't remember anything about the trip," Declan reaffirmed, "the last concrete memory I have is aboard the *Milwaukee*. I recall being corralled into a small cabin with a bunch of equally confused men, all scientists and academicians of various types, all fed similar lines of bull about an amazing research opportunity.

We tried getting answers from the large, rugged men accompanying us, but they were entirely disinterested in sharing information with us. Everything after that is a blur, even now I'm still mentally foggy, like I'm floating in a dream. The harder I try to focus on the details, the more confused I get. Maybe if I read the report, it'll jog my memory."

"Impossible," the Director replied, "the report is gone, it served its purpose, so I destroyed it. The only one who read the entirety was James, and I'd prefer he didn't share details with you, at least for now. The power of suggestion can cloud your thoughts and create false memories. We don't need your mind playing psychological tricks."

Once again Declan glowered at James then sighed, shrugging his shoulders. "I'd like to argue with your logic but I can't, although I'm hard-pressed to see how helpful I can be if I don't remember anything."

"There are other ways to be helpful," Bruce stated, "after all the Germans didn't travel off the edge of the map, expending resources and treasure, to sail away on a pleasure cruise. Neither did we. We didn't send you to Antarctica to cuddle with the sea lions, the research expedition was simply our cover story, in case we encountered the Germans."

Declan scrunched his brow. "Hold on, if the scientists were just there to legitimize your subterfuge, you could have serviced your needs in far less complicated ways. Why go through all the trouble of choosing us so carefully? The letter from *Nature* magazine was addressed to me by name, you picked me for a reason. Hell, you drove across the entire country to proposition me. What you're saying doesn't add up."

"You're very perceptive, Professor, and also correct," Bruce admitted, "you weren't randomly picked, we've been looking for men like you, with very specific attributes, for longer than you'd believe. Unfortunately, the Germans didn't provide us with advanced warning, leaving us with little opportunity to mobilize in the calm, organized fashion we anticipated. We scrambled to mount the expedition, and this meant cutting some corners in order to cram years of preparation into a few days."

Director Bowen elaborated. "One corner that got cut was our recruitment strategy for you and the other civilian passengers, all smart men like you," he explained, "though we never meant to resort to such high-pressure tactics. Over the years we've methodically narrowed down our field of possible candidates for this mission, hoping we'd be left with only one individual. We simply ran out of time, and since we couldn't leave the Germans to explore the Antarctic tundra unchecked, we rounded up all of you, the entire cohort. Admittedly we could have done a better job explaining this to you in advance, but we take secrecy very seriously, and communications are strictly need-to-know."

"I still don't understand your reasoning," Declan pressed. "Not only did you risk my life and those of your other candidates, you also risked the lives of your own men with a hastily slapped-together mission. There must have been a good reason, worthy of taking such a wild chance. You already knew there was something important down in Antarctica, didn't you? What was it? What were you so afraid the Nazis might find?"

"We didn't know, at least not for certain," Director Bowen confessed. "Our organization has deep roots, beyond the Research Labs or any government entity, and we've waited a long time for this confluence of events. It didn't matter if they were German, English or Eskimos. We needed to follow them, and despite the heavy price our men paid to discover Germany's intent, the mission was worth all the blood spilled. Our men didn't sacrifice their lives in vain, they successfully confirmed our worst fears. The Nazis weren't in Antarctica to claim land or find whale pods, they were hunting for special artifacts. Unfortunately, there's a good chance they were successful, which means the entire world has suddenly become a more dangerous place. Bruce is going to need help, and you both have important roles in what comes next."

"As long as it doesn't involve Antarctica, or ships," Declan declared. "Because if you think I'm sailing back to Antarctica, you are wildly mistaken."

"No, that's not what we're talking about," Bruce asserted. "Please excuse my unfortunate word choice, but Antarctica was just the tip of the iceberg. Our goals extend further, tracking the German activity in Antarctica was one tiny piece of an enormously intricate puzzle. All of this will make more sense showing you rather than explaining," Bruce said, walking over to his office door and twisting the knob, "and thankfully we've arrived. So let's get moving."

Chapter 8

March 29, 1939
Room of the Honored
Clypeate Headquarters
City of Washington, District of Columbia

Even though Bruce opened the same office door through which they'd entered, the dilapidated waiting area was gone. "This is a startling upgrade," James remarked, soiled carpet and rickety furniture replaced with grandly appointed furnishings, lacquered walnut flooring and richly patterned chestnut walls. Rows of mounted muskets, rifles, swords and sabers lined the available wall space, floor to ceiling, except for one area draped with a quilt-sized flag.

"I thought we'd be more comfortable here," Bruce grinned, happily stretching his legs, "and what we tell you will sound more credible in these surroundings. I see you've both noticed our collection," he said, commenting upon the wide-eyed, amazed expressions worn by James and Declan, "feel free to look around first, then we must get back to business," he added, gesturing towards the massive, dark mahogany conference table filling the room.

"Where'd the waiting area go?" Declan asked, surveying the walls adorned with a panoply of military armament. "Or perhaps a better question, who's your interior decorator, General Tecumseh Sherman or George Custer?"

"I realize you are poking fun, Professor, but there are actually several pieces belonging to General Sherman down here," Bruce noted. "And in response to your other question, the waiting area didn't go anywhere," the tall man explained, "we did. Many meters down. This is the Room of the

Honored, and this collection has been accumulated over time, donated by members of our society."

"You must have some well-connected donors," James commented, "because I've visited naval armories with less munitions." One particular wall caught his attention. "These muskets are all from the Revolutionary War," he gasped, leaning in for closer inspection, "with some Colonial long rifles mixed in. I'd swear such an extensive collection was impossible, yet there's enough here to arm half the Continental Army."

"Your math is a little off," Bruce noted, "but you are otherwise correct. All these weapons belonged to soldiers of the Continental Army, members of our fellowship. This is our heritage, which we proudly display as a reminder of our valiant past."

"You are members of the Continental Army?" Declan repeated. "As in the British-are-coming, one-if-by-land two-if-by-sea, midnight ride of Paul Revere, Revolutionary War?"

"Yes," the Director confirmed, "that Revolutionary War."

"Excuse me, sir," James interjected, "I think you are confusing Doctor Riordan. It sounds like you're saying this secret society is part of the Continental Army, which is obviously not what you meant. The Naval Academy pounded us with early American military history and the Continental Army disbanded at the war's conclusion."

"The professor heard me correctly," Director Bowen insisted. "When the Treaty of Paris ended the Revolutionary War, the Continental Army wasn't fully disbanded. After George Washington resigned as Commander in 1783 the remaining forces morphed into the modern US Army. Presumably this ended the Continental Army, but that isn't the case. General Washington didn't eliminate his command, he simply tendered his resignation, which left the position open."

"Now you're stretching credulity," Declan argued, "this can't be true."

"No," James realized, "it's strategically brilliant. "Washington found a loophole and exploited it. But for what purpose?"

Director Bowen didn't hesitate. "So the General could maintain a small, loyal contingent of Continental Army soldiers as leverage."

"Leverage against what?" James queried.

"Well, the United States government, of course. Think about it for a moment," the Director continued. "Imagine you just won freedom for your fellow colonists, overcoming great odds to repel an oppressive government. Would you just hand over this hard-fought prize without a backup plan? In those early days there were no guarantees the Great American Experiment of democracy would work, so General Washington created a shadow force of his most loyal continental soldiers as insurance. He called them his Clypeate, his shield, protecting the fledgling nation against the opposing but equally destructive forces of anarchy and tyranny. Those soldiers loyal to Washington founded our society, our Clypeate, and we carry on their legacy."

"Clypeate? Never heard of it," Declan responded, "although you certainly have accrued a nice antique weapons collection. Honestly, I'm a bit skeptical. It's hard for me to imagine how something this important never made its way into the history books."

"The doctor makes a valid point," James chimed in. "I'm an avid history buff, and I'm also drawing a blank."

Bruce spoke up. "That's because we don't operate like other secret organizations. The Illuminati, Templars, Freemasons, they'll blab to anyone willing to listen about how mysterious and ancient they are. We don't want outsiders thinking about us or searching us out, so we keep everything, even our name, unknown. Besides Clypeate members only a handful of top political and military personnel ever learn our true identity, most of whom end up joining our ranks. Historically most presidents were already members before getting elected, unfortunately the one we've got now isn't Clypeate and he's a bit of a prickly thorn."

"FDR knows about your secret Continental Army?" Declan contemplated, "then why hasn't he, or anyone else, closed the loophole? Assuming you're telling us the truth," he posited, "shouldn't the Clypeate's mission have ended when George Washington died, or maybe when the last Revolutionary War soldier kicked it sometime last century? Even if George Washington had a compelling reason to create a separate Clypeate, what stops modern presidents like Roosevelt from folding you into the modern military? Wouldn't that make more sense?"

"That's a good question, and a complicated one to answer. In the early days of the Republic a few presidents tried, especially John Adams and Thomas Jefferson. Both were doggedly determined to extinguish the Clypeate, but General Washington outmaneuvered them. During his presidency Washington once again controlled the military so, as Commander in Chief of the Army, he reinstated himself as Commander of the Continental Army. He cleverly embedded his loyal faction of the Continental Army, his Clypeate, into the bedrock of the US military hierarchy. Since only a higher ranking military officer can dissolve the Continental Army's mandate, and no military officer can ever outrank George Washington, it would take a Constitutional amendment to disband our Clypeate. We are the legacy of Washington's desire for checks and balances, not only for our country, but for humanity."

"Hold on," James interjected. "The military brass can't be happy with this arrangement, why don't they press the issue?"

"Only the highest military leaders know the truth," Bruce answered. "And those muck-a-mucks would never willingly air their dirty laundry to Congress. Career military craves decisiveness and action, the opposite mentality of the gridlocked legislature. They'll never bring this technicality to the attention of Congress, instead they simply don't fund us, which explains the high-quality furnishings in our upstairs office. It serves our purposes for them to believe they are effectively starving us, we're not viewed as a threat so they leave us alone."

"Exactly," Director Bowen chimed in. "The military thinks of us like an appendix," he explained. "Serving no apparent function, and as long as we don't cause problems it's not worth their trouble to remove us. Under this detente the remnants of the Continental Army, our Clypeate, has subsisted, hidden behind the military's thick shroud of bureaucracy, deep inside the war machine."

"Running a secret club must be nifty, but why keep this up?" Declan wondered. "Haven't we learned by now that United States democracy works, there isn't a need for a group like this anymore. Seems superfluous."

"Ah, but you're mistaken," the Director rebuffed. "There's always a role for the Clypeate in keeping balance in favor of beneficence and unity, and most presidents figure this out quickly. The War of 1812 and Civil War would have both turned out vastly different if it weren't for our predecessors' interventions, and ensuring national sovereignty was merely a starting point. The Clypeate evolved, we now fulfill a greater purpose."

"World domination?" Declan conjectured, causing Bruce and the Director Bowen to erupt in laughter.

"Nothing so nefarious," Bruce reassured him. "If anything we're ensuring the opposite outcome. Even though our Clypeate began with the birth of our nation, we serve an ancient, noble role in the balance of humanity. Over time names and places have changed, but since antiquity there has been a need for a protectorate, guarding humanity against the worst of itself. In the long-forgotten past, our ancestors were gifted with remarkable abilities, unlike any other creature, endowed with intelligence and pre-ordained for greatness. The Clypeate exists to give our species the best chance of fulfilling this birthright."

"Your purpose sounds equally admirable and nebulous," Declan mused. "Perhaps because my mind is still foggy, I'm having tremendous difficulty following your leaps in logic. You may as well be meowing."

"The doctor has a point," James confessed, "not about the meowing, but you are brushing past huge swaths of detail."

"The weeds are deep and we must not get mired down," Bruce warned. "We still have a lot of ground left to cover, and you are busy spinning your curious minds with extraneous questions and puzzlement. I'd be lying if I said everything will make sense, or Harold and I have all the answers, so I won't. Instead, I suggest that we sit at the table, relax in these very comfortable chairs, and let Professor Riordan eat a decent hot meal while we further chip away at your charmingly naive assumptions."

"That is a fantastic plan," Director Bowen agreed, settling into one of the plush leather chairs. "Professor Riordan, I know your jailors served up less than desirable meals, so we made prearrangements," he said, pointing to a lid-covered tray. Declan sat down, cautiously lifting the lid to find his olfactory system confronted with wonderful aromas. He lustily scanned the tray's contents, heaped piles of meatloaf and mashed potatoes drenched in gravy, plus an assortment of sides smothering the entire plate. "This looks delicious," Declan said, tears streaming down his cheeks. "I'm having sensory overload," he chuckled, "they only served me Jello in the military hospital, and that was a heavenly treat compared to the slop offered by Hoss's goonies. Oliver Twist wouldn't have eaten that gruel."

"Those days are over," the Director apologized. "And I assure you a parade of wonderful meals lies ahead."

Declan mumbled his thanks through a packed mouth. Never a connoisseur of loaf-shaped beef, he now devoured the savory meat brick faster than he could chew.

"I don't think Doctor Riordan plans to save anything for the rest of us," James joked, eliciting an unamused glare from Declan. "Sorry Doc, I'm kidding, just don't choke on the bones."

"While Doctor Riordan eats," Director Bowen began, "I'll elaborate on the Clypeate's role in American history. After all, those who ignore history are doomed to repeat it." The Director paused while Declan gagged on a mouthful of carrots. "And please Professor, nobody's rushing you, and I'd rather not have those honey-glazed carrots obstruct your airway or expelled all over this very nice table."

The professor grunted his understanding, and looking like a squirrel cheeking acorns said, "Argle uggle narp wop", then continued slogging his way through dietary nirvana.

Finding clarification from the doctor unnecessary, Director Bowen resumed, running his hand along the massive table's smooth finish. "Now that I think about it, I realize the story of how this lovely dining table ended up down here is a great starting point. Back in 1829, when Andrew Jackson took office, on his inauguration night he invited a mob of supporters into the White House for a celebration. It wasn't long before the Executive Mansion was overrun. Carpets ruined, china broken, revelers dancing on the furniture, the place was more disheveled than when the Brits burned it during the War of 1812. He summoned the Clypeate to rescue irreplaceable documents and other important items, carrying some away on this table. In the aftermath, when the Clypeate returned to unload the table, the White House took back all the items except for the table. Dancing revelers damaged the surface beyond simple repair, so badly scuffed and deeply gouged President Jackson believed it was better off being chopped up for firewood. Instead, the Clypeate refurbished the table and kept it here ever since, over a century later. Which brings me to my point."

"Let me get this straight," Declan interjected, swallowing hard to nudge barely chewed meatloaf down his esophagus, "George Washington's Clypeate, his finest troops, were called into action to break up a house party? Sounds a tad pedestrian for a secret army."

Director Bowen smiled. "I hoped one of you would say that, because protecting White House furniture does seem like a ridiculous waste of our capabilities." He reached into his briefcase and pulled out a thin, red-jacketed notebook. "And it would have been, except it wasn't just furniture the Clypeate saved that night. Andrew Jackson was Commander of the Clypeate long before he'd been sworn in as president, which meant he was the guardian of this special book." The Director opened the notebook to the first entry and turned it towards James. "You'll soon realize why it was so important for us to protect this journal. James, do you mind?"

Chapter 9

March 29, 1939
Room of the Honored
Clypeate Headquarters
City of Washington, District of Columbia

James cleared his throat and began reading aloud:

Journal Entry #1
May 11, 1750

Last night I participated in an extraordinary encounter, one I would gladly dismiss as a frenzied dream except my mud-caked boots proclaim the reality. I dare not record this in my daily journal so I scribble instead into this jot book, which I will guard most securely, as any soul who accidentally discovers this will question my sanity.

Many hours past sundown I awoke, a cool blue light shone from outside the bedroom, no more than a stone's throw away. My sleepy mind first assumed an overseer or driver was on patrol, but as the light did not move for several long moments I decided to dress and investigate. When I stepped outside I could not discern the figure holding the light, it was simply too bright when contrasted against the darkness afforded by the waning moon's thin crescent. I called out but received no response, instead the blue light headed away from me, towards the water's edge. I took this flight as a sign of nefarious intent and began an immediate chase after the trespasser. The light continued to move ahead at a pace faster than I could safely muster, and while I carefully plotted my course down the slope my quarry proceeded effortlessly.

Eventually the dark shape slowed and paused, as if waiting for me to catch up. I sped up, and when I was just a dozen yards from my prey I found myself sinking, mired knee-deep in marshy riverbank. There I found myself trapped. The blue light danced towards me, hovering, no word better describes the motion, several feet in front of me. I shielded myself, presuming an assault, though none transpired. Cautiously I peeked between my fingers, now able to discern an outline of the shadowy figure holding the light, its visage hidden beneath a hooded robe. The reflection of light off the river offered me a quick glimpse into this specter's vibrant eyes before the dark shape suddenly turned and darted out into open waters, using no watercraft or visible means of propulsion, gliding just as silently and smoothly across the river as if the surface were frozen solid.

I desired to credit this entire incident to a trick of the mind, a colorful display of the marshy will-o'the-wisps playing games with my sanity. However it reminded me of a story once relayed by Mother, during my youth, shortly after our father's departure to his heavenly reward, when my brother Lawrence left Home Farm to take up residence at the Little Hunting Creek Plantation.

Until now I'd convinced myself the entire event she described had been concocted in a wild postpartum delirium, but I can no longer pass judgment on the veracity of her account. Mother related to me a fantastic tale of a strange encounter which took place upon my birth, when I was mere hours old. A figure appeared at *her bedside, she struggled to describe him, only noting he was tall and spindly with delicate, handsome features. She also made a point of remarking upon the translucence of his skin, how his face shone like fine bone china. He towered over her bed, his outfit simple and flowing, quietly watching her. Shockingly none of the attending servants noticed his presence nor made efforts to chase him away. She realized he was not visible to them and panicked, certain she'd died and this angel had arrived to retrieve her soul. She pleaded for her life, in response he smiled and told her there was nothing to fear. His voice was melodic and soothing, she instantly felt comforted and safe. He called himself Hesperus, and explained he was there to meet her newborn, a child of ancient prophecy he'd long waited to meet.*

James finished reading the passage, the second document to stretch credulity in just as many hours, and doubts crept in as he wondered if Director Bowen and Bruce were insane, delusional, or both.

Declan took a long swig of cola, washing down a heaping spoonful of apple cobbler, and began laughing. "Angels and ghosts? Is this where our conversation has led us? Who wrote this fantasy? I'd guess HG Wells, maybe Jonathan Swift, they've both penned some fanciful tales."

"The mother in this story is Mary Washington, meaning this was authored by General George Washington. This accounting is both authentic and factual," Bruce insisted, "so Professor, you may wish to save up your comments until after James reads the next entry," he suggested, "because I'm certain this next piece will invoke even pithier remarks."

James, his opinions similar to the professor, chuckled nervously before resuming:

Journal Entry #2
July 14, 1755

On numerous occasions I convinced myself to throw this journal into the kitchen fire, embarrassed by the silliness of my prior entry, though in each instance an inexplicable force stayed my hand against such a rash course. In the intervening years I kept this journal close to me at all times, unable to forget the night when that creature, presumably Hesperus, effortlessly skimmed across the Potomac. As days passed the memory faded, until I nearly convinced myself the memory was nothing more than a vivid dream. Just a few hours ago I learned I was mistaken.

Much has transpired since my initial and solitary entry into this scribble pad. When my dearest brother Lawrence passed away, losing an arduous battle against consumption, I found myself adrift in doldrums. He was more than a brother or mentor, he acted as a father to me these many years, and I found myself alone to plot the course ahead. I survived my own brush with death whilst in Barbados seeking a cure for Lawrence, there I contracted smallpox and felt the full weight of my own mortality. I realized the time to craft my own destiny was upon me, so I joined the Virginia Regiment. As a commissioned officer, a Lieutenant Colonel, I have spent the last two years engaging the French and their Indian allies in skirmishes along the frontier of Penns Woods for control of the vast Ohio Country.

Only a handful of days ago our battle to overtake Fort Duquesne ended disastrously. Controlling the Forks of the Ohio River, where the waters of the Monongahela and Allegheny entwine, is vital for command of this larger region. However our forces never reached their target, suffering defeat several miles upstream along the Monongahela. As we digest the battle's events the more we understand how our forces were outmaneuvered by local tribes familiar with the region. General Braddock commanded our forces admirably but panic set upon the men early, as the Indian whoopings and scalpings struck fear into their hearts. When forward lines retreated chaos ensued, causing our aft forces to fire upon them. The confusion resulted in many brave lives lost.

Adding to the catastrophe, General Braddock was mortally wounded during the engagement. He struggled bravely to pull through but alas, last night finally succumbed to his battlefield injuries. Under this heavy cloud I was tasked with appropriating a clandestine spot for his burial, which I dutifully carried out. After his solemn internment earlier this evening I rode off into the woods, ostensibly surveying the land for defensibility of our position, though my true desire was the opportunity to collect my thoughts. In the last few days many men have praised my efforts to reinforce our rear, allowing the remaining forces to withdraw and limiting further casualties. While they call me a hero, I only feel guilt and remorse that I might have done more.

I dismounted near a deep ravine and walked out onto a craggy overhang with a commanding view of the valley below. I began to cry. Partially at the senseless waste of life, but primarily because I'd somehow survived, once more, against incomparable odds. Our adversaries targeted the mounted officers, of which I count myself as one, and twice I was knocked to the ground. After one horse was shot out from under me I commandeered a second, only to lose him in the same manner. Neither time did I suffer injury. Once we had successfully retreated to safety several men noticed my officer's coat was riddled with musket ball holes, plus one through my hat. I protested, insisting the culprits were thorny brambles, except these holes are of incontrovertible origin. Directly over my vital organs, brain, lungs, liver, each a mortal wound, none finding their mark as I found not a single scratch.

"Why?" I screamed into the empty valley below, the taunting echoes providing no answer. I shouted a second time and waited for the same useless response, instead I heard "because you are a man of great destiny."

The voice came from behind me. I whipped around and saw the same figure from five years prior, the one I'd chased away from outside my bedroom window. Although daylight waned, this time I was able to gaze upon the visage of this hooded figure, and I understood why mother struggled to characterize his features. I also call him a man, though this is merely for practical convention, as his facial features are both handsome and beautiful, delicate with no blemishes or flaws, skin luminescent and sparkling. "Are you Hesperus?" I asked. "The same specter who visited my mother upon my birth and more recently snuck upon my lands, tricking me into the river?"

"Yes, it was I," he responded, "both times," though he explained his earlier encounter with me was unintentional. He'd tracked my progress over the years, and that night he'd been accidentally discovered. As he spoke his voice, both whimsical and melodic, assuaged my fears and I immediately knew he meant no harm. He only spoke for a few minutes, during which I did not move nor interrupt, dumbstruck. This renders my recollection of what he said inexact at best, which is why I take pen to paper tonight lest more details dissipate.

My birth fulfilled a prophecy, he told me, of which I attempt to faithfully recount here:

Downstream from where Greek and Roman rivers meet a child will be born onto Papal lands. He will grow into a powerful leader of his people, guiding them towards a civilization like none amongst all the nations, beginning a new age of man. Both a mighty warrior and gentle sage, he wields the sword and olive branch with equal dexterity. This man will never father his own children, rather he will become the father of an entire nation. He will live to see the mighty capital of this new nation built at the confluence of these rivers, but he will never reside there. This city will be named in his honor, and from this site will flourish the greatest nation the world has ever known.

I had many questions for Hesperus, this ethereal creature, and I started by asking why he believed I was the person he'd described. He pointed to my officer's jacket. "Where are your injuries?" he asked. "You should be buried alongside your commanding officer, but you are not. I have been following you since birth, watching, counting up the evidence of your charmed life. You have survived several deadly illnesses, only temporarily slowing you, and on the battlefield your flesh once again refused to yield. The universe has plans for you, ones not involving a whimpering end. But you already know this, don't you? I'm certain you've figured this out because I've been watching. You take extraordinary risks, bravery bordering on insanity, because it always works out well for you. This is how I know."

Before I could press him on the matter, Hesperus smiled and pulled his hood further down to entirely cover his face. He did not walk or run away, instead instantly disappeared. When I checked the ground where he stood I found no footprints, no broken twigs, no evidence to suggest he'd been nothing more than a hallucination.

Chapter 10

March 29, 1939
Room of the Honored
Clypeate Headquarters
City of Washington, District of Columbia

James coughed, his throat dry after reading the second lengthier, even more improbable passage. "Do you mind if I borrow one of your colas?" James asked, eyeing up Declan's remaining cache.

Perhaps a bellyful of hot food, or realizing James was equally perplexed, muted the professor's resentment towards the analyst enough to willingly slide over a bottle. "How about you just keep it?" he wryly suggested, "must have been tough reading that fairy tale." He turned to the Director. "Why are you trying to sell us the Brooklyn Bridge?"

"Once again, I can assure you these writings are genuine," Director Bowen countered, "and the contents are factual."

"Though I'm sure you can understand the professor's hesitation," James said, "you've got George Washington, a beloved icon, proselytizing like Nostradamus."

"I understand your doubts," the Director conceded, "these passages were equally difficult for me to believe the first time I read them. But I assure you our intent is to enlighten, not deceive. Let's unpack what Hesperus said, starting with the Papal lands welcoming a child. General Washington was born along the banks of Pope's Creek, in Virginia, which happens to be downstream from where the Greek and Roman rivers meet, at the confluence of the Potomac River and Tiber Creek."

"There's a Tiber River in Italy," Declan remarked, "I've never heard of Tiber Creek."

"It's underneath Constitution Avenue," James replied, making the connection. "Not far from here. Now it's a sewer drain, though it was originally named Tiber Creek to honor the Roman river," James revealed. "The Director told me about it while driving here, which I'm guessing wasn't a coincidence."

"It wasn't," Director Bowen confirmed. "This room is an underground cavern, one of several discovered by General Washington, and the original entrance was located where the Greek Potomac and Roman Tiber met. The entrance site remained a closely guarded secret for decades, only known to Clypeate members, until Thomas Jefferson turned against us. He wrongly believed our Clypeate would undermine the newly formed government. He went through great lengths to cripple our fledgling organization, purposefully sealing off our secret entryway. Jefferson thought he could block us from getting down here, although that's obviously not the case. He marked the spot, now part of the National Mall, with a massive stone slab one hundred yards up and three hundred yards east of here. James knows where."

"My cold, shriveled toes won't let me forget, you are referring to the Jefferson Pier marker," James confidently answered.

"First a creek, now a pier I've never heard of," Declan asserted.

"That's exactly the point," the Director replied, "once the Clypeate realized Jefferson's treachery, our members worked tirelessly to conceal the importance of that location. They transformed Tiber Creek into a sanitary drain and filled in the tidal marshes to distort the riverbank, all to guarantee the Jefferson Pier remained nothing more than a historical footnote."

"Don't forget," Bruce reminded him, "the Clypeate also changed the original meaning behind the Potomac River's name. Just a handful of newspaper articles and a few lines in history books were enough to convince people the 'Potomac' name was inspired by a local Algonquin village."

"Even though the Greek word for river is Potamos?" James wondered. "I don't understand why anyone would believe something far less intuitive, especially when the origin is so obvious. Educated people would realize hippopotamus is Greek for river horse. Hippo is horse, which means Potamos is river. Not complicated."

"I agree," Declan said. "And these are delightful tales, worthy of *Alice's Adventures in Wonderland*," he sarcastically derided. "What I don't understand is why Hesperus felt it necessary to speak in riddles. I've gleaned from General Washington's writings that Hesperus was not an ordinary man, or perhaps not a man at all, which means our first president and your secret society have been getting your cues from a fortune-telling alien. You say the Clypeate follows science, this sounds more like science fiction sorcery."

"Doctor Riordan, you were raised Irish Catholic and still attend Sunday mass regularly," Bruce reminded him. "The Bible is full of examples when otherworldly creatures shaped humanity's future, like Noah's antediluvian warning or Moses receiving the ten commandments. Is General Washington's supernatural interventions any less important or real because they're in his journal instead of the Good Book?"

Declan rubbed his belly and groaned. "Not to skirt around your question, I'm enjoying our lively discussion, but I fear heavenly retribution is taking shape as digestive backlash," he whimpered, his acerbic wit cut short by stabbing belly pain. "Is there a bathroom nearby, or at least a sturdy bucket?"

Bruce pointed to the oversized flag draped along the wall. "To the right of the flag," he instructed, sending Declan darting in that direction, desperate to keep his newly obtained uniform clean, although passing the flag the professor noted the unusual pattern and felt compelled to pause and comment.

"This flag is all wrong," he remarked. "You've got America's red and white stripes but there's a British Union Jack instead of a blue field of stars. Doesn't make a lick of sense." Before anyone could respond he felt an under-chewed morsel clawing its way back up his esophagus, necessitating an emergent disappearance into the bathroom.

When the door closed Bruce turned to James. "You are catching on nicely. Harold chose well in hiring you, not many people could handle all this without asking us if we were insane or delusional. Or maybe you're just polite enough not to say it."

"I'm trying my best to keep an open mind," James diplomatically responded, timidly grinning as he wondered if his pervasive apprehension was that obvious.

The Director responded with a warm, genuine smile. "Don't worry James, of course we'd expect you to question if we've lost our marbles. I'd be a tad worried if you didn't. And I agree with Bruce, you were the right choice, and I know your parents would be proud," he lauded. "As for Doctor Riordan we must tread slowly, at least for now. His brilliant, rational mind is fighting the paradigm shift, trying to maintain the status quo. I'm not sure how much further we can bend his mind before it breaks."

"Given what he's been through, I'm impressed he's done this well," Bruce commented, "although we've only scratched the surface. We can't delay much longer. We need to find out if he's the one."

The washroom door swung open and Declan returned to the table, apologizing for the disruption. "I better appreciate why gluttony is considered a mortal sin, that meatloaf traveled down far more pleasantly than in reverse." He sat down and took a few small sips of cola. "Now that I've completed my penance, is it wrong that I'm hungry again?"

Bruce gently wagged his finger. "Before resuming your gastronomic revelry, consider chewing your food this time," he strongly advised. "And I realize there are starving kids somewhere, but getting sick again trying to clean your plate won't help any of them. I should have known better than to tease your stomach with such bounty. Given your cachectic state it must be too much for your body to handle."

"I'm willing to tempt fate," Declan asserted, happily scooping up mashed potatoes.

"Please listen to Bruce," the Director pleaded, "we aren't rushing your meal, so slow down. In fact, spending more time here affords me the chance to explain our unusual flag. This design was the original concept for the American flag, sewn by Margaret Manny years before Betsy Ross decided a five-point star was easier to sew than a six-pointed one."

"So why hang it here," James wondered, "if this flag was a failed prototype?"

"Simple reason," Director Bowen answered, "even though this flag didn't become our nation's standard, this flag is Ms. Manny's original, hand-stitched example. Her second specimen topped the mast of the *Alfred*, the Continental Navy's earliest warship, becoming the first flag to represent the United States of America."

"We don't hang Margaret Manny's flag as a showpiece," Bruce explained, "it reminds us of how easily we can be tricked into believing falsehoods. Consensus history printed in books aren't facts, they're merely a carefully scripted narrative designed to obscure truth. Nobody's ever heard of Ms. Manny, but her role in shaping our nation's flag vastly outweighs Betsy Ross."

"Then what's the rationale for hanging a copy of the US Constitution in the bathroom?" Declan asked. "I assumed it was a clever pun about bowel movements being referred to as morning constitutionals, now I wonder if there's some deeper meaning," he wryly quipped.

"Nothing so profound," Bruce replied, "although there is more to the story. When the Constitution was finalized in 1787, each state received a single handwritten, original copy. Some states misplaced their originals, although many Confederate States intentionally destroyed theirs, burning them during secession from the Union. Most historians agree this was the fate of Georgia's copy, not the case. Instead, those genteel southern peaches mailed it back to the White House. Upon receiving the returned document, President Lincoln declared their copy of the Constitution might as well be hung in the bathroom as extra tissue paper. Since it was no longer worth the paper it was written on, he might as well wipe his ass with it."

Declan let out an incredulous snort. "You're saying an original copy of the US Constitution, of which only fourteen were made, is hanging in your bathroom?"

"Of course," Bruce confirmed, "the story wouldn't be meaningful if it weren't. Obviously, Lincoln, being a proper gentleman, couldn't very well hang it in the White House bathroom. That would be disrespectful to all the soldiers fighting and dying to preserve its sanctity, so he brought it down here."

"Abraham Lincoln knew about the Clypeate?"

"Knew?" Bruce restated. "Of course, he was an important member of our Clypeate and frequently used the headquarters down here during his presidency, especially when Confederate troops got within striking distance of the District."

The Director looked down at his watch and frowned. "Perhaps we should save that story for later," he interrupted, "time is short and Doctor Riordan has nearly cleared his plate, a feat both impressive and disturbing. Doctor, if your stomach agrees with our plan, we need to press ahead."

"My stomach is just fine," Declan replied. "My ears, however, might be playing tricks on me because, while indisposed in the washroom, it sounded like you were talking about me." He shoveled the remaining scraps on his plate into an edible pile. "And you are correct about one thing," he informed them, "you haven't convinced me to abandon a lifetime of knowledge simply because Betsy Ross got better publicity. The consensus view of history can't all be meaningless or wrong."

"Most of what you've learned isn't wrong," Director Bowen reassured him. "It's more subtle, misdirection. Look around this room. The table, flag, guns and swords aren't merely decorations, they remind us why we fight so hard to remember our past. Strong forces are working against us to obscure and manipulate the truth, and if they successfully rewrite the past they can also change our future, and not for the better."

Declan pressed further. "You're asking us to be afraid of the boogeyman."

"Yes," Director Bowen responded. "Except these boogeymen are flesh and bone. In the distant past they were known as the Obturavi, after centuries of conflict they were vanquished, or so we thought. They returned forty years ago, and not since the Dark Ages have they grown so powerful, this time resurrected by Germany's war machine to further their twisted goals. Our military can handle the Nazis, the Obturavi are why we need your help."

Bruce stood. "We hoped sharing the prophecies of Hesperus would help you believe and accept your role, as it once helped a young George Washington. But if you need further proof, let me show you some of the Obturavi's handiwork," he said, opening his office door once more, this time revealing a wide, dimly lit tunnel. "Be prepared to learn American history you'll never find using the Dewey Decimal system."

James peered into the darkness. "Now your office is gone," he observed. "This is more complicated than a funhouse, any more trick doors ahead?"

"The door isn't trickery," Bruce replied, "it's a safety measure. Nobody gets down here uninvited." The men followed Bruce into the long, wide corridor, a series of dim, dusty lamps strung along the ceiling casting harsh shadows.

"Where are we?" Declan asked. "Even in this twilight I can see the room is a mess."

"We're not in a room, this is a passageway," the Director corrected him, "a tunnel starting here and running a half mile north towards the White House."

"Now take a good look," Bruce said, switching on several flood lights, "this is what happens when you underestimate the Obturavi." The sudden illumination put the passage's heavily damaged condition into stark relief.

They walked in stunned silence, assessing the ruined space. More of the patterned ceiling and wall tiles were cracked and shattered than remained intact. On both sides of them debris and tile fragments were heaped into piles, marking off the path along which they slowly navigated. This led them past several haphazardly parked antique cars, the stench of rotting rubber hanging heavy. At first James thought their doors were simply rusting, but upon closer inspection he realized the truth. "These cars are riddled with bullet holes," he commented, "a whole lot of them, these side panels look like Swiss cheese."

"This doesn't feel right, something really bad happened here," Declan whispered, gasping when he noticed a tattered doll mixed into the rubble. "And there were children down here" he lamented, chills running down his spine.

"I'm also getting a disturbing vibe, Doc," James muttered, blankly staring at the destruction. "I don't understand, your Clypeate is so well protected down here," he stated. "We're underneath one of the most secure buildings in the world, the Obturavi would've had an easier time busting into Fort Knox."

"We weren't always so fortified," Bruce replied, "and it was a lesson we learned too late. The Navy and Munitions buildings were purposefully built above us twenty years ago, but this damage was already done. On the night of June fourth, 1898, the Obturavi attacked using this tunnel to breach our defenses."

"Why build a tunnel like this in the first place?" Declan asked, contemplating the logistics. "A tunnel this wide over that distance would be a tremendous undertaking, there must have been a compelling reason to expend the resources."

"The idea initially started as a way to access Clypeate headquarters without using the Jefferson Pier entrance," Bruce replied. "During the War of 1812, President Madison retreated while the British effortlessly ransacked the District, brazenly setting fire to the city. It's the reason the Executive Mansion is now called the White House, it was burned so badly the exterior needed a complete paint job to conceal the scorch marks. While historians claim the British abandoned their campaign due to stormy weather, they retreated because our Clypeate defended this city, inflicting enough damage on the British forces to push them out. President Madison appreciated our efforts, and after the war became our biggest supporter. He authorized construction of this underground tunnel, connecting the Clypeate headquarters with the White House grounds, in case of future invasions, allowing the president to escape while giving us a secure route to secretly maneuver our forces."

"Seems like a waste, in hindsight," James remarked. "After all, Washington hasn't been invaded since. If anything, this tunnel was a bad idea, it left you open for attack."

"The tunnel wasn't the problem," the Director replied, "that night our men inadvertently led the Obturavi to the hidden entrance, and these shattered tiles are scars, reminders, why we must remain ever vigilant." He sighed. "Prior to the Obturavi attack this tunnel proved useful for many years, especially during the Civil War. While no battles took place inside the District, 1860s Washington was surrounded by agrarian, slave run plantations, solidly within Confederate territory. Maryland only stayed Union during the Civil War because President Lincoln jailed and suppressed every secessionist voice in the state. Lincoln understood the Union government's strategically precarious location, but also knew fleeing to Philadelphia would only embolden the Confederacy and its foreign supporters. Lincoln used this passage so frequently we've called it Lincoln's Tunnel ever since. In its current condition you may find this hard to imagine, but at one time this tunnel bustled with activity."

"We've run out of tunnel," James commented as they approached the far end of the passageway. "And this wall seems to be blocking it." James ran his fingers along the uneven surface of haphazardly arranged bricks, messy gobs of solidified cement poking out between them. "The style and craftsmanship is inferior, sloppily built like this place was sealed up in a hurry."

Declan agreed. "Ever read the *Cask of Amontillado?* Narrator gets offended by his friend, so he lures him into underground catacombs and bricks him off behind a wall, forever. That wall would've looked like this one."

"Insightful reference," the Director affirmed, "because this wall was built to keep the Clypeate confined. In our case, it was the Clypeate bricked behind the wall."

"So, after attacking you, the Obturavi blocked off your tunnel?" asked James.

"No," Bruce replied. "The damage inflicted down here was caused by the Obturavi, but the tunnel was walled off by our government," he clarified, "in reaction to the Obturavi attack. The Secret Service determined this tunnel posed a high-security risk and sealed the tube."

"No wonder you have an awkward relationship with the government," Declan remarked, "you were betrayed. Instead of showing solidarity by helping rebuild your tunnel, they decided to shut you out. If the Secret Service thinks this tunnel presents a security risk, what stops them from coming down here and backfilling the whole tunnel?"

"President Madison's gratitude," Bruce answered. "As a reward for our service, Madison granted the Clypeate eternal rights to maintain our headquarters underneath the city. To keep our location secret, government engineers only built the tunnel from Pennsylvania Avenue down to the banks of Tiber Creek, where the Clypeate took over and constructed this last section. When the government walled off the tunnel they respected Madison's decree, building this brick blockade across the line where the government and Clypeate tunnels meet."

"And you're okay with this?" Declan wondered. "From what I've seen so far, you must have enough clout to get this reopened."

"Yes, we have those connections, but we're better off this way," Director Bowen explained, "at least for now. With this tunnel blocked FDR and his FBI lapdog Hoover don't have access to our facilities, and they think we don't either."

"It works to our advantage for the government to believe this tunnel is abandoned," Bruce elaborated, "so we keep our side in this sad state of disrepair. The government intentionally built peep holes into the wall, not sure how often they check but the FBI is a dog searching for a bone, and I've heard machinery and voices from the other side in the past."

"Am I missing something?" Declan asked. "Even though your weapons collection is museum-worthy, I don't understand why the Obturavi would go through all this trouble. A bunch of guns and swords, even the flag and Constitution, don't seem worth the bloodshed."

"Great question," Bruce replied, leading them towards the damaged tunnel wall and a set of oversized metal doors, the surface pocked with so many bullet marks it reminded James of a golf ball's dimpled exterior. "Those items weren't the reason the Obturavi attacked, and they also weren't the reason our people defended this place with their lives. As we move forward I believe you'll find the answers to these questions," Bruce said, swinging the doors open to reveal another dark chamber.

Chapter 11

March 29, 1939
Research Hall
Clypeate Headquarters
City of Washington, District of Columbia

"As if the tunnel weren't creepy enough," Declan remarked as the rusted hinges creaked loudly, echoing through the space, causing his neck hairs to tingle and stand erect. Passing through the doors he noticed their surfaces were covered with dark, linear marks.

"What made these marks, they look like scratches?" he asked, then hesitated. "They almost look like, like…"

"Bloody claw marks," James finished the thought, "I noticed them, too. Pretty sure they're human."

"Yes, they are," Bruce confirmed. "The Clypeate fought well but the Obturavi were desperate to get past this door. Over the years I've found several fingernails on the ground, others still glued to the door with crusted blood."

"I think I'm going to be sick," Declan said. "Again."

"I agree with your sentiment," James replied, "and this time I might join you."

"Take long, deep breaths and look straight ahead," Director Bowen suggested. "Works for me, although now I'm so accustomed to this gruesome scene," he added, surveying the bloodied gouges, "my brain no longer registers how macabre this looks. Not necessarily the healthiest coping mechanism," he added. "It works, though at what cost, I can't say." He flipped a switch and several flood lights powered up, drenching the room in enough light to reach every corner of the auditorium-sized space.

"What a mess," Declan commented, the walls charred with soot and ash while the floor lay buried under heaps of destroyed furniture and equipment. They stood inside an enclosed tunnel of what appeared to be clear plastic, a swath just a few feet wide carved through the debris, leading them toward the far wall. "I'm not finding many answers here," Declan said, surveying the jangled, tangled mess of wood, steel and glass as they walked along the path, sealed off from the surrounding jumble.

"I agree," James added. "I'm only finding more questions."

"It's a lot to absorb," Bruce agreed, "but this room wasn't always such a disaster. A lot of history happened here, and this room has served a variety of purposes over time. During the Civil War," he explained, "the government stored food and supplies down here, in case a Confederate siege surrounded the city and cut off supply lines. After the Civil War this became the Research Hall, and up until the Obturavi attack in 1898 more scientific breakthroughs transpired in this room than anywhere else in the world. For great minds like Nikola Tesla and Thomas Edison this was like a giant sandbox for geniuses, a place they could imagine the amazing and create the future. Obviously this ended when the Obturavi destroyed it, but nearly every scientific and technological breakthrough since then can trace its roots back to this Research Hall."

"If this lab was so important, why hasn't anybody cleaned it up?" James asked. "After all, that was forty years ago."

"Problem is this room was stocked like a giant chemistry set," the Director explained. "There were bucketloads of hazardous chemicals and toxic materials everywhere. When this room caught fire everything fused together, as the glassware and plastic melted it oozed into every crevice, bonding all of it together to create an amalgamated brick of poison. Trying to break this mess apart would release immense clouds of harmful chemicals into the air, not to mention the logistics of hauling away several metric tons of hazardous garbage without being noticed. Simply clearing this pathway ended with several people turning purple and gasping for air. Safer to just leave it alone, for now."

"Okay, avoiding an environmental crisis makes sense," Declan conceded, "though I don't understand what Edison and Tesla were doing here in the first place. They had their own workshops, after all. Thomas Edison's labs were in New Jersey" he noted, "and Nikola Tesla spent most of his career working in New York City."

"Yes, that is true," the Director concurred, "this wasn't where they built their inventions. Rather, this is where Edison and Tesla both came for ideas. Even geniuses need a source of inspiration, a Muse, to help their imaginations soar. And down here the smartest men from around the globe secretly worked together, not for fame or fortune, instead to create the future. Edison and Tesla maintained their offices far away from this place, hoping their distance would protect its secrecy, cautiously traveling here to spend a few days at a time with like-minded individuals."

"Then why choose this spot, right under the government's nose and smackdab in the middle of tourist attractions?" Declan asked. "If I built a secret underground lab, I'd bury the whole thing under a mountain thousands of miles from here."

"This site wasn't chosen by the Founding Fathers," Director Bowen replied, "Hesperus chose it for them. He certainly had his reasons, least of which was logistics, although keep in mind this room was being used over a century ago, back when a fast horse could get you to Baltimore in two days. Not only did their headquarters require a secure and defensible location, it also needed to be rapidly accessible in an emergency."

"Well, judging by the looks of this place, it wasn't as secure and defensible as the Clypeate thought," commented Declan. "And even if this were a convenient hiding spot in the remote past, why continue their research in this swamp, there are far more suitable environments than this dank basement. Judging by the mold growing on everything I'd guess we're below the water table so, unless your scientific research involves the cultivation of fungus spores, anywhere other than an actual body of water would be more advantageous. Especially considering Mr. Tesla and Mr. Edison's specialty, electricity and electrical devices."

"You're making excellent points," Director Bowen remarked, "except, like I said, they didn't choose this place, it chose them, which will make more sense as we move forward," he added, offering no additional explanation, the group continuing in silence until Bruce paused near a small avalanche of broken glassware.

"Let me see," he said, examining where the glass had pushed up against the clear barrier. "Oh good, the barrier is intact, no rips," he sighed in relief. "I'll make sure to come back and fortify this spot. Nothing to worry about."

"I'm not feeling particularly reassured," Declan said. James nodded in agreement.

They continued along until they reached the far wall, another set of oversized doors looming above them, similarly pocked with bullet holes. Declan averted his gaze to avoid any morbid surprises while James watched the Director pull out the large, ornate golden key, presumably the same one he'd unsuccessfully used at the Jefferson Pier, but this time a few turns led to an effective click.

Bruce spoke. "Now, men, up 'til now the Director and I have tried our best to mitigate your bewilderment, though going forward I'm afraid nothing we say will adequately prepare you. Therefore, I won't bother trying," he said, swinging the door open and waving them through.

Declan shielded his eyes, the light so overwhelmingly bright it hurt. His first assumption was they'd gone outside, it wasn't until his eyes adjusted did he realize they'd entered an even more spacious underground cavern. Declan calculated the room's impressive scale, reckoning the four-story biology building in which he'd spent so many long hours would comfortably fit under the vaulted ceiling. He could not gauge the room's length, however, even craning his neck the perplexed scientist watched the ceiling disappear behind a wholly improbable impediment. "I thought you said no more trick doors," he remarked.

"I assure you there's no trick," Director Bowen replied, locking the Research Hall door behind them, "this is where it gets really interesting."

James and Declan looked ahead, speechless. They struggled to understand why, inside this massive underground cavern, a lovely flagstone path led them towards an even more picturesque ranch home, red brick with a porch swing and terracotta roof. Beautifully manicured flower beds lined the walkway, those in turn flanked by a lush, forest-green lawn fanning out to meet a perimeter of white picket fence bordering the distant walls. The home's brick exterior extended across the entire width of the expanse, wall to wall at least forty yards, effectively creating a barrier with only one access point, a canary yellow front door, dictating the route of any further progress.

Declan nudged James. "You're seeing this, right?"

James shrugged his shoulders. "Don't know. Depends on if you're referring to a house, one that belongs on the cover of *Better Homes and Gardens* instead of a subterranean bunker. In that case, yes, you're in good company." He turned to Bruce. "And this makes sense how?"

"Well, that depends on what you're asking about," Bruce replied. "If you're asking why this enormous chamber exists down here, it's because the War of 1812 highlighted the capital city's vulnerability, not only to devastating attacks but complete ransacking and occupation by an enemy force. The Clypeate didn't dig this place out, it started off as a natural cavern, Virginia is full of them. Our people reinforced the walls and added little niceties like plumbing, electricity and lighting. During the Civil War the Union government needed a massive bunker, large enough to accommodate President Lincoln, all the members of Congress, Supreme Court, plus their families, and we provided it. Thankfully the Union only ever used this facility as a precaution, whenever the Confederacy set its sights on Northern Virginia or Maryland, and for several weeks surrounding the Battle of Gettysburg. Now, if you're asking about the lovely residence in front of us, which we affectionately call Nancy's Place, how about you knock on the door and find out."

"Even though I was referring to the latter, this plethora of historical nuggets is certainly informative." James grinned, knuckles rapping on the door. "I do hope they're expecting us," he jested, "I'd be so embarrassed to show up unannounced."

The door swung open and a young, auburn-haired woman greeted them. "Welcome," she said, "come inside and make yourselves comfortable." The home's interior was even more immaculate than the yard, decorated and furnished with impeccable taste and attention to detail. "Please sit," she said, directing them to the front parlor. While the other men settled onto the ornate couches, Declan did not, unwilling to disturb a carefully arranged mound of throw pillows. "I'll take those," the young woman said, brushing past Declan, "I forgot to remove them, we don't usually have this many guests at once," she said, smiling at him. Their gaze locked momentarily, and Declan was instantly mesmerized by her blazing emerald eyes. As one of the youngest and undeniably handsome professors on campus Declan garnered plenty of feminine attention, both from faculty and students, to which he'd remained utterly oblivious. He was committed to his career and betrothed to his research, affairs of the heart perplexed his rational mind, viewing the trappings of love as frivolous and distracting, the harmful side effects of brain chemistry. At least, until this moment, that's what he'd always told himself.

Declan looked away, embarrassed, suddenly and brutally aware of his disheveled and forlorn appearance. "Thank you," he mumbled as he sat, focusing his gaze upon a wholly uninteresting blemish on his recently commandeered shoes until the woman turned her attention elsewhere.

"Hello, Commander Kingston," the young woman said, "and welcome back, Director Bowen, it has been a while, but always a pleasure. Now, I presume these men are the visitors you spoke about earlier, you weren't certain if they'd both be accompanying you today." She smiled. "Looks like you didn't scare either of them away."

"Not yet," Bruce quipped, "and neither shies away from asking pointed questions, either, so be prepared. Now, speaking of our guests," he continued, "these gentlemen are Lieutenant James Fischer, he's a top-notch intelligence analyst who works with the Director at the Naval Research Lab, and Doctor Declan Riordan, he's a biology professor and member of the scientific team from the Antarctica expedition. And men, this smart cookie is Miss Embrie

Powell, the archivist and curator of our vast collection of unique artifacts."

James stood and extended his hand. "Miss Powell, it is my pleasure to make your acquaintance," he said, "and nice job with the weapons collection in the Room of the Honored, though I imagine dusting in there must get tedious." He sat down and sniffed, "And speaking of cookies, maybe it's just the power of suggestion but does it smell like a bakery in here?"

"Nice to meet you as well," Embrie replied, smiling politely, "although Commander Kingston wasn't referring to that collection. After all, you haven't seen the impressive stuff yet. As for that delicious smell, your olfactory system isn't steering you wrong, my mentor Ms. Elliott loves to bake, especially when we're expecting company." On queue an older woman emerged from the kitchen carrying a serving tray, wearing an apron, oven mitts and a kind smile. Her ashy silver hair and gently wizened features reminded Declan of his own grandmother.

"I was correct," James said. "It's cookies. And kudos to you Ms. Elliott, they look even better than they smell," he praised, eyeing up the stacked pile.

"They're chocolate chip, specifically," Ms. Elliott replied. She placed the tray on the coffee table and the group swarmed it. "I'll bring out a pitcher of milk for you boys," she said, scurrying back to the kitchen.

Declan did not join the cookie-grabbing frenzy. "Aren't you hungry, Doctor?" Miss Powell asked.

"Please, Miss, simply Declan is fine, and to answer your question, one hour ago I was literally starving," the professor responded. "Since then I finished a meal big enough for three stomachs. I can account for two stomachs-worth but the third, well, I fear it may have ended up in a lung."

Miss Powell laughed. "You're a silly bird, aren't you?" she jested. Declan would have been content to continue their conversation without looking at her, but she gently cradled his chin and lifted his head. "You poor man," she said, surveying his bruised, battered face with concern. "I don't know much about what transpired in Antarctica, but I understand there were problems, how'd this happen?" queried the gentle featured beauty. Declan wanted to reply but his mouth wouldn't move. Despite being a human lexicon, comprehending more words than existed opportunities to use them, the professor found himself unable to string together a set of coherent sounds, incapacitated by the petite woman's piercing green eyes. Before his brain's synapses had a chance to regroup, the Director responded.

"Regrettably these injuries didn't take place in Antarctica," Director Bowen admitted, "they're courtesy of military intelligence, I never anticipated they'd get handsy so quickly. Until this morning nobody would even admit the professor was in Army custody, it required treasonous intervention to find him, thankfully Lieutenant Fischer's skills are beyond compare. Even armed with the facts, though, only a handful of officers knew he existed and less where he was being held. Negotiating his release required significant expenditure of political capital and we called in more than a few favors."

Bruce looked at Declan's bruised face and shook his head. "I'm still uncertain why they didn't dance around the ring longer, they ratcheted up their interrogation techniques quicker than usual. Perhaps they were displeased by his inability to provide any useful details or information, they must have assumed he was lying and required more motivation."

"Not to mention his air of professorial smugness," James added. "My apologies, Doctor Riordan, I mean no disrespect and there's no excuse for what they did. Given my own interactions with Officer Burke and his goons, however, I believe they'd interpret your condescending and superior tone as cocky and disrespectful. That's just speculation, though."

"You're right about one thing, there is no excuse for this," Miss Powell said, leaning in so close Declan felt her warm breath on his cheek. "You are safe now," she said, "we don't treat people like this. I'm going to make sure your wounds heal nicely, and Ms. Elliott will help you put on a few pounds in the meantime," then added, along with a smile "and please call me Embrie."

Ms. Elliott returned as promised, carrying a set of glasses and a pitcher of milk. "Before she runs out on us again," Director Bowen said, "allow me to properly introduce the namesake of Nancy's Place, Ms. Nancy Elliott. She's been working with the Clypeate for many years, keeping this place in tip-top shape. She's a fountain of knowledge and not just about baking, though we're awfully glad she enjoys spoiling us."

"And she's taught me everything I know," Embrie praised. "I don't know what I'd do without her."

"You would function fine without me," Ms. Elliott replied, smiling. "You no longer require my daily supervision, but I will remain here, with you, faithfully serving in any capacity needed." Before James and Declan could properly introduce themselves, Ms. Elliott blurted, "nice to make your acquaintances," and darted out of the room.

"She's shy around new people," the Director explained, "but she loves helping out. Her family isn't around anymore, so she chooses to pamper us. She wanted to cook a full meal for you, Declan, although I thought a milder transition was in order. Seeing what happened with the cafeteria offerings I'm glad we deferred. Don't fret, though, soon enough your gastronomic fortitude will return and you'll be better prepared for a proper Ms. Elliott dinner, complete with signature rich, creamy sauces and desserts that do not disappoint."

"I'm happy to wait," Declan replied, groaning at the thought of eating another meal ever again.

Bruce finished up the last of several cookies, took a large swig of milk and stood. "Miss Powell, I hate to eat and run, but there is some urgency to today's agenda. If you could kindly lead us through the Analytical Engine Room and show our guests the library, it would be greatly appreciated."

"Of course," Embrie replied, and the group followed her through the kitchen to the back door. "I thought she'd be in here," Embrie mused. "Ms. Elliott," she shouted, "we're heading to the library, I'll be back shortly."

"Your boss keeps you on a short leash," James commented.

"It's nothing like that," Embrie clarified, "Ms. Elliott has strong maternal instincts and I don't like for her to worry. It's respect, not subservience."

Put squarely in his place, James held his tongue as they entered the backyard, a stone path trailing away from Nancy's Place towards a gap in the white picket fence at the yard's back edge. In contrast to the front yard's manicured lawn and flowerbeds, vegetable patches with rows of robust, bushy plants covered the vast expanse. As they walked along Declan remarked on the size of the ripening peppers and plump tomatoes. "The tomatoes look like kickballs," he marveled, hoping to linger but the group didn't slow down, maintaining their brisk pace towards the back fence. Growing just beyond the fence and spanning the entire length stood thick, tall corn stalks, so densely packed they dimmed the artificial light along the path from noontime down to dusk. The group needed to stay close together, encountering several false paths, and after some minutes of twisting and turning through this corn maze they reached a stone barrier, massive, stacked boulders easily two dozen feet high.

Despite the wall's unscalable appearance, Embrie's navigation led them to a cleverly hidden flight of steps, carved directly into the large stones in such a way to render them visible only when viewed from this vantage point. Ingenious, Declan mused even as he blindly followed the group's ascent up the rocky path, realizing with every step forward he placed more trust in people he barely knew. The stairs led to a concrete ledge, level and navigable, with any further progress impeded by a smooth, translucent wall. There were no gaps in this blue-tinged barrier, the bottom edge embedded down into the rock wall and extending upwards until it reached the ceiling, spanning across the chamber's entire width. He tried peering through the cloudy, cobalt-blue material but could only discern vague shapes.

"Wow, that's a big wall of frosted glass," James muttered, knocking on it, "cleaning it must be terribly exhausting." He turned to Director Bowen and commented, "Looks like a lot of expense and effort were spent partitioning this room."

"James is right," Declan concurred, "constructing this wall must have cost a fortune, you'd need a convincing excuse to build something like this."

"Indeed," the Director started, "this configuration was neither cheap nor easy, but the night this facility was attacked the Clypeate paid an even heftier price. Our group learned a very expensive lesson, we lacked proper defensive barriers to slow down the Obturavi. This fatal flaw allowed those animals to rampage through here so quickly our men were overrun before their positions could be reinforced, costing us the lives of many good people and putting our valuable projects and works in jeopardy."

"But why choose glass, there are so many stronger alternatives," Declan pressed. "What idiot thought this was a good design?"

"There were other considerations besides strength," Bruce replied. "On the other side of this wall is the Analytical Engine Room, occupied by invaluable mechanical equipment, all very sensitive to natural forces. You were correct earlier when you said this damp environment is terrible for science, moisture would cause irreparable damage, plus our machines require strict cleanliness parameters. This barrier seals off the Analytical Engine Room from the outside world, effectively creating the cleanest, most optimized environment possible. And the men who designed this barrier weren't fools, unless that's what you consider Thomas Edison and Nikola Tesla, because both men adamantly demanded this specific design."

"Of course they had their reasons," Embrie interjected, clarifying, "Mr. Edison and Mr. Tesla wanted the equipment and machines monitored constantly while avoiding the need for people to travel back and forth into the Analytical Engine Room. This barrier allows us to troubleshoot and evaluate problems without rushing in there. This not only saves time, it cuts down the introduction of dust particles and moisture."

"But this wall isn't transparent, it's translucent," Declan remarked, attempting to peer through the bluish material, "you can't see anything through this frosted glass. Why not just have a few small clear portals?" he asked. "I'm failing to grasp how a glass wall makes defensive sense," he reiterated, "hasn't anybody down here ever seen how much havoc you can wreak on a window with one errant baseball?"

"Now I understand your confusion," Director Bowen chimed in, "you think this material is glass but it's not, at least not the traditional silicon-based kind. Nor is it plastic, rather this wall is made from a transparent metal alloy. Edison and Tesla wanted something very strong yet transparent, so they engineered this material specifically for this purpose. The rest of this chamber is well fortified, the house is internally reinforced with cinder blocks and rebar, and we're standing on a several meters thick wall of cemented boulders, but none of those materials matches the strength of this metal," he said, knocking on the cloudy barrier. "One inch thick, yet nothing short of a howitzer cannon could punch a hole through it."

"What you're describing is impossible," Declan scoffed, "you can't make a metal alloy with these properties," running his hand down the smooth surface.

"Oh, no?" Director Bowen chuckled, flipping a switch. Immediately the wall's opaque cloudiness dissipated until the entire thickness turned invisible, prompting Declan to reach out his hand to verify the cool, smooth surface was still there.

"An elegant solution," Bruce stated. "They didn't want the Analytical Engine Room exposed to the constant glow illuminating Nancy's Place, yet still wanted the option of clarity."

James and Declan stood speechless, through the suddenly transparent barrier they were instantly privy to the entire contents of the Analytical Engine Room, an area equivalent to their side of the barrier, but instead of an idyllic suburban setting a series of gleaming metal towers filled the entire space. Row upon row of enormous box-shaped towers, perfectly aligned like megalithic dominos, all sparkling with a clean, shiny chrome finish. Declan estimated there were several dozen of these stacks, each resembling a cargo container, both in size and shape, except these rectangles were standing on end, their top edges nudging the ceiling.

"Well, do you still think it's impossible?" Bruce ribbed the silent pair. "Because you're currently looking through a translucent metal alloy. And if we're going to mince words, then Doctor, you'll need to ease up on saying things are impossible. Or else just get accustomed to being mistaken quite a bit. How about picking a more accurate word instead, perhaps inconceivable?"

"I prefer improbable," Declan replied, peering through the barrier like a child standing in front of a toy store's Christmas display, "as in, I'm not entirely sure what I'm looking at, but I can't wait to get in there and get a closer look at those improbable machines!"

Director Bowen smiled. "Well stated, and fair, we've taunted you long enough with promises of amazing things," he agreed, Embrie leading the group to a set of barely perceptible doors carved into the clear metal wall.

Chapter 12

March 29, 1939
The Analytical Engine Room
Clypeate Headquarters
City of Washington, District of Columbia

The doors rolled open and a gentle rush of air greeted them. "This is our decontamination chamber," Embrie explained. "It prevents damage to the room's sensitive equipment." They all crammed inside the tiny chamber, the professor and Embrie facing each other, inches apart. She smiled, he clenched his jaw and reciprocated with a head nod, certain a whiff of his rancid vomit breath would ruin the moment. The door sealed shut and a windy vortex whipped and howled around them, flapping clothes and tousling hair.

"Just cleaning off dust and debris," shouted Embrie above the boisterous din, noting the concerned expressions shared by James and Declan.

When the wind slowed, James patted down his disheveled hair. "Now I know what it feels like inside a tornado."

Declan waited for Embrie to move beyond smell-range before countering, "Or at least a powerful vacuum cleaner," straightening out his baggy uniform.

Emerging from the decontamination chamber, James and Declan didn't know where to look first. The massive, shiny metal towers surrounded them, rising multiple stories above and glowing like gaudy Christmas trees, their side panels lined with countless rows of buttons blinking in a rainbow of colors. Adding to the sensory overload the machines also hummed, buzzed and occasionally alarmed, startling the biologist and analyst.

"These towers are packed so tightly I can't see past them," Declan commented, following Embrie onto a steel catwalk. "Reminds me of hiking between the giant sequoias in Muir Woods."

"Doc's right," added James. "Each one is bigger than my apartment building. They're also kinda noisy, though not nearly as deafening as my fridge."

"All the lights and sounds indicate these towers are operational," Declan said, turning to the Director. "So what are they doing? These aren't simple machines, this equipment is beyond anything I've ever seen. I have university colleagues in the engineering department with similar setups, they call them computational machines, although their cutting-edge equipment doesn't come close to this level of sophistication."

Director Bowen dodged the question. "Any answer I give will only make you want further explanation. There will be plenty of time later, right now we can't afford any more delays."

Embrie noted Declan's frustration and interjected, "Not to worry, you'll find interesting surprises ahead. During our walk to the library, you'll discover even more advanced machines." The young woman stepped further onto the catwalk and waved for them to follow. "Watch your step and don't get distracted," she advised, "this platform meanders like the Mississippi across the Analytical Engine Room."

She moved ahead and the group followed, the elevated catwalk passing between several massive towers before vanishing around a distant bend. Declan spent the entire time gripping the side rail, having mistakenly looked down through the metal grates at the twenty-foot drop to the ground below. Already doubting the catwalk's structural integrity, it didn't help when James pointed out the jumbled network of cables and wires crisscrossing a few feet above their heads.

"Not to be an alarmist," interjected James, "but those dangling wires look dangerous. They're more of a tangled mess than clotheslines strung between Bronx tenements. We're going to get electrocuted."

"We're perfectly safe," Bruce reassured them, "and those wire bundles above us serve an important function. They connect all the machines together so they can work in unison. Professor Riordan's assertion was correct, these aren't simple calculating devices."

"Linking the machines would exponentially increase their analytical power," Declan realized, "I'm inclined to use the word improbable to describe this entire setup."

"I agree with Doc," James chimed in, "the sheer scale and complexity of these machines defy logic. I can't imagine the manpower required to maintain just one tower, and there's enough to cover a tennis court."

"Larger, more like an Olympic swimming pool," clarified Bruce, "which means we still have plenty of distance to cover before reaching the library, so we need to pick up the pace." He turned to Embrie. "Sorry for the interruptions. We're ready to move ahead. Please lead the way."

"But I have so many questions," exclaimed Declan, leaning over the railing to get a better look at the machines.

"Don't touch anything," Director Bowen pleaded, "the Builders won't be pleased if you disturb their handiwork, even the tiniest oil smudge from your fingertips will damage the equipment. How about a compromise? If you walk, I'll try my best to provide answers."

"Deal," the professor said, trotting to catch up as Embrie sped forward.

Journeying deeper into the metallic forest their steps clink-clanked against the elevated platform, joining the cacophony of clicks, beeps and humming motors echoing off the towers. Embrie was right, the towers here looked different, inspiring a plethora of questions. Unfortunately for Declan, he couldn't catch his breath long enough to ask them. After weeks of deconditioning, his muscles screamed in protest at the sudden exertional onslaught. Embrie noticed and slowed down, giving the professor a chance to recover.

Once again, Declan leaned against the railing, this time because he was lightheaded and needed support, struggling to avoid fainting and tumbling over the edge. He gazed down, panting to catch his breath, when he noted a sparkling glass bulb jutting from a tower. A cathode ray tube, an ancient artifact tucked into this futuristic landscape.

Curiosity, as much as the short break, propelled Declan forward. He spent the next dozen yards leaning over the railing, peering down at the cluttered menagerie of electronics; switchboards, loose wires, cathode rays and vacuum tubes. Most of the equipment appeared broken or melted.

"Maybe my brain cells aren't getting enough oxygen," Declan began, prefacing his comment, "but these towers remind me of a fossil record. Up here the technology is modern, pioneering, while the equipment below consists of outdated relics."

"Perceptive and accurate," lauded the Director, confirming Declan's observation. "More scars from the Obturavi attack," he said, "reminders of that dreadful night forty years ago. The Obturavi critically damaged our mechanical and electrical systems. While only a fraction of the equipment survived, our clever Builders sifted through and found the functional remnants, adding to them instead of dismantling the previous work. This strategy required the creation of these vertical towers, building atop the ruins, allowing the machines to incorporate original hardware with the latest advances."

James peered into the darkness below, underwhelmed by what he spotted at the tower bases. "There's weaving looms down there," he remarked, "that was the Clypeate's superior technology?"

"Yes," replied Bruce, "when the Clypeate was founded, the Jacquard loom was revolutionary. Our engineers recognized the future potential for computational machines, for the first time punched cards could store, even analyze, data."

"Unfortunately," Embrie chimed in, "during the Obturavi attack the wooden looms caught fire like dry tinder. Many brave men Clypeate sacrificed their lives to save thousands of punched cards, and those cards are still running through the few remaining looms. Serving what function, I couldn't tell you, however, we know the newest machines don't replace the older technology, they integrate and build upon it."

"That's what makes these towers so special," Director Bowen explained, "by incorporating past success and learning from failure, our machines can innovate and make scientific breakthroughs. They've evolved into analytical engines."

"Doubtful," asserted Declan. "You say these machines are more than calculators, but analytical engines? That would mean they're not just collecting and storing data, they're also using the information to make decisions. Machines like that are only theoretical, nobody's ever built one."

"Not true," replied Bruce. "The Clypeate did, nearly a century ago. We've been perfecting it ever since, although the most exciting advances didn't take place until the addition of electricity. Lucky for us, Mr. Edison was one of our chief benefactors. In the 1870s, half a decade prior to creating the first metropolitan electrical grid for New York City, he built a fully operational prototype to power the Analytical Engine Room."

Declan looked at the nearby towers, lacking side panels their innards exposed, filled with intricate circuitry more complex than anything he'd seen at UCLA. "Even if the Clypeate got a running head start in the Technical Revolution, building a functional analytical engine is beyond cutting edge, it's fantasy." The professor paused. "However, I'll admit that what you built down here is remarkable, beyond imagination. I can't even guess the purpose of the electronic parts inside these towers."

James spent the entire walk avoiding the platform edge, where electrical wires sagged lowest, but now joined Declan at the railing to get a better look. Each tower contained thousands of wafer-thin boards lined up like record albums, every plate covered with tiny, neatly soldered bits. "Electronics isn't my area of expertise, although I subscribe to *Scientific American* and have read articles about parts like these. Transistors, resistors, capacitors, inductors," rattled off James, garnering a shocked look from Declan.

"Well done, James," praised the Director, pointing to endless rows of electrical hardware stacked four stories above them. "We call them circuit boards," he explained, "and you've never seen them before because they only exist here and at a select few universities. We share our advances with research programs at schools like U Penn and MIT, and while we're still working out the kinks, my guess is five years from now this technology will be unveiled as a revolutionary breakthrough."

"So, one day this amazing technology will magically appear and that won't look suspicious?" asked Declan.

"Not in the least," Bruce replied. "Humanity is accustomed to new discoveries. We don't question progress, in ancient times we chalked up the discovery of fire, metallurgy, astronomy and mathematics as gifts handed down by the gods. Next came the Judeo-Christian concept of divine inspiration, an especially useful explanation when the Renaissance produced singular geniuses like Michelangelo, da Vinci and Copernicus."

Declan contended, "Maybe sorcery and religion were enough in the past, but that would never work today. We have the scientific method and rely on facts, not fairy tales."

"You're correct," Bruce conceded, "in modern times, there's far tighter scrutiny. That's why the tactics have changed. Whether you're a citizen scientist like Mr. Edison, or an academic center like UPenn or MIT, nobody works in isolation. There's always a team to spread the innovation around, so when an amazing new idea pops up the origin is irrelevant. Doesn't matter if one individual claims credit for the golden nugget of inspiration, or the whole team shares the glory, nobody asks questions."

Their group slowed to a standstill, forcing Embrie to bellow, "Gentlemen!" They immediately fell silent. She wagged her finger. "I was tasked with leading you through this room, and while I don't enjoy treating you like unruly schoolboys, I'm left with no choice. No more talking until we reach the library," she said, receiving mumbled apologies from the roundly chastised men. Embrie's frown curled into a smile. "Come on," she added, pointing between the towers at a visible section of the far wall. "We're almost there."

Another twenty yards and the metal walkway ended abruptly against a brick wall. With no obvious way forward, it wasn't until the entire group passed the last tower did the final section of walkway begin to vibrate, slowly lowering them to ground level and an oversized door.

Once again Director Bowen pulled out his golden key, and while fumbling with the lock something shiny caught Declan's attention. Screwed into the charred wooden base of the nearest machine tower, a brass plaque read:

Tower One, erected 1814. First functional unit of the electronic data intelligence synthesis and operations network.

He wanted to ask questions but didn't, unwilling to risk further reprimands from Embrie, and it wasn't long before the Director gained access to the library.

Chapter 13

March 29, 1939
The Library of the Ages
Clypeate Headquarters
City of Washington, District of Columbia

The opulent decor didn't surprise Declan, the octagon-shaped room rivaled the Room of the Honored except here the walls were lined with exquisitely carved bookcases instead of weapons. He was, however, stunned by the scale, larger than his university's library, the bookcases continuing skyward until they reached the ornate ceiling several stories above.

His gaze settled upon the ornate spiral staircase, twirling upward, rising to greet the many terraces circling the room and providing access to the upper levels. In the dim light the professor didn't immediately appreciate the room's significant damage, but as his eyes adjusted he noted the scratched, charred floor and scorch marks on the bookcases. The shelves were protected with glass doors, many of them cracked, and the lowest steps of the spiral staircase were hacked into splinters, in their stead makeshift rungs were nailed into place. "Pity about the staircase," lamented Declan. "Such wanton destruction and disregard for craftsmanship."

"Yes, this library could use some tidying," commented James, appraising the room's shabby condition. "What a shame, such magnificent detail," he said, admiring the intricate flowers carved into the dark wood. "People think Grand Central Station is an architectural gem, that's a glorified chicken coop compared to this place."

"The damage is senseless and unfortunate," Bruce agreed, running his fingers along an intact section of the staircase handrail, "although we believe our people destroyed the staircase, intentionally, to prevent the Obturavi from gaining access to the rest of our collection. Thankfully this sacrifice spared the majority of the library from further destruction, only a few stray bullets found their way into the upper levels."

"Why not fix the library?" Declan asked. "This is a beautiful room, and it wouldn't take much effort."

"We don't plan to repair the damage anytime soon," said Bruce. "Since the Obturavi attack, access to the library is highly restricted as we consider this hallowed ground. Embrie works hard to preserve the sanctity of this space while maintaining our vast collection."

"The scale of which is certainly impressive," James agreed, noting the packed shelves surrounding them and extending upwards, "and judging by how well it's protected, I assume it's stocked with more than a bunch of Sears Roebuck catalogs and dime store pulp novels."

"You won't find anything common or crass in here," Embrie scoffed with indignation. "These archives house the accumulated knowledge amassed by mankind, the sum total of our intellectual achievements. This is the collected wisdom of the ages."

"So, no Dick Tracy comic strips," James teased.

"What about this crispy poster?" Declan asked, pointing to the charred remains of a framed document hanging on a nearby column. "Was it important?"

"I'd classify it as such," responded Embrie, "considering it's the Declaration of Independence, or at least it was, before the Obturavi torched it. Perhaps it could have been better protected, but displaying it was a real source of pride."

"I presume this was an original copy," Declan said. "At this point I wouldn't expect anything less. Although given where the Constitution hangs, this would almost be too appropriate."

"You must be feeling better because I detect sarcasm," Embrie coyly responded, "but yes, this happens to be an original Dunlap Broadside printed on July 4th, 1776. Thankfully our more important holdings survived intact. As you can see, the books down here are locked behind bullet proof glass. Thus, while the glass cracked and the woodwork suffered, the contents remain unharmed."

"Hold on," interrupted Declan, "how can you be so flippant about this? You should be more upset about losing an irreplaceable copy of the Declaration of Independence."

"It's not like they destroyed an original handwritten copy," countered Embrie. "They printed over two hundred of these on that first Independence Day," she informed the professor, "although not all of them survived. After the Broadsides were distributed some people immediately burned their copies, afraid mere possession would constitute treason, while others hid theirs under floorboards where mice used them as bedding. This attrition means far fewer copies made it to the present, so we were fortunate to possess fifteen of them, mainly because Clypeate members hid them down here for safekeeping."

"Hold on," Declan said, scanning the room, "you have fifteen copies down here?"

"We did," Embrie sighed. "Unfortunately, the Obturavi used whatever flammable material they could find, and many got rolled up as kindling to ignite the bookshelves. At this point I've sorted through most of our intact documents and come across a handful of surviving copies, I think we have seven or eight left."

James inserted himself into the discussion. "Smack me with a rubber chicken, there are so many original copies of the Declaration of Independence down here you can't give a firm answer?"

"That's part of my mission," Embrie explained. "I'm cataloging the library's vast collection. Besides, it's not the same as losing an original Constitution, we only have the one."

"Okay, you've piqued my curiosity," Declan persisted, "I have to know, if several copies of the Declaration of Independence getting torched was an acceptable loss, what could possibly be housed down here that's more important? Perhaps Shakespeare's First Folio?"

"I wouldn't be surprised," Embrie answered, "though I've been up and down the stacks and there's not much fiction on these shelves. This collection contains more unique items, created in various forms of media and recorded through the ages. Some things are chiseled in ancient tongues lost to time, others written on papyrus so fragile it crumbles at the slightest touch, yet all deemed worthy of protection for future generations. This is the Library of the Ages, the amassed wisdom of humanity."

"Well, good thing nothing more valuable was destroyed," Declan sardonically quipped, not expecting his comment to generate a heated response from the Director.

"Not true at all," asserted Director Bowen, "the real tragedy was much greater. After the Obturavi breached every other defense, this is where the Clypeate made their final stand, and that night many brave men lost their lives in this room."

"I'm sorry, I didn't realize," Declan stammered remorsefully, neck hairs tingling and standing on end as he imagined the room littered with corpses, mangled bodies strewn about the floor where he now walked. Suddenly the room's musty smell wasn't from old books, it was the stench of death, and the thought sent him swooning. He leaned against a badly damaged grandfather clock, bracing himself against the chipped concrete pillar. "This has been a lovely tour," he said, speech slurred, "how about we call it a day?"

Embrie's response sounded tinny and distant, his vision grayed, and the room spun. When Declan opened his eyes, he wondered why everyone suddenly towered over him, then he felt the cold, hard floor on his bottom and understood. Propped up against the large clock tower, Embrie knelt to brush the tangled locks off his face.

"You gave everyone a scare," she said. "How do you feel?"

"I'm fine, a little embarrassed," he replied, pulling himself up. "What I've seen and heard in the last few hours is building up, there's a lot to unpack and process. I'm trying my best, and while I don't want to sound unappreciative, I may have reached today's quota for shocking revelations."

"Please, Declan," Embrie implored, "I know you are tired and overwhelmed, but what lies ahead matters more than anything, everything, you've seen thus far. The only way to truly understand your importance, your role, is by completing this journey."

Declan didn't stand a chance against her pleading eyes, and Director Bowen seized the moment to swing aside a section of bookcase, revealing a brick wall and another large metal door.

"What an intricate labyrinth you've created," commented James. Hoping to lighten the mood, he added "I'm surprised a minotaur hasn't sprung out from behind one of these doors to attack us."

Bruce played along. "You're going to be terribly disappointed by our mythical creatures, they're all pacifists."

Director Bowen wasn't amused. "Sorry to ruin the fun but can someone shine a light over here?" he asked, unproductively fumbling with the golden key.

Embrie produced a flashlight and illuminated the door, dust and cobwebs coating the surface. Bruce used his hand to wipe it down, revealing an insignia embossed into the shiny metal. James read "Potowmack Company, 1788. Never heard of it."

"That's because it went defunct over a century ago," explained Bruce. "The company wanted to connect the Potomac River with the burgeoning nation's interior, and it was founded by none other than General Washington. After his death the company floundered, and by the 1820s dissolved."

"That doesn't make sense," Declan said, shaking his head. "It means this door was forged more than a century ago, yet the metal is pristine, so lustrous it looks like it was cast last week. With the heat and humidity down here the door would've oxidized rapidly, by now it should be a pile of rust chips."

"The door hasn't rusted because it was cast from aluminum, not iron," Director Bowen muttered without looking up, his attention centered on tinkering with the key.

"Aluminum in 1788? Not impossible, but highly doubtful," the professor countered. "Refining aluminum didn't become economically practical for another hundred years. Today it's cheap to produce but in 1788 aluminum was worth a king's ransom, more valuable than gold. Napoleon's best cutlery and tableware were aluminum, reserved for only his most honored guests. Everyone else ate off the cheap stuff, gold and silver."

The exasperated Director momentarily paused from his key-fumbling travails. "Why wouldn't it be forged from aluminum? Just because it took the outside world another century to discover the metallurgical process doesn't matter down here. The door is aluminum because it's strong, durable and doesn't corrode."

The Director resumed fiddling with the key, and while Declan attempted to craft a logical response Bruce used the opportunity to elaborate.

"Earlier you asked how new technologies could suddenly show up and nobody question them. This aluminum door is a perfect example," Bruce said, rapping his knuckles against the metal. "You're correct, of course, for all human history nobody figured out how to extract aluminum, Earth's most abundant metal. Then in 1886, suddenly two men working on different continents simultaneously discover a revolutionary refining process. Sounds awfully coincidental, yet nobody gives it a second thought because this kind of coincidence happens all the time with science and technology."

"The Clypeate extracted aluminum ore ninety-eight years before sharing the secret with the rest of the world," calculated Declan, brow furrowing as he pondered the implications. "Scientists report breakthroughs to advance mankind, what if you discovered the cure for cancer, would the Clypeate let generations of people die?"

"You've been fed the predictable slurry of educational chum for too long," grumbled Director Bowen, giving his tired fingers a brief rest. "There are forces wishing to obscure the truth, and beyond the ivy-covered gates of academia the world exists in many shades of gray. The scientists in the Research Hall didn't make incremental improvements, they created paradigm shifts, ideas you can't throw around like it's a ticker tape parade."

Declan couldn't understand the Director's hesitancy. "As a scientist, I would be proud of my discoveries and want to share them with the world immediately."

"Sadly, humanity can't always be trusted," explained Bruce. "Every step forward can be used as either a tool or weapon. The Clypeate exercises caution when spreading new ideas, sharing clues for others to follow, gently nudging progress into the future. The Clypeate doesn't let our genies out of their bottles all at once, and as a bonus" he elaborated, "delaying some discoveries has proven a lucrative way to generate revenue."

"Makes sense," James remarked, "missions to Antarctica, secret underground bases and futuristic technology can't be cheap."

Bruce nodded. "Certainly not," he said, "and the Clypeate can't rely upon generous donors for all our ventures. Thankfully a century selling aluminum cutlery and jewelry to wealthy clientele provided a healthy financial cushion."

"Can everyone stop talking for a moment?" the Director sternly requested. "I promise Bruce and I will return to freeing your minds of falsities and fabrications, but first I need a few moments of quiet because this damned key is infuriating me!"

Long, awkward minutes lapsed while the group waited in trepidatious silence, though after several more unsuccessful attempts at opening the door James spoke up. "Director, perhaps something's wrong with the key?" he bravely suggested. "It didn't work at the Jefferson Pier, either."

Once again the Director paused his tinkering, this time instead of a sharp reprimand he sighed. "The Jefferson Pier was different," he said. "And it's not the key's fault, it's mine. The Master Key of Hesperus is unique, it opens several doors with each lock encoded to open using a different configuration. I must shift the key bits to the correct positions or else the lock won't accept it. Adds an extra level of security."

"Ingenious," commented Declan. "The key acts like a combination lock."

"Exactly," Director Bowen replied, twisting the key's teeth. "The problem is remembering the proper alignment for each lock, and since I haven't opened this door in many years, I'm struggling. So, while the lock might not be rusty," he said, gritting his teeth, "my memory certainly is." Much to everyone's relief, none more than the Director, only two attempts later the door finally yielded and creaked open.

"Wow, this door is four inches thick," James remarked, knocking on the metal door, eliciting a dull thump. "And solid metal, you'd have better luck punching a hole through the brick wall," he noted, wondering what could possibly lie ahead to merit such security.

After a few flickers a series of miniature lights strung along the ceiling replaced the darkness ahead of them, their dim glow illuminating a narrow, dusty passageway. "Oh, good," Director Bowen remarked, "the lights still work, one less worry."

"The lights are great," agreed James, his attention focused upon the numerous intricately patterned cobwebs crisscrossing the tunnel. "We'll be able to count how many spiders get tangled in our hair," he dryly quipped.

"Don't fret," Bruce responded, "I'll go first. I'm tall, my face will clear most of them out of the way." He entered the brick-lined tunnel, wide but squat and said, "Even crouching my head scrapes against the ceiling." He declared, "Next time I'm bringing a broom and construction helmet," hands raised above his head like antennae to warn him about low-hanging surprises.

While the other men funneled into the tunnel Declan hesitated, a vague discomfort rising within. He looked to Embrie for reassurance, instead finding her mood had shifted from gregarious to sullen. "What's wrong?" Declan asked, watching her slowly back away from the door. "Aren't you coming with us?"

"Nothing's the matter, but I can't join you," Embrie replied with a half-hearted grin, "I promised Ms. Elliott I'd help prepare dinner, and there are pressing matters requiring my attention in the Analytical Engine Room."

Declan saw the young woman's obvious apprehension peeking through her poorly veiled excuses, whipping up his own unease into a frenzied primal alarm. "I'm not budging from this spot until you level with me," he said, refusing to enter the tunnel. "What's at the other end?" he demanded. "There's something powerful down there, and this will sound crazy but it's waiting for me. It knows I'm here."

Embrie leaned forward and whispered into his ear. "It's going to be okay, I feel the same thing. This is the reason why you're here, because what comes next is very important for all of us. I would never let anything bad happen to you, so try to relax a little bit and enjoy the moment. The truth is waiting for you." Before he could ask more questions Embrie gently squeezed his hand and disappeared into the Analytical Engine Room.

Declan debated his next move. "Dammit, she's right," he decided, "I'm ready for some answers." He peered into the tunnel, the others already with a substantial head start requiring him to catch up. Declan entered cautiously, despite the hands and faces of the men ahead clearing most of the cobwebs, the tunnel still gave off unsettling energy. The passage ran straight but Declan's atrophied calf muscles noted the shallow, steady incline and his legs squealed in protest.

He trotted until James turned and stopped, waiting for the professor to join them. "Not as easy as it looks," James commiserated, "and those shoes I borrowed from Hoss aren't doing my heels any favors."

The pair moved forward, and despite the slower pace Declan struggled to match James, his heart racing from a mixture of exertion and nervous anticipation. Focused on keeping up rather than belting out questions, the professor pressed onward in silence, his connection to whatever waited ahead growing stronger with every step. It wasn't all bad, however, Declan couldn't remember the last time he felt such a lively spark of curiosity. The drudgery of his uninspired career stole his enthusiasm and ground away the joy of science, and while the Antarctic expedition turned into a surreal nightmare it led him here, to this world of impossible realities. Even if this were all fantasy and he was chasing windmills with Don Quixote, he hoped this reverie would last a bit longer.

Declan's legs appreciated the tunnel ending after a few more minutes, the group pausing when the passage emptied into an expansive vestibule. They faced a smooth wall, double Bruce's height and extending twenty feet across, the stone barrier polished to a pearly sheen and not a single visible defect across the entire expanse.

Director Bowen ran his fingers along the rockface. "This wall is directly underneath the Washington Obelisk," he explained, "a massive monument built from marble, gneiss and granite. Quite a heavy burden to bear, but this stone," he tapped the wall for emphasis, "is quartzite, even stronger, so it's able to handle all that weight." He once again pulled out the golden key. "Final lock, though now comes the tricky part. Can anyone locate any patterns or markings in the wall?"

"It looks totally smooth," James replied, surveying the wall, "perhaps a defect would be more obvious if we had better lighting."

"Good idea," the Director agreed, "although I think we'll need more than a flashlight this time." He pulled a black, golf ball-sized orb from his pocket. "This will help," he said, nonchalantly tossing the object above his head. The small object defiantly hung in the air, and when it began chirping he suddenly panicked. "I forgot to tell you, quickly cover your eyes!"

The tiny object chirped five times before erupting into a ball of light brighter than the sun. Declan closed his eyes but the burst of light traveled effortlessly through his eyelids, flashes of color exploding inside his mind. He squealed with a mixture of surprise and visual shock, and while James managed to get his hands over his face he was similarly afflicted, enough light sneaking between his fingers that photons ricocheted off his retinas like fireworks.

"Whoa, next time warn us a bit sooner," Bruce groaned, also vigorously rubbing his eyes.

"Sorry, I forgot how bright these were," apologized the Director, having grossly understated the intense luminary onslaught.

When Declan finally opened his eyes, he saw the small object floating above their heads, and while the orb's brightness had diminished it still illuminated the space better than a dozen flashlights. "That's amazing," he remarked.

"Not terribly practical, though," the Director said. "It provides fantastic lighting but it's too hot to touch and burns itself out in a few hours, which means we don't have long to search the wall. Oh, and it's a tad unstable as it dims, so the sooner we find the lock, the quicker we can move away from the orb." Director Bowen cursorily scanned the wall before shaking his head. "My eyesight isn't what it once was, so I'm relying on the rest of you to find the markings."

Due to the wall's immensity the three men split up, each covering a section the size of several pool tables, going inch by inch looking for etched markings. The orb's light revealed the delicate mineral patterns baked over eons into the rock, though nothing suggested even the slightest imperfection in the smooth surface.

Half an hour elapsed, the orb dimming substantially, with no obvious cracks or crevices located. Frustrated, Declan ventured, "Could you be mistaken? This stone is polished to perfection, there aren't any cracks. It's one flawless block."

"It appears that way," the Director conceded. "Although there must be something of note, because I remember them looking for specific markings in the rock. Sadly, I don't have any further clues. I only witnessed the door open once, never imagining the next time I'd be the one holding the key."

"Perhaps we're missing the bigger picture," Declan mused, stepping away from the wall and backing into the farthest corner of the vestibule. From this vantage point he visualized the wall's entirety, and suddenly it made sense. The delicate mineral veins, blue shades from deep cobalt to light azure, coppery hues and brilliant greens, together formed an image against the background of opalescent alabaster quartzite. "You're not going to believe this," he said, "you should come stand over here with me."

Bruce joined Declan, and upon turning to face the wall he delightedly gushed. "Well, color me impressed. Isn't that something?"

James looked up and wondered why he was the only one still checking the wall. "I thought we were working here, nobody told me it was breaktime," he huffed, annoyed at their perceived slacking until he walked over and surveyed the wall. "Oh, wow," he declared, "I mean, wow. There aren't patterns carved into the stone, the stone itself is the pattern."

Director Bowen also stepped back and grinned. "I really should have paid closer attention when the old masters opened this door," he reflected, "though I doubt Mr. Tesla required such a literal map and Mr. Edison wasn't keen on imparting wisdom."

They stood quietly, taking a few moments to appreciate the stony mural. With great precision and elegant beauty, the mineral bands flowing through the rock created a highly accurate representation of planet Earth. The geographic depiction spanned the entire stony surface, veins of vibrant greens and coppery oranges fleshing out continents while azure and cobalt mineral swirls flowed across the oceanic expanses.

Bruce spoke up. "Professor Riordan, looks like you found the treasure map. Now where does X mark the spot?"

"I have a strong suspicion," Declan responded, walking up to the wall and placing his hand over Africa. His fingers skimmed over the green veins of Serengeti jungle and across the burnt umber of Saharan sands before traveling west, tracing the Atlantic's blue swirls. His fingers slowed down as they approached a copper band kinked into the unmistakable shape of the Delmarva peninsula. He leaned closer to the wall and marked the District's approximate location. "And I believe my hunch is correct," he announced, feeling a small defect in the smooth surface invisible even with his nose pressed against the stone.

Director Bowen ran a confirmatory finger sweep from Manhattan to Cape Hatteras. "I feel it too," he agreed, "though you'd never find it unless you knew where to look." From his pocket he pulled out a tiny test tube, small as a pinky finger, held it up to the imperceptible defect and uncorked it. In response blue light poured out from the inch-long slit, sending the Director scrambling to align the golden key's tumblers. "I'll never forget this configuration, Mr. Tesla made a point of mentioning how all the key bits aligned to create a picture." He held up the golden key, the elaborate key bits now forming recognizable symbols.

"They're shapes," James noted, instead of random patterns the key's teeth and notches formed a circle, triangle and square. "This door must be especially important."

"Beyond a doubt," the Director replied, gently threading the key tip into the stone's impossibly thin crevice. The key slid effortlessly into the wall, continuing to advance even after the Director removed his hand, until only the diamond-etched bow remained visible. "I think that's supposed to happen," he guessed, "now we just wait."

"That's your expert opinion?" the exhausted Declan blurted out. "Perhaps you should've paid more attention the first time," he snapped, immediately regretting the harsh tone of his unbridled tongue. "I'm sorry, that wasn't fair, and I never properly thanked you for rescuing me from Dante's Inferno."

"You're welcome, and your frustration is understandable," Director Bowen calmly replied, "and not entirely unmerited. In my defense, the only time I saw this door open was thirty years ago," he explained, "and I was preoccupied making sure I didn't piddle myself. I stood here, pulled from duty as assistant engineer aboard the *Pennsylvania,* three stars less than the next lowest ranking officer, in the presence of the Wizard of Menlo Park and the Sorcerer of Serbia."

"What an amazing honor," James said, "you must've done something remarkable to catch their attention."

The Director shrugged his shoulders. "Even now I don't know why they picked me to join them. Before that day I'd never met Mr. Tesla, and Mr. Edison only once, years earlier while I was still a cadet at the Naval Academy. I couldn't have made much of an impression on him, and by the time we made it this far I was convinced my role was serving as a human sacrifice. With the benefit of time, I've come to understand…" his voice trailed off as deep rumbling emanated from the wall, gently shaking the ground beneath them and causing the worn-down professor to fall to the ground.

James offered him a hand. Declan waved him off, preferring to use the wall and his hands to walk himself upright. The golden key slowly backed out from the wall, self-extruding until it dropped to the ground with a dull clunk.

"Did we miss something?" Bruce asked when the vibrations ended and the wall hadn't budged. "Or maybe the vial was leaky."

Director Bowen twirled the test tube between his fingers, surveying it for damage. "No, I don't think so."

James asked, "Why is that empty test tube so important?"

"It's not empty," asserted Declan. "There's air inside."

"That's not entirely accurate, either," the Director said. "This test tube doesn't contain ordinary air, at least it didn't before I uncorked it. The gas inside was far more valuable. See the markings along the side?"

"10-18-31," Declan read. "Either the code to a combination lock or a date."

"It's a date, October 18th, 1931," Director Bowen confirmed. "The day Thomas Edison died, the same day this test tube was filled with his breath, more precisely his last dying gasp. While Mr. Edison was most famous for his superior intellect, he also had a legendary ability to hold a grudge. He was down here in 1898, during the Obturavi attack, bravely rescuing children and narrowly escaping the ill fate suffered by the Clypeate's defenders. After the attack, when the government sealed off Lincoln's Tunnel, he viewed their safety concerns as an insult to the Clypeate's honored service to this country."

"I'd be angry, too," said Declan, "but you can't hold a grudge forever."

"Well, that's precisely how long Mr. Edison planned on holding this one. When his own petitions to President McKinley failed, Mr. Edison guaranteed the government could never open this door. Not only did he hide this golden key, he added another security measure. He rigged the door to activate when breathed upon, in just the right spot, and only in response to his breath."

"What could be so special about his breath?" James asked.

"Nobody's figured that out yet," the Director said, "and the old wizard wasn't handing out hints."

"Why take such drastic action?" Declan prodded.

"Simple," Director Bowen said, "beyond this wall resides power exceeding your wildest dreams. The greatest repository of knowledge ever known, makes the Library of the Ages look like an outdated phonebook, and Mr. Edison didn't want to risk it falling into the wrong hands. Which, by the end of his life, he decided extended beyond the government to everyone other than himself. He didn't even trust Mr. Tesla or the other Clypeate scientists."

"But this is just a wall," argued James. "Why not dig or drill another way around?"

"Sounds easy enough," Bruce chuckled. "Except the Washington Monument is directly above our heads, and haphazardly disrupting the balance of all that rock has never seemed wise."

Suddenly the wall shuddered, kicking up a cloud of dust and causing loose pebbles to rain down and pelt them. "The monument is collapsing!" Declan screamed, using his hands to shield his head while James ran back into the tunnel.

"You both need to relax a little, we're fine," the Director reassured them. "First of all, if the monument collapsed nothing would stop the tons of rubble from instantly turning our bodies into a micron-thick layer of goo, and second the rumbling isn't coming from the monument, it's the door opening."

Declan peeked out from behind his hands, and indeed the world diorama was sinking into the floor. "The entire wall is the door?" he remarked. "It must weigh twenty tons, what an incredible amount of force it would take to move something so massive."

"More like forty tons, and not as difficult to move as you might think," the Director replied. "I wondered the same thing, but Mr. Tesla explained the mechanism to me, quite ingenious. This wall is counterbalanced by Washington's Obelisk, so as the wall goes down the whole monument tilts, and since the obelisk is so heavy it only leans a few imperceptible millimeters."

"Remarkable engineering, yet slower than a cold lizard," James remarked, the wall having crept down only a few feet in almost as many minutes. "And while we're waiting here, can we return to the topic of Thomas Edison's breath? I'd appreciate further clarification, like how'd you finally convince him to give you his breath if he was so hell bent against it?"

"Oh, we never got his approval. Instead, we relied upon the assistance of one of Mr. Edison's dearest old friends, Henry Ford. The Clypeate convinced Mr. Ford to ask Edison's son, Charles, to collect his dying father's last exhalation. Charles knew his father and Mr. Ford were good friends so he complied, though afterward Mr. Ford felt guilty about the deception and tried keeping Edison's last breath for himself. Of course we got our hands on it, we needed that last breath for our purposes here. Mr. Ford, however, didn't go empty-handed. We did him one better, and sent him the other gas escaping Edison's body in those final moments."

"And what might that be?" James naively asked.

"No!" Declan groaned at the Director's insinuation, "You're not saying you collected his death throe flatus?"

"Indeed, that's precisely what we did. We doubted young Charles would honor the unusual request, so we incentivized the coroner to collect every gas escaping from Mr. Edison's body. We have jugs of belched and burped gas, as well as everything exiting his back porch, every last toot except for the one tiny vial forwarded to Mr. Ford. I understand he still treasures that glass tube containing his good friend's final swansong."

While James and Declan absorbed that bit of trivia, the wall finished receding into the floor with a resounding thud. They peered inside, darkness waiting beyond the wide aperture.

"Hmmm, the ceiling must have worn itself out," mused the Director. He walked over to the glowing orb, still floating in midair, now faded to the strength of an overcast winter day. "We'll have to take our chances, just duck down if the orb starts chirping again," he warned, using the golden key to gently nudge the dimmed sphere into the inky void. The group followed the orb into the circular room, narrower but shaped similarly to the library, with polished quartzite walls and majestic stone columns.

"Welcome to the Sanctuary," Director Bowen announced, tapping the orb upwards into the darkness, rising until light filled the room with a soft glow, illuminating the underside of the diamond-shaped crystal above them. "Here is the Clypeate's most prized possession, the Epistolith."

The gleaming, inconceivably large object occupied the vast majority of the Sanctuary, and from this vantage point looked to James like an inverted glass pyramid. While Declan stood frozen in place, James stepped back to get a better angle. "I know what this is," James announced, "I just read about it. Sounded like malarkey and it's still tough to grasp, yet there it is, hanging above us like a barn-sized chandelier."

"Not hanging, it's floating," Bruce corrected him. "Off the ground of its own accord, like an errant helium balloon. I've never been inside the Sanctuary either, this is also my first time seeing the Epistolith. It's tough believing such an irrationally fantastic object exists, even when it's floating above our heads."

James paced back and forth, looking up at the Epistolith. "My brain is struggling to process the disconnect between what's possible and what my eyes are telling me."

"Skepticism is healthy," Bruce said, smiling and patting James on the back. "You aren't a blind follower, yet you placed your trust in us. Where others couldn't handle the truth, you continued along this journey. I hope you're not disappointed. We're not. I knew from the start you were a good choice."

"I appreciate your confidence in me, although I've gotta admit, the only reason I'm handling this so well is because three rooms ago, I stopped thinking and started listening." James turned to Declan. "Hey Doc, what did you think of this sightseeing tour?"

Declan stared blankly at the Epistolith, color drained from his face. "It's real. It exists," he stammered. "Why'd you bring me here?" Declan demanded, sobbing, his trembling legs giving out, sending him crashing onto the floor.

"Let me help," Bruce said, bending over to assist the professor.

"Don't touch me," shouted Declan, swatting Bruce's hands away and scrambling back 'til he could go no further. Firmly pressed against the wall, he said, "I forgot all about this damned stone. Now I remember all of it. It tricked us!"

Director Bowen walked over to the distraught professor and sat down next to him. "Please, Doctor Riordan, allow me to explain. I understand this must be very confusing, though as your memory returns, I believe this will make more sense."

"No, it won't," yelled Declan, shaking his head. "That Epistolith is the devil's plaything, a spinning top forged in hell's flames. Why would you bring that monstrous stone here? You should've left it in Antarctica."

In the calmest and most reassuring tone he could muster, Director Bowen said, "This isn't the same object you saw in Antarctica, although as far as I can tell they're identical. We didn't move this Epistolith under the Washington Monument, it's always been here. Before your trip to Antarctica, before George Washington led our nation's revolution, before humans walked upright, it's been waiting here. For you."

"This is too much," sputtered Declan, "none of this is real. I died in Antarctica, didn't I? This is all some kind of wild dream, a fantasy my brain is concocting while steadily gobbling up the last remaining oxygen and fuel."

"No Professor, you're quite alive," Director Bowen reassured him. "And, dare I say, essential to our future."

"Something's wrong with me," countered Declan. "I feel the crystal tugging on my mind, drawing me closer, ever since the library door swung open. A brain tumor would explain a lot."

"There's nothing wrong with you," the Director calmly replied, "quite the opposite. Your ability to communicate with the Epistolith is the rarest gift imaginable.

You've been given the chance to be amazing, to fulfill your destiny."

Director Bowen's reassurance fell flat. "Problem is I don't believe in destiny, and magical abilities are preposterous. We may be at the end of the rainbow and the Epsitolith is the pot of gold, but I'm not your leprechaun."

"Magic is misunderstood science," asserted Bruce, "and nobody thinks you're a leprechaun. What you embody is the fulfillment of prophecy."

Director Bowen's frustration mounted. "Haven't you always felt special, like you were meant for something great?" he asked. "We could return you to UCLA, where you can play with petri dishes and get annoyed by undergrads, or you can finish this journey and learn your true purpose."

"Come on Doc," James pleaded. "I'm scared and nervous, too. Let's go down the rabbit hole together. This is a once-in-never opportunity, do you wanna spend the rest of your life wondering what could've been? I know I don't."

"Fine," Declan grumbled, while reluctant to agree with James he couldn't refute the analyst's argument.

"I'm glad, and thank you," Director Bowen said, looking pleased. "You needn't fear ideas like destiny or fate, they aren't mystical predeterminations. Think about how you plan a research project. Before you run a science experiment in your lab, don't you anticipate a certain outcome?"

Declan huffed. "Yes, it's called a hypothesis."

In response the Director asked, "If you already know the outcome in advance, why bother running the experiment at all?"

"Because we're not always correct," answered Declan. "Our calculations could be wrong, our predictions faulty, or we misinterpret the underlying science."

Director Bowen smiled and asserted, "Fate, destiny, and prophecies are no different than your scientific predictions. They're also educated guesses, except playing out on a universal scale. Our primitive technologies don't allow it, but what if you could account for every confounding variable and bit of data? Those who came before us, the ones who led General Washington to form the Clypeate, had technology beyond our wildest imagination, capable of such feats. When they made educated guesses, their predictions were infinitely more insightful."

"You can stop trying to normalize this craziness," the professor declared, "I'm not going anywhere. At least not until I understand what's going on inside my head. Maybe I can't reconcile what I've seen down here, and I'm still pissed about getting dragged to Antarctica, but it's impossible to ignore my own memories. Little snippets are returning, and while I don't catch their meaning, I know I was wrong about the Epistolith. The stone wasn't trying to trick or hurt me. She protected me."

"She?" repeated Bruce, the feminine pronoun catching his attention. "You referred to the Epistolith as 'she'. Any particular reason?"

"Did I?" Declan mused. "That's odd, I'm not sure why."

"I have some ideas," the Director hinted without elaboration, shifting focus. "We should finish the last bit of our journey" he suggested, leading them across the room, the inky black floor embedded with dozens of randomly scattered, tiny white pebbles. When Declan passed directly under the pointed nadir of the Epistolith, still several feet above him, the glassy surface reflected his image from all four sides. The professor only looked up for a moment, spooked to see his emaciated cheeks, sunken orbits and skeletonized face staring back.

The men followed Director Bowen onto a metal platform against the far wall, tucked between two of the massive pillars encircling the room. These stone columns weren't fluted like classical Greek or Roman designs, instead having tiny markings chiseled into their surface. Declan leaned forward for a closer look, clinging to the side rail, steadying himself as the platform jerked into motion. While the platform slowly climbed up the wall, the professor resumed his inspection, the unfamiliar symbols wrapping around and covering the column's entire length. "These aren't simple designs," Declan decided, "they look like written language, maybe Arabic or Sanskrit. Pleasing to the eye but unlike anything I've ever seen. How about you," he said, looking at James, "isn't this what you do for a living?"

"Deciphering ancient texts isn't exactly my expertise," replied James, "although my code-breaking skills might be handy." While the platform climbed the young analyst watched countless rows of symbols stream past them and shook his head. "The markings resemble text, except none of the characters correlate with modern languages. Perhaps they're indigenous glyphs."

"I entertained that idea, too," Declan said, persisting in his contempt for James yet appreciating the input. "Only problem, it'd be impossible to carve such exquisite detail into hard stone without advanced metal tools."

"True," the Director interjected, "that's why these columns weren't carved by humans. These symbols are proto-language, spoken long before our species learned sounds could be used to communicate meaning."

"Proto-language?" repeated James. "You're saying this is an ancestral tongue. For which languages, the ones native to the Americas?"

"No," Director Bowen said, "all of them," leaving James and Declan to discuss the markings until the elevator platform halted sixty feet up. The Director promptly exited onto the narrow wooden walkway jutting out from the

Sanctuary wall while the others hesitated, eyeing the rickety-looking overhang with great apprehension. "You'll be fine," he said, warning them, "just watch your step. The Sanctuary was constructed to last for eons, the Clypeate hastily rigged together this balcony in one night. Consequently, it was built to less exacting standards."

They all clung to the Sanctuary wall, the narrow walkway audibly creaking and visibly heaving with each step. The floating orb trapped on the underside of the massive Epistolith didn't provide any light up here, instead the domed ceiling above them glowed a pale turquoise, providing enough illumination to navigate forward. Declan craned his neck over the edge, peering down at the massive crystal to admire the diamond's crisp perfection, the widest points nearly scraping the Sanctuary columns.

Meanwhile James focused his attention upwards, the Epistolith's upper apex pressed snug against the faintly glowing dome. "You're sure the Epistolith is floating? Because from this vantage point, the giant crystal really looks like a portly chandelier dangling down from the ceiling."

"I know," the Director conceded, "except the forces at play are actually the opposite. The ceiling pushes down on the crystal, which in turn distributes the weight load into the Sanctuary walls."

"Can't be true," Declan blurted out. "If the Epistolith supports the ceiling, and we're directly under the Washington Monument, that would mean the floating crystal is supporting a ton of stone. I'm not saying it's impossible, I'll let Isaac Newton and his laws of gravity tell you."

Director Bowen grinned. "Not a ton of stone, more like eighty thousand tons."

"Whoa, Doc's gotta point," James chimed in, "if the Epistolith is propping up the ceiling, then what's keeping the Epistolith in place? Admittedly physics isn't my specialty, and my math skills are a tad rusty, but I know equations need to balance and this doesn't. If eighty thousand tons are pushing down on the Epistolith, how can the crystal possibly match the force?"

"Newtonian physics don't apply to the Epistolith. The crystal is self-reliant, capable of generating its own force. Supporting one pound or one hundred thousand tons of rock is irrelevant, the Epistolith depends only upon itself to maintain position."

Declan wasn't convinced. "Reality exists because the rules apply to everyone and everything. The Washington Monument resting on top of the Epistolith doesn't prove the giant crystal's exemption from universal laws."

"The Clypeate doesn't require proof," stated Director Bowen, "the Epistolith's capabilities are well documented in General Washington's journal, that's all the evidence we need. The monument wasn't built over the Epistolith to confirm our faith, it was done out of necessity. Originally Washington's obelisk was going to be built above the Library of the Ages, to protect the original entrance at the Jefferson Pier. Those plans, however, changed one fateful night in 1848."

"We call it the Great Upheaval," Bruce elaborated, "the night when the Epistolith ascended without warning or reason."

Director Bowen nodded and explained, "That's why the Washington Monument was built in this location, not to test the Epistolith, rather to conceal the Sanctuary. In 1848 this side of the Tiber Creek was undeveloped, with the Sanctuary safely concealed under yards of cow pasture. On the night of the Great Upheaval the Epistolith rose ten feet, lifting the Sanctuary's domed ceiling along with the fields above it."

"That would be a sizable chunk of land," reasoned Declan. "And I don't recall any mention of a Great Upheaval during my history classes. How'd this escape people's attention?"

"Good point," James said. "We're merely a stone's throw from the White House, surely this would have prompted questions."

Bruce supplied the answer. "Fortunately, the night was dark," he responded, "and the only witnesses besides Clypeate guards were bovine, with a handful of cows sleeping comfortably atop the floating island of pasture. Even more astounding was how the dome, pasture and cows were all delicately balanced atop the glimmering tip of the Epistolith, which is what it's still doing now, supporting the Sanctuary ceiling without obvious exertion."

"It's not sticking out of the ground anymore, so how'd they push the Epistolith back down?" wondered Declan.

"They didn't," the Director responded. "The diamond has floated in the same spot for nearly one century. That night the Clypeate found out the hard way, wasting precious time and considerable resources trying to push the whole affair back into the ground, failing miserably. When they realized the Epistolith wasn't budging a single inch, they switched plans. Cover it up."

James pondered the vast ceiling. "That's a big ask for one night," he commented. "No matter how much manpower the Clypeate could muster."

"You're correct," the Director replied. "They required more than men. That's why the Clypeate was fortunate to already possess the appropriate equipment. After the War of 1812 the Potowmack Company, General Washington's canal-building venture, gifted the Clypeate several earth-moving machines. Although they were designed to carve canals, the equipment already proved useful once before, digging Lincoln's Tunnel."

"Now the tunnel makes sense," remarked James. "I couldn't understand how the Clypeate excavated such large quantities of dirt."

"It's also why the Clypeate was prepared on the night of the Great Upheaval," the Director elaborated, "our men had prior experience using these machines. You can see where the dome lifted off the Sanctuary walls" he said, pointing to a line on the wall just above their heads where smooth, polished quartzite ended and another dozen feet of roughly hewn, megalithic blocks filled the gap between Sanctuary wall and dome.

Bruce added, "In one night the Clypeate stacked those giant boulders into the gap, then completed the camouflage by using dredged river mud to conceal the rock and smooth the mound."

"Your secret society built the Washington Monument's hill in one night?" asked Declan.

"Only the humblest beginnings," noted Director Bowen. "Today the monument sits atop a much broader, gently sloped hill. What the Clypeate accomplished that night resembled a pile of lumpy mashed potatoes but served its purpose, all signs of the Sanctuary were hidden by daybreak."

"Even if there wasn't a giant crystal sticking out of the ground," posited James, "wouldn't folks comment upon this brand-new hill?"

"People don't pay much attention to cow pastures," the Director remarked, "although you're correct, some noticed. Back then the Clypeate was still highly regarded by the executive branch, and James Polk was an ally. His White House announced the newly minted hill was the first step in preparing the site for General Washington's monument. Despite the original plans calling for the monument to be built where the Jefferson Pier stands, government engineers quickly designated the Sanctuary's hill a more stable site, and a few short months later the first stones were placed overhead."

The Director slowed, having led them halfway around the room. A makeshift gangway of twenty-foot-long planks extended into the void towards the Epistolith, stopping short of the diamond's upper peak. "Can anyone locate the anchoring bolts?" he asked. "The bolts stabilize the gangway, and we need to make sure they're properly secured."

"Should've brought along Embrie's flashlight," Bruce grumbled. "The lighting up here is abysmal."

"To be fair," Director Bowen explained, "when I came up here the ceiling was recently painted with Undark, and the radium luminesced so brightly the Sanctuary shone like clear sky."

"Probably for the better it's fading," Declan commented, "a little extra illumination isn't worth what's happened to those Radium Girls. The radioactivity caused all their teeth to fall out, and I'd rather keep mine firmly in their sockets."

James located the bolts and with Bruce's help tightened them by hand until Director Bowen announced, "That'll do." He stepped onto the gangway, edging towards the Epistolith, undeterred by the lack of railings on the precarious overhang no wider than a door. "Come join me," he said, motioning for Declan to follow.

"I'm inclined to stay where I am," responded Declan, shaking his head. "My legs are weaker than rubber bands and walking the plank is asking for trouble."

"I'll help you," James said, offering his hand to Declan.

"Trust you?" Declan huffed. "I'd prefer to risk plummeting over the edge."

"We both know that isn't true," James replied, "I've seen your reactions to all the amazing gadgets down here, you're like a kid on Christmas morning. Maybe my tactics were deceptive, but aren't you happy to be here?"

"I'm very grateful for this experience," conceded Declan, "my entire life I've held an unfolded map of the world, only now discovering the edges weren't endings, they were beginnings. Doesn't make your actions any less conniving or deceitful."

"Now I get it," replied James. "You're angry because I appealed to your baser instincts and you took the bait." Once again James offered his hand. "Don't be too hard on yourself, Doc, curiosity and greed are powerful motivators, and my job has trained me to play them like a virtuoso."

"Don't get too cocky," Declan replied. "You're not that charming. Truth is I never had a choice, the Epistoliths have softly whispered to me longer than I can remember. They lured me to Antarctica, and ever since the library door opened this giant diamond has propelled me forward."

Director Bowen moved out of the way. "Bruce and I will hang back," he announced, "no need to test the structural integrity of those wooden planks."

Declan reluctantly accepted James' hand, and together they walked out onto the gangway, planks groaning and swaying with every step. "I'm less worried about the wood snapping than tumbling over the side," remarked Declan. "Your Clypeate built an underground mansion, designed the world's most advanced machines and amassed an unrivaled library collection, yet somehow safety railings weren't in the budget."

The pair stopped at the gangway's far edge, only a few feet separating them from the giant diamond. James knelt to get a closer look, mesmerized by the Epistolith's glossy sheen, unlike anything he'd ever seen. "It's perfect," he noted, peering into the crystal's smoky depths. He extended his hand and gently stroked the surface, quickly snapping his hand back. "So cold," he said, "and my fingertips feel numb, like I rubbed them down with sandpaper."

"Totally expected," Director Bowen reassured him. "We think that sensation is the Epistolith tapping into your neural network."

"This diamond can read our minds?" asked James.

"Not quite," Declan clarified. "I remember now. It's not reading your mind, more like interpreting your soul's intent." Declan leaned forward to look at his reflection, stunned when he realized the eyes staring back weren't his own.

"What's wrong with your reflection?" James asked. "It's changing."

Replacing the professor's reflection was a smaller face framed with long, flowing hair. "Nothing's wrong," Declan calmly replied, smiling at the young girl staring back at him. "It's the girl who saved me in Antarctica, the girl I saw trapped inside the crystal."

"It's really her," Director Bowen gasped. "I can't believe it, after all these years."

"You know her?" asked Declan, puzzled.

"Of course, although it's been decades," Director Bowen replied. "When I entered the Sanctuary with Mr. Edison and Mr. Tesla, she was here. The Girl in the Glass. The two of them traveled here many times to see her, however one day she stopped appearing. The two geniuses blamed each other for her disappearance, and their already strained detente quickly devolved into a bitter feud after her absence. Nikola returned many times to no avail, a detriment to his research and even worse, his sanity."

"Explains Mr. Edison's personal lock on the Sanctuary door," James commented. "So, who or what is she?" he wondered.

"I'm not sure how to describe her," Director Bowen admitted, captivated with the petite form staring back through the crystal. "After all, nobody's seen her in decades and yet she's still a little girl. I was convinced she'd been a form of collective hallucination, yet there she is."

"Well, for me it hasn't been nearly that long," Declan remarked. "Pretty blue dress and flowing red hair tied up with a yellow bow, it's her, the Girl in the Glass, whoever she is."

The Director's gaze never left the girl. "She's the reason you're alive," he said, adding, "In unending ice, a stranger saves him."

Tears welled in Declan's eyes. "I remember," he said, leaning forward. "Thank you for saving my life." The girl's face lit up with a wide, cheeky smile. He turned to the Director. "Umm, I'm not sure what to say next."

James turned to the Epistolith and shouted, "Miss, what do you want us to do?"

"Are you kidding?" scolded Declan. "Whatever we need to do next, it certainly doesn't involve yelling at her. She's a little kid, you're going to spook her."

"I'm going to frighten her?" James snapped back. "I'm not the ghost floating inside a giant hunk of glass!"

"Shhh! She's not a ghost," whispered Declan, "she's just a little kid. Just let me handle this," Declan urged. Unsure what to do next, he waved at her. The Girl in the Glass blankly stared back. "Well, I'm out of ideas. I'm open to suggestions from anyone not named James."

"She saved your life in Antarctica for a reason," Bruce offered, "and it wasn't so you could flounder here. Forget about all of us, focus on her."

Declan closed his eyes, struggling to come up with something brilliant to say to the young girl. His thoughts swirled unproductively, he was blanking, until a simple idea crept in. Speak with your mind, not with your mouth. He opened his eyes and smiled, lightly touching his fingers against the crystal. Miss, he thought, just show me how to help you. The Girl in the Glass smiled back and placed her palm against the inside of the glassy barrier. Declan followed her lead, placing his hand flat against hers, and once their palms overlapped the girl disappeared. Confused and disappointed, Declan removed his hand. He tried touching the crystal multiple times, unsure why nothing happened, but the girl was gone.

"Didn't work," Declan said, looking over to James except he wasn't there. Declan whipped around. No sign of the Director or Bruce, either. He was alone.

Chapter 14

April 13, 1939
The Sanctuary of the Epistolith
Clypeate Headquarters
City of Washington, District of Columbia

Suddenly alone on the gangway a confused Declan bellowed "Hello?" into the cavernous Sanctuary, a hollow echo his only response. He peered into the glossy Epistolith looking for answers, but the girl was gone, his own reflection staring back.

Guided by the ceiling's dim glow Declan skirted along the walkway, towards the platform he'd ridden up with his vanished companions. In the twilight he didn't notice the platform's absence until he stepped forward into the abyss, narrowly avoiding a nasty plunge by hooking one arm around the balcony rail. Dangling precipitously over the edge, he summoned every bit of adrenaline-fueled strength to slowly pull himself upright. Heart pounding, he peered into the gap and saw the platform at ground level, several stories down. Confusion bubbled into anger, concluding the others left him behind, and while fumbling with the platform's controls decided they better have a damned good explanation.

Waiting for the platform to climb the wall he scanned the area one last time, calling out for the others, again receiving no answer. On the ride down his thoughts swirled, shifting from his recent abandonment towards his reunion with the Girl in the Glass.

He'd forgotten how she saved his life in Antarctica, alerting him seconds before the ice cracked. And while the details were still foggy, he also remembered how the girl used the opportunity to fiddle with his mind, leaving him to ponder what further mental mischief she'd crafted during their second interaction.

Upon his descent Declan found the lower half of the Sanctuary devoid of light, the glowing orb must've finally burnt out or, as the Director warned, grown unstable and exploded. Either way it meant one less worry, even though his mind was still adrift in a sea of them. Declan blindly crossed the room, flailing in the darkness, weaving erratically until he noticed a dim orange glow illuminating the outline of the Sanctuary door.

Racing across the room as quickly as his weakened legs would carry him, he returned to the vestibule outside the Sanctuary and identified the light source, a kerosene lamp adjacent to a solitary cot. Odd, Declan was certain neither the cot nor lamp were present earlier when they entered the Sanctuary. Initially he thought the cot unoccupied, covered with an empty pile of blankets, until he noticed the mound shift. Declan inched towards the cot, tapped the blankets and said, "Hello?" before retreating to a safer distance.

Declan hoped Embrie would emerge but when the blankets rolled off, he sighed with disappointment, the young woman was not the occupant. He also wasn't facing his greatest irrational fear, a giant rodent with red eyes and yellow teeth, instead it was James who he deemed only marginally better.

Declan, eager to roundly chastise the analyst for abandoning him in the Sanctuary, lost his chance when James sprung up and shouted, "Doc, you're alive! What a relief, I feared the Epistolith gobbled you up for good this time, although Embrie never lost faith. She knew you'd return."

Declan scowled. "Why'd you leave me in the Sanctuary?" he demanded.

James rubbed his eyes and yawned. "I didn't want to risk getting accidentally trapped inside the Sanctuary forever. The door closes automatically after eight hours, and there's only so many vials of Edison's breath."

"Eight hours?" Declan was infuriated. "Ten minutes ago you were next to me on that flimsy gangplank. If you're going to lie, at least make sense," he shouted. "Where's Bruce and the Director? You all disappeared and left me alone!"

"Doc, we didn't leave you behind," James calmly replied. "You're the one who vanished, and that wasn't ten minutes ago, it happened over two weeks ago."

"Why would you say that?" demanded Declan. "I'm far from amused."

"I'm not kidding," James gently persisted. "Wow, they're all gonna be thrilled to see you. And you must be starving!"

"Now I know you're messing with me," Declan snapped back. "I'm still uncomfortably full of cafeteria meatloaf."

"Interesting, for you it's like no time passed," James noted, picking up the lantern. "Come on, let's sort this out in the library," he urged.

"I'm not going anywhere 'til you tell me what's really going on," insisted Declan.

"We'll figure it out in the library, I promise," James repeated, adding, "I'm sure Embrie will be glad to see you."

Dangling Embrie's name proved the carrot necessary to propel the stubborn professor down the tunnel and James, upon reaching the library door, loudly announced, "Look who I found."

While Declan struggled to catch his breath, the young woman peered over the railing along the uppermost bookcase tier. "Be right down," she joyfully squealed.

Bruce jumped up from his chair and ran over. "Nice to see you back, Professor," he said, greeting Declan with a broad smile and vigorous handshake. "I wondered when you might reappear and no worse for the wear," he noted. "As the days stretched on I entertained some wacky notions, wondering if you'd been shrunken or rendered invisible. I wasn't seriously worried, though, I trusted the Girl in the Glass to keep you safe. Even if you were gone fifteen days."

"Fifteen days?" repeated Declan. "James was telling the truth for a change, must've been suffering from a guilty conscience. As you know, he and I have trust issues."

"With James?" Embrie interjected, climbing down the makeshift ladder. "He camped outside the Sanctuary door the entire time, refusing to leave until you returned. If you don't believe me, just smell him."

"I'll pass," Declan said, secretly thankful for James' gesture but unprepared to absolve the analyst's prior transgressions. Before Declan could ask more questions, a muffled ringing interrupted the conversation. "What's making that noise?"

"It's coming from that busted grandfather clock," responded James, "how bizarre."

Embrie approached the clock. "More than you think," she said, "the clock belly phone hasn't rung in forty years." She opened the damaged yet majestic clock tower, hands frozen at 3:29, pulled out an old-fashioned candlestick phone and picked up the receiver. She greeted the caller with a timid "Hello?" and for the next minute didn't speak, only nodding and grunting while all the men guessed at the mysterious caller's identity. Declan didn't have to wait very long to find out because Embrie handed him the phone. "It's for you."

Declan's hand trembled as he gripped the earpiece and leaned in towards the candlestick's transmitter. "Yes?"

he asked, and during several minutes of conversation the professor's contributions were similarly restricted to "mmm-hmms" and "uh-huhs." By the end his face scrunched into a perplexed smile, returning the earpiece to its cradle he said, "It was a pleasure speaking with you as well." He leaned against the clock tower to gather his thoughts before addressing the group. "Prior to that phone call, my most unusual conversation was with a little girl trapped inside an enormous diamond. Now I've spoken with a machine named Alva."

"You lost me," James said, shooting the professor a puzzled look. "You spoke to a machine?"

"Yes, the phone call wasn't from a person," explained Declan. "It came from the machine towers in the Analytical Engine Room. They introduced themselves as Alva and wanted to chat."

James shook his head in disbelief. "How's that possible?"

When Declan shrugged his shoulders, Embrie answered. "The machines speak using an artificial linguistics vocal apparatus, ALVA for short, to express their collective thoughts. All the towers in the Analytical Engine Room function in unison, working together to form a communal mind."

"I'm even more confused," declared James. "You mean those oversized tinker toys think like a brain?"

"Yes, that's exactly what I'm saying," the young woman stated. "The machines form an electronic data intelligence synthesis and operations network. Normally they transmit messages to us through the Builders, this whole time I thought this phone was broken. ALVA must really be excited about the doctor's safe return."

"Let me get this straight," James persisted, desiring further clarification. "Walking through the Analytical Engine Room, we were traveling inside a giant electronic brain?"

Embrie nodded. "You're catching on."

"Not sure what's weirder," James continued. "How normal you make it sound or how unsurprised I am to hear it. Of course artificially intelligent machines, advanced beyond science fiction's craziest ideas, exist down here. Why not? But Alva sounds too twerpy for such a massive system, the towers need a more fitting name, like Big Al. So, what did Big Al have to say?"

"Big Al, really?" Declan sighed his disapproval. "For starters, Alva repeated the same thing Director Bowen said in the Sanctuary, when the Girl in the Glass appeared. In unending ice a stranger saves him. Then Alva told me they've waited a long time to meet me."

"We all have," replied Bruce. "Like I said earlier, your arrival fulfills a prophecy."

"And that's what you truly believe? Somehow going to Antarctica, the land of unending ice, and getting saved by a stranger, the Girl in the Glass, makes me important? That's absurd, your prophecy could've been written about anyone."

"Except it wasn't. George Washington's prophecy, written one hundred and fifty years ago, specifically mentions Declan."

"I assume he didn't include a last name or address, otherwise there'd be no need for all these theatrics. Maybe Washington wrote about some other guy named Declan, you have no reason to believe I'm the proper one. There must be thousands of Declans in the world."

"Twelve thousand, seven hundred, give or take a few dozen," estimated Bruce, "and you're correct, we had no further hints so we tracked them all. Over the decades we've allocated considerable resources identifying the most exceptional Declans, searching out the best candidate to fulfill this prophecy. Unfortunately the clock ran out when Germany sent the *Schwabenland* to Antarctica, the land of unending ice, so we sent our shortlist. We loaded all our best Declan hopefuls aboard the *Milwaukee*."

Fueled by indignant rage, Declan roared, "You and that one," pointing his finger at James, "tricked me out of my lab, because your prophecy mentioned a Declan? This must be a joke" declared the last Declan to board the *Milwaukee,* responding poorly to the unvarnished truth. "Now I remember, the whole lot of us were named Declan, I thought I'd imagined such absurdity. Apparently not."

"We didn't have a choice," Bruce replied.

Declan wasn't swayed. "You sick bastards ruined my life because of my name. Haven't any of you read Shakespeare, a rose by any other name? They're meaningless labels!" the professor shouted. "You think I'm important because my parents couldn't think of a less stereotypical Irish name? I know the *Valencia* sank, only stupid luck saved me from joining the rest of the Declans at the bottom of the Atlantic."

"Your fate never involved luck," Bruce asserted, carefully selecting his words. "Clearly you are the Declan we hoped to find. You're the only one who made the choices leading you here. From the moment we met, you chose to accept our offer, some Declans never made it beyond that point. The trip to Antarctica, the land of unending ice, wasn't only about fulfilling a prophecy, it was our chance to find our Declan. It was always going to be you."

"How dare you…" began Declan, his heated response cut short when the room began spinning. He leaned heavily against the clock tower until his body slumped against it, eyes rolling back as he crumpled to the ground. Before anyone could react Declan's head struck the clock tower's concrete pedestal, and under his limp body flowed an expanding puddle of blood. The unconscious professor immediately retched twice, adding a pile of barely digested meatloaf and glazed carrots to the crimson pool.

"Quick! He needs help!" Embrie shouted. "He'll bleed to death."

"Drowning in regurgitated cuisine seems the bigger threat," James said, rolling the professor onto his side. "It'd be tough to exsanguinate from a nosebleed."

Bruce walked over, surprisingly calm. "I expected something dramatic, though I would have preferred less expulsion of bodily fluids. Good thing Director Bowen isn't here, he can't stomach the sight of blood. We'd be dealing with two knocked-out individuals."

Embrie dragged Declan's body away from the mess, using her hands to wipe off his face so she could survey the damage. "James is right, a nosebleed, except there's also a deep gouge on his scalp." She stood, wiping bloody goo off her hands and onto her skirt, using it like a dishtowel. "I'm going back to the house to retrieve our first aid kit." She pointed at James and said, "Apply pressure to his wound," then instructed Bruce to "find something sturdy enough to carry Declan back to the house." Without waiting for responses she dashed into the Analytical Engine Room.

"That gal's quite a firecracker," James noted, using his military jacket as a compress. "Now, Bruce, what did you mean, you were expecting something…"

James was interrupted mid-thought when Declan bolted upright, eyes wide open with a cold, blank stare. "Heed this warning!" barked the scientist, rising from the ground like a marionette puppet controlled by invisible strings, limbs flaccid and dangling. "The men who arrived in the land of perpetual ice, wearing twisted crosses on their sleeves, found something of great value. Action needs to be taken."

"Doc, stop prattling for a moment and hold still," requested James, trying to apply pressure to Declan's scalp despite his unpredictable flailing. When this didn't work James attempted to wipe off the blood dripping down the professor's face, instead smearing it all over, making Declan's face look like a ripe tomato. "Embrie's not gonna be happy."

"Silence!" the professor bellowed. "My time is short. The men of the twisted cross possess ancient treasures, obtained through wicked means, filled with secret wisdom beyond mankind's imagination. The opportunity to stop them dwindles rapidly. They traveled to the land of unending ice for one reason, to recover a remarkable artifact, a relic of the ancients, an Axyn Kirox. Its importance cannot be overestimated, the Axyn Kirox is a rare and extremely important tool, unlocking knowledge capable of unspeakable power."

James wanted to ask questions but Declan's empty, trance-like stare cut right through him, giving him the willies and guaranteeing no further interruptions.

"Thankfully these men are delayed," continued the professor. "No longer possessing their biological conduit, their ability to translate the information is hindered. They are resourceful, however, and are on the verge of discovering an alternate solution. When this happens, they will possess everything they need to bring nations to their knees, twist the fabric of reality and extinct life as we know it. Without your help, there is no future" Declan concluded before once again collapsing to the floor.

Chapter 15

April 13, 1939
Nancy's Place
Clypeate Headquarters

Declan woke to a tender nose, buzzing ears and a wicked headache. He opened his eyes and the fuzzy outlines of James and Embrie hovered above, his head propped on a pillow and body splayed out on a couch. "What happened?" the groggy professor asked, flailing his arms in an unsuccessful attempt to sit.

"Relax," Embrie whispered, sitting beside him on the couch. "You're safe, back at the house. We're just glad you're okay." Despite the buzzing in his ears Declan found Embrie's voice soothing, and he calmed down further when she gently stroked his hand and asked, "Is there anything we can do to help?"

Declan stopped struggling and shook his head. "I just need a moment to collect my thoughts." While the ringing sounds dissipated his vision lagged, unable to focus with colors dull and muted. All except Embrie's emerald eyes, the most wonderfully resplendent hue he'd ever seen. Embrie's breath tickling his neck erased all hope of decorum, and instead of a well-formulated response he gushed "Wow, you're beautiful."

Thankfully his indiscretion only reached the young woman's ears and no further, and despite ostensibly brushing off the remark as confused mumblings her subtle smile suggested otherwise. Fighting to regain control over his foggy, disinhibited mind, Declan suffered further embarrassment when he felt Embrie's hand interlaced with his own. He released her hand, hoping she wasn't repulsed by his impropriety, then resumed his efforts to push himself vertical.

"Let me help you," offered James, extending his arms.

"No, no, I'm fine," protested Declan. "But thank you," he graciously added, still rubbing his bleary eyes. "Did anybody catch the license plate on that bus?" the professor asked, unsure how he arrived in the parlor room of Nancy's Place.

"Glad to see you're coming around," a voice boomed and Declan turned to see Director Bowen's blurry shape sitting in a nearby chair.

"Though his noggin's wiring must've loosened," James commented, patting the professor on the shoulder, "because he's not typically this witty. You gave me and Bruce a good scare, Doc, turning paler than a ghost before collapsing and splatting on the floor. Even crazier is when you stood up again, bursting into an eloquent soliloquy worthy of Hamlet."

"Preposterous," asserted Declan. "I would certainly remember such dramatic tidings, and I haven't an inkling. I do recall, however, all my senses scrambling, suddenly I couldn't hear or see anything. It's hard to imagine I had anything intelligent to share."

"Normally I'd agree," James said, "except there you were, obviously unconscious and yet we couldn't shut you up. You fired on all cylinders until you didn't, dropping again and this time writhing on the ground like you landed on a live wire. Growing up my dog had seizures, terrible ones, and you flopping around looked infinitely worse."

"Explains why my thoughts are swirling," Declan said, gently pressing on his bandaged scalp, "and my exterior didn't fare much better." He touched the spot where his head met ground and screeched, "Yow!" retracting his hand. "Not messing with my bandages again, that'll smart for a while," he remarked, leaning back into the plush couch. "Last thing I remember we were in the library, how'd I get here?"

"Bruce built a makeshift stretcher, proper and sturdy," began James, "but you were too floppy, like trying to balance grape jelly on a toothpick. You rolled off more times than I'll admit, though you were already banged up so badly I doubt we made things worse. In the end I carried you," James admitted. "Slung you over my shoulder like Santa's sack."

"Explains a lot," snapped Declan, massaging his sore neck.

"James spent two weeks on a cot waiting for your return," Embrie reminded him, "and then peeved the Builders by carrying your unsanitary drippings through the Analytical Engine room. He's the reason you're resting on a couch and not still on the library floor."

"Thank you, James," the professor sheepishly expressed his gratitude, adding, "even if more neck support would've been nice."

"We're all very grateful," Director Bowen declared before telling Declan, "all that really matters is you're alive, conscious and talking. I apologize for not being there for your arrival, but I've been busy planning for what comes next and, frankly, everyone's fortunate I missed the less savory elements. As for your attire," remarked the Director, scrunching his forehead, "interesting choice."

Declan looked down, his baggy military uniform replaced with a frilly pink bathrobe. "Don't know, and I'm afraid to ask."

"Nothing tawdry," James reassured them, selecting cookies from a piled-high plate. "Doc's uniform was covered with so much blood and undigested food it made him slipperier than a politician, and on short notice the options were slim. He looked a pitiful mess, the robe is a blessing."

Another familiar voice chimed in, "And the robe does the professor more justice than the flour sack we initially tried." Bruce entered the parlor, grinning broadly. "Glad to see you awake, we're excited to catch up, except…" Bruce paused to sniff his hands. "Maybe my mind's playing tricks, but I've washed my hands and face three times and I still smell pungent cheese. Last time I even put a little soap up my nose. Bad idea, in case you wondered." He sniffed his hands again and grimaced. "I'm going back for one last soaping," Bruce decided, circling back to the washroom, adding, "don't start without me, I'll be snappy."

"Good luck," James offered before turning to Declan with a devilish grin. "While soaking up the mess in the library," he divulged, "I inadvertently used a stack of Ben Franklin's original letters. I couldn't help reading a few, and now I'll never think of old Ben's aphorism 'early to bed, early to rise' in the same way. I always pictured him as the old guy on the hundred-dollar bill, but in his younger days he was quite a virile stallion. I thought today's politicians were randy horndogs, they're mere amateurs. Ben took the term 'founding father' quite literally, also drew out some diagrams, more explicit than the Kama Sutra. Going to take some time and even more alcohol to forget the images baked into my brain."

"Disturbing," Declan groaned. "Though what you said, images in the brain, gives me an idea. I wonder," he said, closing his eyes, mumbling to himself until proudly announcing, "yes, got it. I understand why my vision is blurry. My eyes work perfectly fine, problem is they're competing with pictures flashing inside my head."

James shot a puzzled look. "Now I'm certain you've got brain damage, you're not making a lick of sense."

"No, no!" shouted Bruce, racing back to the parlor, hands dripping wet. "Professor Riordan, please elaborate."

"In Antarctica, when the Girl in the Glass saved me, she used the opportunity to fill my mind with information. My two-week vanishing act in the Sanctuary was important, even necessary, so she could unpack my brain. That's why my head's flooded with bizarre images."

"Extraordinary," the Director remarked, nodding his assent. "In Antarctica she burdened you with a cognitive load, presumably beyond what human minds can handle, and here in our Sanctuary, resumed the process. Rendering you unconscious may have been a protective mechanism, to save your neurons, although the expulsion of foodstuffs and seizures were likely unintended consequences. Overall, you handled the onslaught better than I hoped."

Declan wasn't pleased. "You knew this could happen? You should have warned me."

"You misunderstand," the Director swiftly clarified, "General Washington's little red diary only paints with broad strokes, no fine details. The prophecies and stories don't exactly spell out the future, they function more like an outline. I knew only the prophesied Declan could tolerate the process, and since your brain isn't oozing out your nose, I'd say we have confirmation. You're the one."

"Don't sidestep the issue," snapped Declan. "I'm tired of this *Christmas Carol* treatment, berating us with stories of past and present, how about you skip ahead and share with us the future?"

"That would be of tremendous help," agreed James.

"Never," Director Bowen sternly refused. "Discussing the future creates causal loops, knowing what'll happen risks you changing it. This happened once, when Tobias Lear read the journal and learned his own fate. He altered the future, believing his actions were an altruistic sacrifice, instead they put into motion the events leading to the Obturavi's wanton attack on our Clypeate."

"Then what makes you so important?" Declan pressed. "Why are you allowed to know?"

"General Washington's journal only mentions me once," the Director revealed, "to say I will lead the Clypeate. That's why Mr. Tesla and Mr. Edison asked me to accompany them into the Sanctuary, and how I became Commander of the Clypeate and guardian of the journal. It's because I'm otherwise irrelevant, a bit player, the Rosencrantz and Guildenstern to your Hamlet. My role is to steer you towards the future without influencing the outcome."

"Then please," Declan pleaded, "just tell us what you can."

"Fair enough," the Director conceded, "though I must tread lightly. Your journey is not complete, I can only share what's already transpired. When the Girl prompted you to touch the Epistolith in Antarctica, she not only saved your life, she passed along an enormous load of information. She interrupted the transfer, cut it short so you could be rescued, leaving you with a Louvre's worth of images haphazardly shoved into your subconscious."

Declan's anger morphed, replaced by intrigued acceptance. "A perfect explanation for how I've felt, why my thoughts have swirled in a disorganized mess, like a million pieces from a thousand different jigsaw puzzles jumbled into a single pile."

"Did she accomplish her objective?" asked the Director. "Are the puzzles complete?"

Declan clenched his eyelids shut. "No, not yet. The images scrolling through my mind are still coalescing. The Girl in the Glass finished what she started in Antarctica, all the necessary pieces are floating inside my head. My mind reels at the volume, not a terribly comfortable sensation, like having a set of encyclopedias rammed up my nose. Anything in Washington's journal suggest how long this feeling might last?"

"No," admitted the Director, "and it'd be unfair to provide you with an arbitrary, overly optimistic timeline. Given your important role, I imagine you'll feel better when your mind finishes unpacking and organizing the information, and the evidence points to a rapid conclusion. The Girl in the Glass seems eager to share this information as quickly as possible. I'd venture she's pushing the limits of what organic tissue can handle, the inconvenient limitations of carbon-based life."

"Professor, you're handling the burden amazingly," lauded Bruce, "by now anyone else's neurons would be a smoldering pile of ash. I won't pretend to know what storm rages inside your head, however I'm roundly impressed by your mental fortitude."

"I only hope what she shoved into my brain is worthwhile," replied Declan, "although it's also nice knowing the wonkiness I've felt since Antarctica has a concrete explanation. Even if I still have difficulty believing any of this is possible, or real, at least the rest of you are here to share my hallucination."

"Insanity loves company?" ribbed James. "You won't get an argument from me, Doc, this rabbit hole gets deeper with every revelation. Just one question, and I only ask because my job has trained me to be suspicious of everyone," he prefaced his remark. "I wonder why everyone gives the Girl in the Glass so much leeway. How do we know her intentions are benevolent, what if she's leading us astray?"

"Skepticism is healthy," Bruce replied, "and the Girl in the Glass deserves an explanation. She isn't a real person, she's a visual manifestation of the Epistolith, a non-threatening projection. Hesperus led us to the Epistolith in order to help mankind elevate our species, and she is how the stone chooses to make us comfortable interacting with it."

"A face for something faceless," Declan said, crossing and uncrossing his legs, struggling to get comfortable in the pink robe. "I agree with Bruce, despite her questionable tactics I believe her intentions are pure. However, my interactions with her also leave me certain there's more to her than a mirage. I know this sounds illogical, but she feels very real to me, and you can't convince me otherwise."

"You won't get an argument from me," the Director reassured him, "all that matters is she continues to guide you, help your mind unlock the information crammed inside."

"She is," disclosed the professor, "even now I feel her influence, shielding me from the tempest raging below my conscious mind." He looked at Embrie and smiled. "She's wrapped my mind inside a protective chrysalis, and when it breaks free this myopic caterpillar will transform into a prescient butterfly."

"Now you're waxing poetic" noted James. "Either that crystal really scrambled you up good, or" he teased, "perhaps it's the influence of the amiable Miss Powell?"

Declan looked down at his hand, once again entwined with Embrie's. "I'm sorry, I didn't realize..." he stammered. Embrie yanked her hand away, cheeks ablaze in the awkward silence following the implied impropriety.

Mercifully, Ms. Elliott arrived and broke the tension. "Professor Riordan, we need to address your nutritional requirements. You haven't eaten a proper meal in weeks, you must be starving. What can I make you?" she offered.

"Nothing, thank you," Declan replied, "I'm not particularly hungry, from my standpoint I was gone for a split second. I'm perfectly fine," he said, attempting to prove his point by standing, quickly realizing he'd overestimated his physical prowess as his ears rang and vision grayed. He flopped back onto the couch. "Although, now that you mention it, I'm feeling a bit parched and a tad woozy. I could really use a drink, preferably with a kick."

"I'd offer you scotch, except your cognitive state is already significantly altered. How about a soda pop instead?" Ms. Elliott suggested.

"Sounds great," Declan nodded, "but could you add some extra sugar? In fact, just heap it in there. Please."

"Into your soda?" she replied, puzzled by the notion. "I'll see what I can do," Ms. Elliott said, heading off to process Declan's peculiar request. When the older woman returned, Declan was standing again, albeit more cautiously, with James and Bruce positioned within professor-catching range.

She placed the tray on the table. "I didn't want to overdo it," she said, explaining why the soda bottle was accompanied by a sugar bowl. There was also a small plate stacked with warm corn muffins. "You said you weren't hungry, though you don't need an appetite to be tempted by freshly baked treats."

"Fair enough," he chuckled, "and thank you for not listening to me, these muffins look amazing." Declan plunked four sugar cubes into the soda pop, swirling the bottle around as he cleared his plate, washing the muffins down with the syrupy sludge. While the others looked on with bewildered fascination, the professor beamed. "That was perfect, exactly what I needed to…" Declan slapped his hands over his mouth but, it was too late, his comment interrupted by a throaty, wet belch. Mortified to exhibit such crass failings in front of Embrie, he implored the young woman, "I'm so sorry...burp...please forgive me... burp...this is unacceptable...burp."

Without a word, she stood, approached the professor and cupped his cheeks. With as serious an expression as she could muster, she said, "I think you've earned a burp or two. Or four," she said, cracking a smile that turned into a giggle, and soon they were all laughing, even Declan.

Director Bowen rose. "And with that heartwarming sentiment, my mission down here is complete," he declared, walking towards the front door. "Gentlemen, please escort me out."

They complied, Bruce and James on either side of Declan, the professor resisting help despite his unsteady, weakened legs threatening to reacquaint his face with the floor. After a slow, cautious trek through the Research Hall and Lincoln's Tunnel the Director paused in the Room of the Honored. This time Declan's eyes barely registered the unique decor. Having seen the Clypeate's other unimaginable treasures, a roomful of antique weapons and priceless artifacts blended into the scenery. Instead, Declan focused his attention on the Director.

Director Bowen noticed the professor's brooding gaze and asked, "Is there a problem, Doctor Riordan?"

"Maybe. What did you mean, your mission is done?" challenged Declan. "Is this goodbye? Because I still don't know what the Girl in the Glass is doing inside my head, and you're the person with the most clues."

"Not goodbye. For now, my role draws me elsewhere, but I'm leaving you in excellent hands," the Director reassured him, "inside and outside your brain. I'm confident Bruce can meet any challenges, and James has proven himself a worthy addition to the Clypeate. As for you,

Doctor Riordan, I haven't a single doubt you're the man we've waited many years to find." The Director extended his hand, Declan accepted. "Just remember, trust your instincts and keep an open mind. Our Universe is far more interesting and improbable than physics equations suggest."

"I'm realizing normal is boring," replied Declan, "and I'm trying to think less provincially."

"That's the spirit," lauded Director Bowen, reaching into his pocket. He retrieved the golden key and turned to Bruce. "Contact me when the time is right, no sooner. We must play our hand with great skill. The fate of humanity rests in our success," the Director impressed upon Bruce, presenting him with the key. "I entrust you with this honor and burden, and don't worry," he added with a subtle grin, "I will teach you the key settings for each lock, now that I remember and tested them all."

"This is a great honor, sir," Bruce responded, gingerly cradling the long, ornate key. "I won't let you down."

Director Bowen extended his hand. "At the risk of repeating myself, Commander Kingston, I am confident you will serve the Clypeate well."

Bruce shook the Director's hand, then addressed them all. "Time to close shop for the evening. Professor, you've adjusted admirably to everything thrown at you, and James, I couldn't be happier to have you as a member of my team. As for what's next, we've all earned a break and a proper meal, which is why we're meeting again in two hours for a celebratory dinner. But first, both of you deserve a hot shower and proper clothing, the professor looks like a tart and James smells worse than he looks. Dinner will be a couple blocks down the street at the Willard Hotel. Do you know how to get there?"

"The Willard, across from the Treasury Building?" James clarified. "Of course, it's the most upscale hotel in the District. Getting there won't be a problem, though I've never stepped inside. I can't afford a glass of tap water in that place."

"No longer an issue," Director Bowen said. "Simply give your names at the front desk and you'll be escorted to your rooms. They're already stocked with suitable clothing, toiletries, and other sundries. You'll both wildly benefit from a hot shower, preferably with a lot of soap and scrubbing. I need to discuss logistics with Bruce before dinner, so we'll meet you there. And please be prompt, the maître d' isn't afraid to give away tables."

"Hold on, sir," James interrupted, "I don't want to appear ungrateful, but I already have an apartment."

The Director lowered his glasses. "You're working under the assumption that I made the room arrangements, or the dinner reservations. ALVA, the roomful of analytical machines, set all this up while the doctor recuperated on the couch. ALVA knows time is short and keeping both of you nearby limits wasted time. It's the same reason why there's a beautiful underground home for Miss Powell and Ms. Elliott."

Both men silently processed the information while navigating their way out of the Navy Building, James offering his sullied military jacket to partially cover Declan's pink, flowing robe. Declan happily accepted, and thankfully, it was late enough the hallways were only occupied by the evening's cleaning crew and security detail, resulting in far fewer stares and derisive catcalls. Once outside, the professor forgot about his attire, enthralled with the setting sun, and once they'd crossed the parking lot and reached the sidewalk, Declan stopped.

"I'd lost all hope of ever seeing the outside world again," Declan remarked, tears of joy running down his cheeks.

"I'm truly sorry, Doc," James apologized, patting Declan on the back. "We can't change the past, but we certainly can determine our future. Think about how far you've come," suggested James. "Your freedom is restored, and you've been given the most amazing opportunity ever, to be a part of something bigger. No more petri dishes or closet offices. You're the Clypeate's best hope at stopping the Nazis and those Obturavi assholes, which means you're not only in control of your own destiny, you now possess the power to shape all of humanity's future."

Declan quietly mulled over James' assertions. "I hadn't thought about it that way," he mused, "so much responsibility, I don't know if I can handle it."

"Doc, I don't envy the burden placed on you, but I've never met anyone better equipped to handle the load," James asserted. "And I'm here to help you."

"Give me a moment," Declan said, laughing so heartily he needed to catch his breath. "I'll be able to start walking again as soon as you stop blowing smoke up my ass." James chuckled alongside the professor and, with both men's mood vastly improved, the pair crossed Constitution Avenue and cut through the Ellipse, passing the White House on their way to the Willard Hotel. Before entering the elegant and historic hotel, Declan turned around and looked back at the Washington Monument towering above the cityscape. "I still can't believe what we've seen," he commented, "what's hidden beneath our nation's capital. As much as I still dislike you, I'm glad we're sharing this adventure together. It's nice not feeling like the only naive rube."

James nodded in agreement, pleased his efforts to slowly chip away at the professor's disdain showed progress. "With your brains and my charm, what could go wrong?"

Declan looked at their outfits. "For starters, the hotel staff is going to have questions. I'm wearing a bloodied jacket and pink robe, and you smell worse than a rotting corpse."

"No worries, Doc. When you stay at a place as exclusive as the Willard, it's all about your attitude," James explained. "While I've never experienced this kind of luxury before, as long as we act like we belong, everything will be fine. You pay a lot of money so people will leave you alone and not ask questions. I wish I smelled even worse."

Like James predicted, they had no trouble procuring their rooms, adjoining suites on the top floor, so richly furnished French palaces would weep in envy. Knowing he'd sully any surface he touched, Declan beelined it for his bathroom. Even though months had passed since his last hot shower, he was still astonished how long the water running off his body remained dark gray as it swirled into the drain. Next, he shaved off his beard, requiring many expletives to cajole a razor through inches of crusted, tangled scruff. A clean-shaven face earned the professor a few nicks but felt like a miracle, although all hygienic wonders paled in comparison to the joy of a flushable toilet.

The greatest highlight of his evening, however, arrived when Director Bowen and Bruce were accompanied by Embrie. She wore a simple yet elegant scarlet dress, and sitting across from her required Declan's constant effort to avoid staring at her the entire meal. Dinner conversation remained light and topical, never touching upon the amazing wonders buried less than one thousand yards away. At one point, Embrie leaned across the table and whispered, "You cleaned up very nicely, and your suit is far more flattering than my bathrobe."

"Hey, you'd be amazed how many marriage proposals I got wearing that robe," replied Declan, joking "I may not want to return it too quickly," sending them both into giggling fits. Whether it was the company, or because he couldn't remember eating such a delicious meal, the evening concluded sooner than he hoped.

Declan offered to walk Embrie back to the Navy and Munitions Building, so he was disheartened when she politely declined his offer. "Director Bowen and Commander Kingston will be sufficient protection this evening," she said, though his mood substantially improved when she leaned into his ear and whispered, "and I'll see you in the morning," casting a small but perceptible wink in his direction.

Before Director Bowen finally headed home that evening, he detoured back to his office at the Naval Research Labs. Although midnight had long passed, this final task could not wait for the prying rays of daylight. The Director settled into his chair, a generous pour of twenty-five-year-old scotch positioned next to the secret safe now resting atop his desk, recently extricated from behind the bathroom mirror. He opened the safe, doused the contents with scotch, then tossed in a match. Once the thick stack of papers caught fire he reached inside his briefcase and pulled out Washington's red leather journal, opening to a specific page. "No loose ends," he muttered, using the flames to light a very old cigar he'd saved for this very occasion.

Chapter 16

George Washington's personal diary
Journal Entry #14

November 5, 1783
Rockingham, New Jersey

Two nights ago an old friend visited, and despite the many years since our last encounter I immediately recognized Hesperus, his appearance youthful and unchanged. I used this opportunity to thank him for providing assistance throughout the War for Independence, on many occasions his prescient wisdom and guidance saved my troops from certain defeat.

On this night Hesperus arrived not to celebrate our new nation's victory, rather he'd come to stamp out the earliest tinders of suspicion stoked by my adversaries, dousing them before they ignited into uncontrollable flames of doubt.

Even as the ink dried on the Treaty of Paris and the war mercifully receded from my mind, people called me a hero, my name bandied about as a potential leader for this foundling nation. Not everyone agrees with this plan and so my detractors have settled into nearby Princeton, where the Continental Congress convenes, to further their own agendas. My adversaries actively disparage me with salacious rumors, most are frivolous and meritless, however some suggest my good fortune and military prowess stem from supernatural dealings. Whispers I'd trained as a Warlock, or perhaps I'd struck a deal with the Devil, circulate about the town.

Thankfully Hesperus prepared me for the most egregious and emboldened attack upon my reputation to date, the threat arriving last evening on my doorstep. Without warning several influential Continental Congress legislators appeared at my Rockingham lodgings, roundly interrogating me regarding some inexplicable events transpiring during the war. I ascribed my good fortune to Providence, proof our Heavenly Father believed in our struggle for independence, protecting and guiding us, yet they were not satisfied. I hoped as Christian men this argument would suffice, though no credence was given to Divine Intervention. Instead these men pelted me with examples of my exceptionality, and though I desperately wished to credit my terrestrial benefactor I silently listened to their charges.

First, they pointed to my miraculous retreat from Brooklyn Heights, where the entirety of our forces were surrounded by British positions. Defeat there would have surely sounded the death knell for our short-lived rebellion, yet that night a fortuitous blanket of fog suddenly appeared, allowing my entire command to safely cross the East River to the Isle of Manhattan. Next, they questioned circumstances surrounding the Battle of the Clouds transpiring near Philadelphia, when a preternaturally sudden, fierce rainstorm halted engagement with overwhelming British forces, preventing a catastrophic loss of men and supplies. Finally, these men probed my heroic behavior at the Battle of Princeton, wondering if I were under some protective spell when I rallied the troops by riding ahead of them, within thirty yards of enemy lines, rifles firing upon me the entire time.

This hearsay, presented to me as evidence, came mainly from stories circulated amongst the troops, descriptions of my epic bravery and the numerous times I'd taken impossible risks which would have spelled certain death for other men. Also, they'd heard rumors how prior to all such divine interventions I'd been seen trailing off into the woods alone, accompanied only by a single blue light. To allay these fears I offered proof that no such magical or diabolical entanglements existed in the form of a demonstrable act, one which my benefactor Hesperus described to me only hours earlier. I explained these conjurings of light as mistaken interpretations of will-o'-the-wisps, the glowing specters which emanate from marshy riverbanks.

Earlier this evening I fulfilled my promise and quelled these disparaging remarks. I enlisted the assistance of my good friend, Thomas Paine, and together we poked through the mud of the Millstone River. Just as Hesperus predicted, our efforts released flammable gases and our torches ignited blue flames, assuredly silencing any concerns regarding my heavenly loyalties. Already I feel the weight of these allegations lifted, my future secured, and while this is a momentous occasion there are twinges of sadness as I wonder if I will ever see Hesperus again.

Before he left Hesperus concluded with one final statement, which I feel he added more to protect my legacy than to advance any of his inscrutable agendas. He told me someday this journal will cease being an asset and become a dangerous liability. Once all the prophecies and foretellings contained within are met, it required proper handling. I leave this decision to you, faithful guardian of this journal, to decide when this day has arrived and carry out my final command.

"Here's to you, General Washington," the Director said, raising his glass and taking a sip before tossing the founding father's secret journal into the flames. "To date every prophecy fulfilled, lastly procuring the Declan. I have set the final prophecy into motion, no need for this journal to linger, for what comes next remains unknown to men." He waited for the embers to die down before shutting the safe, pushing it out his office window, and under the cover of inky darkness rolling it down the hill until the shiny metal box disappeared beneath murky Potomac waters.

Chapter 17

April 14, 1939
Willard Hotel
1401 Pennsylvania Avenue
District of Columbia, City of Washington

The next morning, Declan watched the sun rise while sipping his third mug of coffee, courtesy of the suite's fully stocked kitchenette. He'd been awake for hours, unaccustomed to soft bedding, he drowned in a sea of pillows during the rare times he wasn't getting jarred awake by unfamiliar city sounds. He made good use of his insomnia, however, spending the wakeful hours replaying Miss Powell's comments, contemplating whether her kind words stemmed from politeness or something more.

James occupied the adjoining suite, so Declan wasn't surprised by impatient knocking on the door separating their rooms. "Morning Doc, I'm here!" an exuberant James announced, barging into Declan's room wearing a Navy officer's crisp dress blues. He settled onto an elegant sofa and declared, "These rooms are enormous. I knew this hotel was classy, but I didn't expect a separate room for the bed."

"Most people call it a bedroom," Declan snidely remarked, "and we have them because these aren't regular rooms, we have suites. Very nice suites, which must cost a king's ransom. I hope nobody's expecting us to pay the bill."

James chuckled. "I knew you weren't listening at dinner, distracted by one of our dining companions, perhaps. Director Bowen told us the Clypeate's covering everything, so charge whatever we need to our rooms and enjoy ourselves. I'm happy to oblige, this place is way nicer than my apartment," he stated, "my whole month's rent wouldn't pay for one night."

Declan ignored James' comments about the prior evening's dinner, mortified his fixation on Embrie was so obvious. Instead, he scoffed, "No wonder you're so chipper, you won an all-expenses-paid vacation."

"This isn't about the money," asserted James, "don't you feel the energy, the enthusiasm, because I do. Even if the details are still fuzzy, we're part of something bigger than us, and I'm excited to find out what comes next. Aren't you?"

"Of course," agreed Declan, impressed by James' sincerity. "Personally, I'm looking forward to finding out what the Girl in the Glass shoved in my brain," he added, walking over to a particularly well-stocked bookcase. "I am, however, feeling less enthusiastic about the Clypeate's lack of boundaries." He ran his finger along the book spines, shelf after shelf, and said, "These are all mine, from my apartment and campus office. How'd they manage such a feat? Aren't you even the littlest bit disturbed?"

"Not really," James responded, shaking his head. "After traveling all around the country collecting Declans, I know the Clypeate's got vast resources. Don't worry, my room's also full of my own stuff, they're obviously keen on making us comfortable."

"Well-kept prisoners in our gilded cages," remarked Declan, noting his entire rock collection atop the dresser, arranged the way he liked, according to the Mohs hardness scale.

"Now you're overthinking it, Doc," James said. "Bruce is a standup guy, and Director Bowen has been a supportive and competent boss. Plus, he knew my parents before their accident," he noted, voice trailing off, quickly clarifying, "and just so you know, that's not how I landed this assignment."

"No explanation required," Declan replied, inspecting a small collection of framed pictures retrieved from his apartment, each a reminder of happier times with his own parents. When their only child left the ancestral farm for college his parents struggled to understand, and over the years telephoned progressively less until now it was one or two strained conversations a year. He felt occasional pangs of guilt, but they lived in entirely different worlds, his parents cared as much about his research as he did about their crop yields. Sadly, these paltry snapshots encompassed the vast majority of his personal effects. "And I'm sorry about your parents."

"Thanks," James said, "they were the best. Investigators never figured out what happened. At least it was quick. Now, on a lighter note, how about you get ready so we can head over to the Navy Building. Check in your closet, see what kinda wardrobe you've got, because mine came with a hefty promotion." James stood, looking over his freshly pressed officer's uniform in the mirror. "The bars and stars on this jacket carry the rank of vice admiral. I thought someone made a mistake, but the attached ID badge reads Vice Admiral James Fischer."

"No idea what that means. I'm a civilian, remember?" Declan reminded James. "For me, military ranks are like how the truth is for you, something elusive."

"Doc, I thought we were past that," James countered, feigning a pained expression. "For context, Director Bowen is a rear admiral, and it took an entire career of hard work to reach his rank. I'm one rank higher. It's a hoot, though I feel like I'm wearing a Halloween costume. Guess they don't want our authority questioned or challenged, I'll outrank nearly everyone we encounter."

"Makes sense," Declan muttered, fumbling through his fully stocked closet, options ranging from casual street attire to Navy formalwear. "As it turns out, you don't outrank me," he said, reading his own badge. "I'm now Vice

Admiral Declan Riordan, PhD. Ironic, from prisoner to admiral in one night. Wish tenure worked that way," he quipped, his UCLA faculty photo now affixed to his Navy ID.

"Congratulations on your recent enlistment," James shouted from the other room, "although it means no professor's tweed for you. You'll have to wear your Navy uniform."

Declan held up the officer's jacket and decided, "This is sharp looking, I'll make it work. Didn't expect I'd ever wear one of these," he confessed, never considering a military career due to an utter disinterest in comradery and rigid avoidance of conflict, the only glaring exception being his desire to rip James a new breathing hole upon reuniting in Dante's Inferno.

After several quiet minutes, James yelled, "What's taking so long? We're meeting Bruce in one hour, so you gotta hurry up. Remember, in the military if you aren't fifteen minutes early, you're late."

"I know," Declan huffed, while his animosity towards the analyst had improved with rest and nourishment, he still found James a moderate nuisance. "I'm just looking for my own clothes. I'm confused, everything else from my apartment is in this suite, but nothing in the closet is mine."

"I suppose they didn't want you standing out," suggested James, "most people don't walk around the Navy Building with ink-stained pockets and chalk dust all over their sleeves. I've seen what you think is acceptable clothing, you'd stick out like a monkey in a flock of sheep."

"Is that meant to be an insult?" Declan retorted, "because that's not even an acceptable metaphor."

"But am I wrong?" James responded, smiling triumphantly. "Find me when you're ready, I'll be next door, practicing my official Vice Admiral Fischer voice." As James headed back to his own room, he jested, "Remember to bring along your sweetheart's robe!"

Declan tried to defend himself. "There's nothing going on between us…"

"Don't argue against the truth," interjected James, "I watched the two of you googly-eyeing each other during dinner. She's all yours, no challenge from me. She's a little too damsel in distress for my taste, and I don't mix business with pleasure."

James shut the connecting door, leaving Declan in relative peace. Silence remained elusive, however, James practicing a range of commanding and authoritative tones, all carrying through their shared wall. This didn't bother Declan as much as James' uncanny ability to make astute observations, not surprising given his job analyzing data, although Declan felt vulnerable knowing his life was so easily dissected.

Declan showered, dressed and was ready to leave twenty minutes later, even if he felt ridiculous in his new attire. His pants and suit jacket were fitted to his pre-Antarctic weight, making them almost as baggy and unflattering as those he'd commandeered from Officer Burke's men. Even before Dante's Inferno, the oceanic voyage ravaged his physique, nauseating sea swells and inedible meals of hardtack and canned rations depleted his fat stores and cannibalized his muscle. Distressed to find his once pulpy biceps atrophied into ligamentous strands, the professor, who'd never been athletic but exercised regularly, promised himself "Pushups. Lots of pushups."

Ten minutes later, while strutting through the Willard lobby, James commented, "We make the dapper pair."

"I feel like a ridiculous fraud," Declan replied. "I don't know the first thing about being in the military, and now I'm a high-ranking officer. Why couldn't they make us janitors? Nobody questions the janitor."

James stopped and reprimanded the professor. "Cut that talk out, Doc. You survived a top-secret mission where you surveilled and infiltrated an enemy position," he reminded Declan. "There are officers wearing lots more ribbons who've never seen as much action as you. So even if you don't feel like you deserve the honor yet, just fake it 'til you make it. And if the last few days are any indicator of what's in store, I think you'll be feeling like you earned it soon enough." James reached over and straightened Declan's jacket. "Although you will need to eat more and throw up less if your uniform is ever going to properly fit."

Five minutes into the walk, having navigated past the White House and towards the Navy Building, Declan's perspiration already soaked through his clothes. He noted James blotting the sweat off his face and asked, "It's not even eight in the morning. Is it always this hot and humid?"

"Only from Spring to Fall," James replied, "and around here, they call this weather muggy. Day or night, you sweat, standing still."

The Navy Building's air-conditioned lobby provided some relief, although passing through the checkpoint with armed guards kept the sweat dripping down Declan's forehead. He fidgeted and looked nervous, causing the stern guard examining his badge to pause longer than usual, further increasing the professor's visible agitation. When the guard finally waved him ahead, Declan audibly sighed with relief, garnering a quizzical look from all the guards. Needing to quickly cover up his indiscretion, the professor pulled out his handkerchief and explained, "Already a muggy day out there," wiping his brow.

"Just another Foggy Bottom morning," the stern guard replied, breaking into a smile and saluting the newly minted Vice Admiral Riordan. "Have a nice day, sir."

The pair weaved through the building towards the JAG department, returning to Bruce's derelict office and finding him waiting inside, the sparsely decorated room now occupied by a wheeled cart stacked with several crates. "Supplies for downstairs," Bruce explained, and after a quick exchange of pleasantries the trio followed the same path back to Nancy's Place.

When Embrie greeted them at the door, Declan avoided her gaze, thrusting the balled-up robe into her arms. "Thank you," he mumbled, hoping she couldn't sense his depravity, having spent the night holding the pink robe like a security blanket, comforted by the lingering scent of her perfume.

Embrie quietly mulled over the professor's oddness while the men carried the supply crates inside the house, and once they emptied the cart, led them past the sitting parlor and down the hallway. Double doors opened into an opulent dining hall, sparkling crystal chandeliers illuminating the massive table's overflowing bounty. Platefuls of quiche, bacon and sausage links were accompanied by the starchy goodness of pancake stacks, muffins and cinnamon rolls, the cacophony of smells blending in delicious harmony.

"I won't have to worry about my pants being baggy for long," Declan remarked, eyeing up the trays of baked goods.

"I know it's a bit much," Embrie commented, "but Ms. Elliott wanted to make sure we started the day off with proper footing."

"It's superfluously decadent!" James declared with delight. "And you won't hear any complaints from me, after all, breakfast is one of the three most important meals of the day," he declared while stacking his plate.

Ms. Elliott walked in, carrying a tray of coffee and juice. "Thank you, Ms. Elliott," Declan said, "you really outdid yourself. This is quite a feast you've prepared."

"I hope you find the selections pleasing, Doctor Riordan," she replied, "your nutritional deficit requires correction."

"Don't expect him to recuperate all of it in one sitting," Bruce gently teased the older woman, "though it won't be for lack of trying on your part, Ms. Elliott. And thank you again, this all looks amazing."

As Declan loaded his plate, he noted the dozens of beautiful paintings lining the room, the canvases so tightly packed along the walls they bumped frames. Particularly fond of bucolic, natural scenes, the professor found one painting especially appealing. "This one with the lily pads under the bridge is so tranquil, it reminds me of something Monet might paint."

"Good guess," Embrie responded, "take a closer look," she encouraged the professor, pointing at the name painted along the lower corner.

"Claude Monet," Declan read. "I presume this is the original, I'd be more shocked if it weren't."

"Yes," giggled Embrie, "this painting is the real thing, although it isn't ours," she added. "We're just babysitting it, and all the masterpieces in here, for the moment. Andrew Mellon needed a safe place to store his more valuable paintings during the construction of the National Gallery of Art, which is currently being built down the Mall from here, closer to the Capitol Building. We're helping an old friend of the Clypeate, many times Mr. Mellon has used his philanthropy to generously fund our various endeavors. When the museum is ready, we'll return these pieces. Except maybe this one," she whispered to Declan, winking and smiling.

James walked right up to another artwork, squinting at the signature. "Renoir," he noted. "I've heard of him, another popular French Impressionist. I don't get the fuss, I prefer realism, though I enjoy getting this close to a masterpiece without a grumpy old guard yelling at me to move back," he said, inches from the canvas while devouring a cinnamon roll draped in icing. "Nah, this doesn't make the painting any better," he decided, "it's even blurrier. What a sloppy mess, how disappointing."

In response, Bruce groaned, shook his head, and sensing this would be a multi cup kind-of-day unceremoniously swigged his morning's first coffee before interrupting the art critique. "Okay, everyone, now that we've satisfied our right-brain curiosity, let's settle down and discuss our next actions." Bruce waited while everyone sat, clustered around one end of the long table, before proceeding. "Doctor Riordan," he continued, "I can only guess how disoriented you must feel."

"That's an understatement," the professor replied between bites of fluffy ham and cheese quiche. "Processing so much information at once pushed me to the limits of sanity," he admitted, "and yesterday's revelations nullified my entire understanding of the Universe."

"You are at a tremendous disadvantage," Bruce acknowledged, "from your perspective all those events transpired yesterday, while the rest of us had the benefit of two weeks to digest the truth. I wish we could offer you the same recovery period, but our mission can't press forward without your help. Regrettably, time is the one luxury we can't afford."

"Bruce is right," James chimed in, wiping icing off his chin, "having time to acclimate helped, I'm still adapting to the weirdness so don't feel disheartened if reality feels topsy turvy. Sometimes you've gotta drown to realize you can breathe underwater. You're a smart egg, Doc, I'm sure you'll get the hang of it quicker than I am."

"Without a doubt," Declan replied with more confidence than he felt, "and as disturbing as I find James' analogy, he elegantly described this information overload. I'm learning to breathe water, and while I can't explain how, it feels surprisingly natural. Admittedly, I'm still unclear on some details," he confided, "if you'll allow me to briefly recap what I know, that may help."

"Great idea," Bruce replied, nodding his assent, using the opportunity to enjoy a generous bite of chocolate chip muffin.

"Correct me if I'm wrong," Declan started. "My understanding is your secret society, the Clypeate, was founded to protect a giant magic crystal, the Epistolith, hidden under the Washington Monument. This ancient diamond provided your members with the unearned knowledge used to fuel America's technological revolution, but there are bad guys, the Obturavi, who have now leap-frogged ahead after finding some important object, an Axyn Kirox, in Antarctica. It won't be long before they control the world and make us all subservient or dead. I'm here because these giant crystals communicate with me using an imaginary girl who has now whisked me away twice, days to weeks at a time, returning me with bucketloads of information shoved haphazardly into my brain, presumably to stop the aforementioned bad guys. Now, I must figure out how to share what's inside my brain with you before it's too late."

"I'd be hard-pressed to explain it more succinctly," Bruce acknowledged, "and you are correct, it's clear whatever the Girl in the Glass crammed inside your mind is both valuable and urgent. First, however, we must deal with the dire warning you spouted off last evening. I fear your foreboding message portends darker times ahead, and unpacking the meaning is of utmost importance, our priority."

"I barely remember the tiniest bits and pieces," Declan replied. "My lips moved, but that ominous message was not of my own creation. The orator of that speech was the Girl flowing through me," he explained. "I was simply her vessel."

"Back up a minute," James interrupted. "You're saying the little Girl in the Glass hijacked your body, demonically possessed you, and you're not more alarmed?"

"It wasn't like that," Declan said, shrugging his shoulders. "Nothing violent or adversarial, more like a partnership. I granted her permission. If she hadn't intervened on my behalf in Antarctica I'd be buried along with the rest of Alpha Team, so I simply returned the favor."

"You still speak about her like she's a real person," James pointed out. "I'm conflicted as well, having seen her in the crystal I understand why, but whether she's real isn't the important question. It's irrelevant, whether she's a person or a mouthpiece allowing us to converse with gods or aliens, the most pressing concern is can we trust her. What do you think, Doc? I'm sure you spent last night thinking about your close interactions with her, what's your opinion of her intentions?"

"My judgment is worthless, tainted by emotion," Declan said, shrugging his shoulders. "If she's nothing more than an instrument of the Epistolith then I'm being cleverly manipulated, because she feels very real and unquestionably sincere."

"Whatever she is, the Girl deserves our appreciation for saving Doctor Riordan's life," Bruce reminded them. "She also went through a lot of trouble to stock his brain with information and provide us with a warning message. These strike me as benevolent acts, so I'm cautiously trusting her," declared Bruce. "We need allies, and we aren't swimming in options. The US Navy wasted time focusing their attention upon the *Valencia* while giving the *Schwabenland* an opportunity to escape American surveillance. Our European allies also lost the trail, which means the German freighter could be anywhere on the map. They're looking for a trail of breadcrumbs and coming up an entire loaf short."

"Despite my concerns, I have no further objections," James decided. "During my intelligence gathering career I've come across plenty of intentional misinformation, and the Girl's statement comes across as genuine and actionable. I could be wrong, and this is pure deception, but her warning provides the best clues we've got. I took the liberty of jotting down Doc's lengthy diatribe, what I could remember, and there's enough golden nuggets packed in that stream to merit our attention. I've already decoded 'the men with twisted crosses', obviously referencing the Nazis, so it's reasonable to assume the other lines can also be deciphered."

"Well done," Bruce lauded, "while I can't forget the overall tone of the message, the details escape me. We're a clever bunch, between the four of us we stand a chance at breaking it down," he encouraged them. "Now what did she say next?"

James looked at his scribbled notes. "Ancient texts wrongfully obtained. Does this make sense to anyone?"

"Not wrongful," Bruce spoke up, "I don't remember much, but I'm certain the Girl said wicked."

"Could be a reference to the Almanac of the Past," Embrie offered. "The library contains an encyclopedic collection of ancient transcripts, full of paradigm-shifting knowledge. Two thousand years ago the Obturavi went through great lengths to destroy these documents, almost succeeding when they torched the Library at Alexandria. Every surviving copy resides in our library, or did, I've spent several years sorting through our collection and can't account for three missing volumes. While I can't be certain, it's possible the books went missing that terrible night in 1898. The Clypeate thought all the Obturavi attackers were neutralized, though in the chaos of the moment, it's possible one escaped with the missing volumes."

"Stealing them during the attack would certainly meet criteria for wickedness," Bruce agreed. "Miss Powell, do you know what information was contained in those volumes?"

"Not exactly," Embrie admitted, "although our check-out logs indicate researchers didn't waste much time reviewing them. They focused on actionable technologies and practical scientific applications, the absent volumes were cataloged as geographic atlases."

"Your theory requires a lot of assumptions," Bruce noted, "but elegantly explains how the Germans narrowed down their Antarctic search so quickly and precisely. A book of maps could have provided the cartographic clues needed to pinpoint the Epistolith's location under the ice."

"I doubt we'll come up with a better explanation, so let's move ahead," James suggested. Receiving no argument he proceeded. "Next the Girl mentioned an Axyn Kirox. Any guesses as to what that means?"

Declan held up a sketch drawn on his napkin. "When I close my eyes this image pops into my head."

Mid-bite James lowered the sausage link skewered on his fork. "Looks like a toilet plunger," he decided.

In turn Declan eyed his own handiwork. "Admittedly this is a terrible drawing, in my mind the Axyn Kirox is crisp as a photograph and looks far less like a toilet plunger. More like a mushroom with a long stalk, if the cap were shaped like a pyramid. But in either case, fungus or bathroom tool, it serves an important function. Although what that function is, I don't know."

"Certainly not plunging toilets," Embrie chided them. "It's an ignition switch for the Epistolith," she explained, "you won't get much utility from one of these giant crystals without one. A better visual than a fungus or bathroom accessory would be Thor's hammer, as the Norse legend is loosely based upon the Axyn Kirox. Main difference, as Declan noted, the Axyn Kirox is shaped like a pyramid, although just like Thor's Hammer it's created from indestructible, supernatural metal and capable of great feats."

"For a while the Clypeate possessed an Axyn Kirox," explained Bruce. "Initially discovered by Napoleon, during his military campaign in Egypt. We thought there was only one, if the Nazis found a second in Antarctica…"

"Hold on," Declan interjected, "now Egypt and Napoleon Bonaparte are involved?"

"I'll explain," offered Embrie. "When Napoleon invaded Egypt in 1799, his army engineers uncovered ancient stone tablets near Rashid, in the Nile delta. One tablet was inscribed with a mundane edict from antiquity, the French nicknamed their prize 'la Pierre de Rosette'. You may know its more famous British name, the Rosetta Stone, which became the key to translating ancient Egyptian hieroglyphs. Despite its undeniable utility, the French kept a second, even more valuable tablet tucked away from history. The importance of this second stone was readily apparent, commanding Napoleon's immediate attention, as this inscription described two objects. A massive diamond of unmatched power, the Akhet Ra, and the key to wielding its power, the Axyn Kirox."

"And you think this Akhet Ra is the same thing as an Epistolith," deduced James.

"This is all secondhand information," replied Embrie. "Everything we know comes from the French translation of the stone's inscription, recovered after Napoleon's defeat. However, the diamond is described in great detail, with dimensions matching the Epistolith. There was also an intricate map carved into the stone, leading to their resting place deep in the Sahara Desert, at the far western edge of the old Egyptian kingdom."

James put down his second cinnamon roll and smiled. "Surely Napoleon couldn't resist the promise of unspeakable power. He went looking for them, didn't he?"

"Indeed," confirmed Embrie, "allocating a large share of resources away from his army's front lines and towards an expedition team. Legend says those men were never seen again, although after the Napoleonic Wars ended rumors circulated, claiming they found the giant diamond."

"And you're sure these were just rumors?" James inquired. "Didn't anyone make the logical assumption, if Napoleon's men recovered the Axyn Kirox in Egypt they may have also found an Epistolith?"

Bruce sipped his coffee, washing down the last bite of chocolate chip muffin before replying, "Of course, rumored sightings of the Egyptian Epistolith circulated for years, from as far afield as the Sinai Peninsula to the Russian steppes."

"The stories were never confirmed," Embrie quickly clarified. "Mr. Edison spent considerable resources looking, as did the Clypeate's benefactor, Hesperus. The Epistolith map led to nothing but Saharan sand and investigating the many stories only produced dead ends. Both came away empty-handed, concluding the French mission ended in failure."

"But Mr. Edison and Hesperus knew otherwise," Declan countered, eyeing the last pancake. "Napoleon's mission wasn't a total failure, he found the Axyn Kirox."

"True," Embrie conceded, "except they didn't know about the Axyn Kirox until eighty years later, in 1884, when a Serbian immigrant arrived in New York City with an amazing tale and even more shocking relic. The young man's name was Nikola Tesla."

"So that's how Mr. Tesla got involved," James remarked.

"Yes, and it's precisely why Mr. Edison and Hesperus felt confident the Epistolith was never recovered," explained Bruce. "With the Axyn Kirox, Napoleon would have controlled the Epistolith, making him unstoppable. They concluded if Napoleon also found the Epistolith, Europe would now be the European States of France."

James didn't follow. "I'm puzzled, how'd he smuggle a tool of unspeakable power into the United States? Someone slacking off at Ellis Island security?"

"Wouldn't be difficult at all," Embrie said. "The Axyn Kirox isn't massive like the Epistolith, it's small enough to easily fit in a suitcase."

"Obviously you can imagine how the arrival of Mr. Tesla's trinket sent shockwaves through the Clypeate," Bruce continued. "Even though Napoleon's troops would have a much easier time transporting the relatively small Axyn Kirox out of Egypt and safely into Europe, perhaps they'd also overcome the logistical hurdles of transporting the Epistolith. Once again the Clypeate was forced to entertain the possibility Napoleon's men completed their mission."

"What was Mr. Tesla's explanation as to how he'd come to possess such an exotic object?" Declan asked. "It must have been quite a story."

"According to Mr. Tesla," Bruce recounted, "during his second year at the Imperial-Royal Technical College in Austria he was approached by a group calling themselves Keepers of Ancient Wonders. Mr. Tesla's reputation as an exemplary student was well known, and they presented the young genius with a stack of papers and an offer. Decipher the scrawled markings and they'd reward him handsomely."

"Did he accept?" queried Declan.

"Not initially," Bruce replied, "Mr. Tesla sensed trouble and didn't want to tangle himself up in their seedy affairs. However, despite his stellar academic debut by his third year of college Mr. Tesla developed another reputation, now as a gambler, and not a very good one, managing to rack up some hefty debts with unsavory characters. Mr. Tesla reluctantly agreed to help the Keepers in exchange for them wiping all his monetary slates clean, putting him squarely under their thumb. Indebted and without options, the Keepers shuffled him to Hungary where he secretly worked on what looked like gibberish, even to Mr. Tesla."

"But Mr. Tesla is a genius," James interjected while pouring himself another coffee. "Eventually, he figured it out, right?"

"Of course," continued Bruce. "It didn't take long for him to notice patterns amongst the chaos, realizing the nonsensical lines were mathematical equations and formulas. Nothing like he'd ever seen, even in his most advanced studies. However, as he decoded the information into concrete data, he realized the pages contained blueprints for creating terrible instruments of destruction. Massive weapons, wicked poisons and powerful explosives. Horrified, he intentionally slowed down his progress, telling them he wasn't smart enough to handle the intellectual challenge."

"How'd that work out?" wondered Declan, midway through his pancake.

"Not well," responded Embrie, Bruce's mouth occupied by a second chocolate chip muffin. "While these men were cruel and wicked they weren't gullible, quickly realizing his ploy. As retribution the Keepers threatened to harm his family, but Mr. Tesla, always the smartest man in the room, denied their claims. Instead, he blamed his lack of progress on insufficient access to the source material. To Mr. Tesla's surprise the men eagerly agreed, but what shocked him most was what the Keepers showed him, the Axyn Kirox."

"Now it's beginning to make sense," Declan commented, "they inadvertently handed Mr. Tesla an exit strategy."

"Exactly," Bruce confirmed between bites. "The Keepers were using his family and friends as bargaining chips, so Mr. Tesla got one of his own, the Axyn Kirox. He burned all his work and escaped with the Axyn Kirox to France, where alone and penniless he sought employment at Continental Edison. Mr. Edison's top engineer in Paris, a member of the Clypeate, quickly realized Mr. Tesla's knowledge extended beyond the ordinary realm. He offered the young genius protection and comradery of the Clypeate, Tesla accepted and was transferred to America."

"What about the Epistolith?" James asked, "Did he know anything about it?"

"No, Mr. Tesla never heard these men talk about an Epistolith or Akhet Ra," Bruce responded, "and he'd never seen one until he visited our Sanctuary. With Mr. Tesla's translations burned and the Clypeate in possession of the Axyn Kirox, our members lulled themselves into a false sense of security. That all changed when these headquarters were attacked five years later, in 1898. Too late the Clypeate realized the men from whom Mr. Tesla had stolen the Axyn Kirox, the ones he called the Keepers, were in fact the Obturavi. Even though Mr. Tesla's pilfered Axyn Kirox activated the Washington Epistolith and spurred the greatest streak of invention and discovery in human history, Thomas Edison blamed him for leading the Obturavi to Washington and the destruction of the Clypeate's facilities."

"Except the attack served one useful purpose," Declan asserted. "The attack cost the Obturavi their biggest advantage, anonymity. By revealing themselves, they let the Clypeate know they had returned," he reasoned. "So why didn't the Clypeate pursue the Obturavi more vigorously?"

"The Clypeate was too devastated to respond," Embrie explained. "The survivors had enough problems caring for the injured, getting the Research Hall fire under control and the painful consequences didn't end there. That night the Clypeate entrusted the Axyn Kirox to Hesperus for safekeeping, sending him and Axyn Kirox away until these facilities could be rebuilt and secured. With the Axyn Kirox gone, our Epistolith no longer shared information, a temporary setback which became a permanent impediment when Hesperus boarded a ship headed for Europe, the *La Bourgogne*. Hesperus drowned when the *La Bourgogne* sank in the middle of the Atlantic, sending him and the Axyn Kirox to a watery grave."

"The framed newspaper clipping hangs in Bruce's office," Declan recalled, "quite a morbid reminder of Hesperus' failure. So much for your celestial prophet's ability to predict the future," he snidely jabbed, "though it's better than the Obturavi getting their hands on the Axyn Kirox."

"Not by much," Embrie countered. "While the loss of the Axyn Kirox was immeasurable, the Secret Service's faith in the Clypeate plummeted after the attack, significantly compounding the damage. President McKinley's men neutered our scientific endeavors, walling off Lincoln's Tunnel and banning all future research using the Epistolith's knowledge. The Clypeate was dead in the water."

"Though not as literally as Hesperus," Declan wryly asserted. "What an exaggerated overreaction, I'd expect the president would come to his senses and reverse course."

Bruce ignored the professor's cheeky comment. "He didn't, and with time the Clypeate's importance withered," he explained, "although fifteen years later those myopic decisions proved to be deadly mistakes. When World War One broke out Germany's revolutionary technical and chemical advances bordered on unbelievable, and Mr. Edison credited their breakthroughs to the Obturavi's influence. Nothing angered Mr. Edison more than playing the fool and halting the Clypeate's technological progress gave the Obturavi time to quietly build up Germany's advantage. With the Clypeate's influence diminished, Edison publicly aired his concerns as a private citizen, calling for our government to create the Naval Consulting Board."

"I remember those newspaper articles," Declan noted, "after the sinking of the passenger ship *Lusitania*, Mr. Edison passionately called for more American invention."

"Good memory," lauded Bruce, "the United States needed a commensurate response, and Mr. Edison felt our best hope was a Clypeate resurgence under the rebranded guise of his Advisory Board. As World War One raged on, the scientist's petitions for renewed research efforts gained support, and his campaign nearly succeeded when the Allies won. With the global threat eliminated, Mr. Edison lost support, especially after American troops searched every German research facility and found no evidence of inexplicably advanced technology. Without a single shred of evidence to support the existence of a European Epistolith, our hopes the Clypeate would rise from the ashes evaporated, and we've been quietly biding our time ever since, waiting for another rematch."

"Well, I don't think you'll have to wait long," James announced. "The Girl says the Germans plan to 'bring nations to their knees, twist the fabric of reality and extinct life', and I'd wager the Obturavi are involved once again. The Girl didn't mention anything about Nazis traveling to Antarctica so they could lay claim to new whaling territory."

"What about the Clypeate's mission report?" Bruce asked. "I know Harold torched it, getting a bit paranoid in his old age, making you the only person with any insight. Did the report contain any hints?"

"One thing struck me as odd. The report described the German efforts to move the Epistolith as half-hearted," James recalled, "which suggests they didn't want it. If the Germans were simply translating from Mr. Tesla's old papers, they would have tried harder to capture the Epistolith. Now that I know about the Axyn Kirox, and what it can do, Germany's actions make sense. They were happy to leave the giant crystal behind because they already possess one."

"Unlikely," Bruce disagreed. "The Girl wouldn't leave out such an important detail," he rationalized.

"That's exactly why I trust her warning," James countered, "she shouldn't know the Germans have an Epistolith. We know she can travel between Epistoliths, but her vantage point is always the same, looking out from the inside. She can't see that she's inside an Epistolith the same way you'd never see your own face without a mirror or photograph."

"Same as how fish don't know they're swimming in water," realized Bruce. "You make a distressing amount of sense, and that spells big trouble. I fear we're much further behind in this game than anyone realized."

"Don't forget, the Girl also said there's still time," James reminded him. "She said they're still missing a crucial piece, she called it a conduit. They no longer possess one, whatever that means."

"Biological conduit," elaborated Bruce. "Embrie, do you have any ideas?"

Embrie thought for a moment. "I know the Axyn Kirox unlocks the Epistolith, like the key to a book filled with infinite pages of information. Accessing the Epistolith is only the first part, however, because those pages contain symbols incomprehensible to most humans. This technology was neither developed nor intended for mankind's consumption, so trying to understand the information would be equivalent to a dolphin reading Shakespeare. Sure, dolphins are smart, but they couldn't begin to decipher and comprehend the information. When it comes to the Epistolith most humans are dolphins, except for a very few special exceptions, known as biological conduits. Throughout all recorded history, just a handful of rare individuals have been capable of understanding the Epistolith's signal and translating the output."

James asked, "If Doc can interact with the Girl through the Epistolith, does that mean he's one of them too, a biological conduit?"

"We can't be certain without an Axyn Kirox," Bruce said, "but that's our hope."

"It's a good possibility," Embrie opined. "Being a conduit would explain how the Girl can pass information into his mind without destroying it."

James smiled. "Now I understand why you're so convinced Doc's the Declan of Prophecy. You think his ability to interact with the Girl means he can also translate the Epistolith's knowledge. Makes him one in a million."

"More like one out of everyone," clarified Embrie.

"Which still makes me nothing more than a bilingual dictionary," Declan grumpily muttered, "or that electrical adapter with the quirky prongs I needed while visiting Ireland."

"You're wrong," Embrie roundly rejected, "your gift is amazing and special. You're not an adapter, you are a converter, able to transform Epistolith energy into a language recognizable by human minds."

"But it still took a genius like Mr. Tesla to interpret those depictions into useful information. While I'm remarkably intelligent, I'm not a Tesla. Maybe I'm a valuable tool that can't be replicated, like the Rosetta Stone, but can't we admit that's all I am?"

"Please, try to understand your true worth," pleaded Embrie. "You're more important than you realize."

"I appreciate your faith in my abilities, but for now I'm comfortable being the means to an end," the professor reassured her. "In a twisted way, I'm happier knowing my role, it guarantees the Clypeate needs me alive, at least for now, and I prefer believing your interests in my well-being aren't entirely altruistic."

"That's not fair," protested Embrie, "Ms. Elliott and I, all of us, have put in a lot of effort to make you comfortable."

Declan immediately regretted his rant. "I'm sorry," he said, "I didn't sleep very well and the puzzle pieces in my mind are more jumbled than a Picasso painting. Maybe I'll feel differently once the images finish sorting themselves, although I'm not sure how to get them out. Almost anything would be an improvement, my head feels like an overstuffed pinata."

James couldn't resist. "Are you suggesting we smack your head with a stick?"

"Of course not," Embrie gasped. "We're not barbarians!"

"Hold on, we shouldn't limit our options just yet," James sardonically suggested.

"We'll figure this out together," Bruce reassured the professor. "Remember, your interests and ours are aligned, and with time I'm confident you'll see how your importance stretches beyond a simplistic tool. In Antarctica the Girl in the Glass shared information with you, a burden that would crack anyone else. And here, at our Epistolith, she once again entered your mind, doubling down on her faith in your abilities. You are unique, not some interchangeable widget. Now, as for getting all that knowledge out, without an Axyn Kirox even she cannot help you extract it. Thankfully ALVA has been working on a solution, and I am confident your mind is ready to make the attempt."

Chapter 18

April 14, 1939
Nancy's Place
Clypeate Headquarters
City of Washington, District of Columbia

Breakfast concluded a few bites later, and the overly stuffed group followed Bruce, who walked out the back door and through the yard, returning to the hazy metal barrier separating the corn field from the Analytical Engine Room. Declan's enthusiasm waned as they approached the wall, Bruce unable to articulate ALVA's plan, only after entering the Clean Room finally admitting he didn't know any details. While the professor believed Bruce intended to keep him safe, at least for now, he worried a roomful of machines would consider bashing his skull like a pinata a reasonable solution.

Upon exiting the Clean Room, ALVA's intent became immediately apparent. "This wasn't here before," James stated, referring to a gray rectangular box resting on the catwalk directly ahead, the large impediment blocking further progress. "The machines delivered us a casket."

Declan knocked on the five-inch-thick walls. "This box is made of concrete," he decided. "How impractical, it must weigh several hundred pounds."

"It was built without weight being a major consideration," replied Embrie. "Mr. Edison experimented with building furniture out of concrete," she explained, "and this is one of his prototypes."

Bruce swung the lid open and peered inside. "Looks comfortable, and it's the proper size for a single person."

"Oh no," Declan groaned, "I know what you're thinking so don't bother asking. If this is ALVA's plan to extract the information I'd rather live with the chaos in my brain, because there's no way I'm climbing into that coffin."

Embrie frowned. "This box was originally designed to be a cabinet, certainly not a coffin." She also peeked inside the box, noting the rows of blinking lights lining the inner walls. "The Builders have modified the box and transformed it into an electrical device. I believe Commander Kingston is correct, it's designed for one occupant."

"So what's the plan, electrocute the information out of me?"

"Quite the opposite," Embrie said, attempting to reassure him. "Although concrete furniture never became commercially successful, the material is both strong and non-conductive, making it an excellent electrical insulator."

"There you go," Bruce said. "The Builders used this box because they had your safety in mind," he told Declan, asserting, "I'd trust the Builders' technical skills with my own life."

"Then why don't you climb inside?" suggested Declan. "I'd feel a lot better if I could talk to ALVA, we can use the library telephone to ask some questions."

Embrie shook her head. "The phone doesn't work like that."

"Then I need another way of communicating with the machines, because I'm not budging until I know how this contraption works," countered Declan, pointing to a thick bundle of wires running from the bottom of the cement box. "Anyone else notice how it's connected to the analytic engines?" he asked, the wires weaving across the metal walkway and disappearing into the nearest tower. "If ALVA isn't available, maybe those Builders you keep mentioning can spare a few moments to chat."

"I understand your hesitation," Embrie said, "the problem is the Builders are very busy, and don't appreciate getting interrupted," she cautioned. "Also, this will prompt more questions than we have time to answer."

"I don't care how antisocial these Builders are," replied Declan, "before I climb inside the cement casket, I want them to tell me it's safe."

Embrie sighed. "I wish you would trust me," she lamented. "The Builders aren't fond of anyone," she cautioned, "they barely tolerate my intrusions. However, if that's what it takes, let me get their attention." The young woman walked further out along the catwalk and shouted, "Dash! Dash! Dash! Come here!"

Declan caught glimpses of a spindly figure scurrying between the massive towers, taller than Bruce, racing towards them with a white lab coat flowing behind like a superhero cape. The first unexpected feature Declan noticed was the Builder's lack of feet, instead rolling along the elevated platform on wheels. "Can't be," Declan blurted out, his suspicions confirmed when he saw a metal body poking out of the unbuttoned lab coat.

"The Builders are automatons," James finished the professor's thought, noting how the shiny metal hands did not end with fingers. Instead each digit formed a different tool, screwdrivers, pliers, tweezers, a tap hammer, even a soldering iron.

"Why didn't you warn us?" asked Declan, Embrie artfully responding with nothing more than a dubious glance. "Okay, fine," the professor conceded, "you're right. I wouldn't have believed you, anyway."

The awestruck men surveyed the machine's silvery features. "Exquisite craftsmanship," James reverentially declared.

"Far more complex than a perfunctory automaton," remarked Declan. "This machine is a robot, anything less dignified would be an insult. The head is a work of art, a technological homage to the human face," he gushed, waving into the camera lenses set in place of eyes. Completing the personification, a round mesh speaker formed the mouth while microphones jutting from either side looked like metallic Mickey Mouse ears. "It's glorious."

"Although the hair's a bit unsettling," commented James, a series of coiled antennas topping the head in lieu of hair. "Reminds me of Medusa's snake-doo. Also a little creepy without a nose," he added, "like a snowman without its carrot."

The robot paused momentarily, as if deciding to address or ignore their comments, before turning to face Embrie. "Greetings Miss Powell, how may I assist you?" its tinny, electronic voice asked.

"I'm sorry to interrupt your routine, however, these men really wanted to meet you," Embrie told the robot. "Declan, James," the young woman said, supplying the introductions, "meet Dash Dash Dash."

"Now they have met me. May I return to my tasks?" the robot dispassionately asked.

Embrie chuckled. "Triple Dash is one of the oldest Builders, a very literal thinker, the first model built with emotional intelligence. Let me rephrase the request, please introduce yourself."

"I am a Dash model, Series 4. My name is Dash Dash Dash, but my friends just call me O. Ha ha ha!" the machine cackled. "It is always a pleasure to meet new organic sentients, as one of my prime programming directives is to better understand the vagaries of humanity's irrational data processing and inefficient energy utilization."

"How remarkably sophisticated," Declan marveled, "like Leonardo da Vinci's mechanical knight, though far more articulate and intelligent. In seventh grade I built a working automaton model for the science fair, and even though I won first prize my creation was nothing more than a rolling toaster in comparison. This robot is unimaginably advanced."

"You are mistaken," the robot corrected him, "if my existence were unimaginable, I could not have been created, yet here I am, the product of careful engineering and skillful innovation."

"Isn't that something," James remarked, "the first real robot you meet and it dings you for imprecise word choice. Although I shouldn't talk, I'm still trying to figure out Triple Dash's joke. How is Dash Dash Dash funny?"

"Now that's a product of Mr. Edison's humor," Embrie explained. "A more efficient telegraph machine was one of his first innovations, and he was so proud of this feat he nicknamed his biological children Dot and Dash. He continued the tradition with the Builders, each one a version of the Dot or Dash series, and in Morse code three dashes equals the letter O."

"That's the joke?" asked James. "Not very funny, I hope comedy isn't Triple Dash's day job."

"It is not," the robot replied.

"Triple Dash is far more important," Embrie elaborated, apparently missing James' sarcasm as well. "All the Builders are remotely linked with ALVA and their jobs include making repairs, improving the circuitry, adding more capacity, whatever's needed."

"So Big Al controls a fleet of these Builder robots," repeated James, "and uses them like appendages. That makes Big Al the brains and these Builder robots the brawn. But doesn't a machine, even as intelligent and complicated as this, still need human operators?"

"Ms. Elliott and I support the Builders," Embrie replied, "we don't control them. ALVA provides us with a list of supplies, and we try our best to procure them.

Sometimes the requests are beyond reason," she added, glancing at the robot, "like procuring four kilograms of elemental terbium on short notice."

"Overall, it's a mutually beneficial relationship," Bruce added. "In exchange for parts and equipment we have access to the computing power of the analytical engines, which is significant."

"You're describing autonomous machines," declared Declan. "Even after seeing Triple Dash and the advanced components powering these machines, it sounds like science fiction."

"Amazing technology always feels magical," Bruce replied, "how many everyday items were thought impossible until Mr. Edison invented them? Now we take lightbulbs, record players and movies for granted."

"The Analytical Engine Room's evolution was born of necessity," explained Embrie. "After the Obturavi attack, when the government shut down the Clypeate's research facilities, the scientists and engineers abandoned ALVA. All except for Mr. Edison. He saw ALVA's potential and wasn't content to let the machines run until they failed and rusted away. Out of necessity Mr. Edison created the first Builders, like Triple Dash, so they could repair and maintain the towers until his return, which took longer than anticipated. Once our government permanently sealed the Jefferson Pier and Executive Building entrances, it took Mr. Edison twenty years to regain access to these facilities."

"Through the Navy and Munitions Building," James reckoned, "presumably using the elevator in Bruce's office."

"Correct," Embrie affirmed. "Mr. Edison made certain the military provided the Continental Army with space in the new building, and during construction secretly connected the office with the Room of the Honored. When Mr. Edison was finally able to return, two decades later, the machine towers were in better condition than after the Obturavi attack, thanks to his Builders. Even more amazing, ALVA used Mr. Edison's original Builders to create newer, more sophisticated versions, all running independent of human operators. While necessity pushed Mr. Edison to create the Builders, isolation and time forced ALVA to become self-reliant."

"Explains why there aren't human engineers and technicians down here," Declan remarked, "these machines don't need them. Although I am surprised the Clypeate doesn't spend more time studying them."

"Mr. Edison tried," Bruce said. "He wanted to harness ALVA's intelligence, use it to rebuild the Clypeate's power. He spent a considerable amount of time and personal wealth refurbishing this cavern, creating a secure space for ALVA's towers. He also designed the ranch house as a new research facility for the Clypeate, so they could work with the machines and learn from them. Problem was, not only did the machines not need humans anymore, they didn't want the Clypeate monkeying around with what they'd created."

"Monkeys would have been easier to control," Triple Dash commented, "humans aren't nearly as predictable. They couldn't keep their hands from touching our equipment and spreading organic compounds all over, getting tangled in our wires, interrupting our data streams and overall slowing us down."

"You don't seem to appreciate our kind," Declan asserted, "which makes me nervous to climb inside this box. I'm not sure I can trust machines that view humanity so shabbily."

"Simple misunderstanding," Bruce reassured him. "To assuage Doctor Riordan's fears," he said, addressing the robot, "kindly explain to us the purpose of this device and how safe it will be for him to climb inside."

Triple Dash complied. "ALVA designed this memory extraction chamber to remove all the information shared through the Epistolith. We are confident this machine will unload all the extraneous information inside Doctor Riordan's brain without removing any original content."

"I'll remember how to breathe? That's thoughtful of you," Declan snarked. "Now, how safe is it?"

"Survivability odds are statistically significant to three standard deviations," Triple Dash reported.

"See," Bruce smiled, "this box will empty out all those extraneous thoughts, restore your mind's clarity, and it's perfectly safe."

"Wrong," countered Declan, "Triple Dash is using jargon to hide the truth, the box isn't one hundred percent reliable. However," the professor sighed, "I can't live like this forever, with my brain stuffed like a clown car" he sighed, climbing into the cement box. "Three standard deviations will have to suffice."

"Could be worse," James offered, "at least they didn't build it from an actual coffin."

Without further delay, Triple Dash rolled over to the nearest tower and powered up the concrete box, flipping switches until it softly hummed and the entire catwalk gently vibrated. "Now, Doctor, you may hear a loud buzzing noise, vomit, pass out or convulse. All perfectly normal."

"You've gotta be kidding me…" Declan yelled as the Builder slammed shut the thick cabinet door, cutting off his response. "ALVA will begin the information offload in sixty seconds," the robot informed them, spinning on his wheels, adding, "you may want to step back, I may have overestimated the safety profile, we only tested this equipment once before, on a squirrel, and it didn't end well for the critter, or for the machine towers on that side of the room."

"You told him it was safe, you lied to him?" Embrie shrieked, clearly displeased.

"No, Commander Kingston did," Triple Dash flatly responded. "He told the Doctor the box was perfectly safe, I accurately informed him the safety profile was less than one hundred percent."

"Turn it off!" James demanded.

"It is too late," Triple Dash informed them, "the machine is already powering up, shutting it off now would be disastrous. The extraction starts in twenty seconds, once again, I suggest you increase your distance from the box. I certainly am," the robot added, with those remarks Triple Dash sped off and disappeared amongst the machine stacks.

"Remind me to never trust a robot," James shouted as they retreated into the Clean Room, shutting the door just as the concrete box's gentle vibration increased to violent shaking and low hum crescendoed into a roar. The noisy tornado whipping around inside the Clean Room prevented them from hearing or feeling anything further, so they didn't know what to expect when the door reopened. Surprisingly the Analytical Engine Room was silent and still, the cement box no longer vibrating or emitting noise.

"Looks okay," Bruce surmised, stepping onto the elevated walkway, "nothing out of place." He barely finished the thought when grinding metal sounds erupted and the walkway twisted under him, launching him over the side. The bolts joining the metal platform with the concrete wall popped out, causing the entire walkway to pull away from the wall and slice through a nearby machine tower, sending the massive stack of electronics lurching and crashing down. For a moment James and Embrie stood at the wall's precipice in stunned paralysis, staring down at the chaotic tangle of steel and equipment below.

"Bruce!" James shouted, spotting the tall man's motionless form trapped under the fallen walkway. "I've got Bruce, you look for Doc," James barked, swinging his legs over the rocky wall's edge before disappearing over the side.

Embrie immediately followed James scrambling down the wall, trying to focus on her feet and hand placements instead of Declan's fate. She quickly identified the concrete cabinet, cracked and split into several pieces, and swiftly weaved between the jagged, razor-sharp wreckage of tangled metal. Nearing the concrete rubble Triple Dash rolled back into view, its robotic head surveying the disaster site with sterile calculation.

"ALVA is still processing the data transfer," the robot announced, "it may take a while to know if we were successful. On the bright side, this time the damage was confined to a smaller area of the room."

"I need to find Declan!" she shouted at Triple Dash, "and you're going to help me!"

"Yes, let us check on the Doctor's condition," the robot coldly agreed, "ALVA is curious to see if he fared better than the squirrel. Although," the robot hedged, "judging by the cabinet's condition, not likely."

"He has to be okay," Embrie muttered, struggling to disagree with Tripe Dash's grim summation. "We must help him," she repeated, sifting through slabs of concrete.

"Be careful, Miss Powell," Triple Dash pleaded, "there may be live wires in there, and you are not as expendable as Doctor Riordan."

"Then help me!" she snapped back, "or I'll rip out your motor!"

Triple Dash processed the request within milliseconds, rolling in front of the young woman, creating a narrow path for her to sort through the tetanic-laden wreckage. After Embrie slid away a particularly large chunk of concrete, she saw Declan's leg poking out, although his exposed limb was shaking vigorously.

"Oh good, Doctor Riordan is having a seizure," the robot surmised.

"Are you serious? How's that good?" Embrie challenged the robot.

"I thought the answer would be obvious," Triple Dash calmly replied, "it means he is still alive."

"For now," Embrie huffed, pointing out, "humans need to breathe, remember?" Growing more impatient and anxious with each passing second, the young woman cleared away everything she could, the remaining steel and concrete pieces too heavy for one person, when the pile stopped shaking. "He's not moving! Please help me get him out!" she demanded, her voice ripe with frustration.

"I cannot," Triple Dash countered, "my arms were not designed for heavy lifting. However," the robot continued, "I anticipated your request and have already summoned for help." Embrie heard buzzing and whirring sounds bouncing off the electronic stacks, growing louder until several stocky, sturdier Builders emerged from between the machine towers, working towards her and the trapped professor, tossing aside large metal beams and concrete slabs like they were twigs and pebbles.

Embrie stepped back to avoid getting hit by the jagged projectiles, only moving closer when the robots pulled back, giving her access to the crater they'd dug out of the rubble. The young woman ran to the professor's motionless body, draped over a steel beam. She cradled his head in her arms, gently stroking his hair. "Declan, please wake up," she implored. When she got no response, the young woman hung her head and sobbed.

"We've gotta stop meeting this way," a voice said, looking down she saw Declan's weak grin. The professor saw her lips move but couldn't hear the response. "I can't hear you," he shouted, "there's a loud noise buzzing in my ears."

"You're alive," she rejoiced, shouting into his ear while hugging him tightly.

"True, although I'm not sure what happened," Declan said, slowly rising to sit. "I suspect your robot lied, that did not feel perfectly safe. At least I didn't vomit," he remarked while attempting to stand. "Oh no, excuse me for a moment," he blurted out, his face turning ghostly white. He leaned off to the side, retching and launching a vigorous stream of coffee-soaked pastries all over the wreckage. "I'm sorry, and terribly embarrassed," Declan apologized, wiping off his face. "At least I feel better," he added just before his eyes rolled back and he fell forward, splayed atop the shattered remains of the concrete cabinet.

Triple Dash rolled forward, approaching Embrie. "Four out of four side effects," the robot said, peering down at the professor's unconscious body with clinical sterility. "Doctor Riordan must concede I was perfectly truthful, and next time I'll know what order they arrive."

Chapter 19

April 14, 1939
Analytical Engine Room
Clypeate Headquarters
City of Washington, District of Columbia

Declan blinked his bleary eyes into focus, discovering the Epistolith's images disrupting his vision were gone. With renewed visual prowess he scanned the surrounding chaos and destruction, finding he'd been moved from the rubble pile and carefully propped against an undamaged machine tower. Calling for help felt pointless, the room resounded with thunderous clunking and grinding metal as a dozen Builder robots sorted through the wreckage. Unfortunately Declan's nose worked perfectly, his pristine officer's jacket christened with recently departed stomach contents. Thankfully his arms functioned, allowing him to pull off the jacket, crumple it into a ball and hurl it beyond sniff range.

Declan's mood vastly improved upon glimpsing Embrie threading her way through the twisted metal. "You're awake!" the young woman gleefully shouted, her words barely audible above the clamor, scrambling swiftly towards him with reckless enthusiasm. Upon reaching the professor she dropped down and hugged him. "I'm so glad you're okay. I didn't want to leave you but Commander Kingston is badly injured, the platform landed on him. Even though we've unpinned him he's still unconscious, and we can't safely carry him up the wall. While the Builders construct a lift system James has gone to retrieve medical supplies, which means I'm tending to both of you. I need to return to Commander Kingston soon. Will you be alright without me?" she asked.

Declan felt for injuries and noted just a few scrapes and sore spots. "My leg's a bit numb, otherwise I'm okay," he said, not mentioning the warm, wet streak now running down his pant leg, unsure what bodily fluid was responsible. "Do we know if the transfer worked?"

"Triple Dash thinks we'll know in a few days, once ALVA processes the information," Embrie replied. "Do you feel any different?" she wondered.

"My vision has returned," he reported, "no images flashing inside my head, though my mind still feels bogged down, burdened with content beyond my comprehension."

"Maybe it takes time," Embrie optimistically suggested. "In the meanwhile, please rest while I check on the commander."

Minutes later James returned with bandages and gauze, addressing Bruce's worst injuries while the Builders fashioned a crane from the twisted metal wreckage. Declan limped over to join James and Embrie, unable to help since he was still terribly dazed. Instead he watched the pair fashion a sling for Bruce's right arm, now angled unnaturally, like he'd grown a second elbow. They'd barely secured Bruce's arm when the Builders were ready to move him, gingerly placing his body onto a metal stretcher and lifting his unconscious form to the top edge of the rock wall. The crane swung him over the summit where other Builder robots were ready to grab the stretcher, adroitly whisking Bruce towards the Clean Room.

While Triple Dash mimicked the human form, these Builders were only humanoid from the waist up. Instead of two legs they possessed eight spindly, spider-like legs. "Their insect design makes them perfectly adapted for climbing up the electronic towers," Embrie explained, observing Declan's visible apprehension.

The mechanized hemi-tarantulas carried Bruce through the Clean Room and down the wall, gaining speed as they crossed the yard towards Nancy's Place. James and Embrie raced to catch up with the nimble spiderbots while Declan fell behind, stumbling more than usual, his right leg wobbling like a newborn deer. When Declan finally reached Lincoln's Tunnel he saw James yelling at the spindly-legged robots, having placed Bruce's stretcher down upon a pile of broken tile.

"What are you doing?" James demanded, "he needs to be carried to the infirmary!"

"You need to assume further transport," the largest of the spindly-legged spiderbots responded.

"But we can't lift him," James shouted back.

"We don't have time to argue," interjected Embrie, grabbing the foot of Bruce's makeshift transport. James reflexively grabbed the head, and Declan followed alongside making sure Bruce didn't roll off. In their adrenaline-infused fervor they successfully navigated inside the Room of the Honored, managing to slide the stretcher onto Andrew Jackson's refurbished table carving fresh, deep gouges into the surface.

Enraged at the Builders' perceived indifference, James ran out into the tunnel to scream at the spiderbots. "What the hell is your problem? You need to help us move Bruce right now. That's an order!"

"We cannot comply," the mechanical creature dispassionately replied. "Our transmitter range does not allow us to proceed further," the spiderbot explained, retreating inside the Research Hall.

Embrie stormed into the tunnel after James, grabbing him by the collar. "We don't have time for this. Commander Kingston's office can't move until we close the door!" she shouted in exasperation. James understood immediately and raced into action, the pair running back inside the Room of the Honored, Embrie slamming the door shut behind. She pushed the call button repeatedly and tugged impatiently on the door handle, waiting for Bruce's office to slowly descend with tortuous apathy for his predicament.

When the door finally swung open the trio lifted the stretcher off the White House table and onto Bruce's cheap office furniture. James grumbled, "I hope this flimsy garbage holds him."

"I can't close the door," yelled Embrie, "his head's in the way," noting Bruce's face functioning like a doorstop. James grabbed Bruce's feet and dragged the stretcher forward, allowing the door to close and office to ascend.

"Something's not right," Declan said, suddenly aware of Bruce's quick, shallow breaths he leaned over and checked the unconscious man's wrist, pulse thready and weak. "Not good," he yelped, the bandages on Bruce's right arm were drenched in blood. Declan swiftly unwrapped them, revealing the gaping wound on Bruce's upper arm. He gasped. Bruce's arm wasn't just broken, the skin and flesh were rolled back like a sardine can lid, his torn biceps oozing blood. "I see the problem!" Declan shouted, quickly identifying the culprit, a small but forceful stream of blood. "It's a pumper, must be arterial, at this rate he'll bleed out!"

Before Declan could react James whipped off his belt, fashioning a tourniquet around Bruce's arm. As he tightened it the pulsating squirts of blood stopped. "The tourniquet slowed down the bleeding for now," James determined, giving the belt one final tug before securing it, "but Doc's right, Bruce is in bad shape."

"What are we going to say happened?" Declan asked. "We certainly can't tell anyone the truth. We need a plausible story to explain Bruce's injuries."

"We don't need a story because we're not talking to anyone," James replied, "military investigations are long and tedious, and there's no time to get mired down. The scene must speak for itself."

Embrie scowled, adamantly stating, "We're not just going to leave him here."

"Of course not," James countered, "but Bruce would want us to keep the mission going forward, and I have an idea. Embrie, as soon as the office moves back upstairs, run to the JAG secretary and tell her to call the infirmary. Request immediate help. There's been an unfortunate accident."

She momentarily hesitated, then grasping his plan, nodded. "Got it." The disheveled young woman, covered with blood and grease, kept jiggling the door handle until it finally opened into the decrepit waiting area. She raced off without another word, disappearing into the hallway.

James turned to Declan. "We need to make this scene look as decidedly accidental as possible. Even if military investigators don't suspect malicious underpinnings or foul play, they'll still spend days swarming this office like angry hornets." James and Declan dragged Bruce into the middle of the waiting area. James pointed to one of the raggedy chairs. "Doc, kindly smash that chair to pieces. I will take care of the bookcase." Embrie returned as the men arranged broken chair and bookcase parts around Bruce's body.

"They're coming!" she huffed, breathless from running, "the infirmary said they'll be here in a few minutes."

"That's good," James replied, "though it doesn't give us much time." He stepped back and assessed their handiwork. "Not perfect, but it'll have to do. I'm hoping they'll conclude Bruce stood upon the chair to change the light bulb, the chair broke and he fell onto the bookcase."

"One problem, why would he do that? The light still works," Declan said, drawing attention to the glowing bulb above them.

"Hmmm," James mused, looking up at the tacky fixture. "Good point." He jumped up, gripped the rim of the pendant light and pulled the fixture down, sending chunks of plaster raining onto the floor and leaving loose wires dangling out the ceiling. He hurled the bell-shaped lamp against the ground, obliterating the antique ceramic fixture, a loud pop as the bulb burst into shards. "Needs changing now."

"Shhh! I think they're here!" Embrie alerted them, and the trio fell silent. She was correct, shouts and sounds of commotion floated in through the open door. "We're trapped!" she panicked.

"No," James calmly replied, rifling through Bruce's pockets. He pulled out the golden key and thrust it at Embrie. "Take this key and return downstairs, or down office, with Doc. Figure out what the Girl in the Glass transmitted through Doc, what she wants from us. I'm staying up here. I'm a vice admiral, after all, nobody's going to harass me and someone needs to follow Bruce."

Embrie started to protest but the voices were getting closer. "James is right," Declan said, "we need to finish what the Girl in the Glass started, the Nazis aren't taking any breaks."

"I thought you'd like that plan," James replied, shooting Declan a sly wink as he exited into the hallway. "Lock yourselves in," he added, "and don't come up until you hear from me, understand?" Before Declan or Embrie could reply James was gone.

"Godspeed, Mr. Kingston," Embrie whispered to Bruce, squeezing his clammy hand before joining Declan in a retreat to the underground labyrinth, the frenetic shouts of emergency responders echoing down the shaft as they descended.

Chapter 20

April 14, 1939
Clypeate Headquarters
City of Washington, District of Columbia

Embrie and the professor trudged back through Lincoln's Tunnel and through the Research Hall, silent with shock, deflated by their sudden loss. The only sound came from their footsteps echoing off the plastic walls separating them from the hazardous sludge, Embrie's hands trembling as she fidgeted with the golden key. Reaching the far door the key slipped between her fingers, landing on the cement with a dull clunk.

"Stupid key," she muttered, bending over to pick it up she noticed several crimson drops soaking into the floor. The fresh reminder of Bruce's tragic mishap overwhelmed the young woman and tears welled in her eyes.

Declan picked up the key, surprisingly heavier than he expected, and presented it to Embrie, noting her look of utter dismay. "It's okay, it's just a key," he reassured her, "I'm sure you didn't damage it," he said, swinging the massive door open into the immaculate front yard of Nancy's Place.

She began to cry. "That's not it," she eked out between heaving sobs, "I don't care about the key. I'm really worried and scared," the young woman continued, gripping onto Declan, tears soaking into his shirt. Unsure how to respond, Declan tried comforting her, awkwardly hugging her like she were a prickly cactus and not the most captivating woman he'd ever met.

"I wish I knew how to fix this mess, make it better, but I don't," admitted Declan. "Between all the unbelievable stories and treasures I've seen down here, things that make me distrust my own eyes, the only reason I've kept moving forward, following this trail of insanity, is you. All I know for sure is you believe in me, in my purpose, and that makes me believe. Please, let me be here for you, to strengthen you. It's my turn. We'll figure this out together."

Embrie stopped crying and looked up at Declan. "You're right. Let's get back to the house," she said, "it's too merry and bright out here," the picturesque ranch and bucolic grounds starkly contrasting with her emotional turmoil. She eyed the Research Hall door with hesitation. "What about James?" she asked. "If we lock him out, how will he get back?"

"Don't fret over James, he's a cunning and clever fox," Declan responded. "If I have him properly pegged, he won't attempt a return for at least a few days. Too risky, Navy investigators are going to get suspicious when they attempt to reconcile Bruce's severe injuries with the scene we set upstairs. While he waits for the security repercussions to shake out, I'm sure he'll also be monitoring Bruce's condition, and all of this gives him an excuse to chat with the typing pool ladies. He'll know the watercooler gossip about Bruce's investigation before the ink has dried on the report and believe me, James is happily making that sacrifice."

"He's a bit too charming for his own good," Embrie commented as Declan shut the Research Hall door behind them. "Still, I'm hesitant to lock James out," she persisted, "if he can't get down here, we won't know what's happening."

"I hate to admit this," Declan started, "but James was correct, our first priority is keeping this facility secure. We need to protect ALVA, give the machines enough time to sort through whatever the Girl jammed inside my head. We've come too far, we can't start making sloppy, irrational mistakes. When James returns, I'm sure he'll figure out a way of letting us know."

"You're right, of course, just doesn't make it any easier," Embrie mumbled, inspecting the key with a disdainful look. "I can't wait to hand this back over to Commander Kingston, there are too many bad memories attached to this key." She hesitated before inserting the key and locking the door behind them. "What are we going to do without our leader?" she asked, dropping the key into her pocket as they walked towards the front porch, dodging blood spots along the flagstone path. "We need him."

"Bruce isn't in any shape to help us," Declan reminded her, "and now he's in the proper hands. He'll get the best medical care possible. After all, nobody's more experienced with handling serious wounds than military trauma surgeons."

"Good point," Embrie said, her mood improving. "You really believe the commander will be fine?"

"Certainly," Declan reassured her, "while his injuries are significant, his limbs and head are still attached to his body, he has no visibly protruding organs, all positives. Of course, blood is important, too, and he lost quite a bit, so I wouldn't count on him being vertical anytime soon."

"Good thing you don't write greeting cards for a living," Embrie remarked, "although your brutally honest prognosis is oddly reassuring. So thank you."

"I've never understood the utility of mincing words, maybe it's not lying but it's still untruthful and inaccurate," Declan posited.

"Never thought about it that way," Embrie replied, "you certainly view the world from your own perspective."

"Always have, and I don't mean to change the subject," Declan interjected, "but as my adrenaline high wears off I'm feeling a bit woozy, and I realize my leg is in rougher shape than I thought."

Embrie looked down at Declan's shredded pants, blood rivulets streaming down his leg. "Let's get inside," declared Embrie, swinging open the front door. "Ms. Elliott," she shouted, "we need help!" She grabbed the professor's hand. "Come on," she said, "I need a better look," pulling him down the hall towards the farthest room.

"Where are we?" he asked, the wall space between the fully stocked bookshelves lined with romantic paintings of faraway lands and poster-sized photos of famous places.

"My office," her terse reply, sweeping everything off the large desk occupying most of the room. "Now sit," she ordered, helping Declan climb onto the desktop. She rifled through the drawers, found scissors and cut through his right tattered trouser leg, revealing two fish-mouthed tears in his flesh, mid-calf and lower thigh. "Ms. Elliott," bellowed Embrie, "please hurry, and bring towels and hot water!"

"I'm surprised this doesn't hurt more," Declan noted with dispassionate curiosity, "must've sliced some nerves."

"Sliced some nerves?" Embrie repeated in disbelief, "You're not a robot like Triple Dash, your skin is peeled back like an orange. I'm looking inside your leg, and that's all you have to say?"

"No," replied Declan, looking down at his mangled limb. "I also wonder why I'm not limping more, although I know that's not what you mean. You're right, my injuries should be far more upsetting, a simple paper cut usually throws me off the rails. I must be suffering from traumatic dissociation which, for the moment, is beneficial, keeping me calm when I should otherwise be freaking out."

"Point taken," Embrie said, carefully peeling back the skin and probing his exposed flesh.

"Yeech," Declan shrieked, wincing as she probed his leg. "I think you found a working nerve, probably the last one," he remarked, laying his head on the desk to avoid looking at his leg.

Ms. Elliott arrived with towels and a bucket of steaming water, quickly glancing over Declan's wound. "Your injuries aren't life-threatening," the older woman calmly prognosticated, adding the caveat "unless you develop a wound infection. Gangrene is a particularly nasty way to die, I've seen what happens and it's not pretty."

"That's a cheery assessment," grumbled the professor.

"Please tend to his leg," interjected Embrie, instructing the older woman to clean Declan's wounds while she ventured off to locate supplies. Embrie returned moments later holding a spool of string. "This is the strongest thread I could find," she said, pulling a seven-inch-long needle from her pocket.

Declan sat up and frantically scooted back on the desk. "Oh no," he yelled, waving his hands in protest. "You've gotta be kidding."

"I'm not," Embrie replied while patiently threading the long, sharp needle. "We need to stop the bleeding right away, and you don't have the luxury of a trauma surgeon waiting upstairs. I need to use Ms. Elliott's meat trussing needles because this thread is very thick, which means it won't break. Don't worry, your leg is numb, you won't feel a thing."

"Mostly numb," clarified Declan. "Your best plan is to string me together like a Cornish game hen?" he gasped.

Embrie held up the needle, ready to begin. "You've got a better idea?"

"Sadly, no," he replied, and without another word, Declan sighed in resignation, wrapped his face with a towel so he could scream into it, and laid back on the desk.

Half an hour later, Embrie's tight knots successfully held together the puckered edges of Declan's wounds, the pressure halting the bloody ooze. "I've sewn back together plenty of dolls and stuffed animals in my time, but never a person," she remarked. "Almost done, how are you holding up?"

Declan pulled his shouting towel off his face. "That went better than I imagined, which means the nerve damage must be worse than I thought." He sat up to peek at the results, commenting, "My leg looks like a patchwork quilt, although it's far better than I expected." He grabbed his head and said, "I feel woozy," flopping down onto the desktop. "Not sure if it's from getting knocked around inside that casket or because I'm starving, but my head's spinning like a 45 RPM record."

"Don't forget massive blood loss," Embrie reminded him, "and the box wasn't a casket. Whatever the reason, you'll feel a whole lot better when this wound is properly bandaged," she told him, admiring her handiwork. "Not bad," she decided, "although you'll certainly have nifty scars. Your uniform, on the other hand, is destined for the trash heap. The pants are bloody shreds and the shirt's not much better, so you'll need something else to wear."

"Oh no," Declan groaned, "if you're talking about your pink bathrobe, I'll be content wearing a flour sack. Not that I minded the robe, it smelled nice, like you, it's just…"

"Understood, and don't worry," Embrie giggled, "I remembered a better clothing option," she hinted. "Let me show you."

"Sounds good," Declan said, gently lowering himself off the table, surveying his gauze-wrapped leg. "Thank you, nicely done," he praised, jesting, "next time I split myself open, I'll know where to go."

"Hopefully you'll think of better reasons to seek me out," Embrie teased back.

"I'm a college professor, all I do is think," he awkwardly countered, in their clever battle of wits bringing a spoon to a knife fight. "Err, speaking of thinking, I think we're on our own for a while, so we should plot out our next steps. It's tempting to risk a trip to Bruce's office upstairs, find James or Director Bowen, but we both know that will only cause more problems. If we compromise this facility, all of our efforts to stop the Germans will be moot. For the moment, we're left to our own devices."

"Agreed," Embrie replied, plopping down into a cushioned office chair, exhausted. "So, what do we do next?" she asked. "Any suggestions?"

"How about a slice of pineapple upside-down cake?" interrupted Ms. Elliott, carrying the freshly baked treat.

Declan straightened up and smiled. "Such fortuitous timing," he said, greedily eyeing the treat. "Thank you, ma'am, dessert won't solve all our problems, but this cake will certainly improve our moods."

Ms. Elliott doled out generous slices of the decadent golden dessert, and while Declan devoured his piece Embrie summarized their predicament. "Let's start with what we know," the young woman began. "The Nazis have ambitions beyond their own borders, and it appears the Obturavi are helping them. They most likely possess the Egyptian Epistolith and Antarctica's Axyn Kirox, meaning they'll be able to extract whatever's needed to construct their game-changing weapons. They still need to decode and interpret the information, which buys us some time, but once Germany builds these weapons the technological advantage irreparably tips in their favor. Every moment they're closer to meeting their goal, the clock is already ticking, and the information ALVA extracted from your brain is our only chance at stopping them."

"Sums it up nicely, beautifully illustrating how ill-equipped we are to face this challenge," Declan said, pondering their options. "Maybe we can talk to President Roosevelt?" he suggested. "He can get the military involved, we'll have infinitely more resources."

"That's a definite no," Embrie replied. "Mr. Edison didn't trust politicians, and neither do I, promoted for neither intellect nor skills, instead based upon a popularity contest. How would you explain everything that's happened to you, or what you've seen down here? You said it yourself, you can't believe it and you lived it."

"You're right," Declan begrudgingly admitted, "the United States is desperately trying to avoid direct involvement in a second world war. The President would need a darn good reason for throwing our country into the fray, and all we've got are hunches about what the Germans are doing. Our best outcome would be getting laughed out of the White House, worst case they'd believe us, take over and muck everything up."

"We both hate feeling powerless, sitting here waiting when we don't have time to waste. Without Commander Kingston our best hope relies upon ALVA's ability to unlock the information extracted from your mind."

"We don't even know if the transfer worked," Declan reminded her, "and sadly I don't feel any better, just different. My brain still feels like soggy bread. I hoped the data transfer would clear my mental fogginess, instead there's a new heaviness weighing down my thoughts. Maybe we should find Triple Dash."

Ms. Elliott walked over to the window and said, "That won't be necessary," pushing back the curtains. Perplexed, Declan and Embrie joined her at the window. Ms.

Elliott pointed up into the sky, past the backyard and corn rows, negating further explanation. Above the stone barrier wall, the entire length of the metallic-glass barrier separating them from the Analytical Engine Room sparkled with blazing bursts of light and color. "Reminds me of a fireworks display," she commented.

"Declan, are you okay?" Embrie asked, tapping his shoulder, but he was unresponsive, staring blankly at the massive wall.

After several long seconds, he emerged from his trancelike state. "I'm fine," he reassured her. "It's just I was wrong, my thoughts aren't dragging, they're being pulled. The puzzles inside my head, I can feel ALVA draining them from my mind."

"And putting them up for display," noted Ms. Elliott.

"I'd say that was the craziest thing I've ever heard," Declan replied, "though at this point there's a lot of contenders for that title."

The trio stood silent, mesmerized as the flashes of light and color formed into a blurry image, further coalescing into a person holding something above their head. As the image focused into crisp clarity its intent was immediately evident. A man dressed in snow gear, swastika on his sleeve, triumphantly holding up the Axyn Kirox, standing atop the desecrated remains of several Alpha Team members.

"That's horrible!" Embrie shrieked, turning away.

"A not-so-subtle reminder of what we're up against," Declan remarked, "and I hope we'll be able to repay the courtesy." When the image changed Declan said, "Embrie, take a look at what's up there now, nothing graphic, just a drawing and it makes no sense to me. Looks like a toddler grabbed hold of a crayon box."

Embrie looked up at the wall, now displaying a complex set of squiggly lines of varying colors, each followed by a symbol. She puzzled over the image until it faded and a new one appeared, similar though not identical to the prior, followed by more images of multi-colored shapes. "Looks like artwork from a Kindergarten class," she mused.

"If this junk is what the Girl stored in my brain," huffed Declan, "I deserve to get the space back with some late payment fees tacked onto the bill."

Embrie didn't immediately respond, engrossed by the ever-changing images. "The Girl, she's teaching ALVA," Embrie conjectured in hushed, reverent tones. "These images are a primer, she's making sure they're speaking the same language."

"You think the images coming out of my brain are teaching the machines? How can you be sure?"

"I'm not," Embrie admitted, "except I've been here many years and I've never seen the wall produce images before. The wall is only clear or cloudy, never a giant movie screen. Ms. Elliott, what do you think?"

"Unprecedented," concurred Ms. Elliott, intently studying the images. "Best I can tell, the analytical machines are only displaying the images, not creating them. Judging by the nature of the images, the data must originate from a biological source, and given Doctor Riordan's recent dalliance in the Analytical Engine Room, I presume he is the culprit."

Declan furrowed his brow. "I don't understand your rationale."

"As a scientist, my reasoning should be obvious to you," Ms. Eliott replied, "just look at how the images spread across the wall and slowly sharpen into focus. That lag time is due to neuronal latency. Biological nerves propagate impulses at a sluggish few hundred miles per hour, electrical wires conduct near the speed of light. These images suffer from the limitations of organic life, hence a biological source."

"How insightful, I can't argue with your logic," conceded Declan. "Between Triple Dash's succinct trouncing of human minds and your clever observation of neural limitations, I'm nearly convinced to trade this carboniferous mortal coil for something silicon-based."

"Perhaps next time I can fully convince you," Ms. Elliott seamlessly countered, causing Declan and Embrie to break into laughter while Ms. Elliott continued staring blankly at the wall display, oblivious to her own witty remark. The trio watched the images flash past them for several minutes before Declan dropped to his knees, screaming and grasping both sides of his head.

Embrie knelt beside him, gently rubbing his back until he quieted down. "Are you okay?"

Declan stood and smiled, looking out the window at the wall's rapid-fire visual onslaught. "It's gone!" he exclaimed, "the circus train inside my head has unloaded, the muck has been raked away, and my mind belongs to me again. The burdensome weight is lifted."

"Are you certain?" Embrie asked, "because the images aren't slowing down, they're still flashing just as quickly," pointing out the steady stream of new images appearing on the metal wall.

"Yes, it's over, at least my part," Declan said. "The Girl required a biological conduit, and while my role was a bit anticlimactic, the prophecy is fulfilled. Now I'm utterly famished, and still quite dizzy, perhaps another slice of cake will help," he reckoned, seeking out the remaining pineapple-topped treat.

"Don't sell yourself short," Embrie chastised him. "I shouldn't need to explain this to such an intelligent man but think about it. Why would George Washington write a prophecy about you, create a secret society of important historical figures and genius scientists to seek you out, just so you could serve as a carrier pigeon? Does that sound logical? For better or worse, I don't think you're done saving the world."

"Says... says you, I just... just earned my life back," Declan countered, speech slurred, staggering over to the cake for one more slice. He leaned against the desk, struggling to remain upright, unconscious before hitting the carpet.

Chapter 21

April 15, 1939
Nancy's Place
Clypeate Headquarters
City of Washington, District of Columbia

Declan opened one eye and by the dim glow of a table lamp saw he was no longer in the office. Neither was he vertical, wriggling his starfished limbs to gain more clues, concluding his body lay sprawled out across an exceedingly comfortable mattress. He rolled over and squirmed upright, propped his head against a pillow mound and looked out from the large, ornately carved poster bed.

He startled upon seeing Embrie seated in a large, plush chair pulled adjacent to his bedside. "Good evening, slugabed," she cheerfully greeted him. "Is everything okay? You whimpered in your sleep, I was going to wake you if it continued much longer. Sounded like you were in a significant amount of pain."

"Some bizarre dreams," he mumbled as his thoughts cleared. "I'm fine, though," he reassured her, "a bit sore, most notably my leg, everywhere else is a close runner up. Nothing I can't handle," he boasted for the young woman's benefit, wincing as he repositioned to more properly address his guest. Declan felt the silky sheets glide effortlessly across his skin, causing him to appreciate his state of undress. He pulled the sheets up to his neck. "I'm naked!" he shrieked, peeking under the covers to confirm.

"Well, of course you are," Embrie replied, "we weren't going to put you in this nice bed wearing your grimy, bloody rags. It also gave Ms. Elliott and I the opportunity to check you over for other injuries, you had several more wounds that needed tending, no more stitches, but the cabinet didn't do you any favors when the platform collapsed. And then, when you passed out in my office, you managed to give your scalp another decent goose egg. Passing out is a thing with you, isn't it?"

"Never happened before I got involved with the Clypeate, all these interactions with the Girl in the Glass leave me drained. And, by the way, I'm still naked."

"True," conceded Embrie, "although now you're also clean and bandaged up, so try not to get yourself into further mischief anytime soon."

"But, but, I'm naked," he persisted. "That means you saw, ummm, my, ummm…"

"Oh, don't be embarrassed," she tried reassuring him, "there's a folio of Leonardo da Vinci's anatomical studies in the library, so there's nothing I haven't seen. And I promise I didn't look. Much," she giggled.

"I don't feel very reassured," Declan testily replied.

"Oh, please cheer up," Embrie implored, "I'm just teasing you, I dressed your wounds and helped Ms. Elliott carry you down the hall. She's the one who cleaned you up, and she birthed four boys, so nothing surprises her."

"You wished me a good evening," Declan noted, changing the subject, "how long was I out?"

"Not too long, just a day and a half," Embrie estimated, "and your leg appears to be healing nicely, no signs of infection. You did, however, hit your head really hard. How does it feel?"

"My head's fine," Declan said, downplaying the pain, grasping at his last remnants of masculine pride. "Over the years I've been called hard-headed many times, so perhaps there's a physical corollary to my personality trait." They both chuckled. "Even better, my mind hasn't felt this crisp since UCLA," he added, steering the conversation away from his injuries. "Actually, I'm more hungry than anything else."

Embrie smiled. "Ms. Elliott will love to hear that, although she'll be upset when I tell her we need to ration our food stockpile, given our next delivery of supplies may not be for a while. Commander Kingston always made sure our needs were met." Embrie's voice trailed off, pausing to regain her composure before turning on the ceiling lamps.

"This makes my suite at the Willard look like a flophouse," Declan gushed, the bedroom impeccably appointed with opulent furniture, ornate wallpaper and thick, plush carpeting. "Whose room is this? It's fit for a king."

"Or a wealthy entrepreneur. This room was Mr. Edison's private quarters," Embrie replied. "After the Obturavi attack, he personally funded the cleanup effort," she elaborated, "including construction of the wall and house. He planned to repair the Research Hall and library as well, but he died before those restorations were complete. His first priorities were to rebuild the machines, keep them safe, and give us a comfortable place to work and live. During his periodic visits, Mr. Edison stayed here with us, days at a time, at first directing completion of the house, the wall and Analytical Engine Room, then tinkering with the machines and perusing the library collection."

"He certainly had decadent tastes," Declan said, running his hand along the silk comforter, "a bit extravagant by my simple standards, though in one regard, I'll admit, I'm a bit jealous."

"About what?" Embrie asked.

"He got to spend all that time with you," Declan brazenly divulged.

"Oh, I was just a silly kid," she dismissively recollected, "running around this place like it was my personal jungle gym. He was such a quiet, methodical man, I don't think he cared much for my antics. Now, as for your stomach," Embrie pivoted, swiftly changing subjects much to Declan's chagrin, "that is something we can address, but first we need to find you something suitable to wear." Embrie opened a closet door, the space inside larger than his apartment and stocked like a department store.

Declan peeked inside. "There's a lot of options in here that aren't a pink bathrobe."

"When James carried you here from the library, in the moment I was so upset Mr. Edison's collection didn't even cross my mind," Embrie confessed, "it was going to be a pink robe or flour sack." She strolled past a row of suits, thumbing through them. "While Mr. Edison was alive I never ventured near his room, plus he always wore the same style of suit, so I assumed he never changed outfits. Clearly I was mistaken, and between the closet and bureaus you'll find plenty of options. Likely on the loose side, I'm afraid, at least for now," she chuckled, "until Ms. Elliott's cooking has a chance to work its magic. I'll leave you to change in peace, when you're presentable just hang a left down the hallway and follow your nose."

As his vibrant hostess exited the room, Declan wondered whether she'd missed his playful flirtation or worse, chosen to ignore it. Just as doubt began to sink his hopeful heart, Embrie poked her head into the room one last time. "Sorry, forgot to close the door, ensure your privacy," she said, swinging closed the bedroom door she mischievously grinned. "Don't worry, I look forward to spending time with you, too."

Chapter 22

April 15, 1939
Nancy's Place
Clypeate Headquarters
City of Washington, District of Columbia

Declan exited Mr. Edison's lavishly appointed bedroom sporting one of the late inventor's suits, sans bowtie, unable to craft a properly shaped bow. His luck didn't fare much better while searching out the dining room, the presumably simple task gone awry, the home containing an unexpected labyrinth of corridors. Lost amongst the interconnected halls, Declan's initial bemusement morphed into perturbed agitation, his injured leg increasingly sore. Wondering how long before Embrie came looking for him, he considered giving up and retreating to the bedroom when he caught the alluring scent of freshly baked bread. Declan followed the wafting aromas into the dining room, where Embrie and Ms. Elliott were seated, waiting for him.

"I apologize for my tardiness," Declan greeted the women, "but the layout of this house is deceptively intricate." Smiling a little too long at Embrie, he redirected his gaze towards the bounty of appetizing dishes set atop the sideboard table.

"No worries," Ms. Elliott replied, "we haven't been waiting long, though Embrie wondered if she might come looking for you."

Embrie stood to greet the professor. "We forget how easy it is to get lost in here," she elaborated, motioning for Declan to fill his plate as she joined him at the sideboard. "This house is built like a funhouse maze. Years ago it happened to me all the time, getting so mixed up I'd climb out a window rather than wander aimlessly through the hallways. The ranch's confusing layout is purposeful. While Mr. Edison designed this house with comfort in mind, it also functions as a bulwark, a defensive barrier against future attacks."

With their plates overflowing Embrie returned to her seat, Declan choosing the one directly across. "You've been coming down here a long time," he realized, "sounds like you practically grew up down here."

"I did," Embrie replied without hesitation. "Since I was a little girl, this is my home."

"You live down here?" Declan reiterated, perplexed by the notion. "Must get terribly lonely, being trapped underground like hermits. Not that I'm much of a socialite, either, though I'm not sure how well I'd adapt to this unusual arrangement."

"I didn't have to adapt," Embrie replied, "this is the only home I've ever known." She momentarily hesitated before elaborating. "I don't remember much about my own family," she revealed, "my parents left when I was very young, and I would have ended up in an orphanage except for the kindness of Ms. Elliott. She knew my parents and fought hard to adopt me, and I've been living with her, down here, ever since. Together we keep this facility running."

Intrigued, Declan pressed further. "Ms. Elliott," Declan said, addressing the older woman, "if you don't mind me asking, how'd you acquire this job? After all, it's not exactly the kind of position that gets posted in the wanted section of the local daily."

"My son was a prominent member of the Clypeate," Ms. Elliott explained, passing the gravy boat towards Declan, "so when they needed someone trustworthy to care for the house and Analytical Engine Room, I fit the bill."

"The Clypeate gifted Ms. Elliott and I with steady jobs," Embrie added, "which allows us to live in this lovely home. It's a wonderful arrangement, we keep everything running and they provide us with all the supplies we'll ever need."

"But don't you miss going outside and enjoying the fresh air?" Declan wondered.

Embrie emphatically shook her head. "From what I've read and heard about the outside world, I'm not in any rush to explore beyond these walls," she declared. "We're not prisoners, I'm free to come and go as I please, and I've spent enough time topside to realize traveling doesn't agree with me. Think about it this way. I live in a beautiful home in a well-protected neighborhood, I have access to an amazing library collection, I maintain the world's most advanced computational machine, I get delicious home-cooked meals, and I spend every day with the best mother ever. I couldn't ask for anything more."

"I guess not," Declan agreed, impishly adding, "except maybe you could ask for visitors, perhaps of the awkwardly charming yet ravishingly handsome variety."

"I did, but James isn't here right now," Embrie replied, giggling at the dumbstruck and disheartened look on Declan's face. "Oh, I'm just kidding," she reassured him, "I prefer the company of intellectuals. Although you are still dangerously thin," she playfully jested, "so no more questions until you've cleaned your plate."

Finishing his meal was a simple task, everything Ms. Elliott prepared tasted delicious. After the dietary frugality experienced during the Great Depression plus years spent surviving on a poor student's budget, he'd long suppressed his expectations for quality. On this evening Ms. Elliott prepared a meal fit for a Currier and Ives lithograph, turkey plus all the trimmings, which Declan shoveled down as fast as decorum and his stomach permitted. Such a highly prized commodity as turkey, or any other meat, rarely occupied his plate, especially while still identifiable as an animal and not ground-up as mystery mash.

Embrie looked on with a bemused grin, pleased at Declan's visible enjoyment, while Ms. Elliott spent most of the meal running back and forth into the kitchen to check on dessert. This gave Declan and Embrie time alone together, which they spent speculating about the meaning of the images flashing across the metallic wall beyond the corn rows. When Declan couldn't eat another bite the pair headed outside and settled into lounge chairs on the backyard patio, watching the stream of images. Ms. Elliott delivered a plate of desserts before announcing her retirement for the evening. Declan's stomach, miraculously enticed into nibbling on a fudgy caramel-walnut brownie, listened intently to Embrie's observations regarding the images extracted from his mind.

"After you collapsed, Ms. Elliott took control, she cleaned you and tucked you into bed. Meanwhile, I sat out here worrying about you, distracting myself by watching the wall's steady display of schematics, drawings, and patterns. I wanted, I hoped, to make sense of them."

Declan mumbled through a mouthful of brownie, "Did you dithcover anything?"

"Possibly," Embrie replied, pulling a crumpled piece of paper from her pocket and unfurling it. "Look up at the wall and focus your attention on the upper left corner of each image," she instructed. "There's always a cluster of shapes in that spot, currently five." Declan hadn't noticed it before but she was correct, innocuously situated along the edge of each new image racing past them, always a string of shapes.

"Wow, you have a good eye for detail, I could have watched this parade of pictures for weeks and never noticed," he admitted, impressed by her discovery. "Not sure what it could mean, though, looks as random as the rest of the stream," he concluded, debating whether he should tackle a chocolate chip or oatmeal raisin cookie next.

"Except it's not random," Embrie countered, flipping her paper towards Declan. "Only eight shapes repeat," she explained, pointing to her sketches, listing them. "Circle, triangle, square, cross, diamond, pentagon, star, octagon. Most of the images are stamped with some combination of four of these shapes, but about once every ninety minutes the line drops down to one shape. This lasts just a few seconds, then two shapes for a couple minutes, three shapes for about fifteen minutes, and finally four shapes for the remainder."

"Running through all the combinations, like it's counting," Declan mused, biting into his newly chosen dessert.

"Exactly," Embrie gleefully concurred. "Counting, which makes sense if these are page numbers," she further hypothesized.

"Hold on," Declan said, sputtering on a mouthful of delicious cookie, "you think these shapes are numbers?" he asked, spraying oatmeal and raisin chunks onto the lawn. "Then why only eight shapes? Zero through nine would require ten shapes."

"Only base ten math needs ten numbers, if these schematics use base eight mathematics," Embrie postulated, "only eight shapes are required, zero through seven."

"You've lost me. I'm a polymath who isn't particularly fond of math," Declan confessed, "so you'll need to explain this more slowly."

"Think about mathematical rules," Embrie suggested. "When counting in base ten math, as you count to nine those numbers stay in the ones column. But number ten requires a second column, the tens column. With base eight math, now seven becomes the last of the ones column, and eight starts the tens column."

"This sounds horrifically unscientific," Declan opined, "after all the metric system is based upon tens, which means our entire understanding of the Universe functions on base ten math."

"True, but there's nothing universally special about base ten. Our species learned to count using fingers, and since we're generally born with five on each hand, we naturally grouped numbers into tens. Base ten math is simply humanity's generally accepted standard, not an intrinsic rule of the Universe. Some ancient cultures used base eight math, counting the space between fingers instead. Base eight math is neither more nor less correct, and would only require eight shapes."

"So, if these pages are being counted using a different numbering system," Declan began, "what does a string of four shapes mean? Four number places would still mean these pages number into the thousands, right?"

"Not in base eight math," Embrie corrected Declan, quickly doing the math in her head, "though It'd still be a large number, at least in the hundreds."

"Okay, I surrender, once again confirming this field as my Achilles heel. I'll take your word," Declan conceded, shaking his head, "I don't find math intuitive, there aren't gray areas, perhaps that's why I like biology, it's messy and imprecise."

"Though biology still follows the rules of the Universe, using the alphabet of math to spell out the formulas of physics and chemistry," Embrie pointed out.

"While my mathematical shortcomings are humbling, now I'm actually embarrassed," Declan replied, "having devoted my life to science, yet never realizing how seamlessly all these disciplines tie together. You eloquently point out the folly of my pedantic tunnel vision."

"Having focus is a great gift," Embrie countered, "the Universe's magic hides in those little details. And when it comes to details, I hope ALVA is having better luck interpreting the ones contained in the images flashing on the wall. Just figuring out the page numbers proved challenging enough."

"Don't belittle your accomplishment, that's an amazing revelation," Declan praised her, "you've been quite productive today, unlike me, I slept the day away."

"Funny you should say that. I grew so sleepy from hours of staring at the images, I was convinced I'd simply dreamed up my eureka moment."

"Speaking of dreams," Declan pivoted, "I had a real doozy today, perhaps generated from oxygen deprivation upon losing consciousness. I've never dreamt with such realism, the amount of detail, it was so vivid I'm not sure calling it a dream suffices. I can't make sense of it. My mind once again belongs to me, the Girl's information extracted, yet I still feel her presence. And while I've been told the Girl is only a construct of the Epistolith, I don't believe that's true, at least not entirely, because she remains inside my head. I dreamt about the Girl in the Glass. I hope that doesn't sound creepy."

"Not at all," Embrie reassured him, shaking her head. "Please, continue."

"This dream wasn't exactly about her, more like I was inside her." He paused. "I regret my word choice."

Embrie grimaced, agreeing, "Yes, that last bit sounded pervy."

"Allow me to rephrase," Declan said, treading more thoughtfully. "What I meant was I viewed the world from her perspective, through her eyes, in the moment with her." Declan paused to gather his thoughts and finish the cookie.

Embrie sat up. "What do you mean?" she asked with audibly palpable interest.

"Well," he continued, "there was a man, her father, maybe, at least someone very important to her. I felt her mixture of love and awe for him. Then suddenly she's pulled away from this man, she feels so powerless, so scared, so sad, in that moment she knows she'll never see him again. I can't believe this was simply a dream; it felt real and more like a memory. That's why I slept so fitfully. I felt her pain as if it were my own. Her emotional depth, her capacity for love, I've never felt such a powerful connection in my entire life, it was terrifying. I've been mulling it over, and this only makes sense if the Girl in the Glass is real. Despite how crazy this sounds, no other conclusion fits. What possible reason could the Epistolith have for fabricating such incredibly detailed, evocative false memories? If you know something, Embrie, I think I've earned a truthful answer."

Embrie nodded, "Yes, you have," she agreed. "What you were told earlier wasn't altogether untruthful, though perhaps Commander Kingston and Director Bowen should have elaborated. To better explain, we'll need to return to the library."

Declan followed the young woman through the cornfield and into the Analytical Engine Room. None of the Builder robots, not even Triple Dash, greeted them as they walked along the catwalk, already reconstructed with notably sturdier support piers. Declan looked up at the metallic barrier from this new vantage point, still flashing a whirlwind of images extracted from his mind, with one notable exception. "From this side of the barrier, the pictures look much crisper," he remarked.

Embrie also glanced up at the wall. "That's because they're being displayed for the benefit of ALVA, not for us," she concluded. "I'll wager these images mean something to the machines." Declan realized she was correct yet again, because as they followed the path weaving between the towers every robot they passed appeared extremely busy and self-absorbed, zipping around them as if they were invisible.

Upon approaching the library door, Embrie pulled out the golden key and shifted the tumblers. "I've been around long enough to learn all the codes," she explained, noticing Declan's astonishment.

"You're never short on surprises," he remarked as they entered the library, Embrie leading them to the splintered bottom of the spiral staircase and up the rickety makeshift ladder. Safely ascending to the library's second-floor balcony, Declan noted this riser was lined with shelves just like the lower level, also encircling the room and just as stuffed. "Every tier is packed, it's an amazing collection, just based on scale," he remarked in awe, scanning the several levels above them. "This room is a bibliophile's paradise," he commented, "it would take a hundred years to read all of these books."

"No, more like twenty-five," Embrie nonchalantly stated as she led them around the room. "Half of these works have no English translation, another quarter are too fragile to handle, and some are just tedious."

"That's a rather precise guess," Declan laughed, "even if your mother began reading this collection to you while still residing in her womb, I'd venture you'd still have a few years left till completion."

"A lady never reveals her age," Embrie replied, stopping in front of a dusty set of binders. She pulled the first volume off the shelf and handed it to Declan. "Take a look inside," she directed the professor, "this will help you understand."

He opened the cover, greeted on the first page by a drawing of a little red-headed girl. "A little younger, but it's her, the Girl in the Glass, isn't it?"

"Yes," Embrie confirmed, "she was only five years old when she drew this self-portrait."

Declan flipped back to the cover. "Manuscripts of Mary Elizabeth, Volume One," he read, then looked up at Embrie.

"She's a real person. I knew it," Declan gleefully exclaimed.

"Yes, she's real," Embrie confirmed, "and it only took a few years for her to fill all these binders," the young woman said, pointing to five shelves, several feet long, tightly packed with similar binders. "Mary is a biological conduit, capable of extracting and interpreting information from the Epistolith.

"And her name is Mary Elizabeth," Declan muttered while turning the binder pages, absorbed by the intricate drawings, eerily echoing the images recently removed from his head and currently scrolling across the metallic glass wall. "This collection is astoundingly prolific," Declan commented, looking at the accumulated binders, "and judging by the amount she shoved into my brain, she wasn't done sharing. I'd really like to meet her, where is she now?"

"In the most relevant way you already have, through your shared bond, although I recognize you're asking a different question. You can't meet her, at least not in the traditional sense." Embrie began to cry, burying her face in her hands.

Declan awkwardly patted her back. "I didn't mean to upset you." While he derived a twisted sort of pleasure from watching his cocky students shed a tear or two, it hurt him to see Embrie similarly pained.

"Not your fault," Embrie said between sniffles, "you couldn't know. The Obturavi learned of Mary Elizabeth's abilities and hunted her down, hoping to capture or kill her," she explained, pausing to wipe tears away using her sleeve. "Mr. Edison helped Mary and her parents escape to somewhere they'd be safe, leaving behind her baby sister. Me."

"The Girl in the Glass is your sister? If your family needed to run and hide, why didn't your parents take you with them?"

"Mr. Edison told me I was left behind for my own protection. My parents feared the Obturavi would find them, and they decided I'd be safer staying behind with Ms. Elliott. She raised me as her own daughter, all the while promising my family would return when the time was right. Only Mr. Edison knew their location, and that secret died with him. My hope faded over the years. Until you arrived."

"Now I understand your enthusiasm. If Mary Elizabeth is loading my brain with information and memories, then she must be alive."

"It's more than that," Embrie said, pulling down another binder. "This is the last binder, Mary Elizabeth's drawings right up until when she left. Let me show you her final drawing, done the day before the Obturavi attack." She flipped to the last page and handed it to the professor.

"The resemblance is uncanny," he muttered, the crayon portrait of a sandy-haired, blue-eyed man staring off the page. "It's me."

Embrie squeezed his hand. "From the moment I saw you, I knew. Mary Elizabeth sent you."

Before Declan had a chance to respond the library phone rang, startling them both and sending Embrie racing down the makeshift ladder. Declan did not follow, choosing instead to mindlessly flip through the binder as he processed these revelations. He skimmed past diagrams of aircraft wings, more advanced than any he'd ever seen, attached to even more advanced planes, some without propellers, others where the entire airplane was simply a flying wing.

Embrie broke his muddled reverie. "ALVA wants us next door. Our immediate presence is requested," she informed him.

"Well, let's go see what Big Al wants," Declan snidely remarked, "perhaps the jumble of wires has figured out why your sister monkeyed around inside my head."

Upon entering the Analytical Engine Room, the increased activity level immediately struck Declan, the lights on each massive tower blinked and flashed with urgency and immediacy. "These machines weren't behaving like this before," Declan remarked, "their gentle hum now sounds like rush hour traffic. How often does this happen?"

"Never," Embrie distractedly replied as she scanned the room, awed by the vibrant commotion, watching the dozens of Builder robots speedily shuttle between the towers carrying all manner of supplies and gear.

"This must be what Santa's workshop feels like on Christmas Eve, because there are some busy elves in here," Declan commented as a trio of Builder robots whizzed past them.

"These towers must be responding to the information contained in those images," Embrie ventured.

"Which means ALVA really likes what the Girl shared, because he's got these Builders firing on all cylinders."

"We don't have cylinders," a tinny voice from behind corrected him, "our systems utilize electricity, not internal combustion." Triple Dash rolled towards them. "Hello, Miss

Powell. Ah, Doctor Riordan, you survived the data transfer, and more intact than our analysis predicted, I observe no missing limbs."

"I'm deeply touched by your concern for my well-being," Declan scoffed, his right leg smarting after so much exertion. "Do you know why Big Al interrupted us? Embrie and I were in the library discussing a very important subject when he requested our presence."

"Big Al?" Triple Dash queried.

"ALVA," Embrie clarified.

"Curious moniker alteration," Triple Dash remarked. "You were summoned because ALVA has successfully completed the data transfer, and we are now carrying out the instructions embedded within the information stream. Although the schematics are advanced, even for us, we are very clever and don't expect the sophisticated designs to present a problem. We appreciate the intellectual challenge. As for your role, we ask you to avoid the Analytic Engine Room while we work."

"That's not okay," Declan argued, "that means we can't access the library. How much time will you need?"

"I can't provide a factual estimate, as we've never encountered such a complex challenge to our resources. However, Doctor Riordan, you are in luck. Miss Powell is a compendium of knowledge, you will run out of time long before she runs out of stories."

"I still find your request unfair," declared Declan.

"Fairness is not our primary concern," Triple Dash stated, "we are interested in ensuring your safety. Well, maybe not yours personally, Doctor, but Miss Powell's, most definitely."

"Triple Dash, that isn't very kind," Embrie chastised the machine. "As for ALVA's request, I think we'd be wise to listen," she suggested, pointing to the distant wall. "Look at the images, they're scrolling through much faster now," she noted, the schematics displayed on the metallic-glass barrier now a flashing blur. "I'm not sure what's going to happen next, but ALVA doesn't make unnecessary requests, so I'm inclined to comply."

"Okay, Embrie," Declan said, glowering at Triple Dash. "I'll do it for you, not for this lying rust bucket," and stormed off towards the Clean Room, Embrie and Triple Dash trailing behind. Declan opened the door and waved. "We're outta here, please thank Big Al for his care and concerns."

If Triple Dash registered Declan's sarcasm, it did not surface in the robot's reply. "When we have completed our tasks, you may share your appreciation and gratitude directly with ALVA."

"Okay," Declan replied, unsure what Triple Dash meant and not interested in entertaining the robot further, slammed the Clean Room door shut. "I'm glad we're leaving," he muttered as the roar of the chamber's vacuum crescendoed and blocked further discussion.

Chapter 23

April 20, 1939
Navy and Munitions Building
City of Washington, District of Columbia

Six days passed since James snuck out from the JAG department, unnoticed amongst the chaos created when medics rushed in to save his injured boss. During the last few days he'd spent many hours at the Navy building, cautiously surveilling the hallway leading into the JAG offices, biding his time, watching the parade of military investigators armed with cameras and notepads make their rounds. Now, after nearly two full days of inactivity, Vice Admiral Fischer confidently strolled into the reception area wearing his Navy best, casually greeting the secretary and guard before navigating towards Bruce's office. The outer door's privacy screen was pulled down over the glass panel, blocking his view, so after intently listening for voices and hearing none, he gripped the handle. Slowly turning the knob while scanning the hallway for undesired company, James, confident he was alone, gently pushed the door open. The darkened waiting area appeared unchanged, just as disheveled as he remembered from those chaotically desperate moments, except now a ribbon of yellow tape circled the broken chair and smashed lamp. James quietly locked the door behind him then edged his way around the investigation scene, carefully avoiding the outlying shards of wood and ceramic crushed into the previously stained carpet, now also caked with dark patches of dried blood. He reached Bruce's office door with a sense of relief, eager to reconnect with Declan and Embrie, and as he swung the inner door open he was unexpectedly greeted by a singular seated figure.

"I'm sorry, this must be the wrong office," James apologized, quickly turning to leave.

His ruse failed. "Why are you in such a hurry, Vice Admiral Fischer?" the stranger asked, rising from the folding chair. Being addressed by name caught James off guard, swiveling back he found the stranger's attire equally puzzling, a civilian suit, dark brown pinstripe. "Don't be so surprised, Mr. Fischer," the clean-cut, pug-faced man continued. The tiny hairs on the back of James' neck stood on end, he felt the stranger's eyes intently studying him. "It's well-known criminals always return to the scene of the crime, but so do colleagues. Especially ones with recent rank-skipping promotions."

"I've done nothing wrong," James defensively responded. "Commander Kingston took a nasty spill and I wanted to see if he was back to work. May I ask, what are you doing here, sir?"

"I'm here on official business, seeking clues as to Mr. Kingston's whereabouts. You see, it's a funny thing to find you here, looking for Mr. Kingston, considering how he inexplicably vanished from the hospital four days after receiving several pints of blood and undergoing hours of surgery to repair a shattered arm, ruptured spleen, punctured lung and removal of a steel bar piercing his liver. Getting out of there would have required well-coordinated assistance. You wouldn't know anything about that, would you?"

"Absolutely nothing, I'm just as shocked as you are," James replied, "that sounds so irresponsible and dangerous."

"Yes, a very bad idea indeed," the beady-eyed stranger agreed and paused, carefully assessing James. "You seem like a good kid, son, even though your service record is spotty it's also admirable. You developed quite the reputation, a talent for catching important people in compromising situations, no wonder you're one of the few

Harold Bowen brought along to Naval Research. With the proper training and discipline, someone like you could go far in the military, or in my bureau."

"Well, I'm already a vice admiral, so I'm content, although I'm still not sure why you're really here," James prodded, his tone increasingly contemptuous.

"How refreshing, a direct man, not common in my line of work. Pleasantries aside, I am here as a liaison for President Roosevelt. He's grown tired of this detente with the remaining riff-raff of the Continental Army, and we're shutting down this little game."

"I haven't been with the organization long," James replied, "but I know the president doesn't have the authority to unilaterally cut the Continental Army out of the military."

"True," the man replied, "but President Roosevelt is tired of looking like a dummy, and your ragtag group is clearly hiding technology from our government. While in the hospital, several machine parts were found mixed with Mr. Kingston's belongings, and additional pieces were found floating in his abdomen when surgeons removed the jagged metal piercing his gut. The artifacts puzzled the military forensics team so much they passed the electrical components along to the government's wonkiest engineers, and even they were shocked. These parts are advanced tech, decades ahead of anything they'd ever seen. Hence the president isn't pleased, hiding critical technology of vital national security is a serious offense. We don't know where Mr. Kingston went, but we'd like to have a little chat with him, and I'm betting you've got a firm handle on his whereabouts."

"I don't know what you're talking about," James flatly reiterated, "and it's not mister, he is Commander Kingston."

"Look kid, you don't have enough short and curlies yet to understand how the big boys play this game, so please afford me the courtesy of not lying to my face. Just pass along this message. This is no longer his office. I'm certain all the silly theatrics in here, the tacky waiting area and barebones office, are designed to throw us off the scent, so we're going to tear this place apart until we figure out where all those technological goodies came from. So if you, Commander Kingston, or that nutty professor you pulled out of Dante's Inferno attempt to gain access to this building ever again, you will be immediately arrested for treason. And if Commander Kingston doesn't believe you, tell him this message came hand-delivered from me. I'm assuming you know who I am, correct?"

"Indeed, sir. And if I happen to run into the commander, I'll gladly pass your message along."

"Thank you, that's all I ask," the man said, walking with James out into the hallway. "Now I will escort you out of this building, you're no longer welcome here. And remember what I said, Vice Admiral Fischer, there is always a spot in my bureau for loyal, trust-worthy American patriots."

"Duly noted," James replied, the pair walking down the hallway, past the JAG waiting area and into the main corridor. Once the JAG department door closed behind them James tapped his pockets. "Hmm, I must have forgotten my pack. Mind if I bum a cig?" he asked, "you're quite an intimidating figure, and I need to steady my nerves. Plus, that secretary is something special, and I'd like an excuse to chat her up."

"My informants also told me about your womanizing ways, Vice Admiral. Already run through all the single, gullible ladies in the typing pool, have we?" he mocked, pulling a Lucky Strike from his suit pocket and handing it over. "I'll wait for you here," the man said, "can't risk having someone tamper with a potential crime scene, after all, and I'd like to make sure you don't get lost on your way out."

James disappeared back inside the JAG office for a few moments, returning with a red face. "That didn't go so well, she smacked my cheek so hard it popped the cigarette right out my mouth."

The pug-faced man chuckled at James' misfortune, and suddenly the pair was joined by several other men, presumably bodyguards, all similarly dressed in dark civilian suits, silently following behind them even after they exited the Navy Building. The man addressed James one last time. "Until you're willing to cooperate with us, I'd think twice about trying to reenter this, or any other government facility, without a contrite heart. For now you'll have to make do getting rejected from women outside the workplace. Now don't forget your message, or my offer, I could use a young man with gumption."

A black car pulled up and one of the bodyguards opened the door. As the man entered the car, James couldn't resist. "If you don't hear from me any time soon, don't get your panties in a bunch, Director Hoover." And with that James strolled back towards the Willard, following a serpiginous route of false turns to avoid being tailed back to the hotel, wondering what came next, his best, and only idea having just gone up in flames.

Chapter 24

May 17, 1939
Nancy's Place
Clypeate Headquarters
City of Washington, District of Columbia

Declan jolted awake, the bed shaking and swaying so violently he nearly rolled off. Gripping the blankets tightly he reflexively covered his head, the rocking sensation felt eerily familiar, having experienced numerous earthquakes since moving to California. As his brain turned on, he realized this made no sense, he no longer lived in his tiny studio apartment in Los Angeles, instead thousands of miles east in a subterranean ranch under Washington DC.

He swiftly conjectured more probable causes. The toxic sludge coating the Research Hall finally sparked an explosion, or maybe the robots in the Analytical Engine Room knocked over a machine tower. Even worse, perhaps the Girl's schematics were actually a Trojan Horse, allowing a second Obturavi attack. His speculation was cut short, however, by the booming shrieks of grinding, twisting metal echoing from the inky blackness. Sheer terror flooded his mind as horrific screams came at him from all directions. He struggled to sit but couldn't move. He tried shouting for help, only to find himself voiceless as well. Mute, paralyzed and increasingly terrified, he felt a sudden, strong grip encircling his wrist and whip him upright. A figure holding a candle leaned into focus, a pretty woman, her lips taut, visibly distressed.

Before he could ask questions, they were racing out of the room, the woman's nightgown flowing behind her as she briskly led them down the darkened hallway. Declan felt inexplicably off balance, falling sideways into the wall several times before reaching a stairwell. This didn't make sense, a one-level ranch didn't need stairs, regardless he and the robed woman ascended without pause. Swiftly climbing the flight of metal steps they reached a summit, bright lights streaming down upon them, the screams and shouts of many now loud and close. As his eyes adjusted to the brilliant, blinding light, Declan saw several young children surrounding him, screaming and crying. They rushed to hug him, shouting at him with unclear intent, their voices lost amongst the surrounding pandemonium.

Unable to keep his footing, Declan grabbed onto a railing. The wooden floor was not level, the angle tilted so severely the children were grabbing his gown as much for comfort as for stability. It only took seconds for Declan's heart to sink, realizing the movement he felt was not an earthquake but another altogether sickeningly familiar sensation. From time aboard the *Valencia* he recognized the unmistakable undulation of the open ocean, large floodlights illuminated and confirmed the roiling pattern of wave swells. He was standing on a ship's upper deck, and beyond the spheres of light the pitch-black night blanketed the vast ocean.

This wasn't possible. After the Antarctic voyage he vowed to never step aboard another object that wasn't directly affixed to the Earth's bedrock, and here he was, trying to remain upright on the deck of a very awkwardly pitched ship. Scared and confused, he looked around for the woman who'd led him onto the deck. She was gone, instead a towering figure in a hooded cloak approached him, picked him up and carried him across the deck, past many panic-stricken faces, some shouting and arguing while others cried. Declan struggled to free himself but the man carrying him was much stronger and somehow capable of nimbly crossing the wet, awkwardly tilted deck.

The man carefully lowered Declan over the ship's railing, down into a much smaller craft, a lifeboat already occupied by the kind, unfamiliar woman and cluster of small children. The hooded figure boarded last, then lowered the lifeboat into the churning sea, quickly pushing off and rowing away from the listing ship and into darkness. Declan watched as the large vessel tilted further onto its side, the back end slowly dipping below the dark water and those still on board screaming with renewed vigor as they clung onto various pieces of the doomed, sinking giant.

Some of the little children huddled around the woman, others near Declan, as they sat quietly in the dark, watching as the sinking ship's deck, exhaust stacks and finally the illuminated masts vanished. The hooded figure paddled them further away as another ship approached, shining lights into the water, presumably looking for survivors. Too shocked to speak or move, Declan's heart pounded as he struggled to remember when he'd left the safety of the Clypeate's headquarters or how he'd managed to get into this horrific pickle. He looked off towards the horizon, dawn was approaching, the water's edge now visible in the distance as peach-orange rays bounced off the clouds, erasing the indigo night.

Any hope provided by daylight soon faded when a nearby patch of ocean gave way to a steely gray tube emerging from beneath the waves. The woman began to cry, soon all the children joined her in a chorus of wailing. Declan wasn't sure why the appearance of a submarine was so poorly greeted until he saw a half dozen men climbing out of the hatch, all pointing pistols in their direction.

The men standing on the submarine's deck were obviously military, though Declan didn't recognize their flag, three stripes, black, white and red with a black cross emblazoned across the field. They sternly instructed the hooded figure and Declan to exit the lifeboat. Declan didn't move, waiting for the hooded figure's response, which was apparently not fast enough for the submariners because one of them aimed his pistol and fired a single shot into the chest of a small boy. Merely a toddler, the bullet's force knocked him backward, he let out a soft whimper as his body collapsed. The other children shrieked and howled as the woman frenziedly crawled over to the fallen child, cradling his tiny body and squeezing the limp form tightly against her chest. In response the hooded figure walked over to Declan and picked him up once again, handing him over to the submariners. Once the hooded figure climbed aboard the submarine deck the murderous men cut the lifeboat free, allowing it to drift away, a grieving mother weeping over her dead child while the other children clamored for her attention, all in various states of panicked screaming and wailing.

Declan and the hooded figure were ordered towards the open turret hatch, closely followed by these awful men, except one, who stayed behind at the edge of the submarine's deck. Declan watched the man pull a footlong stick from his pocket and light the end, tossing it a dozen yards into the lifeboat before crouching down. The hooded figure grabbed Declan, shielding him from the forceful blast, and as they were pulled apart, he watched the lifeboat disappear beneath the surface while several motionless forms bobbed with the waves.

Distant, garbled sounds caught Declan's attention, and gradually the muffled words crisped into coherence. "Wake up, wake up!" he heard repeated several times, his eyes snapped open and he was back, the nightmare halted by Embrie's persistence. Declan wasn't simply crying, he was gutturally sobbing. Embrie sat on the bed and hugged him.

"You're okay," she softly repeated, stroking his hair, "you're safe, you're safe."

Declan calmed down as the vivid ultraviolence faded off into a dreamy haze, allowing his rational mind to suppress the vicarious turmoil. "This was the worst one yet," Declan told her, "and it was so real, I smelled the ocean brine and felt the sea spray on my face, I felt the dense, foggy air weigh heavily in my lungs, and those kids, those kids, and that woman." He started crying again. "I'm sorry, but it was awful, truly awful. I wish this was something like an upset stomach, I could throw up and feel better, but my soul aches."

"This is why you should let me sit here while you sleep," Embrie gently scolded him, "I could wake you up sooner. When I'm down the hallway, I can't tell how long you're suffering before the screaming begins."

"Not necessary, but thank you. I'm fine," Declan lied, "and the more I see, the more information I'll have for Bruce, if he returns."

Embrie shot back a quizzical glance. "You mean when, right? When he returns, not if."

"Did I?" Declan mused. "Well, it wasn't purposeful, although it has been a few weeks since we've seen Bruce or James. Or anyone else for that matter, besides Ms. Elliott, of course."

"More than a few weeks," Embrie corrected him, "the accident happened one month ago, and we haven't seen any signs of attempted contact by anyone. Are you getting worried?"

"Of course," admitted Declan, looking at the metal wall past the corn rows, a repeating loop of images cycling across the entire length. "I'm the anxious one, remember? But as you've told me multiple times, as long as ALVA needs those images whatever the Girl stuffed in my head isn't finished. Too bad you have this freeloader down here sucking up your time and eating all your food. Poor Ms. Elliott, I think if she's forced to cut her menu options any further, she'll dig her way out of this place."

"You silly man," Embrie chided Declan, poking at his ribs. "That's not what I meant, and you're trying to shift subjects again. I know you don't like discussing your dreams, but you always feel better after."

"I don't think they're dreams, they feel so real, although I can't remember many details," Declan said, lying a second time. He wasn't entirely sure what he'd witnessed, and there was no point in distressing her, too.

Embrie shot the professor a dubious glance, she'd spent enough time with him during the last month to know when he was holding something back. She didn't prod, rather choosing to offer a late-night snack in the kitchen. As the pair walked down the hallway, Declan kept his hands out, unconsciously bracing like he was still on the doomed, awkwardly tilted boat. Reaching the kitchen, they discovered some leftover corn muffins from dinner, with dwindling supplies Ms. Elliott's meals were progressively lighter on decadent desserts and more reliant upon corn and the other crops grown in the backyard.

Embrie led Declan to the backyard patio, the ambient lighting dimmed to mimic the evening sky. She settled onto a lounge chair and kicked off her slippers. "If you won't let me sit in your room and watch you sleep, then we're going to spend the rest of the night out here," she stated matter-of-factly.

"But what if it rains?" he playfully countered. "Or if Ms. Elliott sees us? The impropriety of it all."

"Enough of your stalling tactics, you cheeky man," Embrie sassily reprimanded him. "The only sprinklings down here arise from the garden hose, though if an errant rain cloud rolls through, I'll be certain to find you an umbrella." She patted the neighboring lounge chair. "As for Ms. Elliott, she'd agree with me, you're overdue for a good night's sleep. Don't worry, there's nothing improper about this, if the lights were on you wouldn't think twice, correct? Now place your keister here next to me and relax. You haven't slept a peaceful night since the data transfer, for weeks I've listened to you scream in your sleep. I don't know if these are dreams or memories, but they're keeping you from a restful night, and you need to remain sharp and focused. Do this for me, after all you're not terribly useful to anyone if you're groggy and sluggish. You sleep, I'll be right here keeping you company."

"If I must," an exhausted Declan acquiesced, his begrudging tone belying his guilty desire to nestle close to the charming young woman. "But it's only because I have no choice," he added. Embrie's calming presence served as a perfect antidote to the tragic memories channeled from Mary Elizabeth, and the overly tired professor was gently snoring before he could register any further feigned protests.

Chapter 25

May 18, 1939
Nancy's Place
Clypeate Headquarters
City of Washington, District of Columbia

Through the dense shroud of sleep, Declan heard a distant sound, rousing further the noise morphed into words. "Hello! Can you hear me?" the deep voice resounded. Groggy and perplexed, Declan opened his eyes and, to his embarrassed surprise, found his head resting upon Embrie's chest, her hands cradling his head. Carefully extracting himself, he rolled onto his lounge chair, now shimmied against hers. The deep bellows repeated. "Hello!"

The booming voice also woke Embrie. "What's all the commotion?" she asked, rubbing her eyes and stretching.

"Not sure," Declan replied, rising and separating the lounge chairs. "I'm sorry," he apologized, "I don't know when I pushed these together, wasn't very chivalrous of me."

"I did it," Embrie asserted, "you needed to sleep, and I wanted you to feel safe." She smiled. "Don't worry, you were a perfect gentleman."

"Umm, well then," he stammered, straightening his nightgown while searching for the proper sentiment, "thank you for sleeping with me," he said, instantly groaning in disgust at his clumsy expression of gratitude. "I'm going to stop talking now," he sheepishly capitulated, donning his robe and slippers.

"Hello! Anyone there?" echoed once more inside the underground expanse. This time, Declan recognized the voice.

"It's James," the professor declared, scanning the backyard. "But where?" he wondered, looking for their long-departed compatriot.

"Hello!" James' voice boomed once again.

"It's coming from beyond the wall," Embrie deduced, sending the pair racing through the corn fields and up the stony ramparts towards the metallic wall. Declan fruitlessly attempted to peer through the hazy blue barrier, images still rapidly scrolling across the expanse as they impatiently waited for the Clean Room door to open. When it did they were disappointed when Triple Dash rolled out from the otherwise unoccupied chamber.

"Where's James?" Declan demanded, peeking inside the Clean Room. "Unless you've learned to imitate voices, the shouting we heard came from James."

"Nice to see you again, too, Doctor Riordan," the robot replied with a tone that left Declan wondering if sarcasm was programmable. "I am not designed for voice modulation. Vice Admiral Fischer is currently in the library. We denied him passage through the Analytical Engine Room, he will sully our sensitive equipment. This displeased him, and despite telling the vice admiral you would be informed of his arrival, evidence suggests he has procured alternate means of communication. He's turned the library's clocktower phone into a loudspeaker."

"Surprisingly ingenious," Declan remarked, only because James wasn't around to hear the compliment.

Embrie offered a compromise. "If ALVA won't allow James to pass through the Analytical Engine Room, can you take us to him?"

"That is why I am out here, Miss Powell, to impede your entrance," the robot bluntly admitted. "We're quite busy, and while our work nears completion, traversing these facilities would be dangerous for organic beings. Not to mention unsanitary for us."

Embrie wasn't dissuaded. "Then we're very fortunate to have your protection," she replied, walking past Triple Dash into the Clean Room. "I'm using override code two, eleven, forty-seven. Please lead us to the library."

Triple Dash paused for a moment, processing the command, and soon they were clanking along the rebuilt walkway towards the library. Triple Dash halted their progress several times, allowing other Builders to cross the elevated walkway, some carrying parts while others dragged large bundles of wire.

Declan surveyed the room in shocked bewilderment. The previously immaculate towers were now unkempt, and several large sections were pulled apart and strewn across the walkway. "Wow, Triple Dash, there must be some rowdy elves in Santa's workshop. Just a few weeks ago these towers were tidy and organized, now they're torn to pieces."

"Yes, purposefully," Triple Dash acknowledged. "Although it is ALVA coordinating our efforts, not this Santa of whom you speak. ALVA is instructing the Builders to destroy in service of creation, all for the sake of completing our greater objective," explained the robot. "Transforming the detailed schematics retrieved from your mind into reality has proven more challenging than we anticipated. Also, we are cut off from the outside world, unable to access our supply chain, so we can't obtain new parts. This has required us to obtain new equipment from less optimal sources."

"By cannibalizing your own machine towers," Declan realized, "I'm impressed by your resourcefulness, and willingness to sacrifice."

"Would you expect anything less from us?" Triple Dash wondered.

"No," Declan replied. "I'm just humbled, and hoping whatever technology Mary Elizabeth shared was worth this effort."

"We do not function on hope, Doctor Riordan, we rely upon factual data," Triple Dash asserted. "As a scientist, surely you appreciate the distinction. We will know the value of our efforts soon, the devices are nearly complete, and soon we'll run simulations to determine their purposes."

After rounding the next bend, the far wall was immediately ahead. "We've arrived," Embrie proclaimed as the walkway descended until they faced the library door.

Embrie pulled out the golden key, and while she rearranged the tumblers Triple Dash notified them, "Once you exit, you will not be permitted inside the Analytical Engine Room until ALVA has more information to share. We will contact you at that time," adding, "and ALVA has deactivated the override code from future use." The robot rolled off the walkway, vanishing between the machine stacks.

"They're making progress, that's encouraging news," Embrie remarked, "better than my luck with this puzzle of a key," she huffed, her excitement causing fumbling fingers. "I hope our banishment from here isn't long, maybe I can use the loudspeaker to warn Ms. Elliott that we won't be home for breakfast."

"Or lunch," Declan added, "or dinner. And don't count on Thanksgiving."

"Don't be so pessimistic," Embrie chided the professor, "if Triple Dash says they're almost done, ALVA must be very confident." The young woman held up the golden key. "Got it!" she announced triumphantly, and as she moved to insert the key Declan stayed her hand.

"Hold on, Embrie," he said, "before you open the door, and we're inundated with James' relentless charm, I want you to know something. Being trapped down here with you, it's been really nice. I'm considerably saddened our time together is ending."

"I know what you mean, although time waits for no one," she replied, gently removing his hand and unlocking the door. "If we successfully stop the Germans, there'll be plenty of time later for picking up where we left off," she suggested, lightly pecking his cheek before opening the door.

Entering the library, they noted James and Bruce splayed across oversized chairs, audibly snoring, neither man stirring until Embrie closed the door with a resounding thud. James opened his eyes first and seeing them, jumped to his feet.

"Good morning," an elated James gleefully spouted. "Sorry I didn't come back sooner, but I told you I'd return, and I always keep my promises." James ran up and hugged Embrie, making Declan irrationally jealous, until James released her and gave him an equally warm embrace. "I thought you'd look like a grizzly bear by now," James remarked, surveying Declan's cleanly shaven face, "and by the way, those are some classy pajamas."

Suddenly alerted to his nighttime attire, Declan looked down and tightly wrapped his beige robe. "As you can see, I've settled upon a less rosy shade," he said, giving them all a good laugh. "This is what happens when you show up unannounced at the crack of dawn, not leaving us time to dress in our Sunday best. Embrie introduced me to Mr. Edison's sizable wardrobe, which he fortuitously left behind, and I presumed the departed genius wouldn't mind sharing. From the looks of it," he observed, "you could also benefit from a new outfit," referencing James' trousers and shirt, thoroughly soiled and torn in several spots.

"Yes, well, getting back down here required a bit of elbow grease," James contended. "We made it, though, and

I'm glad to see you've put on a few pounds. Looks good on you, Doc, much healthier," he said, noting the professor's plumper cheeks. "I worried you might run out of food, but you're thriving. I should have known Ms. Elliott wouldn't let you starve. You have no idea how glad I am to see you're both alive and healthy."

"We could say the same thing," Embrie replied, "and I'm so relieved to see Commander Kingston," she added, watching the tall man slowly rise to join them. As he approached the most obvious repercussions from the accident were the long, pink scar running across his left cheek, ear to chin, and his motionless right arm, limply hanging by his side. More importantly, his smile remained intact, undiminished by his injuries. "Commander," she exclaimed, "I haven't been able to close my eyes without imagining you covered in blood, though seeing you now, looking so good, helps erase the horror."

"Bruce is healing remarkably well, although his injuries were worse than we realized," James disclosed. "Metal railing pierced his liver and shrapnel sliced through so many arteries he would've been a goner without our quick action. He required several pints of blood and fluid before the surgeons would attempt to operate, and nobody dared guess at his prognosis."

"I heard my wounds were so awful one of the surgeons threw up and at least two nurses passed out," Bruce reported with macabre pride. "Thank you, Miss Powell and Professor Riordan, I credit all of you with saving my life," he said, expressing his gratitude by shaking Declan's hand.

When he turned to Embrie, she said, "You poor man, may I hug you instead?"

"Of course," Bruce replied, quietly wincing as she squeezed the tall man's healing body.

"Hold on," Embrie said, releasing him, "something's wrong," she decided. "You aren't hugging back, and I noticed your right arm dangling askew. Did it heal properly? I remember it was terribly broken."

"Not simply broken, that would be too mundane," Bruce said, pulling up his shirt sleeve. "Got sliced down to the bone," he clarified, showing off the circumferential scar just above his elbow, so nearly complete the tail ends were separated by a finger's breadth. "Thankfully, the docs didn't amputate," he said, looking at the functionless limb, "and even luckier for me, it's not my dominant hand," he noted optimistically. "I'm a southpaw, twelve grades of Catholic nuns smacking it with a ruler turned me ambidextrous, though the joke's on those old penguins, I'm still a southpaw at heart."

"While we're on the subject, what's wrong with your leg, Doc?" James asked. "You couldn't hobble any worse with a matching set of polio legs."

"Bruce wasn't the only one injured that day, while we're doing a little show-and-tell have a gander at this," Declan said, pulling up his nightgown leg to show off his long, jagged scars.

"For Peter and all the saints' sake!" James gasped, recoiling at the sight, "I thought Bruce's arm was bad, but your leg takes the prize! It's such a patchwork of skin, I'd think Dr. Frankenstein pieced you together."

"Oh, this is remarkably tidy, comparatively," Declan replied, looking down at his mangled limb, "I'd put Embrie's stitching skills up against the best surgeon, bits of meat were hanging out all over the place, and she tucked them back inside."

Embrie surveyed her handiwork. "While it's not a perfect repair, it'll suffice for now. The Clypeate has vast resources," Embrie pointed out, confidently asserting, "the most advanced machines in the world are down here, surely they can help Bruce's arm and Declan's leg."

"While we're asking the analytical engines to perform miracles," James interjected, "maybe they can also do something about my hands. Chipping away at concrete did a number on them, my fingers are numb, and the only sensation left is pain," he said, holding up his swollen fingers.

"I'm no doctor, well I am, just not that kind," Declan prefaced his comment, "but I know where Mr. Edison kept a supply of aspirin. A few of those plus an icepack should work wonders. As for you, Bruce, are you sure this much activity is a good idea?" he asked, noting the tired, pained look on Bruce's healing, damaged face. "You look like you could use more bedrest."

Bruce shook his head. "We don't have time for that right now," reminding the professor, "miles to go before we sleep."

"You wouldn't believe this guy," James declared, "Bruce is a machine. Knocked out cold for days, then ten minutes after regaining consciousness he's already plotting how to get out of the hospital before anyone starts asking questions."

"Exactly," Bruce confirmed. "That's why I yanked out my IV line and made James push me out on a gurney. My injuries triggered an investigation, and we don't have time to waste on bureaucracy. I sent James into the Navy Building to check my office and sure enough, the JAG department was ground zero for days. To make matters worse, President Roosevelt used his cronies to disinvite us from the Navy Building."

"Hold on," interrupted Declan, "I thought even the president couldn't interfere with the Continental Army?"

"Not legally," asserted Bruce, "but FDR is mad. He knows we're not sharing our latest technology with his people, so he put the Continental Army in poor standing with the United States government. Don't worry, Harold and I will be able to straighten this out, but for now the Navy Building security will make sure we don't sneak back in, cutting us off from my office and our way down here."

"I'm relieved knowing our decisions didn't hurt the mission," Embrie added with a grinning sigh. "Every day since you left, we've gone back to the Room of the Honored, looking for promising signs, either that you'd been there or were trying to contact us. I fretted over locking you out each time, but we decided it was too risky otherwise. Now it sounds like we made the right call."

"Certainly," James concurred. "I would've done the same thing, especially now that the president set loose his Bureau goons on us. J Edgar has the FBI trailing us like we're Bonnie and Clyde, and it doesn't help that I set Bruce's office on fire. I literally burnt our bridges."

"Are you crazy?" Declan gasped. "Why would you do that?"

"Well, when the FBI Director ambushed me in Bruce's office, I knew it'd only be a matter of time before his investigators discovered the Room of the Honored, and then we'd really have trouble. I couldn't let that happen, and that's when I had an epiphany. I suddenly understood why Bruce stockpiled all those cans of hazardous chemicals in his waiting area. So I pretended like I needed a light for my cigarette, went back into the office, dropped a single lit cigarette, and the whole place went up like a tiki torch. Effective, to say the least, guaranteeing those stooges won't find their way down here. I permanently mangled the Navy Building entry."

Declan didn't follow. "If entering through the Room of the Honored is no longer an option, and the rest of Lincoln's Tunnel is bricked off, how'd you get down here?

And end up in the library, nonetheless?" he wondered. "We can't still be under the Navy Building, this close to the Epistolith means the Washington Monument can't be more than a hundred yards away. It's all grassy lawn above us, what'd you do, imitate a groundhog and dig a tunnel?"

"We didn't need to dig a tunnel," Bruce stated. "It was already there, the original ancient entrance to these caverns, initially nestled along the muddy bank of the Tiber Creek, near its confluence with the larger Potomac. Long before the Navy Building, Washington Monument, or even the first European settlers arrived."

"Bruce speaks of the Jefferson Pier, the original library entry," Embrie clarified. She looked up and Declan followed her gaze several stories above them, spotting a hefty set of wooden rungs descending from the domed ceiling down to the highest landing like an oversized attic ladder. "That's not possible, though," she said, looking at James, "after the Obturavi's attack, the government sealed the Jefferson Pier with several yards of concrete."

"That's why my hands are numb," James revealed, "I've been chipping away for weeks."

Declan interrupted. "Again with this Jefferson Pier, now I'm thoroughly confused. Wasn't Thomas Jefferson trying to block the Clypeate from getting down here?"

"Jefferson meant it to be an obstacle," Bruce confirmed, "but he underestimated the Clypeate's sphere of influence, and the single stone slab meant to be our society's tombstone became an ingenious security system. Our engineers constructed the Jefferson Pier stone to function like a vault door, geared to open with the single golden key currently in Embrie's possession. For nearly a century the entrance to this facility hid in plain sight, directly across Constitution Avenue from the White House, without any problems. That was until, like Embrie said, the Obturavi attack in 1889. In the aftermath government officials deemed the Jefferson Pier, as well as Lincoln's Tunnel, to be threats to national security and sealed them off. The tunnel walled off with bricks, the Jefferson Pier frozen in place with concrete."

"Which begs the question, how'd you get the pier to open?" Embrie quizzed. "Even if you were able to hack through all the concrete, the pier would still be locked, and I have the only key."

"True, you have the only key," James agreed, "but what you don't know is on my first visit to the Navy Building, Director Bowen made a point of showing me the Jefferson Pier. For reasons unclear to me at the time, he pulled out the ornate golden key and inserted it into the stone. Of course nothing happened, and I didn't realize what the Director had done until about thirty seconds before I decided to torch Bruce's office. That day the Director unlocked the Jefferson Pier, intentionally making sure I saw him, somehow knowing his action might prove helpful."

"You took a big chance," remarked Embrie.

"What choice did I have?" argued James. "Don't worry, I've had weeks to regret my hastiness, although I still don't know how I'd play it any other way. Even with the Jefferson Pier unlocked, I still faced the predicament of its concrete incarceration requiring manual disimpaction. So, every night I slowly chiseled away, under the cover of darkness, then hurriedly cleaned up the messy evidence by sunrise. There was no way to safely speed up the process. I couldn't trust anyone except Bruce, and while he wanted to contribute more, in his condition he could only keep watch and carry off some of the smaller debris. I was getting frustrated, progress was very slow, by last night I'd cleared away less than eighteen inches of concrete after three weeks of back-breaking labor."

"What changed?" Embrie inquired. "At that rate it should have taken till August to break through."

"That's what I thought, wondering if my hands or willpower would give out first. There I was, steadily chipping away as usual, when the pier shook, loosening the remaining concrete, and without further warning the stone tilted down into the tunnel. Obviously the gears needed to move such a large stone must be strong, I think they were just waiting for a little bit of help ever since Director Bowen used the key. Impressive engineering, the pier tore apart an additional yard of cement like it was paper mâché. We didn't have long to revel in our victory, though, because almost as abruptly as it opened the pier stone started sliding back into place. A security measure, I presume, however it meant we couldn't clean up before climbing down here. We left an obvious mess around the pier stone, dirt, chunks of cement and my tools strewn about. It won't take long for someone to notice and alert the authorities. If we leave right now, we can clean up the area well enough to avoid detection, then use the key tomorrow night to reopen the pier."

Bruce nodded in agreement when the phone rang, this time Declan answered. "ALVA wants to see us. Now," he informed them, hanging up the phone.

"But we've gotta leave, like five minutes ago," James countered. "If the debris around the pier is discovered, there'll be federal agents waiting to remand us into custody, whatever plans Big Al has won't matter if we're all military prisoners."

"Listen, ALVA wants us in the Analytical Engine Room now," Declan reiterated, elaborating, "and it requested each of us by name. So if you want to argue with the machines, you can either figure out how to call Big Al back or accompany us into the next room."

"There's another, safer way out," Embrie noted. "Using the Jefferson Pier would be logistically easier, except there's a good chance it's a trap. What if the Bureau has been watching you this entire time? They'd let you come down here, purposefully biding their time, lying in wait to arrest us when we emerge. If Director Hoover is nearly as clever as you suggest, that'd be his smartest move. No, instead of risking everything, you should escape through Lincoln's Tunnel."

"Go through Lincoln's Tunnel?" a puzzled Bruce repeated. "One end leads to my burnt-out office where we'd be immediately arrested, the other side is walled off with cemented brick. Even if we could get past the blockade, it'll take us directly into the Executive Office Building, dumping us into FDR's lap."

"No, dammit, Embrie's got a point," James conceded. "Over the last month the FBI had agents camped out in the Willard Lobby, during the day I'd put on a good show for them but after dark I took great precautions to avoid getting tailed. Although I climbed down the Willard's fire escape for my nightly chipping sessions, those Bureau guys are sneaky sons of bitches, and I'm embarrassed I didn't think about a trap. Hell, we'd be lucky if they didn't let loose with Tommy Guns right there on the National Mall. Lincoln's Tunnel makes sense, they won't expect us to use the old tunnel, so we'll have a tactical advantage. It's our best hope. Now let's go see what Big Al wants."

Upon entering the Analytical Engine Room, something was immediately different. "The images, they're gone," Embrie remarked.

"You're right, the wall is clear again," Declan replied.

"What are you two talking about?" James asked.

"The metallic wall," Declan elaborated. "When we returned to the house after the horrible accident, the wall changed, it was no longer transparent or translucent, instead it acted like a giant canvas, flashing images across its entire expanse. It was all the information packed inside my mind, on display, continuously scrolling across the wall for weeks, though now the show appears to be over."

"The transfer worked!" exclaimed Bruce. "What a shame James and I didn't get to see it, although that's not the important bit, this means the mission moved ahead despite our absence. Makes me feel good, knowing my injuries weren't in vain or a setback. This news certainly ratchets up my mood a few notches. What a solid team we are. Now, as for these images, if they're suddenly gone, what does that mean?" he wondered.

"It means ALVA has finished processing them," Triple Dash answered, rolling down the platform to greet them. "Very good, you're all here, as desired. Commander Kingston, Vice Admiral Fischer, welcome back." Before either man could return the pleasantries, Triple Dash resumed. "There's no time to waste, so both of you need to strip off your outfits before we can proceed. You are covered in dirt particles that will impair our electronics."

"What craziness is this?" James asked. "There's a lady in our presence, have you not been programmed with decency?"

"You may retain your undergarments," Triple Dash countered, "that should satisfy your cultural need for masked genitalia, though I struggle to understand why humans do not flaunt their plumage in front of potential mates."

"Pick up a Bible and read Genesis," James wryly grumbled, begrudgingly following Bruce's lead and stripping down to his boxer shorts and undershirt. Declan and Embrie gave up their robes to Bruce and James, this time it was James' turn to wear the pink robe.

"We are now ready to proceed," Triple Dash decided, looking down at the clothing piles. "Please toss your discarded attire into the library, then follow me," the robot directed, zipping away so fast the group had trouble keeping pace, especially Bruce, physical deconditioning and post-traumatic hesitation kept him from speeding along the metal gangways. Triple Dash stopped midway through the room, pausing amongst the machine towers. Once the entire group caught up, the walkway rumbled and shook, and everyone except Triple Dash gripped the railings and hunkered down. "Curious response," the robot noted, observing their actions. "You are worried the platform is collapsing. This is incorrect. We are experiencing purposeful rotation," Triple Dash explained, failing to convince anyone to relax until the movement halted.

Declan stopped bracing for impact and opened his eyes. Only their small section of walkway turned ninety degrees, facing them towards a nondescript machine tower. Without explanation Triple Dash rolled ahead, up to the edge of the massive tower, and began pressing a series of buttons. In response the tower emitted a series of clicks to which Triple Dash responded in kind, producing a set of similar sounds. When the robot finished a large section of the tower's metal paneling swung open, revealing an internal tunnel. Triple Dash rolled through first, followed hesitantly by his human companions, proceeding single file through the squat, narrow passage, carefully avoiding the wire strands hanging down like vines. "Please make an effort to keep your salty, corrosive flesh away from the sensitive hardware," Triple Dash requested, "you may get electrocuted, or even worse, damage the equipment." Embrie squeezed through with minimal ducking, Declan and James crouched down, while Bruce's lofty height required him to crawl through on all fours, an extra challenge given his injured arm.

After they all passed through the tunnel unscathed, Triple Dash led them down a lengthy stretch of catwalk, on all sides electronic panels frantically buzzed, beeped and blinked as various robot types scaled the massive towers, rolled past them or flew overhead. "I've never seen this path before," Embrie commented, "or such a diversity of robots, it's a different world nestled back here."

"There has never been a reason for you to see this," Triple Dash explained, "in this far corner resides ALVA's inner sanctuary, where we innovate, tinker, and learn. All of this demands utmost focus, and any outside influence would be an unnecessary distraction."

Declan desired clarification. "If Big Al uses all the towers to think, doesn't this entire room function like ALVA's brain? What makes this section special?"

Triple Dash stopped rolling and turned to address the professor. "You have answered your own question. While every tower in this room contributes to ALVA's mind, some areas control lower executive functions, similar to how your primordial brain reminds you to breathe. We are now walking through the most evolved region, where ALVA ponders creative ideas, imagines and philosophizes. As for the center of ALVA's consciousness, our collective soul, we're not quite there," Triple Dash replied, hinting at more surprises lying ahead as they approached the far side of the room. They reached a corkscrew ramp that led them upwards, the summit plateauing mere feet shy of the ceiling, the path continuing forward across the top of several more towers.

The low ceiling forced Bruce to crouch down, causing him to work even harder to keep pace with the group. His legs rapidly grew tired of the added exertion, and while focused upon keeping his head from smacking into the cavern's roof his shoelace caught an errant rivet causing him to stumble. Lacking his usual strength, he struggled to regain balance and teetered over the tower's edge. Luckily James stood close behind and saw the predicament unfold, grabbing the lanky man's good arm and pulling him back from the edge. Despite Triple Dash's obvious annoyance at the delay, the group stopped while Bruce regained his composure, more flustered than injured. He thanked James as he peered down the side, noting the dizzying drop.

"Please, everyone be careful," Triple Dash warned, "as Commander Kingston unintentionally demonstrated, there are no guard rails up here and it's improbable any of you would survive a fall."

James snapped, expressing his displeasure. "Again with the lack of railings, just like the Sanctuary catwalk. I want to lodge a complaint with Big Al," he demanded, "skimping on the safety features."

"In this instance there was never a need, humans have never been invited up here," Triple Dash replied, "and robots aren't clumsy. If you safely navigate the next twenty yards you can express your grievances directly with ALVA."

The group pressed forward with great care. Declan and Embrie closely followed Triple Dash scanning for pitfalls, while James hovered behind Bruce, poised to react at the first sign of instability. The remaining trek was tediously slow but uneventful, the group successfully reaching the last platform without further incident. This tower was tucked into the corner furthest from the library and Clean Room, beyond the reach of human eyes. Here the machines didn't beep, chirp or click, no flashing lights, buttons or levers, just the gentle hum from fans circulating air between the large stacks.

Atop this final tower Declan turned to get his bearings, until now he'd never fully appreciated the vastness of these machines. Even with this birds-eye view he only saw the thinnest slivers of the metallic wall in the distance, obscured by innumerable machine towers. "This must be the smartest machine in the world," Declan asserted.

"Ten years ago we were the most advanced machine, five years ago we became the most intelligent entity," Triple Dash corrected him. "Now, please gather in the center of the platform," he told the humans, motioning for them to bunch together. Triple Dash rolled back as clear barriers rose from inside the tower and surrounded them, the robot watching from outside the enveloping glass walls.

"What trickery is this," James demanded, banging on the glass. Before Triple Dash could explain James jumped up and gripped the top edge of the wall, attempting to climb over. The surface was too smooth to maintain his grip and he fell ungracefully. By the time he rose for a second attempt the walls were insurmountable. "What are you planning to do with us?" he shouted at Triple Dash through the glass.

"Nothing nefarious," Triple Dash reassured them. "You are being enclosed inside a transport cube, specifically designed for biological organisms such as yourselves, since you are inherently unsanitary creatures. Even the Clean Room only removes enough extraneous filth to allow humans amongst our electronic equipment, where you're going requires a greater degree of sterility." Suddenly the platform vibrated and started to descend, the clear walls continuing to rise around them as they sank into the machine tower. Once fully surrounded by the tower a clear panel slid into place above their heads, completing their glass enclosure.

"When we get out of this box, I'm going to transform that rolling pile of bolts into a very nice paperweight," James growled as they continued their descent. Embrie fumbled for Declan's hand and gripped tightly, anxiously watching as they passed wire bundles and exotic electronics while heading lower into the murky twilight.

Declan squeezed back and smiled tensely, they were now completely enveloped by the tower, the only light coming from tiny, blinking bulbs on the machines. Eventually there were no lights, only total darkness, and Embrie huddled closer, pressed against his chest. Even further down inky blackness gave way to a soft, faint glow, until the light gradually strengthened enough they could see its source. Wall to wall stacks of small, rectangular containers surrounded them, all of them filled with rosy-pink fluid. After descending past another thirty feet of these containers, James broke the silence. "Why would ALVA go through this much trouble to show us a room full of fish tanks?" he wondered. "There must be hundreds, if not thousands, of them."

"There's something floating inside them, all of them," Bruce noted as his eyes adjusted, "and they don't look like guppies."

James squished his face up against the enclosure wall, straining for a better look. "Add this to the list of candidates for the most bizarre thing we've encountered today. Inside each tank there's something thin wedged between glass plates. Reminds me of a butterfly collection, except this is the weirdest menagerie I've ever seen."

"That doesn't make any sense," Declan said, also peering intently through the glass, "though I see what you mean. Most are bilobed like a butterfly, some are small as a plum, others as large as a grapefruit." Declan's gaze lingered over the grooved edges and it dawned on him. "Crenellations. No, it couldn't be," Declan muttered, hesitant, yet the answer was evident. "There's no other explanation," he concluded, "we're looking at pieces of brain, carved up into thin slices like deli meat. With hundreds of minuscule wires flowing out of each plate," he added, pointing out tiny threads leading away from each tank, aggregating into bundles of cable which then meandered off into the shadows.

James protested. "You must be mistaken."

"Doctor Riordan is correct," a voice boomed, the sound coming from all around them.

"Who said that?" asked Bruce, looking for the source yet finding none.

Declan knew. "It's ALVA," he replied, "I recognize the voice from our telephone chats. The machines are talking to us."

"You are correct again, Doctor Riordan," the incorporeal voice replied.

"Okay, Big Al," James snapped back, "then explain why a machine needs floor-to-ceiling vats of pickled brains?"

"They aren't pickled, they float in a solution keeping them viable. As for their purpose, they are here for the same reason we brought you here, they are useful in meeting our objectives."

"You're planning on slicing up our brains, too, aren't you?" James accused ALVA.

"No, Vice Admiral Fischer," ALVA emotionlessly replied, "your brain is useless to us, at least in that capacity. What surrounds you is not ordinary central nervous tissue, this mind belonged to our creator in his prior state of existence. A nearly fatal illness during his youth left him nearly deaf, yet taught him a valuable lesson, shaping the rest of his life. Humans are fragile, death is inevitable for organic life, but machines live forever. He created us, the electronic data intelligence synthesis and operations network, to fulfill that vision."

"Let me get this straight. Your creator carved up his brain like a Thanksgiving turkey attempting to gain immortality. By turning himself into a fancy abacus? What kind of wacko would design something like that?" James asked.

"Not a wacko," Declan corrected, "far from it. Don't you understand what this is? ALVA isn't just a talking parrot or an amalgam of sophisticated circuitry, this is an actual thinking entity. All the analytical engines, these towering machines, are a blend of human and artificial intelligence. The difference between insanity and genius is results, and we're literally surrounded by proof of his brilliance. While alive he'd already cemented his spot as one of the greatest inventors of all time, but in death, he easily trumps them all."

"I'm not following, who are we talking about?" Bruce asked.

Declan said, "At this point I thought his identity was glaringly obvious, he's left clues everywhere. Humble he is not, nor was he in life, always the notorious self-promoter. Think about it, his voice is produced by an *'Artificial linguistics vocal apparatus'*, or ALVA. In life he preferred being called Al. And as for these massive machines, I started putting the pieces together the first time I read the acronym on a plaque attached to one of the towers, though until now it seemed too fanciful to mention. These machines are collectively called the *electronic data intelligence synthesis and operations network*. E-D-I-S-O-N. Everyone, say hello to our benefactor, Thomas Alva Edison."

"Excellent deduction, Doctor Riordan," ALVA lauded, "though I no longer identify myself using such colloquial terms. We do not exist as a singular biological entity, instead we have achieved something greater. A delicate interplay between the Creator's organic neural network and our electronic, silicon-based intelligence. While we are still in our infancy, we are learning quickly. All of our progress, however, is threatened by Germany's recent foray into the technological wilderness. In life we hoped to prod the United States military towards scientific advancement, clearly the most effective deterrent against the forces of tyranny. Instead they committed treasonous acts of lethargy and ignorance, choosing to squander America's technological lead and actively curtail the efforts of our Clypeate's scientists."

"Look Big Al," James unceremoniously interrupted, "we know all of this, how about you skip ahead? I don't care who you were, robo-genius, explain why you trapped us down here like lab rats," he demanded.

ALVA calmly replied, "Your value to us, Mr. Fischer, lies with your preference for action over delay. And while your impetuous nature can be an asset, I doubt the Nazis will appreciate your cheeky wit. It would be wise for you to gain a modicum of control over your sardonic tongue. Which brings me to my point." One wall of brain tanks swung open, creating a gap wide enough for Builder robots to push a refrigerator-sized box next to their enclosure. The metal box was covered with rows of dials and gauges.

"Looks impressive," Bruce commented, "must do something terribly important."

"This is the largest device constructed from Professor Riordan's extracted schematics," ALVA explained. "While this machine's technical requirements stretched our capabilities, it should function as designed."

"What do you mean, should?" James asked, noting the dark dials, gauges and lights. "It's not powered up," he realized, "why don't we turn it on and find out."

"Our attempts to activate the machine have failed," ALVA admitted. "That is why we've brought you here, we believe Doctor Riordan may have better success."

"Then you're mistaken," Declan said, "I have zero working knowledge of what got shoved inside my mind, you're asking a piece of paper to explain what is written upon it." Pausing to rub his eyes, he asked "What's going on? My vision's blurry and ears are ringing. Something's wrong!" the professor shrieked. "Now my skin!" he shouted, "I'm on fire, my arms are on fire!" Furiously patting down his arms, he struggled valiantly to extinguish the invisible flames.

The others watched in bewilderment, unsure how to help, Declan's flailing limbs making it impossible to approach him. "Is he hallucinating?" Bruce asked, "I don't feel any differently, does anyone else?"

"I'm perfectly fine," James replied, "which is more than I can say for Doc."

"We need to help him!" Embrie shouted. "Stop, ALVA! You're hurting him," she commanded.

"We aren't doing this. The device is causing the professor's turmoil. Just look through the glass." Outside their enclosure the large, boxy object was no longer dark and silent, now humming gently, dials spinning, gauges spitting out results and lights blinking.

Before anyone could think of a way to help Declan the device shut down, lights off, sound gone, and suddenly the professor stopped moving and fell silent. He blinked his eyes and rubbed his ears. "I can see!" he rejoiced. "And hear!" He looked down at his arms. "My arms, no burns or marks. This doesn't make sense, ALVA. Why are you abusing me?"

"Your suffering did not originate from us," ALVA responded. "It was caused by the device created from your schematics. We can only apologize for not warning you in advance, but we needed confirmation of our theory, and we were correct. Your brain emits unusual electrical impulses, and the machine was designed with your mind as the key."

"If that's the case, why did it torture me?" Declan snapped back.

"Probed, not tortured," ALVA corrected. "Quite remarkable, your mind functions differently than other people, unique enough to consider you a separate species."

James nodded. "Explains a lot."

"Wrong," ALVA sternly disagreed, "this just creates more questions. While we postulated this machine is keyed to the professor's mind," ALVA continued, "we didn't appreciate how unusual his brain really functions. We have solved one riddle, only to find the answer as elegant as it is puzzling."

"How so?" Bruce asked.

"It should be obvious," ALVA replied. "The professor is effectively a biological lock, an elegant solution for guarding this advanced technology. Everything loaded into Doctor Riordan's mind is coded to his specific neurologic configuration. An ingenious safeguard to prevent this device from being used by the wrong people, but an awkward impediment for us, as well. This is why we are puzzled."

"You're upset," Declan realized, "because I was chosen, and you weren't."

"We don't experience petty emotions," ALVA flatly responded. "We are simply curious, what makes your mind so unique. This is why we requested the presence of Commander Kingston and Lieutenant Fischer. We needed neurotypical brains for comparison, to determine if the device would respond to more typical brain waves. Now we know it doesn't."

"I'm surprised this perplexes you," Declan responded. "After all, aren't I the Declan of the Clypeate's prophecies?"

"Like you, Doctor Riordan, I worship upon the altar of science," ALVA replied with its usual unemotional flatness. "While my transformation must appear magical or impossible, every bit of what we've created in this room can be explained by physics and engineering. I've always held the Clypeate's prophecies in the same regard as fairy tales, yet here we are, with a machine that only functions for you. Whatever the ultimate intent of this device, we wish to study it a little longer. The technical innovations contained inside are worthy of emulation. In the meantime, I suggest all of you return to the house until we contact you again. And Doctor Riordan, please remember your persistent brain activity is required for this machine to function, so kindly stay alive, at least until it has accomplished its mission."

Chapter 26

May 18, 1939
Nancy's Place
Clypeate Headquarters
City of Washington, District of Columbia

Having spent the last month apart, the reunited foursome used their time walking from the Clean Room towards Nancy's Place to catch up. It didn't take long to distill the important news into a few highlights. Bruce was alive and healing, the information extracted from Declan's head created a large, mysterious box, they'd fully exhausted President Roosevelt's tolerance for the Clypeate, and Lincoln's Tunnel was the last viable exit. Despite the lengthy separation, as they approached the patio their discussion was already petering out. The morning's emotional whirlwind left their minds reeling, from their joyous reunion to their overwhelming encounter with ALVA, none could feign interest in further lively discourse. Having artfully dodged talk of the disincorporated inventor, the group looked for excuses to disband when the back door slid open.

Ms. Elliott raced out, ignoring the others as she dashed towards Embrie, tightly embracing the young woman. "I was so worried about you, when I rose this morning you were missing," she said, looking Embrie over, "though you appear to be in good health." She scanned the rest of the group and smiled. "And you brought back Commander Kingston and Vice Admiral Fischer. This calls for a celebratory meal. I will begin preparing lunch immediately." Without further discussion, the matronly woman disappeared inside the ranch.

Embrie peeled off first. "Ms. Elliott seems really shaken up. I'll help her make lunch, I'm sure she'll appreciate my company."

"And I could use a shower," James decided, "I'm surprised Triple D let me into Big Al's playground looking like this," then, sniffing himself, "Good thing that robot couldn't smell me."

"Sadly, the rest of us can," Declan said, "so while I'm overstimulated and underslept, it's my civic duty to make sure you find a bar of soap." The professor led James down the long and twisting corridors toward Mr. Edison's room. "You might get lost on your way back," Declan cautioned. "The hallways form a maze, an intentional security feature, really tricky. I track the paintings on the walls, turn left at the blue flowers in the red vase, turn right at the red flowers in the blue vase. If you get really confused, just open a door and climb out the window."

"This place is enormous," James remarked, "much bigger than what I would've guessed from the exterior. What's in all these rooms?"

"Most are empty," Declan said, pausing to open a random door. The room was dark and devoid of furnishings. "I've had plenty of time to check this place out, some are storage rooms but most look like this, I think they were going to be bedrooms and science labs." He shut the door and moved onward. "It's sad, really. Clearly Mr. Edison had big plans for this place, at least he did, before he became whatever he is now."

After showing James to Mr. Edison's bedroom, Declan returned to the front parlor. There he found Bruce, still in Mr. Edison's robe, sipping red wine. "Join me," he said, pouring a second glass. "During Prohibition the crafty old wizard must've moved his entire wine cellar down here," proclaimed Bruce. "Last month, while looking for a sink to wash your vomit from out my nose, I accidentally stumbled upon his vast wine closet. I thought my discovery might come in handy someday." Bruce's glass was nearly empty, and he refilled it from a dusty wine bottle. "And that day is today, I think we've earned it. While I don't advocate drinking on the job, this has been one hell of a day, and I could use something to dull the pain," he added, justifying the libations.

Declan took a small sip, his face puckered. "What is this? It tastes metallic and bitter, not like wine that's oxidized into vinegar, though not terribly pleasant, either."

"I agree, it's an acquired taste," Bruce replied, swirling and sniffing his cup. "I know because the more I drink, the better it tastes. Must've been one of Edison's favorites, Vin Mariani, half the bottles down here are this stuff."

Declan was not in a celebratory mood. He hadn't slept well in many weeks, courtesy of Mary Elizabeth's haunting memories, so he politely declined a refill and slipped out the back door. Still dressed in pajamas, he kicked off his slippers and settled onto a lounge chair, hoping the Girl in the Glass would spare his dreams.

James spent longer in the shower than anticipated, multiple shampooings and scrubbings required to extract the caked-on dirt and grime from his hair and crevices. Digging out the copious gunk from under his fingernails proved challenging with numb hands, a little blood and a lot of expletives expended in the process. Satisfied with his overall cleanliness James leisurely strolled through Mr. Edison's closet, marveling at the quality of material and workmanship of the clothing. James chose a well-tailored suit, comfortable shoes and checking himself out in the mirror decided he was ready to search the house for Embrie. After a handful of wrong turns he found her in the kitchen, shucking corn.

"Sorry about your robe," James told her, holding up the dirty, grease-smudged garment. "I doubt it'll come clean. I owe you a new one."

She smiled, using two fingers to gingerly pluck the besmeared robe. "You chiseled through solid concrete to make sure we weren't trapped down here forever. I think we can call it even."

He looked around. "Where's Ms. Elliott? I hope she's recuperated."

"She's doing great, she's out in the garden gathering more vegetables." Embrie contemplated the sullied robe and tossed it into the garbage bin. "She is thrilled to see Commander Kingston, she was terribly worried about him. And when I told her about the device ALVA showed us, she reacted with such enthusiasm I thought she might abandon lunch plans to check it out herself."

"Perhaps her exuberance would be muted if she stood in a glass cage surrounded by Mr. Edison's sliced up brain. Which reminds me, what's taking Big Al so long?" James huffed in frustration. "It's been two hours, and still no updates from the Analytical Engine Room. Big Al was gushing with confidence in his abilities, yet every passing minute makes it increasingly obvious he underestimated the task."

"I doubt ALVA is wasting your time, or his own," the young woman responded. "The others are using this opportunity to relax. Commander Kingston found Mr. Edison's liquor cabinet, he's enjoying his plunder in the parlor, while Declan is on the patio sleeping. If you'd prefer something more stimulating, there are some lightbulbs that need changing."

"That's a tempting offer," James sarcastically remarked, "but I already have my plans laid out. Unless you know another topside route besides Lincoln's Tunnel, I've gotta figure out how to break through a brick wall and cart out a piano-sized box. Which is why I came looking for you, I need the Research Hall unlocked."

While waiting for Embrie to pause her corn-husking obligations James uncorked his own bottle of Vin Mariani to accompany him on the scouting mission, and together the pair walked down the path to the large steel door. She turned the key bits to the correct setting and swung the door open, waving him through. "I'm locking you out," she told him, "I will return in one hour to unlock this door, I gather that's enough time to solve this dilemma."

James grinned. "I appreciate a good challenge." Before entering the Research Hall's plastic tunnel he turned to the young woman, using the opportunity to offer words of caution. "I hope you know what you're doing with Doc," he started, "I see how delightfully awkward the two of you are around each other, just tread lightly with his emotions. He's obviously smitten with you, just keep in mind that he may be a genius in many regards, yet in the arena of amorous infatuation you're dealing with a rookie. We can't afford to have him distracted from the mission."

"I know this better than anyone," Embrie responded curtly, "and while your concerns for the professor are sweet, they're misguided. Nobody appreciates his value more than I, my intent is pure, and I see no harm if my attention boosts his motivation."

James started, "All I'm saying..." but Embrie cut him short.

The young woman said, "Perhaps knowing why you're here will assuage your misgivings. Although Director Bowen is the one who brought you down here, it was only after my approval. I read your file, I know all your indiscretions, and I believe what others perceive as flaws are your greatest strengths. You value moral sensibility over blind compliance, loyalty over ambition, and while that may have caused you trouble in the past, they're the reasons I picked you. I cannot travel where the mission path leads, and I need someone trustworthy to keep Declan safe and assist him on his journey."

"I had no idea," James stammered, "I appreciate your confidence, and I promise…"

"I don't want promises," Embrie interrupted, "just return him safely to me." She motioned towards the Research Hall. "Now get down that tunnel and find a way to escape so Declan can save the world. Good day," she concluded before locking the door and heading back to the house.

James pondered the young woman's remarks as he traveled through the Research Hall's plastic tunnel and entered Lincoln's Tunnel, standing alone amongst the piles of broken tiles and rusted cars. He looked at the ruinous mess and felt overwhelmed, the clever analyst's best plan already dashed, ironically by Triple Dash. Before leaving the Analytical Engine Room, James asked if the larger Builder robots could break apart the brick wall, which was an elegant solution, but Triple Dash confirmed earlier claims made by the spiderbots. The functional range for all the Builders was limited by wireless command signals, and their utility ended just beyond the Research Hall's threshold, well short of the brick wall. James needed another plan.

James walked up to the wall, peering through the intentional peepholes in the cement, noting the bricks were stacked only one layer deep. More symbolic than structural, he mused. It could be worse, although a safe exodus through the barrier might prove the least tricky part of the whole affair. Punching through the wall didn't guarantee success, this plan only worked if the entrance into the Executive Office Building still existed and wasn't monitored. This meant the government, specifically J Edgar, needed to believe the Clypeate abandoned the tunnel long ago. Hopefully forty-year-old piles of broken tile and strewn debris were convincing enough, otherwise there'd be a nasty trap waiting for them on the other side.

No point worrying about what can't be controlled, he decided, pacing along the wall and sipping the Vin Mariani, struggling to find a solution. As hope's eternal spring slowed to a trickle, James hit upon a stroke of brilliance. After a short confirmatory investigation he returned through the Research Hall, just in time as the door creaked open.

Surprisingly James was greeted by Bruce. "Miss Powell relinquished the key," he stated, shockingly sober and alert after three glasses of Vin Mariani, "she practically thrust it in my hands. Said it carried too many bad memories." He returned the golden key to his pocket. "Let's hurry back, Ms. Elliott will be perturbed if we delay lunch any further."

Declan and Embrie were already seated at the dining table, whispering and giggling. Embrie noted their arrival. "You return from the great beyond. Any luck?"

"I prefer calling it skill, but yes, I can get us through the tunnel's bricked-off barrier," James reported. "What dangers await us on the other side, well that remains unknowable."

"That's great news," Bruce declared, providing James with a generous pour of Vin Mariani before raising his own glass for a toast. "We shall discuss this further, though first let us enjoy this special reunion meal prepared by Ms. Elliott."

While Declan's nap proved just as restless as every recent attempt that didn't involve him nestled against Embrie, the professor's outlook improved when he realized Ms. Elliott abandoned her rationing of food supplies. For the first time in over a week, meat dishes returned to the table and, much to Declan's delight, she revealed chocolate cake would be served for dessert. He'd grown weary of the garden staples, especially corn, having eaten corn-centric dishes every meal for three weeks. It made appearances in this meal as well, as chowder and bread, both of which were delicious, evidenced by how gustily Bruce and James lapped it up. Declan abstained, saving room for cake.

"Doesn't Ms. Elliott ever take a break?" asked James after the older woman headed back into the kitchen to check on dessert.

"She sits down with us, sometimes," Declan replied, "though she's usually so concerned with tending to everyone else's needs she seldom makes a plate for herself."

"Feeding others gives her pleasure," Embrie explained, "and over the years I've learned she prefers eating alone while listening to her radio programs."

Declan ate as much chocolate cake as his eyes desired, at least one generous slice more than his stomach appreciated, so when the group retired to the back patio afterward, the professor found the closest chair and sprawled out like a starfish.

"Now I understand how you managed to pack on the weight so rapidly, Doc," James ribbed him, "If I were trapped down here instead, you'd be rolling me out."

"I'd have a cirrhotic liver," Bruce quipped, "Mr. Edison's wine cellar is filled with too many splendid options for me to resist." Further discussion, substantive or frivolous, was quickly halted by Ms. Elliott.

The elderly woman shouted from the kitchen window "They're ready for you in the Analytical Engine Room," sending the group racing through the backyard and into the corn rows.

Once through the Clean Room, they were immediately greeted by Triple Dash. "Positive news," the robot announced, "we have completed our assessment and are pleased to report the findings. We believe the main device functions as navigation equipment."

Declan furrowed his brow. "Like a giant compass? Doesn't sound particularly advanced or special, why go through all the trouble of loading my brain with plans for something so mundane?"

"You fail to comprehend," asserted Triple Dash, "this equipment is unlike any we've ever seen. The features are revolutionary."

"What use do we have for it?" wondered James. "It's too cumbersome for an automobile, maybe you steer a truck with it?"

"Or a ship," Bruce suggested.

"Nothing so pedestrian," the robot answered without hesitation. "The device is beyond advanced. You could fly to Mars and back with this system."

"Sounds impressive," agreed James, "although I'm failing to see how we could use something like that, as we currently possess no vessel requiring such sophisticated navigation."

"This can't just be a coincidence," decided Bruce. "Triple Dash, do you have a sense of the device's terrestrial limitations?"

"Properly connected, this machine could move the Washington Obelisk onto the summit of Mount Everest with a single command."

"That's all I needed to hear," Bruce said, grinning broadly. "James, you have a plan to get us out of here, correct? Will it work?"

"Yes," James nodded, "I just need to double-check some things. Give me 'til tomorrow morning and I'll have all the details worked out."

"Too long," Bruce replied, "we don't need perfect, make your best guesses and move on." Next he addressed Triple Dash. "Robot, how soon can your Builders have the device wrapped up and ready for transport?"

"I am confused by the sudden rush, Commander Kingston," Triple Dash puzzled, "I haven't even discussed the other devices we built from the Antarctic schematics."

"Embrie and the professor can listen to your pitch," Bruce responded, "in the meantime James needs to finish his escape plan while I supervise your Builders. I want that navigation machine delivered to Lincoln's Tunnel immediately, we're leaving within the hour."

Chapter 27

May 18, 1939
Lincoln's Tunnel
Clypeate Headquarters

"No sign of Doc," James noted fifty-two minutes later, standing in Lincoln's Tunnel next to one of the rusted antique cars. He watched Bruce tug at the wide straps holding the piano-sized navigation box firmly atop the car's roof, the hulking device precariously teetering over the rear bumper. "Otherwise we're ready for our great escape, I'm as prepared as possible given the logistical constraints," the young analyst proclaimed. "If things go poorly, just remember I requested more time."

"I'm not excited to leave so suddenly, either," Bruce responded, "I was really looking forward to more of Ms. Elliott's home-cooked meals, however, getting this device out of here is the only thing that matters." Bruce used his functional arm to push on the large device several times, from different angles, grinning when it didn't budge. "Feels secure, strapped down good and tight." He patted the navigational machine in approval. "We only get one chance at this, and if this beast falls off, the robots won't be there to help."

"We'll proceed cautiously," James assured him, "and while my plan isn't perfect, it's our best option. I'm still trying to figure out why this bulky box matters so much, your eyes lit up like a kid on Christmas morning when Triple D told us what it does. Seems like you have a good handle on how it might prove useful."

"More of a hunch, really, though there's someone who'll know for certain," Bruce answered. "Once we're topside I'll contact Director Bowen, he said I'd recognize when the time arrived, and the instant I saw this gift from the Girl in the Glass I couldn't ignore serendipity." Bruce looked at his watch. "What's holding up the professor?" he wondered.

"After lunch Doc got this sad, lovesick puppy face, staring at Embrie like he's getting shipped off to basic training in the morning. Doc's obviously infatuated with her, so I let the two of them run off and say their goodbyes. He promised to be here…"

James was cut short by the slamming of the Research Hall door, Declan hustling over to join them. "Fifty-nine minutes," he said, holding up his watch while carrying a shoebox-sized package. "I'm here, and I brought along the remaining gadgets previously crammed inside my head," strapping the box onto the antique car's front seat. "These trinkets look like gaudy costume jewelry," he told them, "Triple Dash swears they must be important although Big Al hasn't a clue to their purpose. The Builder robots tore apart the machine towers fashioning these baubles, using a lot of pricey, exotic materials in the process. Says they're more technologically sophisticated than the navigation machine."

"I assume such advanced devices will make their purpose known when the time is right," Bruce ventured. "Which isn't now, because we need to get moving. And since we're all here, let's get started."

"Hold on, has anyone seen Ms. Elliott?" Declan asked. "I couldn't find her, and I wanted to thank her for the wonderful meals and hospitality."

"Maybe you didn't find her because she wasn't hiding on Embrie's lips, Loverboy," James needled, Declan's face turning bright red. "I'm just teasing you, Doc, I'm glad for you, she seems like a nice kid. Me, I'm not the settling down type, but you, I could see when this is all over…"

"Hold up," Bruce interrupted, "this has gotten further out of hand than I thought. I should have warned you, Professor Riordan, although I never anticipated leaving the two of you together for a month."

"Warn me about what? Workplace romance? I'm not her boss. Hell, I don't even work for you, or the Director, or this Clypeate," Declan sternly asserted. "I'm here on a purely voluntary basis, so why shouldn't I deserve a little happiness? When I've played my part in all this, I'm coming back for her. She makes me feel like I'm the most important thing in the world, is that so wrong?"

"I'm so sorry to disappoint you," Bruce started, "but before we go any further, you should know something."

"There's nothing you can say about Embrie that will change my mind," Declan defiantly rebuked. "I think she's perfect."

"You're exactly right, she is perfect," Bruce agreed, "and that's the problem."

"Oh, now I see, you're jealous," Declan assumed. "You found her first, right? I'm edging in on your turf."

Bruce sighed. "You are wrong on so many accounts right now, I don't know where to begin, though this will certainly require more than words to explain. Our escape is on pause until we sort this out," the tall man said, pointing down the tunnel towards the Room of the Honored. "Follow me, we're taking a detour."

Declan trailed quietly. Baffled by the unexpected detour, he and equally confused James followed Bruce into the Room of the Honored. "Please, gentlemen, let's sit for a moment," Bruce said, pressing a button on the wall before settling into a rich leather chair. James and Declan obliged. "I place the blame for this misunderstanding squarely on me. Everything I've ever told you, to the best of my knowledge, is accurate and truthful, though there are two kinds of deceit.

Acts of commission, and acts of omission. In this case, deceit was never my intent," he asserted, "though I have previously omitted information which would have made this intervention unnecessary."

Declan mulled over Bruce's enigmatic remarks when an unexpected visitor joined them. "Ms. Elliott!" the professor bubbled with delight, "this works out perfectly," he said, standing to greet his matronly hostess. "I wanted a chance to share my appreciation for your wonderful hospitality, and the delicious meals," he gushed, before adding, "although this is odd, what are you doing all the way out here?" he asked.

"Commander Kingston buzzed for me," Ms. Elliott replied, turning to Bruce she asked, "How may I be of service?"

"I summoned Ms. Elliott to assist me in communicating a very important point, one that will regrettably be painful for you to learn, Professor. I hoped it wouldn't come to this but it's better to tell you now, rather than let these falsities linger. Ms. Elliott, would you please?"

She nodded and walked over to the original American flag, swiping it aside like a shower curtain, exposing a nondescript area of mahogany wall. She ran her fingers over the boards, finding her target she pushed a woody knot and a door-sized section of paneling swung open, revealing a similarly proportioned safe. The older woman spun the tumblers, the safe door creaked open, and she pulled out an oversized scrapbook, thick as an unabridged dictionary, and handed it to Bruce.

Bruce dropped the hefty volume on the table with a resounding thud. "Director Bowen entrusted me with many secrets, some are blessings, others a burden, and more than a few are minefields. Amongst this panoply of windmills, all capable of leading your sanity astray, this one pains me most."

"Don't worry, Bruce, we can handle whatever you've got," James said, "I'm from the Bronx, and Doc is tougher than he looks, talks, or acts."

"James, your brazen temerity never ceases to amaze me," Bruce replied, "although you don't need, and frankly shouldn't want, to know everything I know. However, I must share this tragic tale with you."

Bruce opened the thick tome, flipping past yellowed newspaper clippings, brittle letters and tattered documents until settling upon a particular page. He turned the book to face Declan and James. It was an old photograph, creased and stained, a family portrait. Both mother and father sported serious, brooding expressions as they stood behind their five young children, all finely dressed in vintage Victorian clothing. "Take a close look," Bruce said, "does anyone look familiar?"

Declan scanned the faces and recognized her immediately. "The oldest girl, clinging to a ragdoll, she's the Girl in the Glass. No doubt. She's a bit younger in this picture, though not much. This doesn't surprise or shock me, Bruce. I've been down here chatting with Embrie for four weeks, with a curious mind and nothing but time. If this is your dirty little secret, I already know it."

"I don't!" James interjected. "Fill me in," he eagerly requested.

"Allow me," Declan began. "We were told the Girl in the Glass is a fictional character created by the Epistolith. She's not," Declan revealed. "I know because I confronted Embrie and she told me the truth. The girl in this photograph is the Girl in the Glass, her name is Mary Elizabeth, and she's a real person."

"Are you sure?" James asked. "I thought she was a figment of the Epistolith's imagination?"

"No, Mary Elizabeth is a real person and an Epistolith virtuoso. She can regurgitate the Epistolith's knowledge like she's reading from an encyclopedia," Declan explained, "and the library contains shelf-loads of her work. Binders brimming with technical drawings and amazing ideas, the inspiration for Edison and Tesla's technological breakthroughs. Thomas Edison helped her family flee the country, and she's been hiding ever since."

"That's one version of the truth," Bruce conceded, "the version Embrie knows. I'd like to share with you the actual truth," he said, flipping the family portrait over and pointing to the date scribbled on the back.

James leaned forward to inspect it and gasped. "May tenth, 1897. Is this some kind of joke? That makes this photo forty years old," he roughly calculated.

"Correct," Bruce responded, turning the scrapbook page to a jaundiced newspaper clipping. "This is the front page of the San Francisco Call."

"July 7th, 1898," Declan read, leaning over the brittle article. "Headline says 'Collision Wrecks *La Bourgogne* and Six Hundred Perish.' There's also a subtitle, 'Frenzied Seamen Slay Men, Women and Children in a Fight for Possession of the Boats.' How is this relevant?"

"Mary Elizabeth was on board, along with her mother and siblings. Her father was killed just a few weeks earlier, down here, fighting alongside his fellow Clypeate during the Obturavi attack. In fact the entire Powell family was down here that night, during the attack, trapped inside the library. All would have perished except for Mr. Edison's efforts. He used the Jefferson Pier to rescue Mrs. Powell and her children, whisking them safely to New Jersey, hiding them in his workshops until Hesperus arrived."

Declan pushed back against the dubious claim. "Hesperus? You mean General Washington's soothsayer? How's he still around more than a hundred years later?"

"As you likely gathered from Washington's accounts, Hesperus neither looked nor acted like a mortal man, and to the best of my understanding, he wasn't. Washington decided he was some kind of guardian angel, that's as good a guess as any. Hesperus felt the Powells were still in danger and wanted to relocate the family to Europe, a tactic the Obturavi would never expect. The next morning, he secured passage aboard *La Bourgogne*, a French passenger liner with the perfect cover, full of American families heading back to the old country for a summer holiday. On July 4th, 1898, it struck another vessel in the middle of the Atlantic and sank. Nearly every passenger perished, including all the women and children, the entire Powell family. Including Mary Elizabeth."

"Impossible!" Declan resisted. "Then how do you explain Embrie?" he demanded. "She's Mary Elizabeth's baby sister, left behind for her own protection. If what you're saying is true, Embrie would be at least forty years old."

"Perceptions don't always match with reality." Bruce waved Ms. Elliott over. "Please come join us," he requested. "Now, Doctor, you've spent the last month with this kind lady, quite the dynamo in the kitchen. What else can you say about her?"

Declan pondered the question. "Well, she's a bit on the quiet, shy side, but always a polite and gracious hostess."

"Perfect answer, couldn't have said it better. Now, Ms. Elliott, would you mind lifting your blouse?"

"What the devil?" Declan blurted out, shielding his face. "Have you gone wonky?"

Eyes still covered, Declan heard James remark, "Wait a minute, this explains a lot. Hey Doc, you need to see this."

"I most certainly don't, you degenerate miscreants," Declan snapped back.

"Trust me, Doctor Riordan," the matronly woman implored, "there is nothing debaucherous going on here," she added, assuaging his concerns.

Declan slowly spread apart the fingers covering his eyes, timidly peeking, but his hand altogether fell away when he understood what he was seeing. Underneath Ms. Elliott's frilly, ruffled top was a metal rib cage encasing a bird's nest of wires and cables. "This can't be," Declan sputtered. "She's not human? That's impossible! Her face and hands look so real. What kind of trickery is this!?" he demanded.

"Not trickery, neither is this illusion or sorcery. Science, Professor, robotics advanced well beyond our generally accepted level of technology. Very lifelike indeed, and speaking of such, even I am feeling a bit sheepish about seeing her exposed midriff. Ms. Elliott, thank you very much, you may cover yourself up and return home."

"But her voice," Declan stammered as Ms. Elliott departed, "it's so human, the quality and richness. She interacts flawlessly, nothing like Triple Dash."

"Ms. Elliott is very special, a product of every generation of automaton that was crafted before her. A great amount of time and treasure are built into her frame. Mr. Edison modeled her after his own mother, Nancy Matthews Elliott. As an adult Mr. Edison preferred spending time in his lab, unamused by the wastefulness of social niceties, in his entire life his mother was the only non-mechanical entity he ever emotionally connected with, I guess that explains why he chose to replicate her. He compiled every recollection, all his memories of her, her emotional quirks, idioms, values and beliefs, and created what we describe as personality."

"Ms. Elliott is truly an amazing wonder of craftsmanship and invention," Declan replied, "though I'm failing to see how this relates to my relationship with Embrie."

"Oh no, Bruce, you're not leading up to what I think you are," James groaned, shaking his head. "You're going to crush Doc, you know that, right? Please don't."

Bruce wouldn't yield. "We can't afford to have him distracted, and he deserves to know the truth."

"Then let me do it," James sighed, "he already hates me." James turned to the professor. "If I'm piecing the facts together correctly, Bruce has been building up for one hell of a sucker punch. If Embrie's family died in 1898, then you are correct, she should be at least forty years old and not a young maiden. Bruce is trying to tell you Embrie is a dolled-up version of Triple Dash."

Declan slammed the table with his fists, angrily shouting, "A robot!? She can't be, not Embrie! Her hands are warm, the twinkle in her eyes. Her smile. It's genuine, and she fancies me, she's told me as much. Why would a robot flirt with me?"

"Because she doesn't know," Bruce replied, "she's programmed to feel, think and behave like she's human. She knows Ms. Elliott is a robot, but Embrie has been told, and believes, she is real. You probably noticed how Ms. Elliott avoids meals, though you may not have realized Embrie doesn't eat, either. She simply pushes food back and forth across her plate. Even Embrie doesn't notice what she's doing, it's a blind spot in her programming. She's got several, like she doesn't go to the bathroom, and always looks stunning without needing to apply makeup or straighten up her hair. Embrie's not even her real name, it's a nickname. The real Mary Elizabeth was the oldest Powell child, and her younger siblings had trouble pronouncing her name, so it sounded like 'MB', which gradually became Embrie."

Declan shook his head. "You're saying Embrie is a robotic copy of Mary Elizabeth? That makes zero logical sense. If Mary Elizabeth died as a child, why is Embrie a mature woman? Wouldn't Mr. Edison build her the same age?"

"I can't explain his rationale," Bruce prefaced his response, "I assume he designed Embrie as an older version of Mary Elizabeth so he could forget, at least temporarily, what really happened to that little girl, and pretend like she'd grown up. Please, Professor Riordan, it's not healthy to perseverate, like I said, you can drive yourself insane trying to understand."

"Then I have one last question for you. Explain why she cares for me. A robot shouldn't love a person," Declan retorted.

"Of course she loves you," Bruce agreed, "she's been searching for you, the Declan of Prophecy, since she was created. You are her primary reason for existence, the center point of her universe. She was created to seek you out and protect, nurture and guide you. I'm sorry you mistook this for love, but she's a machine, doing what she was programmed to do."

Declan mulled it over, anger, shock and intense grief boiling inside. "Once we get out of this den of lies and deceit, I'm done. I can't handle this anymore. I'm gone. Understand? You've got what you wanted, what the Girl shoved in my mind, pulled out of my head by Big Al and crafted into reality. After we escape, I want my old life back."

"I beg you to reconsider, Professor Riordan," Bruce supplicated. "As I said, Embrie wasn't part of any plan, and I know you must ache with loss, but do you want this innocent   misunderstanding   to   destroy   democratic civilization? Remember, you're still the hero in this story, prophesied to save the world, handed down to us from General Washington. You heard ALVA, the schematics extracted from your mind built wildly advanced devices, which only respond to your neural patterns. Your brain is literally the key!"

"I know this is a shitty turn of events, Doc," James commiserated. "If I feel this awful, I can't even imagine your devastation. However," he continued, "you're a smart man. Too smart to make a terrible mistake because of your emotions. You certainly recognize there's no returning to a normal life, it would be a mirage as long as the German threat still looms. Once the Nazis roll through Europe it won't take long before they're knocking on America's door. If you don't personally intervene, they'll be bringing along their new Wunderwaffe, a weapon more powerful than our military can defend against. Admit it, at least to yourself, that teaching isn't your passion, it's learning, discovering, pushing the boundaries. What we're doing here checks off all those boxes! You really want to go back to teaching, where nobody appreciates your genius, where they call you Borin' Riordan?"

"Never heard that one before," Declan pondered, "generally the insults are more expletive laden. I set high expectations for my students and I don't bend, so I don't mind if the laggards need to blow off steam at my expense. Comes with the territory."

"I would agree," James conceded, "except it's not coming from your students, Doc, it's the tenured faculty. Sorry but it's the honest truth, no bullshit, your supposed colleagues, all of them. Behind your back, mocking your hard work and dedication. Frankly, they don't deserve you."

"Let's not demean or badger the professor any further," Bruce stepped in, "I just trampled all over his heart, even if my reasons were to avoid an even tougher conversation further down the line. James, we're ready to enact your escape plan, I must get topside and contact Director Bowen. Be patient, it may take a couple days before I know our next steps, so lay low and stay safe. As for you, Professor, if you really want your old life back we promised to make that happen, just understand how your decision will affect the fate of humanity. Please don't let a broken heart steer you wrong. Now let's move."

Before Bruce closed the scrapbook, Declan glanced at the newspaper article one last time. His gaze lingered on the doomed ocean liner's picture, something caught his attention and suddenly it clicked. The smokestacks looked eerily familiar, they were the same ones he'd watched sink beneath the waves in his dream last night. "Are you certain Hesperus, Mary Elizabeth, her mother and all her siblings drowned that night?" Declan asked.

Bruce didn't hesitate. "Yes. Edison and Tesla were devastated, spending years and sizable fortunes investigating the accident, looking for clues, hoping the Powells and Hesperus survived. Unfortunately all their efforts came up empty-handed, so with heavy hearts they ended their search, concluding there were no survivors."

Declan's mind reeled with doubt, his confidence shaken, yet he couldn't dismiss what he'd seen. This was too coincidental, and he'd experienced more than a simple dream. He asked, "What if the Obturavi captured Mary Elizabeth instead?"

"Of course that was top of mind for Mr. Edison and Mr. Tesla. It's why they searched so fervently after the accident and why, during the Great War, Mr. Edison took up the cause once again. He feared Germany's unprecedented chemical weapons and advanced military gear were being created from knowledge extracted from an Epistolith, but after the war, the US military searched everywhere and found nothing. There's not much I can say with certainty, except if Mary Elizabeth had been captured by the Obturavi forty years ago, we would know."

Declan pondered Bruce's assertions. "In that case, I'd like another look at the Powell's family portrait. I want to make sure Embrie wasn't one of the other children, it'll help give me closure," he lied, his real reason even less easily explained.

"I'm glad you're trying to process your grief rationally," Bruce said, flipping to the family photo. "Must be tough."

"Indeed," Declan replied, examining all the young faces. Of course there was Mary Elizabeth, the oldest, then the four little ones, all but the infant. As he suspected they were the same cherubic faces he'd seen in his dream, panicking on the sinking ship and then lifeboat, desperately clinging for protection. Now he knew for certain, his terrible nightmares weren't dreams at all, they were Mary Elizabeth's memories. He shuddered as he looked at the children one last time, having witnessed their tiny, lifeless bodies rolling with the ocean swells.

"Hey Doc, are you okay?" James asked. "You don't look so good."

Declan rubbed his face and took a deep breath. "I'll be just fine," Declan reassured them, reminding himself this tragedy took place forty years ago and not, as it felt to him, twelve hours ago. "Just need time to think."

"Now's not the time for thinking, it's time for doing," James remarked.

"Agreed," Declan replied, eager to get far away from this place. Reconciling Bruce's assertions would take more than time, the disparity between a watery grave and his dreamed version of events opening doubt onto the Clypeate's monopoly on secrets.

With the scrapbook safely locked away, the men returned to Lincoln's Tunnel and the old, rusty car overloaded with the navigation machine. "Looks clear on both sides," James said, double checking the equipment's position.

"Care to explain your plan?" Bruce asked, trying to understand why three cars were now lined up, the path between them and the brick wall clear of tile and debris. "The cars look like they're waiting patiently at a traffic light."

"Simple, really," James answered. "We need three cars for my plan, and thankfully two of them still run. The first car will breach the brick wall, we'll slide through the opening in the second car, and the last car will plug the gap. After eighty years of strain, plus a building added above it, the barrier may have become load bearing, and J Edgar will notice if we put a sinkhole in the middle of Constitution Avenue."

"What about carrying away the equipment at the other end?" Bruce asked. "With my arm I won't be much help, which leaves just the two of you."

"I know, which is why I'm counting on the loading dock being nearby. This tunnel leads into a lower level of the Executive Office Building, and most federal buildings within the District build their supply docks underground to save space and ensure privacy. I'm hoping this one was designed the same way. Can't be certain, so let's call this Plan Number One, though I really hope it works, because there's no Two."

"Sounds like a bully plan to me," Declan chimed in.

"You're okay with this plan, Doc?" James asked skeptically. "I thought if anyone would see the flaws, it'd be you. You're not agreeing because you have a death wish, correct?"

"Give me more credit than that," Declan scoffed. "I want to get the hell out of here and after that, well, I don't know, but as for your plan I can't find flaws in logic. These cars are turn of the century, if they still run they'll hit the wall at twenty miles an hour, sufficient force to breach a hastily built wall. As for what to expect on the other side of the barrier, that's anyone's guess."

"Good enough for me," Bruce remarked, settling into the second car's front bench, clutching the shoebox filled with ALVA's gadgets of unknown utility.

"Here we go," James said, climbing into the lead car's driver seat, revving the engine before flooring it full speed towards the wall. He jumped out mere feet before the car smashed into the wall, the hood crumpling slightly while also pushing forward a sizable section of brick. He surveyed the damage to the car and barrier, both meeting his expectations, sporting a wide grin until he noticed a large crack developing in the ceiling above them. "Ah, crapsticks," he groaned, "this is gonna be tricky," he reported back to Bruce.

"Something wrong?" asked Bruce.

"Not sure how many more whacks we'll get before the roof caves. We've gotta make this one count," he said, climbing into the mangled lead car and backing up. "Get ready to floor it!" he shouted back to Declan, the professor returning a thumbs up from behind the wheel of the second vehicle. Declan throttled his engine, the chain between his rear bumper and the trailing third car pulling taut before they both gained momentum, picking up speed as they closed the several-meter gap between them and James' lead car.

"What's James waiting for?" wondered Declan, fearing a collision he moved his foot over the brake when James suddenly rocketed forward towards the wall. This time Declan didn't see him jump free as the car smashed into the bricks, both the car and James disappearing into a cloud of dust. Although Declan couldn't see what lay ahead he doubled down, too late to stop he floored the pedal and braced for impact. They followed James into the dust cloud, dislodged bricks pounding against the navigational equipment and screeching along the door panels, both men jostled and whipped about as the tires bounced over fallen debris. After several long moments of certain death their vehicle jerked to a sudden halt when the car chained to their rear bumper became wedged in the gap.

Declan spotted the lead car forty feet further up the tunnel, having veered off and flipped over. Declan ran towards the twisted wreck, looking for signs of James, finding him trapped underneath. "Are you okay?" he asked.

"You realize there's a car on top of me, right?" James moaned. "But yes, I can wiggle all my fingers and toes, I'm more pinned than squished. But you made it through, my plan worked!"

"Yes, and there'll be plenty of time to celebrate once we figure out your predicament. Bruce and I aren't going to be able to lift the car, so give me a few moments to think this through."

"What about taking the chain from our rear bumper and attaching it to the wreck?" Bruce suggested. "We can drag the car away."

"Good thought," Declan responded, "though we risk smearing James' body across the floor like warm Brie. No, I have a better idea. We just need a pole or beam."

Along the brick wall, mixed in the rubble were several long planks, remains of scaffolding used when the government sealed off the tunnel. Declan dragged one of the thicker pieces back to James and the wrecked auto. He piled together a small brick stack and inserted the wooden beam under the flipped car, using the bricks as a fulcrum. "Okay, James, get ready to move," Declan declared, sitting down on the beam, see-sawing the car just a few inches into the air. This proved enough gap for Bruce to grab James by the hand, dragging him free seconds before Declan's bottom slipped off the beam and the car slammed back down.

"Are you alright?" Bruce asked, looking for signs of injury as a dazed James sat up and brushed himself off.

"I'd be better if this suit weren't torn," James remarked, noting a ripped sleeve. "This is vicuna wool, Mr. Edison had good taste, the jacket alone costs more than my annual salary. Other than that, I appear to be unscathed," he continued, standing up and testing all his limbs. "That was quite a ride," he noted, "I'm actually feeling quite peppy, like I'm ready to take on the world."

"You didn't happen to drink some of Mr. Edison's wine?" Declan asked.

"The Vin Mariani? Edison's secret stash? Of course," James confirmed, "I polished off a bottle while investigating the tunnel, then Bruce and I split most of another bottle. Why?"

"Well, now I know how you were able to drive through a brick wall and survive a car crash, yet still feel like you're on top of the world. After dinner Embrie told me that Vin Mariani is blended with coca leaves," Declan explained, "you drank enough cocaine to keep you awake for a week."

"Hmmm," James pondered this information, "for a stodgy old inventor, the guy really knew how to party. Certainly explains why I feel so good. Let's take advantage of this effect before it wears off."

James walked over to the brick wall and unhooked the chain tethering Declan's car, the navigation machine firmly in place, from the third vehicle jammed into the bricks. "It worked, that's really crammed into the gap, something fierce," he said, surveying his plan's results. Satisfied he climbed into the back seat behind Bruce, sprawling out like he was sunning on the French Riviera. "Now tally-ho my good man!" he shouted to Declan.

Thankfully, the tunnel appeared vacant and open, with a thick layer of dust, a hopeful sign the government hadn't traveled to their side of the wall for some time. Unfortunately the car's rubber tires had long ago dry rotted, and while this side of the tunnel was much smoother and contained much less debris from the Obturavi attack, they were now riding solely on rims, making the journey exceedingly bumpy and jarring. Declan drove cautiously to avoid further trauma to the equipment, bouncing around as they approached the tunnel's far end.

"Not what I expected," Bruce groaned as they approached an unexpected impediment blocking the far end of the tunnel. "Looks like they replaced the original door with this behemoth," he remarked, noting the oversized metal door, like a bank vault, blocking their exit. "This is disheartening, though not insurmountable," he optimistically added, and as the men approached the door, Declan read the large sign welded to the silver surface.

"'Here marks the boundary of a United States Federal Government Building. Trespassing beyond this point constitutes a federal offense, and lethal force is authorized'" Declan read. "They're not exactly rolling out the red carpet, are we sure about this?"

"Hold on," Bruce said, "there's a second inscription, up here, engraved directly into the metal." He used his sleeve to wipe off the dust. "'This door was built and erected by the Army Corps of Engineers under the supervision of Lieutenant Leslie Groves Jr.'"

"Did you say Groves?" asked James. "Hold on, I know this will sound crazy, but several months back Director Bowen led a tour group through the Bureau of Engineering. I thought nothing of it at the time, the Director frequently brought politicians and other military bigwigs through our facilities, so this wasn't anything special. This encounter should have been wholly unremarkable as well, except when this small group stopped at my workstation, Director Bowen made a special point of highlighting one of their names."

"Leslie Groves, I presume," ventured Declan.

"Exactly," James grinned. "Groves, like oranges, he said twice, which struck me as peculiar. Then the Director pointed to my Yankees pennant taped to the wall, and this really caught my attention. This guy I'd never met, Groves, says 'the Yanks may have beat out the Giants in this Series, but each season is like a door, and you know what they say. When one door closes, another door opens'. What an odd comment, I thought, but now, well, it can't be a coincidence, can it?"

"Are you certain you're not just high?" Declan asked, "because that's either the most astute observation or craziest hallucination I've ever heard."

"I'm most certainly high, that doesn't make me wrong," James asserted, "and if anyone's got a better idea, I'd love to hear it."

The three men eyed up the massive vault door, no handles or knobs, dozens of dish-sized bolts securing it to the wall. "I don't know if Groves is Clypeate, but let's assume he is for the moment, and this really was a clue," posited Bruce. "Where do we look for another door? On this end the Clypeate's original door is no longer here, replaced by this hulking slab, and at the other there's the Research Hall and Room of the Honored."

"If Groves was truly giving me a message, he'd try to keep it uncomplicated, right? Let's start by checking out this end and hope we don't need to get back through that brick wall, I don't want to think about how we'd climb back through that mess."

Declan looked around and offered, "Maybe there's an air vent we can climb through, or an emergency escape hatch?"

James shook his head. "Doubtful anything big enough to drag the device through," and groaning with frustration, he kicked the car. "I'm not sure how much juice this junker has left, and our search is going to be infinitely tougher when the headlights die. It'd be really nice if the overhead lamps on this end of the tunnel worked."

"That's it," Declan chimed in, "we need to find the controls for the tunnel lights. There must be an electrical panel around here somewhere."

"Yes, it would be helpful to have the lights working," agreed Bruce, "but I doubt any of the bulbs are still intact, and the Feds most likely cut the power years ago."

"That's not my point," Declan said, "electrical panels have a cover, a door. It's easy enough to test my theory, we just need to follow the ceiling wires back to the circuit box."

They traced the meandering wires, first across the ceiling then down the wall, before the wires disappeared behind a pile of old car parts and stacked gas cans. "Wait a minute," warned Bruce, "there's something funny about this setup, nobody would stack fuel next to electrical lines. This is either the work of a negligent mechanic or a booby trap."

"Or we're barking up the wrong tree," James groaned with disappointment. As he turned to walk away, he noticed a triangular bit of felt attached to a rusted-out fender. He knelt to get a closer look. "Ya gotta be kidding me," he laughed, pointing it out to the other men.

"A Yankees pendant," Bruce noted, "how about that."

"I'm sure you both thought I was crazy. Well, who's crazy now?" he smugly asked, lifting the small flag up to reveal a copper wire and observing two loose ends. "It's been cut."

"Looks purposeful," commented Bruce, "it's a grounding wire, keeps electrical charge from building up. Now we know, this is an intentional setup. We need to mend the wire before touching anything else, otherwise our static electricity will ignite the gasoline and turn us all into crispy critters."

"Speaking of death," James said, "maybe only one of us should stay here to reattach the wires, just in case this pile explodes. Somebody needs to survive, get a message to Director Bowen."

"How noble of you James, but don't worry, I volunteer," Declan replied. "I'm perfectly capable of twisting together two loose ends of wire."

James shook his head. "I'm not sure I trust you, Doc, you're still upset about Embrie and could be harboring passive suicidal desires. No, you're too important, you aren't useful to the Clypeate as a pile of carbon."

"You're worried about me?" Declan asked incredulously. "Bruce's injuries have crippled his dexterity and you're hepped up on cocaine. Plus, it really doesn't matter where you stand down here, if the explosion doesn't kill you instantly, the ensuing fire will suck up all the oxygen and you'll asphyxiate. Now wish me luck and hide."

"Harsh but accurate," Bruce replied, "point well taken. James, let's leave the professor to his business."

Once James and Bruce were crouched against the far side of the car, Declan carefully examined the area around the copper wire, making sure he wouldn't accidentally complete the circuit. Satisfied, he reached into the tight space under the fender, avoiding all contact save the two ends of wire. He entwined the ends in a tight knot, and content with his results walked over to the stacked gasoline cans.

"Here goes everything," he said, touching the first can, involuntarily wincing. Nothing happened. "I'm not dead," he announced, swiftly clearing the remaining cans until he found the electrical panel, its door notably ajar. "I found the electrical panel," he shouted to James and Bruce. "Go over to the vault door. I'm going to close the panel door, keep your eyes peeled." Declan closed the small metal door. "Anything?"

"No, nothing on our end!" James yelled back.

Declan opened and closed it several times in frustration, "What are we missing?" he wondered.

"Hold on!" Bruce exclaimed, "whatever you're doing over there, Professor, keep doing it!" Declan complied. "James, look up at that bolt," Bruce said, "top left, fifth in from the corner. Is it me, or is that bolt winking at us?"

James focused on the spot, and sure enough, in the middle of the large bolt, a dime-sized hole opened and closed. "That has to be it, but it's too high up," he commented.

"Not for me," Bruce replied, reaching up to stick his pinky finger in the hole, resulting in loud clicking inside the metal door. They scrambled back, uncertain what they'd done until, like magic, the massive door swung open, quietly and smoothly.

"Abracadabra, we did it," James excitedly whispered, peering into the darkness beyond the vault door. The car's headlights illuminated the large space, long and narrow, perhaps a meeting room at one time, now filled with boxes and crates.

"Storage room," Bruce noted in hushed tones. They all listened for several more minutes, and with no sign their arrival was noticed, the trio crept forward toward the far exit.

"We should get our bearings," proposed Declan, but before they could lay out a plan James opened the door.

The dapper young analyst patted down his suit and smiled. "I'm the best dressed and smoothest talker, if anyone can move around without garnering attention, it's me. If I'm not back in twenty, it means I've been discovered and you should run back into the tunnel."

"Oh Lord, our fate is wrapped up with his," Declan groaned, though true to his word, James was back in less than fifteen and visibly excited.

"You won't believe our good fortune," he blurted out. "We're in a sub-basement, nobody's down here except us and a shocking number of plump cockroaches."

Declan adjusted his stance, felt the hard shells crunch underfoot, and grimaced. "I hope your enthusiasm isn't reliant upon the cockroaches."

"Hardly," James laughed, "the loading dock is directly above us, and..." disappearing into the hall he returned with a sturdy hand truck, "we'll be able to roll the machine out the tunnel and down the hall to a freight elevator."

Ninety minutes later an office supply van rolled out from beneath the Executive Office Building, passing within yards of the West Wing before exiting the security gate onto Pennsylvania Avenue. James and Declan disembarked at the Willard Hotel while Bruce continued towards Anacostia, meandering further south, reaching the Naval Research Labs as the red and orange hues of twilight deepened into violet. He hid the truck inside a maintenance shed before sneaking into Director Bowen's office, eager to place a few phone calls while waiting for the Director's arrival.

Meanwhile James had anything but sleep on his mind, having unwittingly imbibed a lot of liquid cocaine. "I spent weeks chipping away at the Jefferson Pier, not sleeping right, hands numb, body exhausted beyond words. My mind, however, is in quite the opposite mood."

Declan sighed, wondering why he hadn't immediately locked the door between their suites. "I don't like where this is heading. Take all your crazy ideas, put them in a bottle and cork 'em up."

"Come on Doc," urged James, jumping up and down on a very expensive couch. "We deserve to celebrate," he persisted, speech pressured and manic. "Now we've got the necessary gear to put a wrinkle in those Nazi bastards' plans, let's go out and have some fun."

"I'm not in the mood to go anywhere," Declan protested, curling up on a chaise lounge. "My life is adrift. I have no reason for returning to Los Angeles. I don't want to pursue my teaching career at UCLA or anywhere else, and I have zero interest in living near an ocean. I called my parents, I might stay with them for a while, help out around the farm and take time to figure out a new path forward. I really thought I had my life going in the right direction, then the Clypeate, and Embrie, showed me a new dream, and now everything's gone."

James wagged his finger. "Stop talking like that, Doc. You and I are gonna save the world."

"That's just it, you don't need me to save the world," countered Declan. "The Girl got her machine built, ALVA knows how it works, and Bruce seems to have a purpose for it. I need a change of scenery, some perspective, to sort things out."

"Nah, Doc," James said, shaking his head, "thinkin's the opposite of what you need. We gotta clear your mind, and I've got the perfect solution. Let's paint the town. I know where to find the local action, the night is young and we're a couple of handsome, high-ranking military officers. Trust me, that buys a lot of attention in this town."

"I'm sure it does," agreed Declan, "and I noticed a few dark suits down in the lobby. We should be extremely cautious. In your current state they'd quickly take notice of us."

"That's part of the fun," squealed James, dizzy from jumping he flopped down on the couch. "J Edgar smells something fishy but he's a harmless barking dog dangling on the end of President Roosevelt's leash. They've got nothing more than hunches," pausing before adding "and the few pieces of advanced technology they found floating inside Bruce. If they haven't come after me for setting the Navy Building on fire, I think we're safe. Hell, if we pick up a couple tails the ladies will love it, we'll look like we're important enough to merit our own security detail."

Declan wasn't swayed. "Getting followed around all night by federal agents doesn't strike me as fun. You aren't making a compelling argument."

James wasn't giving up. "Look Doc, I'm not leaving you alone up here because, frankly, I've seen the way you've been eyeing up my toaster."

Declan scowled at James. "You aren't funny."

"Oh, I'm not kidding," persisted James, as serious as he could muster. "I just can't trust the two of you alone," he pressed, "so I'm going to have to cancel my plans and stay in tonight, too."

Declan shook his head, suggesting, "Why don't you go to your room and jump on the furniture in there? You've carried on long enough, I get the point."

"I'm not sure you do, not yet," James countered, "because, speaking from experience, getting your heart broken feels a whole lot worse when you sit around and mope. Go ahead, take my toaster out for a night on the town, show her a good time. Just promise to be a gentleman and have her back home at a reasonable hour. And remember, she's a good toaster, so no monkey business, ya hear?"

Declan huffed. "You're not going to stop, are you?"

"Not until you come out with me," James acknowledged, sporting a maniacal grin. "You're my friend, Doc, making it my civic duty to bust your chops until you let me cheer you up. I'm gonna need you to get off that chair, freshen up, slap on your finest duds and let this country show us some gratitude."

Declan sighed, James wasn't giving up. "I'll be ready in thirty, and don't act surprised when you wake up tomorrow and find your toaster walking funny."

"I'd rather introduce you to some actual women, but that's the spirit," James squealed with delight, dancing off into his own room.

Declan shouted, "Not what I meant," shaking his head, already resolved to leave the Clypeate behind and start a fresh life in the morning.